SOMEDAY

a love story

and stories about life and death love liberrty cats and dogs cakes and other stuff

e.a. rogers

iUniverse, Inc.
New York Bloomington

SOMEDAY
a love story

Copyright © 2009 e.a. rogers

This is a work of fiction. All of the characters, names, incidents,
organizations, and dialogue in this novel are either the products
of the author's imagination or are used fictitiously.

The novel SOMEDAY and the short stories following are fiction. The front
cover photograph is of my mother Blanche Venable Rogers on her wedding
day. The character Anna's approach to breast cancer is taken from my mother's
experience. The novel does not detail the life of my parents, or specific
individuals. Other novels with reference to events mentioned in SOMEDAY
include SAINTE LILLLIAN'S MISSOURI, and MELANIE'S CHOICE.

Reader please Note: The town of Sainte Lillian is named after a Welsh Sainte
from the dark ages who spent her life loving the Lord and working to help the
impoverished. Miraculously, she cured the sick, fed the hungry and brought
peace to warring clans. Wherever towns are named after her many women
embody her spirit of love and selflessness. And so it is in SOMEDAY.

iUniverse books may be ordered through booksellers or by contacting:

iUniverse
1663 Liberty Drive
Bloomington, IN 47403
www.iuniverse.com
1-800-Authors (1-800-288-4677)

ISBN: 978-1-4401-8267-9 (pbk)
ISBN: 978-1-4401-8266-2 (ebk)

Printed in the United States of America

iUniverse rev. date: 11/6/2009

DEDICATION

It is with great love and pleasure I dedicate this book to my family: Samantha, Levi and Noelle, Howie and Mollie and their kids, and Lynn Louise and Einstein. With special thanks to Cathie and Ron for their part in making so much joy possible.

A special thanks also to my friend DeAnna Davidson for technical support.

PART ONE

Anna's Diary

Dear Dear Patient Diary

First of all Dear Diary I apologize for neglecting you all this time. My life has been so turned inside out and upside down lately, the last thing on my mind was writing about crops or weather or brother Jethro's antics. It's time for more than that. I want to take hours and days and weeks and the rest of my forever to tell you my deepest secrets. Be warned, I'll be writing things I never ever thought I'd think, let alone write.

One beginning is when I was so close to being 11 years old I decided I already was 11 and didn't let anyone tell me different. Not even momma. Momma gave me one of those looks one day and said it was past time to tell me facts about men and women. She said these were facts of life, and since she knew I was going to turn into a woman someday soon, I needed to know important things.

I looked at her and wondered if she felt alright. How could I turn into a woman? That didn't make sense. I wondered if I would look in the mirror one morning and "poof," my reflection would be that of a full grown woman. I thought my life was fine as it was, so I told her that. Word for word.

Momma smiled. She said she felt that way once but then she became a full grown woman. I couldn't believe her. My momma had never been anything but my momma. My mouth got so wide open that for the first time in ages, words wouldn't come out.

Because I was staying really quiet for practically the first time in my entire life, momma didn't waste a second. She started telling me the most outlandish things. She said a few years after starting their monthly stainy time, young women started looking at young men in a different way. Not only that, young men stopped acting foolish and fighting all the time and looked right back at the young women. Next thing you know wedding bells were ringing.

I knew about weddings because along with funerals they're important social events around Sainte Lillian's. There's more food at funerals, but weddings draw the biggest crowds. Ordinary looking young women turn into princesses in white gowns. Grooms are always so clean and dressed up, folks hardly know them. Something else I noticed, while the princess brides look so happy, the grooms always look scared to death. I never got around to asking momma why. Anyway, when I was "11" pretty princesses and cake were what I liked best about weddings.

I knew men and women got married. So why was my momma making such a fuss about it? I didn't get a chance to ask, she just jumped right in to tell me. And what she said didn't make a lick of sense. Knowing purt near everything the way I did, I didn't believe her.

She said married women had to do their duty and let men have their way. She got all flustered and didn't say their way with what but since I was "11," I told her what I knew. I said, "I know grown men are big and strong and open doors for, and tip hats to ladies. Most of them are nice with kids too. Cept of course banker Crabtree but he's not nice to anybody. And momma I know most men work hard. Men are doctors and preachers and own stores and shoe horses and work farms like daddy. I guess they have to have their way else hard work wouldn't get done. Momma why are you so flustered about men having their way?"

Let me tell you, she surely looked funny, her face all red and all. Momma poured herself another cup of coffee in her big white cup, the one without any cracks or chips in it, and cleared her throat. She took so much time I decided to help her some more.

"I know boys and men are different than girls and women momma but I figure God made them that way so we'd know the difference. I like them a lot momma." Then I told her since we'd talked enough about boys and men I wanted to know more about stainy time. And why she had such a funny look on her face. I asked her if men had stainy time, did it mean full grown women were messy and spilled things on their dresses and had to dye them or something. The more I thought the more confusing it got. But what else could a stainy time be? Then I wondered if every woman was messy and she was warning me to be more careful so I wouldn't have a stainy time.

Since she was still not saying anything, I decided to tell her what else I knew about boys because I watched them all the time...

Momma tried to swallow a sip of coffee and coughed something awful. She coughed and gagged, and carried on for ever so long. Then it took her forever to talk... Finally, and I remember this like it was yesterday, she said; "Folks have told me you hang around boys a lot daughter. That's why we're having this talk. Fact is daughter; this here talk is a bit overdue."

Momma never called me daughter. Never. That name hushed me faster than a hand over my mouth ever could. Momma always, always, always called me "Sweet Anna." Now you know and I know Sweet is not my first name but momma always said it like it was.

Daughter sounded funny. Her voice wasn't soft as usual, but different, like she was upset with me. And her face was turning even redder. My momma was delicate and pale. She never got a red face even in summer because she wore a sunbonnet. Was she feeling poorly?

I thought maybe if I told her some of the things I wondered about, she would feel better. Like how I noticed about the time boy's legs got longer their voices sounded different and they wrestled a lot. They reminded me of roosters in the chicken yard way they strutted around and all. And the way I laughed when young men got all tongue tied and bashful around pretty girls. Land sakes, they'd known one another all their lives and now they acted so strange and bashful around girls. And men: I wanted to know why they ate so much? Why did they chew tobacco? Why did they grow whiskers? And a hundred more things.

Finally, momma found her voice and I didn't get another word in edgewise. One thing she didn't have time for was time for questions I answered all by myself with another question. She especially didn't have time for questions neither of us could answer like why? Why covered a lot of ground on our farm and around Sainte Lillian's. I wanted to know why barns burned and bees stung and some folks were sad all the time. Everything was important to me and could be --should be-- answered after a "Why?"

Momma talked so fast she didn't leave me room for one single word. Not only that, she looked everywhere but directly at me. That was scary. And her face got redder all the time. I didn't know what to think, but I knew in order to hear every word I had to listen twice as fast.

All my life up to this very minute my momma was known as a woman that didn't talk all that much. When she did, she was real sparse with her words. I wouldn't say stingy, because momma was not stingy, but, she knew when to talk and when not to. Just like sugar in her apple pies. She knew when enough was enough. Now she used so many words if this were a pie and her words was sugar we'd have to feed it to the pigs. And they would have been pigs over it. I wonder why.

Momma said yes indeed, most men were nice, but there were other things I needed to know. I knew a lot and told her so. She stopped talking and sighed and if possible got even redder.

Momma was a good artist. She could draw everything. And she did. She drew exactly what she thought I needed to know and I learned real fast I didn't know much of anything. Her pictures scared me nearly to death.

I pointed. "Preachers do that?" Then it hit. My daddy was a man. My momma was a woman. "You and daddy do that?" I pointed at a drawing of a man and woman in bed together and...well, never mind what they were doing. I don't exactly know how to describe it anyway. Back then, when I was calling myself 11 years old, thinking about what men's trousers hid made me want to cry.

Momma said I shouldn't be afraid. She said this was absolutely necessary because men were planting seeds into their wives. She said the seeds grew into babies. The babies grew up to be good Christians and helped keep the world safe for democracy.

I looked at the pictures one more time and stopped her right there. I pointed at the man drawing. "Daddy plants seeds in the ground and doesn't use that," I said. And besides, women don't have gardens down there." By now momma had spilled most of her coffee She was having trouble holding the pot steady as she poured some more. She sat down and put her head in her hands like she was either praying or thinking.

I sat like a good girl, waiting. Land sakes! It was hard for me to sit still. I wanted to know why. Finally momma looked up and smiled. She said what was planted in fields and gardens were different kinds of seeds. I opened my mouth to ask if man seeds looked like corn or tomato or pepper seeds. I wanted to know exactly what man seeds looked like. She put a finger over my lips and said I needed to stop asking so many questions and making our talk so difficult. She said I had to listen. She said if I was quiet she wouldn't get so flustered and could explain a lot better' Momma said man seeds didn't look like seeds at all… My mouth was open again but I remembered in time. She said, "These man seeds fertilized a woman's egg." This time my words came out fast and loud. "Momma women don't have eggs! Chickens and ducks and turkeys and robins and crows and…" "Daughter!" she said and I knew she knew what I was telling her. Then she put her whole hand over my mouth. I was so shocked!

She stared at me for the longest time then went right back to what she was saying just like I hadn't interrupted.

"Once the egg is fertilized," she said and looked at me again, like she was wondering if I'd ask what kind of fertilizer went down there. Truth is I knew about fertilizer that came from the hind end of cows and pigs. I didn't want to think about that going there! I sat still and quiet and let her talk. "The seed and egg grows in the woman and becomes a baby. When law abiding freedom loving God fearing Christian ladies let men have their way the world is a better place."

My eyes and my mind went back and forth from momma to her pictures. Momma said men planted food crops during the day and baby seeds at night.

This time my words just tumbled out like I'd seen spilt great northern beans run all over the floor when I dropped a cup full. "That's an awful lot of planting momma. It's a wonder they have time for anything else." Momma was having a terrible time with her coffee.

While she was coughing, I thought maybe men did their night planting every night to make sure seeds would sprout. "Are there bad seeds in men just like in the grain sacks?" I asked.

Momma had such a time of it then, I thought she'd never answer. At least waiting gave me time to think about families like ours with only two children. In fact there weren't more than five or six children in each and every family all around Sainte Lillian's. Maybe the seeds dried up. I wanted to ask her but thought of something else. I asked momma if farmers shared seeds why people didn't get baby seed from Mr. Kirkpatrick. Last I heard there was 17 little Kirkpatrick's at their farm. Seems to me he would be happy to share, I said.

Momma poured her cup of coffee in the slop bucket. That was not like her! Momma never ever wasted anything. She gave me a real serious look, like she had a lot to say and had to choose her words right careful like. Since I didn't have any more questions right then, I folded my hands neatly in my lap and smiled up at her.

Momma didn't say one single word about my idea, but she let me know baby seed planting was done between one man and one woman united in marriage under the laws of God and man. She said this was a very good thing... Then she got even redder. Redder than the barn after a fresh coat of paint. Why? What was she thinking?

Why if seed planting was so nice did she have trouble talking about it? I put what she said and the way she acted and her pictures together and didn't know what to think. That was odd. I always knew what to think. Two seconds later I wondered if Christians were all men planted. In two more seconds I decided if freedom and democracy ever got around to depending on me the world would be in big trouble.

Momma rinsed a rag out in cold water and wiped her red face and arms. She said it was getting on to supper and we'd have to talk more later. Besides, she said, she'd done her Christian duty for the day. We never got around to talking about these things again which means we never covered stainy time.

My girl friends told me some stories but it wasn't until a few years later I found out about stainy time on my own. Momma was probably trying to be delicate when she called it stainy time. If she'd spoke the whole truth she'd have called it what it is, big, messy cramping stinking time. There, that covers it.

When I was 14 and having my first "wonderful experience with stainy time," my daddy said what with times as bad as they were, he had no choice but to hop a freight train. There was plenty of work out there in Cali for nia. He'd make a lot of money on the fruit farms and construction and all, and then come back for us. He painted a right pretty word picture. Said we would see cactus and cowboys and have more oranges than we could eat, and the climate would be much better for momma and Jethro. He sounded excited and sad at the same time. I wanted to know why but knew by then to not ask every why that came to the tip of my tongue. Anyway, the oranges part sounded wonderful to me because the one we got in our Christmas stocking was never enough. And what was an avocado and was there really nothin' but an ocean of salt water after Cali for nia? And what good was salty water? Water was for drinkin' and washin'. A body couldn't drink salty water without gettin' sick. I know. I tried.

I remember the morning daddy left us. Momma and Jethro and I stood by the kitchen cook stove. Daddy stood in the open door looking at us for what seemed a long time. So long my legs cramped. Finally, he blew his nose on his red handkerchief, adjusted his suspenders, said our names real low and slow like he was chiseling them on his brain. Then he turned and just like that, walked out the door. We heard the train whistle and knew if he was leavin' he had to go. I remember how crackly his voice was and the way his shoulders slumped when he walked out... I wanted to cry but if he was brave enough to leave and seek our fortune, I had to be brave and smile. He promised we would be together real soon. We didn't know then we'd never ever see him again. All the Good Lord let us know then was we had to work hard and keep the farm. All we did was work and momma saved the money daddy sent every month.

One weekend near my 16th birthday, our local Valentino who'd been makin' a pest of himself for weeks sided up to me after school and said he was in love with me. I almost said why? But minded my manners and said "thank you very much," and smiled. Then he up and said if I loved him the way he loved me, we'd go to his hayloft and get necked and do the things momma had told me about.

I told him we were not man and wife and furthermore would never be. He laughed and reached for me and said people didn't have to be married and he could prove it. It was like he was calling my momma a liar. When he returned to school after a two day absence he stood in the hallway, looked right at me through his swollen black eyes and lied through his swollen lips. "Terrible fight. Three thugs from South Saint Louis jumped me." I cleared my throat and he shut up right quick and slunk away. I didn't know I could hit that hard.

Not long after that, I decided to become Charter member and President of the Sainte Lillian's Association of Men Haters. I came up with a plan to insure swaggering overall wearing stinkin' animals got my message. Slow and easy, a little change here, another change there till it seemed I was always downright sour looking ugly. What man would look twice at me? Be glad dear diary you don't have eyes. Telling you this is more than enough.

I draped my bone skinny frame in long ugly granny dresses and pulled my hair back in a bun so tight my eyes ran. My eyebrows once so carefully plucked and arched like movie stars did, grew together. They looked like two wooly worms joined together over my nose. I hated them. What little cosmetics I had went in the trash, and my beautiful dime store genuine imitation pearls went into a drawer. Ugly lace up black shoes a granny wouldn't wear and thick soled barn boots replaced my half way decent shoes.

Every dress I was partial to went into the Missionary barrel at church. It didn't hurt that much to part with my calico dresses, pretty and bright as they were. But let me tell you, saying goodbye to my lavender dotted Swiss dress with the soft white underskirt and collar and cuffs momma made was another story. I cried like a baby then, and cried again when my patent leather shoes with the beautiful black bows joined them. My consolation came in knowing in some far off place with a name I'd never heard a poor missionary lady would rejoice over almost new clothing. Especially my beautiful lavender dotted Swiss and the patent leather shoes.

The memory of the first public appearance of the revised new/old me stands out... On a busy Saturday morning market day, I hitched up my courage and walked straight back into the deep dark back room of Sainte Lillian's Hardware. Now they didn't have a sign that read women and dogs keep out, but even in emergencies women didn't go there. They'd stand at the counter and holler but never, ever did they go back there where it smelled of oil and grease and men were having private man talk. Never. Dogs? Well, by that time, I thought men and mangy dogs were so much alike, if there was a sign dogs would heist their leg and wet it down.

Saturday morning, mid-winter. Men of every size age and shape as long as they were old enough to shave and chaw gathered around the pot bellied stove for man talk.

This particular Saturday I made my move, the bell above the door that announces customers wasn't loud enough to suit. I needed attention and to get that I needed noise. I grabbed a white hickory ax handle and hit that little bell so hard it sounded like a church bell. I knew folks in the street heard it above wagon sounds. For sure and certain that noise grabbed the attention of the pot bellied crowd. They looked up and saw me walking back there hands on hips, ugly scowl on my face.

To a man they looked down much quicker than they'd looked up. Peter Eric White said "well sir," and nothing else came out of his mouth. Ken

Green added "and then I says," and whatever he said he was fixin' to say he didn't. After a split second of stone cold silence, noise coming from the men den reminded me of a hornets nest after it'd been kicked by a mule. They didn't look at each other. They didn't look at me. They made noise. A lot of noise, really fast and garbled. I was invisible to every man there and that was perfect... I knew no man worth his salt would look twice at me. In fact if drunk as a skunk seven days a week Jasper Johns got a good look at me, it'd probably scare him sober. It was all I could do to not click my heels together and laugh out loud.

I never told momma why I was changing, but considerin' it had taken awhile and I was overworked and she was turning sickly, I figured she didn't need the bother.

When my twenties got closer and closer I couldn't believe the face staring at me in the mirror wasn't twice that. It was like my stick in the mud drab life just aged me all over. With frown lines and wrinkles, I was downright sour puss looking ugly. And set in my ways, let me tell you. I looked the part of an old maid lemon sucking school teaching spinster. At school all it took was one look from under my bushy brows and overgrown farm boys knew to take their seats and shut their mouth... Especially the Mouser boys. Those boys were the most rambunctious determined to not learn anything oversized louts I ever saw. Yet it took them less than five minutes to learn first hand that "Miz Anna didn't take no truck from nobody." I busted up more of their fights than they could count. And they started learnin' and liking it.

As the saying goes, even the best laid plans of women and girls can be blindsided. My downfall was dreams. After daddy left for Cali for nia, and momma and Jethro were still so sickly, most of them were about having him home and them healthy. Sometimes my dreams of food were so vivid I couldn't eat breakfast because I was so full of dreamed about and dreamed eaten pot roast and fried chicken and roast turkey. In my dreams we had so much of everything we felt blessed to share with the less fortunate. In reality, if there were folks less fortunate, we were in a big heap of trouble. Still, I dreamed and prayed, and hoped.

Different dreams showed up as I grew older and more womanly and in spite of myself, developed a nice figure. I worked myself to exhaustion at school and at the boarding house and fell into bed absolutely determined to not dream that dream. Sadly, that only made it come faster. Got to where that dream was what I looked foreward to.

I loved that dream. It always started on a beautiful spring afternoon. Everything in my world was perfect. Wearing a store bought green dress with a deep green ribbon in my long red gold curly hair, I was standing in a lane near a blossoming apple tree. The light wind brought the scent of apple blossoms. I felt the lightest touch of green ribbon against my cheek as I stared up at the most handsome man in the world. With his strong arms he pulled me up beside him on his magnificent chestnut stallion. Man and horse were perfection. My perfection. We embraced and then trotted off to a place called Happy Ever After.

Even when I was so committed to my man hating role that I felt bound with unbreakable chains, stuck in concrete overshoes and tied to a whipping post, that dream came every night. Then it happened. The L word. Not like. Heavens no, not that silly non- committal word.

Dear Diary you're probably not ready for this and my hand shakes as I write it because I've never before written about love. There, I wrote it! I am head over heels in love and love is the most beautiful wonderful thrilling word in the world. When I write it, I hear music.

I'm not sure which day God created love. Maybe it was love that inspired Him to create everything else. Heaven, and earth and everything in, on, above and around it.

Regardless I'm at the point where I now want very much to do my part keeping the world safe for Christianity and democracy. It puzzles me though, thinking how kids born in the Ozarks can do things like that, save the world and all. Seems to me we should just live and do the best we can. Anyway, since I've promised to tell the truth the whole truth and absolutely nothin' but the truth, I will. I can hardly wait, and that's the truth.

My very real and very handsome prince is a poor farmer who rides a brownish mule. And the land we're riding off to is a good sized farm a few miles down Maple Brook Road. It's just loaded with potential.

Translated, my true love and I have years of back breaking labor ahead but we'll make it work. Best of all, we will raise our children as freedom loving Christians, and live in our house until our dying day.

My mind started giving me trouble once I admitted I was in love. It seems I became two people. There's the happy full of joy and hope me and the other me, not trusting, and miserably unhappy. Not only that, an angel sits on my right shoulder and whispers encouragement and a demon sits on the left laughing at my dreams. If they weren't yelling at me, they argued and yelled at one another. I went from miserable to happy at least a dozen times a day

The new me with the help of my angel was full of joy. The old familiar me, nurtured for years by demonic doubt did her best to end my newfound hope.

She said I was behaving like I was twin to happy pie-in-the-sky angel and setting my sights on a poor farmer was downright stupid. Why couldn't

I think money for once in my life? She said heaven knows money would solve our problems. She said love and poverty mixed together had as much chance as a snowflake on the Fourth of July. She said if nothing else what love did to my momma should have taught me that much. She demanded I give up my dreams for a better tomorrow and face reality. She said her definition of wasted time was time spent on writing a diary; that I should forget love and get to work.

All life has ever been for me is reality and drudgery and I'm sick of both. Reality is a daddy that walked out and never came back. Reality killed my momma when she worked so hard to keep the depression from ruining us, and left me with a sickly kid brother to raise and a boarding house and farm to run. Before we spend a cent we pinch it. Twice. We're up before sunrise and in bed at dark so we don't have to burn candles or kerosene lamps. I hate reality. I want to live. I want to forget my childish man hating promise and have the love and life a man and woman share.

My angel kicked the grump aside and said by working together and sharing dreams, my love and I could have…no, she said would have. a wonderful life and I'd be a dad blamed addle pated fool if I let her talk me out of my chance for happiness.

Demon pulled herself out of the pit and snarled "Happiness! In the middle of this world wide depression you don't stand a snowball's chance in hell! This pit bull has you, your brother Jethro and your poor Prince Charming and all Sainte Lillian's by the throat and its squeezing hope out of you!" She wasn't finished. "You and everyone else in dirt poor jobless Sainte Lillian have as much potential as cold greasy dishwater. Worse! None of you know it. You sing about a better tomorrow and peace in the valley and work yourselves to death. You're all so blind sided by false hope you don't see how hopeless you are.

Angel charged. "Life is not that bad! We have more than hope; we have faith in the Lord and American ingenuity. We know bad times don't last forever!"

Demon sneered. "I was referring to day old dishwater you ferment and mix with scraps to feed the hogs."

The thought of our lives in this peaceful Ozark valley being compared to pig slop made me ill. I was ready for war but she didn't care. With a voice as irritating as a fussy crow, she shrieked "Stay busy! Get rid of your stupid useless romantic dream!" Stop writing foolishness in that diary." Then in case she'd missed anything she pulled all the stops to remind me of years of poverty, of daddy never coming back, of the way momma died, of how hard and cruel life could be.

When it was that bad, it's a wonder I could breathe; let alone milk Bossie and Maudie. But I had to keep going because I promised momma on her deathbed I would never give up; that Jethro and I would stay together if I had to work around the clock. Sometimes, I do.

Two voices: Voice one, "Stick with reality. Voice two: "Don't let dreams die. Dream! Live! Love! Laugh! Hope!"

With my angel near, I felt beautiful, like I was wearing a pink chiffon gown and satin slippers. I could close my eyes and see me and my love dancing in the silver sheen of moonlight as violins played The Missouri Waltz.

Facing the unknowns alone, there were times I very much wanted to but could not force myself to forget about my love and our dreams. Staying the course was probably the hardest challenge I'd ever faced. Considering my life thus far, that sentence was a real mouthful

Dear Diary I've told you about the hungry days and about momma coughing up blood night after night. Sometimes dear friend you are like a towel soaking up all my tears and pain. I feel awful putting you through this.

Finally, I decided enough was too much! I tossed both demon and angel into a boxing ring and walked away. "Fight it out," I said and with shaking knees and a tear streaked face, I walked away, said my prayers, went to bed and slept like a baby.

In the morning, my bedside Bible was open to One Corinthians Chapter 13. I read about loves promise, its unquenchable hope and patience and looked over my shoulder to see my angel painting a "No entrance" sign on doubts door. Across the door she pinned a banner with "The greatest of these is Love." And then to finish it, "If God chooses, I shall but love thee better after death." I'm pretty sure these were the last lines of Elizabeth Barrett Browning's poem How Do I Love Thee?" Love won. I was free! I had tomorrow and tomorrow and tomorrow and my diary to record everything and the biggest case of nerves any woman in love could ever have. I wanted to write everything. Smiling angel on my shoulder whispered "pour out your heart and don't forget one single thing.

Free at last to write, I couldn't find a starting place. I wrote like I was stuttering and actually wasted paper. That made me think how unhappy momma would be as we never wasted anything.

I sat at my desk like I was kissin' cousin to those big old moss covered rocks down north side of the creek bank. Them rocks been sittin' there since God put them there, full or fossils and who knows what'n all. Seasonal rains and winter ice haven't moved them in hundreds of years. There I sat thinkin' about rocks and their secrets like this was more important than my life. I could probably have written stories about rock people; but when it came to telling you dearest companion about my love and dreams, I was mute. Frozen. As silent as the secret keeping rocks.

Lord knows I'm not a coward. I was afraid. All the "what if's" stared me in the face. What if I wrote about my love and our dreams and they disappeared? No life together, no love, no James Samuel, nothing. Worse, my caterpillar eyebrows would be back.

One thing I'm certain sure of, the way my hand cramps I can't write any more today. Maybe tomorrow.

I'm Back Dear Diary
Trying Again

My angel promoted herself to top drill sergeant in the Army of love. And like others of her ilk, her job was to turn green enlistees into willing and obedient warriors. Naturally, I was her favorite dumb, green; knock kneed, tongue tied scared to death Private. Dear Diary she ordered me to toe the line and write everything. "This is history. Write of your love," she said." I tried to tell her there were secret wonderful thing I didn't want to write but she didn't care. She says everything has to be written so I will never ever forget. I've already told her a million times I'll never forget but she turns a deaf ear. Sometimes I think living with my demon was easier.

If I turned to the left, my nagging sergeant was there. No matter how I tried to avoid her, she was there. She perched on my shoulder. She said I was under orders to write the truth, the whole truth and nothing but the truth. So help me God. "Write here. Write now! Right now!"

Since I'm such a dumb private, I proceeded to argue. I learned real quick that dumb privates never argue with sergeants. Tears didn't work. Next up, excuses and I had some doozies...my hands hurt, I had a headache, I couldn't think straight, I felt dizzy: They didn't make it either. She said while I was still innocent and pure I should write. Blushing would be good for me she said.

From all indicators, the Higher Power had more serious matters to attend, because the mercy I desperately needed was just a word circling the earth.

Was I to write about his kisses, his touch, the wonderful breathless way he made me feel? Mind you, while we never violated God's laws about purity, there were grey areas. Memories reminded me I wanted what I wanted, did what I did and enjoyed every minute. Thinking about James Samuel's kisses makes me tingle all over.

Now Dear Diary according to the dictates of my sergeant I am duty bound to write everything. That's just like a tough old sergeant; telling a newly enlisted private what to do and then forgetting to add the how to's of doing. Sergeants!

In my mind's eye, it was like telling a first time baker certain ingredients were necessary to bake a cake. Then," good luck. Make sure it's the best cake ever. Without experience or a recipe how does the baker know step one from step ten? Was my writing to be like a spice cake? If so, how much cinnamon was too little or, for that matter, too much? At least James Samuel makes me feel spicy, so that's a good start. Maybe.

Dear Diary after all this, I'm still stuck. I don't know how to unlock my heart. And I know I don't know how. I know facts are emotionless and love is wonderful! Love makes the sun shine. Love makes the rain come and flowers bloom. Love, is exciting! Love is everything!

I smiled and looked at the yellow roses in the blue vase Momma bought at the five and dime right before she got serious about dying. It's like the roses are a gift from her.

I brushed a tear away and my eyes rested on my cookbook collection. Momma treasured cookbooks. Since I've strayed so far and also because not a hand full of people know this, and since I'm stalled, and since I'm so desperate to get started, I'll write some memories of momma. I do wish my sentences were shorter. At least my activity with pen and paper keeps my domineering sergeant quiet.

Momma insisted good cookbooks were full of history. She said the more varied the collection, the more a person could learn about lives and times forever past. Her favorites were old cook books with as many household and medical suggestions as recipes. She said the way they covered everything between the bookends of life made hard to come by money worth the cost. More than once, she said "Sometimes, I think how people long dead watch over us while we use their books."

Her favorite is from England. Its pages are thick like they're printed on oiled cloth. Momma would let me and Jethro touch it only if our hands were clean and dry. Even then she stood over us like a mother hen ready to pounce if her chicks strayed. When it's opened after being on the shelf awhile a thick musty perfume fills the air. I told momma it was releasing memories of long ago. Momma said I had a real imagination and smiled like she agreed with me.

Then she showed me how one subject followed another. Salting and curing pork could be on one page and the next would cover 'laying in.' She said that was childbirth. For the longest time she real quick turned a few pages. She especially didn't want us readin' them pages with drawings of dead bodies and what they did getting them ready for buryin'. We could read on bathing though. That was awful funny. The book said taking a bath more than once a week could lead to sickness. I don't know why they believed that or how they got away with it. In those days people must have stunk to high heaven.

Momma said I could help her with recipes, but she didn't want me reading other things till I was grown up. When she was busy at the kitchen pump, I flipped a few pages and saw the dead body pictures, the drawing of a naked man on a table. People wearing thick aprons stood around the table and...Well, never mind! I shut the book so hard momma heard it. She looked at me with one of her eyebrows raised up real high. I hung my head and for once in my life, I didn't question momma at all. I decided it was best to wait for everything that book had to say till I was all grown up. At least 13 or 14 years old. Momma said it would be mine when I got married and someday I could share it with my daughters. Like she knew something I didn't. Me? Daughters?

Momma was a wonderful cook with or without that book. Yet, she always made sure to use its recipe for Christmas Plum Pudding. By midsummer we were drying and storing suet, grapes, plums and lemon and orange peels. This had to be ready to mix, mould, steam and store in the pantry before Halloween.

Momma gave me my best birthday present ever on my sixth birthday right after we started steaming the pudding. With softness in her voice and a look on her face I'll never forget, she said I was old enough to make biscuits.

I felt so important; I didn't think to reach for the porcelain doll. Of course it was a very pretty doll with a painted face and painted dark hair. It was wearing a dress exactly like my favorite blue flowered calico Sunday go to meeting dress. But, what was a doll when compared to making biscuits for the first time?

I had to stand on a kitchen chair to reach the counter top and my apron was a dishtowel. I was six years old. I could make biscuits!

I mixed the flour and salt and lard together with my hands. When it was crumbly we stirred in the buttermilk a little bit at a time. We did so much pour, stir, and mix I thought we'd never get done but time came when it was perfect. Sprinkling flour on the counter top for the dough was easy. I put so much down it was like a cloud and we all sneezed. Momma said I had to dust the furniture later. Then I plopped the biscuit dough smack dab in the middle. There was such a big round hill of dough staring me in the face and I knew from watching momma there was a lot of work ahead. I picked up momma's big old wood rolling pin and nearly fell from the chair. That thing weighed almost as much as me! I worked really hard controlling the dough and the pin at the same time, and flour went everywhere. We sneezed and momma laughed. My momma laughed something she had not done in the longest time. On my sixth birthday I made biscuits, momma laughed and the biscuits were perfect. Even daddy said so.

How memories play with me. Look where a little side story led. I promise to do my best to ignore side trips. However, if I must write all my dictating sergeant demands, necessity dictates doses of my yesterdays are necessary.

Speaking of, guess who just snuck into my thoughts. She growled, like she was an English Professor, and ordered me to focus. To make sure I understood, she repeated that all important 'f' word over and over again. "Focus!" Pause, big growl. Again, "Focus!" Longer pause, louder growl, and one more time louder and clearer' Focus!" If my angel sergeant wants focus; focus she will get. But it will be my way. Slowly. Eventually.

I was staring at the paper when a soft silence filled the room. I welcomed it and felt the warmth of momma's arms around me. Take my word for it, silence can be comforting. Then, the breeze brought music of contented birds and rustling leaves into my room. It was like a blind had opened to let in light.

Dear Diary and Dear Sergeant, since I am now willingly obedient, I will write my love story. And, it will tell everything. Maybe too much. We'll see. I guarantee this will not be a run-of-the-mill he said she said cold hard facts.

Dear Diary, the best idea I've ever had is writing my love story as a letter to my children.

James Samuel Ernest Owen and I are looking forward to doing those things my momma told me about. Oh my! That's the first time I ever wrote anything like that. I feel like I'm blushing all over. James Samuel and I: Mr. and Mrs. James Samuel Ernest Owen will have at least a dozen children. If I have my way six boys and six girls. James Samuel says he wants 12 daughters. When I pointed out he'd go broke paying for 12 weddings, he laughed.

Back to the point: since this is my diary and our story I will write so our children will know everything about our love. Well, o.k., not everything but probably more than enough. As my wedding day is months away, weeks away, days and hours and seconds away, I have plenty of time to write.

As for our children, they will be here soon because my dear boy promises we'll get them started on our wedding night. I can hardly wait. If that reads like I'm some kind of loose woman maybe I am. Yes, I'm blushing red again, maybe even redder. But I won't blot a word because that is exactly the way I feel. Tomorrow, the letter begins.

My Darling Children,

There are many important facts to cover my darlings. One: I, your mother, Miss Anna Augusta Verona Parker (who will become Mrs. James Samuel Ernest Owen and then your mother), began these letters on a lovely May morning mid way through my twentieth year.

Two: Believe that now and for always I will be head over heels in love with your father James Samuel Ernest Owen. We are so much in love nothing will ever get us down.

Three: Be aware these musings will not be in a specific order. Focus will be my way, guided by leadings of my heart and memories. I guarantee this is a true story. As such it is more than the love of one couple. Our community, the way we live and events that shape us are important. Most importantly this story is about God's timing that brought love-- and you to me.

It would be wonderful if the desires of our hearts came as naturally as it does to royals and the self made American rich. That is if there are any left in this terrible life sucking depression. But I learned a valuable lesson a few years ago from old Aunt Vora and I must pass it on to you. My prayer is what you learn may help shape your lives as it continues to influence mine.

This happened about the time I decided to accept the inevitable fact that women have a stainy time and stopped wishing I'd been born a man. Momma and aunt Vora and I had been picking blackberries on a hot bramble filled hillside since sunrise. It got hotter and hotter. I felt like the sun was burnin' a hole through my midsection. It didn't help at all that I was in my stainy time, or that my puny little brother was supervisin' from under a shady tree. Maple tree as I recall. We were sweating in the hot sun. Jethro on the other hand kept himself fortified with a sack of sugar cookies and a jug of ice cold spring water.

Looking at him in the shade only made my head ache. But, Glory be! That headache was nothin' compared to my aching back. If that wasn't bad enough, my troubles kept mountin' up. That headache wasn't half as bad as my backache, and them two combined were nothing when stacked up against my stainy time cramps. Only thing that kept me from pukin' was an empty stomach. Then there was the "pleasure" only women endure wearing pads home made from rags not fit for anything else. Because blood just soaks through, they're as thick as a bath towel folded over. If that's not bad enough, the safety pins holding them in place front and back on my home made belt are so big the whole mess can be seen when wind blows my dress close. I walk like there's a man thing between my legs.

That should be enough, but since I'm sworn to tell the truth, the whole truth and nothing but, I'm going to. I don't like it any more than you do so keep on reading. Not only do I have to wear these awful things nearly five days every month, I also have to soak the blood out in cold water and wash them and get them ready for the next time. I wanted very much to burn them every day, but couldn't. Why? Because, you see, we're so poor we have no choice but to use and re-use until they rot. And momma didn't mean just a little wear and tear here and there rot, she meant falling apart when you touch them rot. Even then momma made me use the salvageable little bits and pieces as filling between stronger layers of stained rags.

Last month, Momma told me to cheer up; by the time I was 50 years old, I wouldn't have to worry about such things. So I did the math. If things don't change, that's 350 months, 1,750 days. Oh why couldn't I have been born a man?

To top off my troubles this miserable hot morning sweat poured off me like I was a hot hog. Even worse, I stank. Combined sweat and stainy time stench together, I smelt almost as bad as rottin' potatoes.

To be certain there were no other likely winners in the Miss Miserable Personified contest, my talent act was moans, groans and long loud compaints. To say I excelled is putting it my way but nicely.

What we didn't have was breaking my poor heart. Daddy was gone, momma was working harder and getting sicker, and it seemed all my brother had strength to do was gather eggs, eat, and whittle. And believe me, that boy can do both.

All we had was work today, and tomorrow, and more work the day after that, and for weeks and months and years. And for what? We managed taxes paid, a roof over our heads and food in our bellies. If you call vegetables and oatmeal and meat once a week food. I picked berries in the hot sun and moaned and groaned.

Momma picked her berries and didn't say a word. Aunt Vora picked hers and said a lot of "Hummm's" Nothing else. She made that irritating noise every time I moaned and groaned.

When I stopped to blow my nose she must have thought I'd run out of moans and groans because next thing I knew, she started preachin'!

I'd no more got my hankie used and tucked into my apron pocket before she started in.

"Child you're makin' me tired. You're remindin' me of them there folks Moses led out of slavery."

Like a good stump preacher, she took a deep breath and gave me a long look...the kind that says "Now think on that for a spell."

That didn't take long. She hadn't wiped sweat from her forehead before I had my thoughts about that bossy old woman ready. I fixed her good with a sour look and then I said "You tell her momma." I knew momma would tell her what was what.

Momma didn't say one single word to Aunt Vora. What she did was give me one of very few but very effective stern looks. Then she said in her usual soft voice "Hush your fussin' daughter. Listen and learn."

That quick I forgot about the way I smelt and pains all over my lower body, and my headache and everything else. I thought my back would break plum in two the way I stood up so fast. I let out a little yelp and then looked at momma till I thought my eyes would pop right out of my head. I had been certain sure momma would tell Aunt Vora some real facts of life. Turned out I didn't know what I thought I knew. For the third time in my life, momma had used *that* tone of voice, and called me "daughter." It was like being whipped.

With that one word I was no longer her "Sweet Anna", but "Daughter. Bad girl. Girl that should know when to hush and learn." I had enough sense to know what was coming would tell me what was what and probably be life changing to boot. I turned toward aunt Vora.

She took time to smile at momma before she started preachin' like she'd been savin' up. "Them there families were followin' Moses to the Promise Land the Good Lord done set aside for them.

Then she just looked at me like she thought I was dumb. I looked right back and to prove I wasn't, said "Well, everybody from Sunday School on up knows that."

Momma cleared her throat. I knew what that meant. Now I had the added burden of convincing my momma I wasn't mean, dumb, or had forgot my manners. I figured the best way for me to do that was to shut my mouth. Hard as it was, and it was hard, I did. Bit my lip as a matter of fact, but my mouth stayed shut.

Aunt Vora went back to teachin/preachin. "Set free from slavery meant their kids wouldn't be took from em, means they could work for themselves, most important of all means they could worship the One True God. They could sing and pray and praise. They didn't' have nothin' to fear. And Child"--- She gave me another one of those looks, the kind that starts on your outside and bores a hole in your heart and mind. "All they did was gripe."

Momma always said I was a bright child. I was catchin' on.

"It's true they didn't bring along much food and when that ran out all their victuals was this here manna stuff God provided with mornin' dew."

She pulled a blackberry briar from a shady spot, shook off morning dew and, began to pluck thumb sized blackberries slow and easy like all the time watching' me. She knew I was thinking about our manna. Blackberries and wild greens and hickory and black walnuts and fish and squirrels and such.

Maybe I did moan and groan too much. I grinned sheepish like at Aunt Vora and then looked down. I felt awful thinkin' I was like one of them freed Israelites that moaned and groaned all the time.

Then she spoiled it. "Maybe we ain't got much, but rich folks waited on hand and foot livin' in fancy mansions are the ones that ain't got nothin'. Child they've never picked a blackberry or dug potatoes or got their hands dirty. No sir they ain't got nothin'!"

Now I was back where I started-- only madder. I knew what nothin' was because we had plenty of it. The rich on the other hand have never smelt an empty pot or drank or wore nothin'

I knew momma would tell Aunt Vora she'd gone too far. No two ways about it. I knew momma wouldn't tell me to hush. Waiting for momma to speak up, I felt a touch of sympathy for poor old overworked Aunt Vora. The way we lived hard scrabble one step away from losing everything lives, we had to be among the poorest of the poor. Our hands were chapped and dirty because we didn't have no choice. And Aunt Vora had just said filthy fat cat overly fed overly dressed rich folks didn't have nothin'. I'd take a tow sack full of that nothin' any day!

I knew for certain sure this time my momma would set her straight. Wouldn't you know it, my lessons weren't over. All my poor overworked sickly momma said was "Amen sister." I learned long ago once momma got in that amen corner she was as good as stuck.

Aunt Vora, like she'd heard angels singin' amen, kept on preachin.' "Sure they got money and all the things it can buy. Look at what else they get with it." She looked at me like she wanted an answer...

She wanted an answer? She would get an answer. Maybe not the one she wanted, but I didn't care. My list was long and my steam was up. Now, at long last, it was my turn to preach. Thank the Good Lord; the only sound out of my mouth was from my empty growlin' stomach.

Then Aunt Vora said for all the good things rich folks set their minds to havin' they plum forgot not a bit of it goes with them when they die. Then like she felt bad about what she was sayin, she said there's folks rich and poor alike believin God as long as God gives them things. They pay no never mind to the greatest gift of all. Folks that don't accept Jesus Christ as their Lord and Savior gonna wake up judgment mornin' just like that fella who let Lazarus die of starvation. The tables sure was turned when he woke up in hell. He begged God to let Lazarus put a drop of water on his burning lips and God said No!"

Momma said "Amen.

At long last my mouth stayed shut all by itself. I always studied my Sunday school lesson and listened to the preachin,' and knew that story. This was maybe the first time I'd realized it was more than a made up story but about real people, just like us. Like history repeating itself generation after generation.

Aunt Vora wasn't through with me. "What matters for all folks everywhere is believin' what Jesus taught and doin' what He said. Just like that verse in Chapter One of James that says if we only listen to the word and don't do what it says we're only lyin' to ourselves. The Bible ain't there to just read, it's our guide book and we're lost in the wildness without it." I thought she meant wilderness but realized she meant what she said.

"Anna it's past time for you to stop your downward slide. Count your blessings child. Get busy, Look around and name them one by one."

She musta figured my mind was stuck somewheres, so she helped me a little. "We're livin' in the promised land.Times be tough, but we ain't alone. Take lessons from your momma and praise the Lord."

Considerin, it would take a lot more to convince me our address was the Promised Land, but I decided Aunt Vora was on the right track. Especially about thankin' the Lord for our blessings and of course my momma. If there was ever a woman always patient, kind, giving and forgiving, that was my momma. For certain sure, I had a very long way to go.

I looked long and hard at Aunt Vora. Past the way she was there, to the way she lived. In spite of losing her husband and only son in that terrible railroad crossing accident, peace was always in her eyes. Little Charlie Richard and his pa was walkin' the rails when little Charlie fell over and his foot got stuck real bad. Big Charlie Richard worked hard as he could to get little Charlie Richard out of that stuck boot. There just wasn't enough time is all. Pickin' up speed for steep hills, the train barreled around Poker Flats curve. The engineer did everything he could; train brakes screamed and screeched, and the whistle blew so loud folks knew somethin' was up. When he coulda run and saved his own life big Charlie Richard grabbed his son and held on tight. He hid little Charlie Richard's head in his chest so all his son felt was his daddy's strong arms, all he saw was his daddy's red plaid shirt, and all he heard was the solid strong louder in his ears than the train whistle beat of his daddy's heart. Both of them wound up dead. Horribly horribly dead.

Deep lines formed little gullies on her wind rough sun burnt face and arms and the washed out grey dress she wore everywhere, hid the real Aunt

Vora. I knew hungry folks counted on her, and her rough work worn hands had the healing touch. Folks said when she walked into a grieving home light and peace came in with her. I realized 'Poor Aunt Vora' wasn't poor at all. She had a storehouse of riches. Better still, when she opened her eyes in heaven, she'd be happy as could be with Jesus and her two Charlie Richards.

On that hot Ozark hillside under a clear blue sky, truth hit me like a bolt of lightening. Here I was thinkin' I had the world figured out and I'd just learned that I not only didn't have the answers, I was a long way from bein' smart enough to have the questions. All that thinkin' made my eyes wet.

I learned later that time with Aunt Vora was an epiphany or defining moment in my life. I vowed to work harder counting my blessings and chastised myself for having such a negative opinion of the spoiled pampered snobbish rich folks. Poor things. If only they knew.

Truthfully wanting to be positive and being positive was pretty hard at times. Watching momma waste away made it awful hard.

Now to put all this into a nut shell: Among other things like awakening my faith, Aunt Vora taught me it's better to look at the real world and the way real people live and love than to waste time moanin' about what we ain't got. That brings us to here and now.

God put your father and me together. We share reality and dreams (Lord knows that's a combination of opposites) Never thought I'd be thankful for hard work but we're gonna need all our stored up experience to make dreams come true.

Have I told you lately your father is unbelievably handsome and that he loves me dearly? To say I love him is not enough. There are so many shades to my love. I love the respect he shows his parents, the gentle hand he has with children, the way animals know him to be a friend. He can't carry a tune in a bucket, but his voice is music. His laughter redefines happiness. The strength of his love shelters me from storms.

Oh dear, just when I was in the mood, good old ever present duty called. I doubt anyone could write when cows need milkin' roosters are crowin' and squealin' pigs chase each other around the pen.

Tuesday

My darlings,

I am so happy. Even more so when I remember that not that long ago, my life was nothing but chores, chores, and more chores. Now, because I'm thinkin' of your father and you I fill my days with song…whether the cows and chickens like it or not. Time now for the story about when I stopped wondering and decided I definitely was falling in love…

Our first date was one of the biggest surprises in my life. We had dinner at the Audubon, which as you know is not only the fanciest but the most elaborate and dare I say it? Yes, I shall, the most expensive restaurant this side of Saint Louis. I knew all about the Audubon because as a little girl I'd stand with my face smushed against the lace curtained window and stare in at all the beautiful people and dream about someday waiters hovering around me. They were dressed so fine and always bowed from the waist and served everything so fancy. And here I was surrounded by waiters and a table loaded with china and stemmed glasses. James Samuel acted like he'd been there many times and the waiters sure worked making him happy. He sent a salad back to the kitchen because the dressing was too oily.

The food was very good, cheeses and fruit first then James ordered something he called escargot. When they brought the steaming dish to the table I asked him if they'd made a mistake. "They're snails," James Samuel, I said and he said they were not plain ordinary garden snails, but imported from France, and he said that word again "Escargot." I told him if it looks like a snail I don't care what he called it, it was still a snail. I ate one because James Samuel said he'd developed quite a taste for them. The hardest part was holding that snail all drippin' butter and garlic sauce in a little round thing and using a tiny fork to pull it out and then…oh never mind, It didn't taste that bad, but snails! I was really glad for the little dishes of sorbet between courses. Especially after the snails. Truthfully though, since I am being truthful, I'd rather have "cleaned my palate" (don't ask) with home made ice cream…only I reckon it wouldn't have done the job.

I'd rather remember the lace table cloth, the smiling waiters, the way they served food with such a flourish, the different plates for everything, and the forks. Forks for this, forks for that, forks for something else. Tiny cups of coffee strong enough to grow hair on a hard boiled egg is another story. So is the chocolate mousse. Speaking of coffee, I think it was there I started saying my coffee needed more cream and sugar.

After dinner we took a leisurely drive to the old mill covered bridge and walked toward a secluded bench. There James Samuel told me I had to hear about his past. Not some gossip version but the truth from his lips. He knew what he was doing when he grabbed my hands because in minutes, I wanted to run. I wanted to forget everything about him.

I remember his voice, the truth shining from his green eyes as he said as difficult as the telling was on his part and the hearing on mine, I had to hear about his sinful ways from his lips instead of some gossip mill version. Both were bad he said, but he was the only one able to tell the whole ugly truth.

"I was mad about everything, and blamed the bigwigs in churches, politics and business for the depression. I didn't respect nothin' or nobody including women. Fat as a hog skinny as a rail, I didn't care if they was bald or bleached blonde, what they sounded like or smelt like, if they was drunk or sober. They were willin' to be caught, and I sowed my share of wild oats."

Most of the time till then, James Samuel and I had kept eye contact. Now hard as he tried, he couldn't keep it up. The grassy picnic spot was more interesting than my blue eyes. I remember wanting to touch a lock of coal black hair that fell across his forehead. I remember trying to listen while a part of my brain escaped as he shared these awful ugly stories… Not made up stories. They were his stories. His history.

Now as far as worldly ways go, I was about as green as just sprouted corn but I knew enough to know the man I wanted to love had confessed sexual intimacy with many women. He could be father to children he would never know. It was like my breaking heart was being trampled by hobnail boots.

Memories of my life of pain rushed back. I was about four when momma's twin daughters were born. I thought they were dolls until she told me they were my sisters. I had two sisters. That meant I wouldn't be alone, and there was someone-two some ones- for me to love. I was so happy. They were so small. Their weak cries sounded like mewing kittens. Momma wrapped them in cotton bunting and fed them warm milk and sugar water with an eye dropper but it didn't do any good... They died. One after the other; same hour, same sad day, both of my sisters died and I was alone again. Momma and daddy cried and that made me sadder. Because they cried, I cried myself to sleep every night. It was dark and quiet at our house for a long time.

Brother Jethro joined our family the summer of my sixth year. He was the sickliest puniest baby folks had ever seen but he sure liked to eat. I don't say Jethro was ugly to be mean, but to tell the truth. There wasn't a thing about baby Jethro that invited a second glance. Except from us and usually that was to make sure he was breathin'. Skin on bone he was and bald. Momma named him Jethro Patrick after his daddy and grandpa. She said they were both good strong Christian men. I said sometime I would call him Ro-Ro. She didn't like that much but when I made up silly songs with his name she smiled.

Momma finished crying over my sisters and then was so scared for Jethro she cried again and worked even harder. She took in washing so Jethro could have tonics.

Troubles and heartache piled up one after another. Jethro was eight when daddy headed out west to make our fortune. He said we'd all have to pitch in and work harder, but in the long run our ship would come in and we'd live on easy street. He wasn't joking about working harder. When he carried most of the load life was hard enough. With him gone it was worse. The three of us had to run the farm and boarding house. There we were: momma, a sickly woman, puny allergic to work Jethro and me against the world. Jethro was good at eatin' and whittlin' but not much else. I was skin on bone, not much bigger than momma and she wasn't more than a shadow. The difference is I was all muscle and strong as most men. I went to school and worked sunup to sundown.

Momma saved every cent daddy sent home, and never stopped working. She got it bad in the chest and coughed and sweated. Like I said, she never was bigger than a shadow but with all that coughing, she got smaller and weaker. There were days she coughed so hard she couldn't stand upright. But she kept on workin.' Momma said she'd fix herself with mustard plasters and onion cough syrup the way her momma did. Sickly as Jethro was, the way she figured it out doctorin' for her would take money away from Jethro's tonics.

Momma never got better. She kept on workin' when her chest cold turned into the consumption and that's what killed my momma.

27

Jethro and I made it through the next few years by the skin of our teeth. Then James Samuel came into my life and I felt hope for the first time. And now this. The man I wanted to love forever was telling me unspeakable things. Why couldn't he hint at some of it and skip some? Better yet, why didn't he keep his mouth shut? Seconds later, my questions were washed away in the flood.

"I headed up the counties moonshine network. Me and the boys, we trafficked our Ozarks, went crost to Illinois, down to Kentucky, had outlets in Ohio and Arkansas. Ours was the best, left the competition in the shade. Loved that shine. Makin' it and drinkin' it and the money pourin' in wasn't bad either. There wast nothin' me and the boys couldn't do or buy. We were as smooth as the shine, so good that John Law didn't know our names."

His voice changed, became the voice I knew. "The morning my life changed forever, I'd made more cash money profit the night before than we'd made in five years of back breaking farm work.

My plans was coffee, a platter full of mammy's Sunday special sweet potato pancakes and then finalizin' our business deal. Had lard buckets and sacks full of money hid away, and plenty of women willin' to work".

I almost asked what kind of work, but his eyes were so sad I didn't dare. Somehow, I knew this work didn't involve cooking, or bending over a wash board.

"It's a good thing pappy didn't know about my saved up money or my plans. Y' see back then I thought his talk about salvation and faith and bein' born again and washed in the blood of the lamb and havin' a personal relationship with Jesus wasn't real. I thought it was just religion and I knowed too many religious shiners to buy into that. Pappy said knowing Jesus was a way of life and I'm certain sure if he'd knowed about my money he'd a burned it.

That Sunday mornin' he was about through with me. He said Jesus hadn't gave up on me but he was about to and mammy started cryin'. Pappy said since I wouldn't go to church, I could catch up on spring plowin'. He said I smelled like a stinkin' drunk and the best way to get that out of my system was out there in the field. He said I'd better hope the mules could stand the way I smelt cause he wasn't sure about the good Lord, and he was certain sure he and mammy couldn't.

Didn't have time for more' n a biscuit and a cuppa lukewarm coffee before he had me headed to the south forty. As I recall, the sun was no more than gettin' acquainted with the trees. You know the way it is early mornin' down t'the hollers with mist low to the ground? He took a deep breath and actually looked at me like he remembered I was there.

"The way what is? Did he mean life? Was I supposed to say something? I opened my mouth to ask while my brain tossed thoughts around like the wind tosses dandelion seeds. I wanted to tell him to not say another word about moonshine, or willing women or sin money. Or stinkin' mules either for that matter. I wanted my safe wonderful world and my dreams of family back. But I didn't get a chance.

"The fed up way pappy was talkin' brought to mind learnin' the razor strap way when I was a kid. Back then, when pappy said "jump!" in that tone of voice, all I had to do was ask "how high Pappy?" before my feet left the ground." He paused like he'd lost his place on a page and then quick as a wink, found it.

"We were an ornery team those old mules and me. They didn't like pullin' that old plow any more than I liked cussin' them and pushin' it. Here I was with the worst"--- He looked at me, and looked away as if he wondered I'd heard about such things. Then he told as much of the truth as he could. "Headache, I had the worst headache," he said and looked to see if I'd caught on.

I didn't understand why after telling me about moonshine and wild women he hesitated to say "hangover," but that's a man for you. I didn't exactly lie or pretend I just looked him in the eye and did my best to smile a sweet innocent smile. You might say "that's a woman for you."

Fighting tears, but determined to leave nothing untold James Samuel cleared his throat and looked at his hands. At long long last, he realized what his strong grip was doing to me. For five minutes he came up with new ways to say he was sorry.

Apologies I didn't need because by then I was captured; not by his strength but by my need to know. No matter what he said, my heart and mind refused to make a sound decision until the story ended. Somehow, I knew our future-- if we were to have one-- depended on my silence.

My eyes must have told him what was in my heart because he seemed to gain more confidence. "Well, where was I then?

This time I answered and felt smug about getting something said in this conversation. "Midmorning," I said and as my hands were free, I arranged myself more comfortable and closer to him. Not exactly leaning on him like a loose woman you understand, but a lot closer. My focus now was this man and this story as if nothing else mattered. Because now, nothing else did not the depression, the doing without and the long dark road of unknown. I knew if I ran I'd never forgive myself because all of our tomorrows and all of my dreams were waiting.

"Ahh yes! I was takin' the mules down creek for a rest, and I needed to get outa that sun. We neared a shaded place where water ran cool and

I heard singin'. Then I recalled mammy said the Free Methodist Church was havin a mornin' baptism"

His smiled like he heard the voices again and his eyes! I've heard about eyes glowing like there were lights behind them, but until this moment I'd never seen such a thing. His eyes glowed, like they were full to runnin' over with joy.

"There was this clear tenor voice floatin' through the trees. Pastor Dave it was. Used to hear him at the Gospel Barn. Remember?"

I said "yes," and nothing else because thinking maybe he did shine business back of the Gospel Barn gave me the shivers.

"Pastor Dave's voice carried up the hill like it was on wings. I noticed old crows after grubs stopped to listen. Wasn't a thing I could do but stand there and soak it in."

Next thing I knew he made a noise that was almost as shocking as his story. Never in my life had I heard anyone do to one of my favorite songs what James Samuel was doing as he threw his head back and let loose. The only way to describe the indescribable is to say what came out of his mouth was a mixture between a cross cut saw and a bullfrog. A bullfrog with a sore throat. Sparing me the whole thing, he sawed through the chorus:

Will there be any stars any stars in my crown
When at evening the sun goeth down
When I wake with the blest in the mansions of rest,
Will there be any stars in my crown?"

I love music so much. It never occurred to me the Good Lord was up to that kind of merriment. James Samuel's solo left me speechless but he was in such a hurry, he didn't notice that, or the look of shock I couldn't hide.

"It was like I was on automatic while I tended them mules. With them outa the way, I started some serious thinkin'. True, I was makin' money but I wasn't doin' a bit of good with it. Thinkin' about it and the way mammy looked mornings when I staggered across the yard hurt me down deep" He reached for his red bandana.

Soon as he finished wipin' his eyes, I grabbed his hands with my version of a vise like grip. He told me to not fret. "I finish what I start. I always do," he said

Next thing three of the prettiest female voices I've ever heard were singin' Just as I am, which happens to be my mammy's favorite song. Them words hit me right between the eyes and smack dab center of my heart. Before I knew it I was singin' along at the top of my voice. I found myself layin' in the dirt like I'd been knocked down while the song worked its way through me. Right then and there in that rocky field surrounded by spring greenin' trees and hearin' those words comin' up from the creek, I turned my life over to the Lord. It was the most wonderful thing I ever done. A feelin' of joy and forgiveness washed over me. It didn't come and go real quick like either, it kept buildin' up. Just like pappy said, I was bein' washed in love and comin' out clean. I knew the good Lord was welcomin' me into His family and didn't mind I smelt worse than them old mules. And somethin' else I'll never forget: The field was covered with a golden glow, t'was on the trees, everywhere.

Once I stopped shakin' and blubberin' me and them mules finished plowin' in record time. We got to the barn about the same time the folks got home from church. They took one good look and knew right off their prayed for miracle had happened. I managed to stop blubberin' long enough to tell the story. Next thing you know, I wasn't the only one bawlin.' Mammy got all weepy and pappy said the angels were rejoicin' in heaven cause a lost sheep had come home. He asked if I'd be willin' to share my testimony at evenin' vespers.

Pappy knew there was a time if I even thought about talkin' in front of Bible quotin' church folks I'd have cussed a blue streak. No getting' around I had to talk nice in public, but now, me bein' new born so to speak, I could tell he wondered what kind of language I'd use.

"Why pappy says I, and I cleared my throat big time while he stood there lookin' like he was wonderin' if I was his son. Then I looked him straight in the eye and said "Pappy that's about the best idea in the world. He sat down real fast. Mammy started singin' and praisin' the Lord."

I was ready to do it right then but mammy started to laugh her happy laugh. She gave me a hug bigger than the one she gave me when I was lost in the woods and half the county and their hounds was huntin' me.

"Son, she says to me, it'd be a good idea if you took a bath first. Then she gave me one of them looks I hadn't seen in years. She said "While you're scrubbin' and I'm cookin' your pappy needs to burn your stinkin' overalls. Lord knows, ain't nothin good been around them and I don't fancy dirtyin' wash water."

That's my mammy. When she takes charge, she takes charge! Meek as lambs me and pappy followed directions while she cooked up a feast. In no time, she'd fried up a couple chickens, some taters and onions with lotsa black pepper, stewed two quarts of tomatoes, wilted lettuce and had a pineapple upside down cake in the oven. Let me tell you, we feasted. There wasn't a cake crumb left over.

The way I paced, it's a miracle I didn't wear holes in the kitchen linoleum. Me! The bootleggin' rich man who hadn't been to church more than three times my adult life and them was for funerals, could hardly wait to get there.

You should have seen them church folks faces. First off they looked kinda shocked and maybe a little afraid. Once I got into the story though, that changed. Kinda reminded me of the glow at the field. He paused… "Well, if you had a little hand mirror, you'd see what I'm talkin' about. Your face is every bit as shiny as theirs."

I didn't need a mirror to know my eyes were wet and I couldn't hide my smile. Most important, I knew the feeling in my heart was real. This was love. I was in love.

Then we sat in silence wrapped in one of those long pauses that comes to cement things. I knew it was time to put my doubts aside and listen to the song in my heart.

James Samuel chuckled. "I snuck down to the church long after midnight and left enough cash to pay off the mortgage, hire old man Hardgrass to reroof, and fix up a few things like rottin' floor boards and pews nearly fallin' apart. There was enough to help some down and out families too. Best of all, they may think they know, but they'll never know for sure where that came from. You're the only person that knows and I know you won't tell a soul.

I had to join his laughter. I could picture Preacher Marley finding that money and the rejoicing it caused. I wondered how James Samuel was able to sit with a straight face when the windfall was announced at Tuesday prayer meeting. I had another question to put aside as my dear boy hadn't finished his story.

My business partners Pete and Joe and old Silent had to hear first hand my part was done. Confessin' to these good old boys scared me a bit seein' as how we'd come that close to getting' rich. But I knew if I was gonna confess to bein' a Christian, I had to not only talk the talk but also walk the walk.

Somethin' I said musta made an impression cause the fellas said if finding the Lord could turn a hell bent feller like me around there had to be somethin' to it. The lot of 'em was in church with me the next Sunday, and they been pretty regular ever since.

James Samuel wiped his eyes to clear laughter tears. "At the church alter prayer time I promised the Lord I'd stop chasin' wild women and marry a good Christian lady. Just to show him how serious I was, I up and told Him I didn't care if the woman he picked for me was bowlegged, bucktoothed or fat as a hog as long as she loved and served Him."

Then he did one of those man things with his eyes and gave a real wolf whistle, and said, "Sure am glad the Good Lord had you in mind."

When James Samuel and I go into eternity I will still remember that day. And I'll treasure forever the nudging from the Lord that kept me there when I wanted to run away.

Have I written I absolutely love your father's every smile and thought and movement? It is like we are one. I can tell you I love him with my whole heart and how much he loves me. The best I can do is pray that together, everything we do will show you how wide and deep and true our love is.

Thursday

My Darlings,

Reading the first few letters made me realize that once again, I've put the cart before the horse. Now that the supper cake is baking, I'll hitch up the old grey mare and head in the right direction. In yet another attempt to begin at the beginning, we shall take the first steps of the journey your father and I started to find you.

Another of my work myself into exhaustion days was almost over. In four hours after evening milking and cleaning up after supper I'd be done. Yippee! Strike up the band!

I was restin' in the old porch swing, sippin' a glass of lemonade and waitin' for Jethro to bring the mail. The hand fan Pastor Del gave me after momma's funeral made a pleasant breeze. Pastor Del said it reminded him how much momma loved yellow roses and the 23rd Psalm and since both were on the fan he wanted me to have it.

I smiled thinkin' about momma and then saw Jethro runnin' home from the post office. He was in such a hurry little furry red road dust clouds marked his path. Funny things those clouds, they're heavy with dust but slow to settle back to the road. When Jethro got to our gate, I spotted the white envelope he was waivin' back and forth. Land sakes, if only he'd put that much effort into his chores!

Jethro collapsed on the porch. "It's for you," he said and commenced to ignore me and use it as a fan. The nerve! It was my letter. I got a real letter once in a blue moon, and I wanted it. Sometimes I want to yell at him, but I did promise momma to be kind. Besides, with his blond hair plastered across his forehead and his tongue hangin' out he reminded me of a tuckered out Cocker Spaniel pup.

I didn't say a word, just watched and waited to snatch it. When the letter went to his left, I tiptoed to his right. He didn't know what happened. I moved to a spot dappled with sunlight and shade near the old fashioned yellow rose trellis, and leaned against it careful like so those nasty little thorns wouldn't prick through my blouse. Sunlight and leaf shadow played with my hands in the warm afternoon breeze that loosed the soft peppery perfume of our yellow roses.

All the while I had the strongest feeling my life was about to change forever. It's one of those fancy words like prescience or foreknowledge that means you know something before you have proof. Know what I mean?

At the envelopes far left corner in dark black ink and a very bold and masculine hand I read a strange name. A name without a face to go with it: James Samuel Ernest Owen. My mind played with his name. "Is he called James, or James Samuel of Jimmie, or J.S.E.?"

Pretending he wasn't watching or the least bit interested, my snoopy brother had presence of mind to grab a white pine board and pull out his pen knife and whittle. He was so busy 'not watching me,' he whittled it down to a toothpick.

I turned so brother couldn't read my lips, and whispered "James Samuel Ernest Owen' I decided then and there I would call him James Samuel. I turned in time to catch Jethro watching me. I smiled. "Have you finished carving the wooden angels for your girl friend?" I asked innocent like. He mumbled something and reached for another piece of white pine. That left me alone to repeat the magical name James Samuel over and over. As I did goose bumps formed on my arms.

I am keeping my promise, sharing exactly what happened before I read the letter. The envelope lay against the fan's yellow tea roses as I looked out over the Ozark hills. As the yesterdays floated through my mind, it was like part of my life had ended. I took time to wonder about the meandering line of my tomorrows.

Then Jethro called in a way too familiar feel sorry for me voice. "So tired," he said expecting me to wait on him like momma and I did when he was small and sickly. He was neither now and I was past being sick and tired of his whining. It was past time for him to grow up.

"Jethro I just fetched a bucket of fresh ice cold spring water. You know where it sits on the table inside the kitchen door."

True to form, he groaned as if taking 30 steps would take his last breath.

"If you think you could eat a few, there's a jar full of sugar cookies in the pie safe." Jethro could never resist sugar cookies. Somehow he found the strength to rescue half of them.

Thank the Lord, Jethro's outgrown ugly. He'll never make handsome, but packin' on 50 some pounds and growin' a foot didn't hurt. My promise to momma aside, I don't see how doin' everything for him will help him grow up.

It was an early April morning near sunrise when momma died. Soft rain promising renewal had been with us overnight. No wind, just the soft washing cleanliness on the tin roof and against the windows. Peaceful. Comforting. As rain clouds were breaking, momma came back from where her dark night had taken her. Her eyes found me first and then went to Jethro. She whispered our names...

We knelt at her bedside and I placed our first fragile yellow rose buds in her hand. Yellow buds. Pale, almost white and so tiny, curled into themselves, their leaves just greening up. She loved yellow roses so. Momma smiled. She used the rest of her strength to place Jethro's hand in mine."Promise," she said and I knew she meant I had to watch over Jethro and keep him well. Jethro knew he had to promise to stay with me.

We said "Yes momma," at the same time as she looked toward the door. A great beam of sunlight like a pathway was at the threshold. Momma smiled and said "Patrick" in a soft loving voice full of joy and then, just like that, she stopped breathing. Or what had passed for her taking breath for the longest time. Little bright red foam bubbles were on her lips. Tiny bubbles. Bright red.

For ever so long we wiped bubbles away as momma coughed and struggled. Short gasp took air in and frothy bubbles brought it out. I never thought these small sounds were our way of knowing momma was with us until suddenly and forever that small quietness was stilled. It was then Jethro and I learned that silence is the voice of the dead.

Momma looked happy and pain free. I remembered that and all Jethro and I had been through in the years before her dying as we cared for her and shouldered the work of boarding house and farm. Jethro really surprised me when he took on more of the work load. He chopped wood, hauled water, and worked the fields like he'd been doing it all his life. Glory be, it didn't hurt him a bit. Fact is, he got stronger, and bigger and taller. Past ugly, just like I wrote.

For two years only a few close friends thought they knew how bad momma was but with flu epidemics and all they were so busy she never told them. Up until the holidays, her friends were over for quilting and tea.

They were as surprised as everyone after Christmas when she never got over that chest cold. Her dying came so fast folks couldn't believe it.

Our 'friendly town banker' and his missus were first to come callin' after the funeral. When I say first, I mean they were at the door before I had my hat off. I heard them knocking and all I could think of was the sound of rocky Ozark soil bouncing off momma's coffin box. I could see shovels full of red dirt and stone covering my momma. My momma all cold and still; and one shovel full after another kept weighing her down. I wanted her to push the box lid aside and get out of there. I wanted my momma. The hurt wasn't going to be over for a long long time.

Oscar and Rhoda Mae Crabtree marched right in like they owned the place. There he was skinny as a rail, dark suit, dark hair, long hawk nose, skin like it's never been touched by sunlight. And by his side Rhoda Mae every bit as skinny and purt near twice as ugly. I often wondered if they lived off bread and water just so they could hide more money under their mattress and all over their big old house. Folks said a body'd need a treasure map to find it all. Sure made folks feel good thinking bankers trusted lard buckets and mason jars more than their own bank.

Crabtree's lips said one thing, their eyes another. Not for one second did I want that crow faced old woman to hug me or pat me on the back. She poured on sympathy and condolences while her eyes traveled the living room and calculated the price of everything momma and daddy owned. She spotted the applesauce cake on the kitchen table and her nose started sniffin' for coffee before she remembered to reach for her hankie and wipe her tears. Dear Rhoda Mae was so distraught. She was so concerned for our welfare now that Jethro and I were poor orphans.

Banker Crabtree had Jethro cornered. He told Jethro we were too young to manage a farm and boarding house, and we would loose everything. The 'honest' banker's best advice "motivated by Christian concern for our welfare of course, was for us to sell out." As good Christians with our welfare at heart, they couldn't stand the thought of house and land going into foreclosure. They didn't want us to loose everything at auction the way some folks round about did. They were willing to shoulder our load. Knowing how anxious we were to go on with our lives, they would help us pack up and move. And then that nasty greedy old man put nearly a thousand dollars cash money on momma's kitchen table. Right by the cake. "That should cover everything," he said, by everything he meant everything down to the cake and the last rusty nail. To them, what momma and daddy had worked and momma had died for didn't matter a hoot in a hand basket.

Because they were older and supposedly wiser, and because momma taught me to respect my elders, I was doing my best to be polite. After all, some folks still respected them, and they were among Sainte Lillian's leading citizens. Whatever that meant. But when Rhoda Mae rubbed her hands over momma's black walnut pie safe and said "And I'll gladly give you three dollars over and above what's on the table for this here pie safe," it was my last straw. When she pulled out her little black change purse and started counting money, my face turned whiter than cold ashes. She looked up just then and probably, thinking I wanted more money, said real grudging like, "Well, four dollars then, but not a penny more."

Jethro was seconds from exploding. If the Crabtree's stayed another two minutes, I'd join him. I had to do something before we turned these so called leading citizens of Sainte Lillian's into bitter enemies. Before Jethro's fuse hit his dynamite, I got between him and our sympathetic callers. Then sweet as you please, I thanked them for their "true Christian concern" and their offer. Hard as I tried, I couldn't call it a generous offer. "We will be in touch," I said. Quick as a wink I grabbed that awful pitiful little pile of money and shoved it into Crabby's hat so fast it bent two of the three black feathers on the brim till they would never be straight. And I wasn't a bit sorry either. Truth be told, wish I'd broken them off.

Jethro opened the door, and to make momma proud, I walked them out. Our banker acting like he'd never been turned down in his entire life, spluttered nonsense. His Mrs., who'd just decided to help herself to cake and coffee said "Well, I never!" In a voice that reminded me of someone slipping on cow flop. She was purely disgusted. We'll never know what she never because I shut that door really fast.

The Crabtree's didn't know Pastor Del and Lara busy putting food away in the pantry had heard everything. Before I turned around, they flew out of the pantry. It was like they'd been waiting to catch the Crabtree's in one of their crooked deals. Me and Jethro stood by the front window, kinda hiding behind the lace curtain and watched the whole thing. The Crabtree's were backed up against their shiny town car looking like they were being' whipped and Pastor Del had that stance he always uses when preachin' a good sermon. We didn't hear any laughin'. Jethro said he knew they weren't talking about the weather. You don't know how bad I wanted to sneak out and around the well house to hear but I didn't dare. Funny thing, we never heard from our so called concerned Christian friends again, and, not once did we have a bit of trouble at the bank. In fact that old banker was downright courteous tippin' his hat, opening the door and everything. Gossips takin' in his changed behavior had a field day but nobody knew nothin'.

It seemed miraculous at year's end when without counting the money under momma's mattress; we came up with two hundred and thirteen dollars cash money. I counted twice and then had Jethro count it three times while I paced.

After his third count, Jethro let out a war whoop. He said our sum total was two hundred thirteen dollars and one Indian head penny. He added that just to tease me. "Got any more surprises?" I asked. He dug through pockets and drawers and added fifty cents. We felt rich, because this was our total profit after taxes, patching' the roof, buyin' yards of material for shirts and dresses, two pairs of coveralls for Jethro, new barn boots, a Jersey milk cow, a batch of broody hens, and...oh dear, this sounds like bragging. Momma was all for hard work and thankfulness, but dead set against pride.

I'm thankful momma taught us to never turn folks away that needed a meal or a bed. Just like her, I stir oatmeal in the soup so something will stick to their ribs. We always haul out the washtubs after they eat. Landsakes, some of these folks need more washin' than do the clothes on their backs. What breaks my heart are little hollow cheeked kids and sad lookin' men and women with nowhere to go. They stay with us for a night or for a season. That they can't afford to pay us cash money don't matter none, because without their help we couldn't run the farm. Momma taught us real good. We know paybacks don't have to be money.

Before I forget, remember when I wrote about being 14 and all that moanin' and groanin'? Well, then I thought we were bottom of the barrel poor, and that folks couldn't be worse off than us. Then the depression got worse, and those that was worse off started knockin' at our door. We had a house, we had a door, and we had food to share. I can't forget the little kids. Scrawny little things, seemed like they didn't have a childhood.

As I looked across the lawn toward the rolling Ozark foothills, dressing up in afternoon shade, my thoughts were peaceful. The smallest every day ordinary things seemed to call me. Blue white haze settled in for the evening like a blessing. Contentment was a soft blanket covering our little world.

I smiled as the peep frog orchestra tuned for our evening concert. When cows started talking it up about milking our concert would begin in earnest. Bullfrogs would sing bass, night birds trill harmony and our valley auditorium would fill with nature's music.

We are surrounded by beauty... Momma could draw and paint. Jethro can if he has a mind to, but that's not often. He whittles. I do word pictures like the beauty of the first ruby red flush of berry leaves, the emerald green of clover against the old gray split rail fence. Poor fence, it's been there long as I can remember and it's still standin' strong. Not two feet from that fence and sometimes shuck up against it is an old narrow bare earth path that follows the fence line where blackberry brambles grow. Bare red gray soil and creamy yellow sandstone are packed and worn smooth by human feet and bovine hoof. Momma said where we live and walk and pray Indian children used to play. Makes me wonder about the stories the earth keeps secret.

Jethro finally gave his jaws a rest from sugar cookies and started serious whittlin'. When he whittled like that, his mind was on girls. In fact, Jethro is smitten by anyone in skirts. Any girl; diaper size or older, short or tall, bouncing round or beanpole straight gets his devoted attention. If he can't amaze younguns, he does his best to charm widow women. As long as there's a female in his sights, Jethro is plum happy.

How many times have I wandered from my dear boy? Don't answer! This is necessary to tell you not only who we are but how we live. It's like these side roads lead to the baked cake.

Baked cake?

Oh no!

Way Too Much Time Later

My darlings,

I surrender. Even though you and James Samuel are paramount in my thoughts, chores must come first. Cows can't milk themselves, and I can't train chickens to not lay eggs in barn rafters, upended buckets and the well house. At least I'm on to their tricks.

I'm breaking my rule writing by candlelight but at least I'm not letting anything burn in the oven. Since you're probably curious, I may as well confess. The cake intended for two suppers wasn't exactly brown. It was so badly burnt I doubted pigs would eat it. Wrong. Pigs are such pigs they eat anything including burned ginger cake. At least they didn't fight over it. Not only was the cake burnt, the cook stove was purt near stone cold. To top that, the entire house smelt. It took forever to air. Even after I fumigated with boiling vinegar water, the smell hid behind doors and in back rooms.

For dessert, boarders and brother Jethro had to be satisfied with canned peaches. One look at my face everyone knew to be thankful and very quiet.

With the strange smell mystery solved and dessert dilemma covered, it's time to return to my first letter from James Samuel. All the while I was lost in memories; it nested snug and close to my heart as if it had found its home. As I read I felt a life time had passed and another was beginning.

James Samuel Ernest Owen was not a man to beat around the bush. He wrote he'd heard about me from mutual friends and wanted to call on me soon Mutual friends? Who? When? Where? I had no idea, and he gave no clues!

41

Right after we did the dishes, I told Jethro I had something important to do and he could add dishwater to the pig swill and get them fed. He was all set to argue there was nothing' more important that feeding pigs cause when we fed them they got around to feeding us, but I didn't give him a chance. He didn't even get out a what? Or a why? I stomped my foot and said "Scat." And for once in his life he listened.

Before I had time to wonder, James Samuel's second letter was in my hand. In no time we were using penny stamps fast enough to make my head spin. And you know, he never said who gave him my name. He hinted it was a very respected community leader. I knew right away it wasn't Oscar or Rhoda Mae Crabtree.

James Samuel wrote he couldn't resist knowing more about a school teacher who was raising her younger brother yet had time to run a boarding house and farm and play piano at church. That sounded like something Pastor Del would say but I knew not to ask because he'd just look at me and smile that smile of his that's answer and not answer.

James Samuel asked me to describe myself and all I could think of was if I did it would scare him away. So I wrote instead of how I feel about life and why I love our Ozarks. I told him I love the Lord and working to help others, and music, and making biscuits and cookies, and sewing, things like that.

His next letter said another mutual acquaintance that he would not name because he promised, told him I was prettier than a China doll and he couldn't wait to meet me. I thought whoever we both knew was probably blind in one eye and couldn't see out of the other. This mutual acquaintance had never seen me milking cows or mucking the barn.

I'd mailed him more than a dozen letters and had purt near twice that many before we met. My heart skipped several beats. I knew more or less what to expect, but seeing him in the flesh took my breath away. He was… Handsome, you say? Oh no, much better looking than handsome.

As he stood in the kitchen doorway framed by evening sunset my first reaction to his handsome face and strong muscular build was this was a cruel joke. He looked so much like Clark Gable. On second glance I decided Clark Gable was not that good looking. Also, that movie star doesn't have sparkling green eyes or hair that dark and thick. And, I'm willing to wager (though I daren't tell Jethro I'd wager a cent) Mr. Gable doesn't have the habit of running fingers through hair that turns into curls whenever it's touched. By the time I got around to my third thought, I knew any man that good lookin' could not be real or interested in me. I was wearing my only dress not made from a flour sack and the way it hung on my skinny frame made me crimson with shame. If I wanted this man, I knew I had my work cut out.

On the positive side, my dime store glasses, awful tight hairdo and wooly worm eyebrows were gone, and I didn't stink. Oh yes, I've been told I have a nice smile. Admittedly that's not saying much, but it's a start.

Never mind me. I'd rather write about your father. I know, I know, I've told you a FEW times how very handsome he is but, there's no harm in repeating. On first sight he impressed me more than any boy or man I've ever seen and that includes stars of stage and screen and, that Gable fellow. James Samuel was so real. In case you expected me to say handsome, I will. He was so handsome! Handsomer. Handsomest.

When we sat on the old porch swing, I let him hold my hand and, much to my shocked surprise I wished he would kiss me. I'd known him face to face for an hour and I wanted him to kiss me! I've never admitted such thoughts, and my dreams never went near my reaction to him. I never knew I could feel this way. I *Blush all over remembering* what I felt and wished. Truth is told, and that's enough of that.

As my old demon would say, if the way I felt meant I was being courted and liked it, it also meant trouble spelled with big letters. Letters big as a barn. James Samuel, standing there in nice slacks and a button down shirt and handsome as any man could dare be; and me, Anna Augusta Verona Parker plain and ordinary lookin.' Talk about an odd couple! Every dress I owned made from flower sack cotton or rejects from the Missionary barrel screamed they could only belong to a spinster school teacher. My red gold hair curled nicely but it didn't take a college professor to know me and fashion were complete strangers. A granny wouldn't wear the old fashioned lace ups for school. Unmentionables won't be.

How could that handsome man look twice at me? (Just for fun, one of these days I'm going to count how many times I've used the H word) I knew before his blinders came off, I had work to do. My hair had never been styled. I'd never owned a store bought dress or nylons, or fancy shoes and my rough red hands made me ashamed. I had to take a crash course in pretty and the sooner the better.

It took a year's supply of courage, but I did it. Bobbed hair, new dresses, and nylons. Shoes that wouldn't last a week in a barn, and flimsy unmentionables. That won't be. Give me cotton any day.

One purse and one hat wasn't enough. Coordination was the key. Black, Blue, White and Brown. All essential. And cosmetics. Lip rouge and face powder... Nylons, not the ugly coarse brown cotton stockings I hate and detest. Nylons, fancy sheer as a spider web nylons! Six pairs went into the growing stack because the sales lady said I couldn't do without them. She put her right hand in one stocking and pulled it down her arm to show how nylon enhances the skin. She said seams down the back kept nylons straight. I almost said there wouldn't be a problem if nylons didn't have a seam but for fear she'd consider me a country bumpkin bit my tongue in time. I hid my rough hands and knew we wouldn't worry about one little old run if I dared try that.

She was shocked when I asked about garters but she covered it real good with a little gasp, and then she lowered her voice. "Garters have just gone out of style." I said "Buy, but, how?" Meaning to ask how to hold the stockings up, but she was ahead of me. She said for the modern woman-- and oh, the way she smiled at me told me she knew I was an up and coming modern woman—a garter belt was an absolute necessity. She laid them across the counter top and if men had been anywhere near, I'd have died. The idea, displaying a personal feminine item in public! But, since men weren't around, I took a good look. Suspenders that hold up men's britches is what they reminded me of, only they fit around a ladies waist and have straps front and back with an odd looking closure at the end. I was half a mind to stick with garters, but something told me since she knew me to be a modern woman I'd better act like one, and asked her to add three to my growing pile.

When the bill came to over fifty five dollars, guilt hit me smack in the face. I spent that much because a handsome man was courting me! Thinking what that money could do at the farm made me want to put everything back. However, with life long responsibilities on one end of the scale James Samuel on the other, there was no contest.

I chose my new royal blue dress, daringly knee length with the added attraction of a flared skirt and middy waist for our first real date. The color set off my red gold hair and made my blue eyes even bluer.

Dressed an hour before James Samuel came; I walked all over the house in my new shoes. Finally, his knock; five fast beats followed by two slow. I swallowed twice, and for the hundredth time checked my reflection in the mirror. I was so pale. Quickly I pinched my cheeks and flipped my hair like the beautician taught me and walked with lady like steps to welcome him. Slowly, carefully, a heartbeat at a time I opened that door with my soft hands.

Whatever James Samuel intended to say didn't make it past his lips. He stood in the doorway with his mouth and eyes wide open. I stood at the door with my mouth wide open. He always came to call in casual clothes like green work pants and such. Course he was always clean and neat and looked wonderful, but I'd never seen him in a blue pin striped suit. Handsome? No, more like gorgeous! We stood there staring at one

44

another, and the more he stared the bigger his eyes got. He rubbed his hands through his hair and then stepped to the side so he could look behind me. When he decided we were alone, he cleared his throat and the way he said my name was more question that greeting. I giggled and that made him blush. First time I ever saw a man get that red.

Now, back to what happened after his confession. He proceeded to make that noise he called singing. I heard most of it, understood less than half, but clear as a bell, he sang "I'm knee deep in daisies and head over heels in love."

I'd never used the L word around him. I'd thought it, but considerin' everything, I wasn't ready to say it.

Maybe James Samuel knew he didn't dare sing again, so he said it. Slowly. I shook my head. Twice in as many minutes he'd made it clear he was in love with me. I was so flabbergasted; I just stared at him with my mouth wide open. I hope my daughters you never do that. It's unladylike, and looks like a fish out of water.

Enough about me.

James Samuel didn't stop with that thing that was supposed to be a song. He took me by the shoulders and turned my head up until there was nothing I could do except close my mouth and look into his deep green eyes. I felt I could drown in them.

"Miss Anna Augusta Verona Parker I fell in love with you the first instant I saw you standing in your kitchen. The evening sunlight turned your curls into a halo. I thought *"James Samuel you're in trouble*. I couldn't say a word. You gave me the sweetest smile and my heart turned over. I wasn't three steps inside your kitchen door and I was in love."

Naturally, my response was brilliant. I said "but, but, but," and faded. There wasn't enough air. Trying to recover, I escaped into my dream world. There, when my handsome hero declared his love I said "Oh my darling" and swooned." He would catch me in his strong muscular arms, and we'd ride off into the sunset while he sang to me. In my real world, I didn'tknow a thing about swooning so it's a good thing I didn't try and my dream lover's voice was the voice of Nelson Eddy, not that bullfrog rusty saw combination James Samuel called singing. Naturally dreams and real life never sat down and planned, so this is what I got.

James Samuel chuckled. He said he would love me forever. Every beat of his heart was my name. Every waking moment he saw my face and I filled his dreams. "Did he stand a chance with me?"

My mind replayed our day, the way he made me feel. Did he have a chance? Does the sun rise every morning?

Much as I wanted to throw myself in his arms and smother him with kisses I decided to be demure. I said I needed time to think. That little lie was no sooner said than I wanted to kick myself.

James Samuel was holding me in his arms and I knew he wanted to kiss me as much as I wanted his kisses but I said he was moving too fast Yet all the time I wishing he'd move faster.

On that bench near the covered bridge, we talked about if we, then we and our lives would be...Both of us wanted our own farm where we could live off the land and make a profit. What we didn't agree on we agreed to work on.

When we walked it seemed natural for James Samuel to keep an arm around me. I felt safe.

The next evening in the moonlight, James Samuel kissed me for the first time. It's a good thing he did because I was tired of kicking myself. I couldn't force myself to stop him. His first kiss was deep, tender, passionate, and made me dizzy. I pulled him close because I didn't want him to stop. He knew. He didn't.

Sometimes it seems I'm taking this whole truth thing too far. I'll try and tone it down.

On my birthday, James Samuel brought a lovely pair or fawn colored gloves, two three pound boxes of chocolate covered cherries and framed pictures of his family. Margaret Ellen his mother wears her pure white hair in a crowning braid. Her eyes sparkle and her smile says she's proud of her family. It was easy to love her. However, Carl Humphrey's picture with a scowl worse than banker Crabtree's gave me pause. Real quick, I put it aside. My dear boy said his pappy has a soft heart "Especially around beautiful women and one smile from you will melt his heart like it did mine." I really blushed.

He has three brothers and four sisters and for the life of me I can't remember their names. He says I shouldn't worry, I'll get used to a big family. He said his mammy ordered kids with dark hair and green eyes and got what she ordered eight times. "As for me, I want girls that look just like you," he said, and you guessed it, I was red again.

Every day, every hour, I thank God for bringing us together. Every night after prayers, I light a candle and read his letters over and over. Then I cry myself to sleep. Jethro asked how I could cook breakfast with puffy eyes and a drippin' nose and I told him I wasn't cookin' with my eyes and nose. He said nobody else was sickly. He said he's seen me cryin' when I milked our jersey cows. Snoopy, that's what he is.

On the wings of a storm, my dear boy was here on November 11. When storm winds blew worse, I began to feel sad and lonely because

I knew he wouldn't drive in that terrible weather. Trees were blowin' down and rain was so thick a body couldn't see their nose in front of their face.

A hot fire in the cook stove made a liar of the storm and kept me busy. A big pot of chicken and dumplings courtesy of an old hen that stopped layin' highlighted our supper menu. I just started dropping dumplings in the chicken broth when a great gust of wind nearly blew the kitchen door off its hinges. "Made it," said a very wet James Samuel and I couldn't decide whether to faint, scream or drop the bowl of dumplings. Fortunately, one of the boarders grabbed the bowl and my dear boy got me just as my knees wobbled. I didn't mind getting wet across my apron front but I did mind having such a wet man holding me. Before he could catch his death, I sent him back to Jethro's room with orders to change. I thought Jethro was tall enough but with James Samuel trying to fit in brother's clothing, I learned different. He stretched every seam to the breaking point.

Later, we built a big fire in our stone fireplace and tried to find privacy on the horsehair sofa. Tried. As if we didn't know they didn't need to check the storm or a book or find the checkers. I blush to admit they didn't stop us. James Samuel said we made love. I said I didn't know how we could do that seein' as how we were completely dressed. Then real quick, I confessed that whatever we did, I liked it very much. It was hot in that room long after the fire turned into ashes. Yes, my darlings use the red crayon again. I must stop telling you everything.

After a fun trip to Saint Louis in James' Model T, we shopped nearly every jewelry store before we found our rings. Then James Samuel pulled out a wad of cash big enough to choke a draft horse. I knew it was bootleggin' money but before I could say anything, James Samuel winked and smiled. You should have heard those sales people. "Yessir Mr. Owen, Wise choice Mr. Owen. Your bride will cherish this ring forever Mr. Owen." Mr. Owen this, Mr. Owen that. I got dizzy.

James Samuel wanted me to wear my engagement ring then, but I balked. "Sir", I said in my most proper school marm voice, "Unless I'm dreadfully mistaken, you have yet to propose marriage.

He gave me a look, did that thing with his hair and grinned all over his face. My dear boy's proposal was ten times better than was Rhett Butler's to Scarlet O'Hara Wilkes Kennedy. And very very public.

When he fell to his knees, clerks and jeweler and shoppers stopped what they were doing to cheer and applaud. Never one to miss opportunity to put my foot in my mouth, I said "Do what?" I blushed till I felt my hair smoking. James Samuel swept me off my feet, kissed me, and to calls of "kiss her again," carried me out. Then he wouldn't give me the ring.

When we neared Sainte Lillian's Jethro decided to pull over and take a walk. Then my dear boy held me close and asked if I would promise to be his forever and he hoped I wanted the same promise from him. We promised together. And he slipped the ring on my finger. A long line of honking cars full of gawking people picked just that moment to pass. So much for privacy.

I hold my ring up to the light to watch my diamond twinkle like a star and wish on it. Oh my darlings, it would take forever to tell you the wonderful things I wish about you and our life as a family

New Family New Beginnings

My Darlings,

We turn another page and bring you closer.

Saturday we had dinner with his parents at the Owen Family farm which is half way between Sainte Lillian's and De So To. Just think, we lived this close and never once met. James Samuel figured that out. He said then we weren't worshiping at the same alter. Just another way to prove he's not only handsome but extremely intelligent. Smart even (private joke).

He said he reckoned his home place was big enough. Then he laughed. "It had to be bigger than a cottage, with us kids and grandma and grandpa till they passed." Just like a man, he left out the house was a crowning jewel on a big hill with six great big bedrooms. He also 'forgot' to mention his pappy and grandpappy used their own oak to make all their furniture. The beds are long enough for Abraham Lincoln to stretch out Every piece of furniture was solid oak and so much nicer than anything store bought. His ma said doing it their way took forever, but the wait was worth it. "For about three years our dining room table and chairs were two by fours across saw horses," she said as she pointed out the table big enough to seat twenty.

Also, even though my dear boy is so muscular and put together so well, other than carryin' on about his momma's sweet potato pancakes, he never bragged a bit more about her cooking. If all this furniture and her table spread put together were to surprise me, it worked.

"When I saw the loaded table, I looked outside for late comers. "Shouldn't we wait for everyone?" I asked. "Mom's used to cooking for a big family" James Samuel said, and loaded my plate. Embarrassed, I smiled weakly and tried to not look at the pork roast, beef stew, chicken and dumplings, fried pork steak and beef and noodles. Of course all that meat needed potatoes and gravy and vegetables and bowls of sauces and six different relish dishes including watermelon preserves and apple butter for our biscuits bread and cornbread And the best pickled green peppers I'd ever tasted. Because I didn't want to hurt their feelings, I sampled everything.

Dessert? Of course! Ma Owen wouldn't be able to hold her head up if we'd left the table without dessert: I don't want to think about my seconds.

Coffee? Tea? Bi-carb?

Wanting to compliment her again on the excellent meal, I no more than said "Mrs. Owen" than she gave me a really cross look.

"Anna I can't take it any more!" I froze and turned pale. I'd used my best manners and been so polite and respectful. What had I done? I looked at James Samuel for help and all he did was grin and do that thing with his hair.

Before I could manage as much as a "'but, what?'" she laughed. "Girl in no time you'll be Mrs. Owen. You'll have to get used to calling me mom Owen because I don't want to known here abouts as the elder Mrs. Owen."

Carl Humphrey snorted and she whacked him with a dishtowel.

We laughed together, and as we did dishes she told stories about my beloved's childhood. When he begged for mercy, she laughed. "I've been looking forward to this for years," she said. James Samuel had two choices. Wisely, he chose to sit back and take it.

Mom Owen said if she lived to be two hundred, she would never forget the day her hair started turning white. "Before his third birthday, James Samuel was still pretty much a momma's boy and did everything with me. Never gave me a lick of trouble. This changed on a Monday washday right after his birthday. As usual, he helped with the wash by handing me clothespins. When he got tired of that, he gave me rocks. I said "No thank you sweet boy," so he decided to watch red birds on the hawthorn bush. "Momma see pretty birds," he said. I kept an eye on him, told him to stay close, and went about my work.

When I finished the sheets and pillow covers, he was gone. I searched the lawn. Then thinking he'd gone in to nap, checked the house. I looked everywhere; the well house, the chicken coop and the barn. It was like he vanished into thin air. Let me tell you, I was scared nearly to death."

Dad Owen took over as mom stood arms akimbo staring at her son. "Ma rang the dinner bell and got me out of the field and we got ourselves a search goin'. All the while we're sick to death with worry and that boy didn't even know he was lost. He just followed those birds into the woods and when he was hungry, he ate his fill of blackberries. When he was thirsty he drank from the creek. When it was nap time he curled up under a big oak and slept. It was near dark and he was still asleep when hounds bayed discovery."

While his ma and pa had a good laugh, my dear boy sank even lower in his chair. Can't say I blamed him.

The story continued. Make that stories. "Between age three and 12, he kept us busy. He took old bed sheets and pine slats to build wings and fly from the hayloft. That was a broken arm. He dared the twins to skate on Covey Mac Pherson's thin pond ice. They didn't. He did. That was a whopping ear infection and pneumonia. He chewed green tobacco and threw up his socks for a week." She sighed and gave me a sad mournful look. "Anna what he did was plain curious normal boy stuff."

Normal. She said normal! I thought Jethro was bad enough but this! Oh my goodness! Until that minute I thought six sons just like James Samuel were ideal. Maybe that's why he wanted 12 daughters.

I could either think or listen. I listened. "When he was 12 stands out," she said. He moaned. "Mom not that one!" He slunk way down in the chair until all I could see were a few dark hairs sticking straight up over the chair back.

"Do tell," I said, and sat on the arm of his chair. He was more interested in running fingers thru his hair than looking at me.

I pointed."Before I forget would you tell me later when he started doing that?"

"Anna honey you didn't stop a thing, you just added to my story. That habit started the summer of his 12th year. That was another time he nearly scared us to death and his pappy was tired of talkin' to him. This time he yanked that boy by the hair of his head and told him to start thinkin' before he got kilt in one of his hair brained schemes."

James Samuel's moans didn't work. "Your intended was a real rascal, especially that summer. Being partial to my sweet potato pancakes the way he is, he planted a sweet potato patch over the hill there. She pointed out the window beyond the red hollyhock bordered kitchen garden. "Tended that patch right well he did. Mornin' and evening he carried water and hoed down nettles and weeds.

The morning he found ground hog holes all over that patch he ran to the house madder than a hornet and hollerin' his head off.

Carl was leavin' the barn when he saw that boy runnin' outa the storage shed with a lard bucket full of carbide in one hand and a full bucket of well water in the other. Even though Carl was hot on his heels yellin' at the boy to stop, James Samuel kept on runnin'. He was in no mind to listen to nobody or nothin'! He had carbide and water down the main hole and was reachin' for his box of matches when Carl caught him. Only by the grace of God, Carl was able haul him away. When they got back here, Carl had James Samuel by the back of his neck and the top of his head. Never have I seen Carl so scared, mad and relieved at the same time. He was nearly cryin' while yellin' at the boy to learn to think. Over and over, yellin' 'James Samuel Ernest Owen think! Think before you do things. Think about other people. Think! Think! Think!" Every time he yelled think, he gave James Samuel's hair another good yank. It worked. At least now we know when he's up to somethin' because he starts with his hair."

I knew enough to know if James Samuel had lit that match, I'd be a devout spinster with wooly worm eyebrows instead of a devoted head-over-heels in love bride-to-be.

Once again I looked at James Samuel. He was playin' with his hair and makin' kissy lips. "I'm thinkin' now," he said. Mom Owen gave me a wooden spoon. I read her mind. He read ours. He ran.

Three times around the kitchen on top of a full dinner, wore us down fast but it didn't stop Mom Owen. As stories continued, I couldn't help but wonder if her hair had turned completely white before James Samuel was 13, and also, how many guardian angels he put out to pasture.

He was quiet for a spell" she said and then added she should have known he was up to something because he was fooling with his hair and he wasn't missing meals.

He was readin' every Zane Gray novel he could get his hands on. Then he got books on desert survival from the lendin' library. Since we ain't nowhere near the Wild West, I was more curious than worried. I kept watchin' and wonderin' and waitin.' Came the day he killed a batch of rattlesnakes and brought them home for me to fry up for supper."

As one 'adventure" followed another, James Samuel sank lower into his chair and my eyes got bigger. The things he didn't do wouldn't fill a page of lined paper.

"James Samuel when I said we had to have six boys just like you, why didn't you tell me what I was getting into?" Pa Owen laughed so hard he nearly fell from his chair

Mom Owen gave me gingerbread to take home and just as I was ready to ask, she gave me an envelope full of his favorite recipes. She whispered "Mostly all you have to do is cook. A lot. I marked his favorites with stars."

The Wonder of it All

My Darlings,

If I burned midnight oil every night, letters would be nothing but chores, chores, and more chores. Something tells me you'd loose interest after the first descriptive of pig swill and cow flop. But just for fun, there is something almost artistic about corn cobs, potato peel and chicken bones floating in dishwater. "Enough!" you say. Very well, besides it's much more fun focusing on the wonderful events bringing us closer.

Earlier when doubts were driving me up the wall, I had no idea that together James Samuel and I could work so well together. I could no more bring up a nagging thought and we would talk it over and work it out.

He solved Jethro's need for a cook/housekeeper at the boarding house in five minutes. Give or take a day or two. A few church friends interviewed, and Jethro hired Irene Kranz. She's young, she's blonde and blue eyed and I sense romance in the air. It gets better: For room and board, her brothers Larry and Bill will help work the farm.

Ah yes, there's even more excitement! Stop reading right now and look at our house! Focus on your own rooms: walk in closets, built in book case, and desk and wide window seats. Everything built like it was ordered. Right? Right! From your windows enjoy the beauty of our orchard. Each spring take time to appreciate the wonderful blossoming lilacs as you walk our circular driveway. On cold nights when blizzards howl I know you enjoy curling up with a good book by the fireplace. Are our porch swings a must on pleasant evenings?

That's right; I'm ready to tell you something else about your wonderful father. We went for a short drive one cloudy wind swept afternoon and parked near an old gate by a side road. "Let's take a walk," he said, and I said "Don't put that on my tombstone." He gave me a funny look and took my arm.

He acted like he didn't understand that I was scared out of my wits. There in front of God and anyone driving by, he kissed me and picked me up like I was a sack of sugar and carried me past signs warning "Trespassers will be shot." He said we had to walk around, and hard as I tried convincing him otherwise, "No" was not the answer he wanted. "Just up the hill. We won't walk the fields or woodland, or orchard," he said. As if we could.

He was determined to walk. I was the exact opposite, and did everything I could think of to get my message across. Was he daft or deaf? Did he care how I felt? Couldn't he see I was scared nearly to death? Did what I wanted matter to him?

So I spelled it out loud and clear. "James Samuel this land is all that's left of the Covey-Mac Pherson holdings."

He interrupted."Yes, my love, I know." He gave that smug smile again. And did that thing with his hair. Again.

I was closer to the boiling point. "James Samuel listen to me! They may be out of state, but you saw the signs. They've hired men to shoot trespassers. We're trespassing. Getting shot isn't part of my life plan." I planted my feet and refused to budge. It was like not moving when a bulldozer said "excuse me, would you mind if I pushed you aside?"

He bowed from the waist extended his arm for me to hold and with a perfect French accent, said "Come with me, there's nothing to worry about." Whether I liked it or not, my left arm went into the crook of his right and we went for his walk. Actually he went for a walk. I went for a drag. To top it off I was really scared. I know, I've told you that, but I was so scared telling you twice won't hurt. Wind was picking up and it was getting colder by the minute. We were alone. If we were shot who would know or care? We'd walked past those terrible signs. Would cawing crows announce our death in the morning?

Imprisoned by his grip I had no choice. I balked at every step, stumbled over stones, stalled, bawled, cried, and protested. Nothing worked. My voice went in his right ear through the vacant place his caring brain was supposed to be, exited the left ear and joined the unfriendly wind.

He pointed toward an overgrown orchard. I stared long and hard wishing wishes I dared not wish aloud as the chilling breeze brought the bittersweet perfume of wasted fruit. Bittersweet perfume and bittersweet wishes combined to make me even more miserable. "To think Covey-Mac Pherson let this go to waste! Thinking about the poor folks who needed this fruit makes me so sad. Please James Samuel take me home."

James Samuel was neither sad, upset, nor afraid of sharpshooters. This full grown handsome man, the man I thought I wanted to marry was acting like a little boy full of excitement...or devilment.

"Over there, he said pointing toward the setting sun, "are acres of fallow fields just beggin' for corn and oats. There's acres of woodland, and the pond I fell in when I was a boy, a deep creek and two big barns, a stone spring house where water runs cold, and, and, and..."

"James Samuel take me home!" I shouted, I yelled, I stamped my feet.

Once again he smiled that smug smile that was making me so mad. Once again, the hair.

"I shall," he said and picked me up and started walking. Not down to the safety of his car, but up the long winding rocky unfriendly hill.

His voice tensed. "Anna whatever you do don't open your eyes until I tell you it's safe!"

I was so afraid I nearly wet my pants. I knew he'd spied sharpshooters taking aim and he didn't want me to see our killers.

His voice was shaking when he whispered "Anna don't be afraid. Remember, I'll love you forever."

I leaned into his chest thinking the last thing I'd smell on this earth was the sweetness of his cherry pipe tobacco. I told myself at least I no longer had to think about when I would die because death was coming and we'd go together. I told myself it could have been worse, I could have been alone and fallen in the pig pen and broke my neck. My only problem was me talking to me didn't help

He stopped and it sounded like he was holding back laughter. He gave me a big hug and a bigger kiss and then put me on my feet turning me so my back was against his rib cage and I was snug in his arms. He said "Open."

Every which way I looked, my eyes filled with a great gray tumbled tumbling held together with baling wire, tar paper and dirt thing. Thing. I could have used other words but pity made me call it thing. Maybe once it was a house. Was it ever a home? All window glass was broken shards. There were more holes in the walls than walls to hold the holes. What was left of the roof sagged to the right, slid to the left, and wasn't visible in the middle. Did people...no, they couldn't have. How could people have ever lived there?

I heard James Samuel's voice coming from a long distance. Twice he said it, then I understood "Darling what do you think?" Then he ran his fingers through his hair. Twice. I found enough voice to croak "What do I think about what?

"Our home," he said. I did not look at him or back toward the orchard or west toward the fields and woodlands. My eyes were glued to that dilapidated pathetic rundown piece of junk he had the nerve to call home.

I was not dreaming.We were still there, and he had said ---

"What did you say?"

"You wanted me to take you home. I did. As of this morning, this is our home."

Did I say something? Did he? His mouth was making shapes like words were coming out and he looked so smug and proud. The cat swallowed the canary look was all over his handsome face. I remembered once telling you he was intelligent and smart. Him! And why now of all times did I have to think of his handsome face?

He said, "It has a nice dry basement. We'll have to burn the dead rats and squirrels, but once that's done..."

That's as far as he got. Had I thought about the James Samuel prankster, the boy grown into man bringing bad habits with him? Did I think about that thing with his hair? I did not. Did I think he was kidding? Same answer. What I did was loose my temper old maid spinster school teacher style. With bared fangs and smoking nostrils, I took aim and fired. "James Samuel Ernest Owen this house is a disgrace to the county, to the entire state, to the Ozarks as a whole. Coveys and Mac Phersons should have had their sharpshooter's blast the living daylights out of a farm manager that let this happen."

He stuttered, he stammered, he tried my name but all he did just fueled my fire. "James Samuel this farm has potential but I will not...You will not... Furthermore, our kids will not set one foot in this..." I stumbled for descriptive, couldn't find enough decent or adequate...and just pointed toward the rundown object of his delight. "We will burn this mess and renovate one of the barns," I said, and followed that wisdom with what we should do, would do, and had to do as soon as his head was on straight.

When I ran out of breath and steam, he let out a great big whistle and a quartet of big men led by Carl Humphrey came out of hiding; the lot of them laughing fit to be tied and swatting James Samuel on the back. Whether they heard my explosion or not, I didn't care, but if they said anything about it, I had more.

James Samuel finally remembered I was standing alone and ran to hug me close. He said where the house was, was perfect considerin' the view and well house and all the potential. Besides, he never did fancy living in a barn. Renovated or not. He wanted a house and he had our plans ready.

Big men. Quiet. Shy now their monkey shines were over came to me hats in hand The twins Joe and Pete Brown who wouldn't go river raftin' but didn't mind bootleggin' said their how do's and backed off.

Two down, one to go! And this one was the biggest tallest rawboned man I'd ever seen. If I hadn't been so steamed from what James Samuel pulled, I'd probably have ducked behind him before looking up. As it was, I stood my ground, craned my neck and finally found somewhere between earth and sky, the smiling face of George Herbert Wallace Bush a.k.a. "Silent." From his treetop high face, came words too soft and low for me to understand but since he'd said something, and opened a dialogue, I said," James Samuel has talked of you for so long it's a pleasure to meet you at last. I looked at Pete and Joe and smiled and then craned my neck again, and laughing said "And you especially Silent."

Next thing I knew this silent soft spoken giant began telling stories about my dear boy I knew for certain sure his momma didn't know. And you can bet your bottom dollar she wouldn't have believed a one of them. I mean who ever heard of a teenager swimming both ways across the Mississippi River just to prove he could? Toppled over outhouses on Halloween and Limburger Cheese under the Christmas manger were but child's play to this quartet. As I recall, Silent said him and the twins just went along for the ride when James Samuel came up with something.

Then Silent interrupted himself and said, "And Miz Parker, mam," and I said "Oh, I know we'll be the best of friends. Please, you must call me Anna." That stopped the stories faster than blowing out a candle would snuff out light.

Shuffled feet brought up clouds of dust. Dust followed by silence that stretched. Without thought I shifted weight from left foot to right and back. Somehow, I managed to keep smiling. And somehow I recognized Pete's soft voice. "Miz Parker mam that wouldn't be fittin' wouldn't be fittin' a'tall."

James Samuel said normally they're a rowdy bunch but since they think I'm refined they didn't want to fright me so they used their best manners He said they'd do anything for me but if they lived to be old as Methuselah, they'd never know what I saw in him. I said I'd tell them but he said that wouldn't be wise it would embarrass them and it wasn't wise to embarrass reformed bootleggers. Now that I think about it, he was foolin' with his hair the entire time. That man! Notice I didn't write 'that handsome man!

His orders to me were cut and dried.. "Have supper ready for hungry men and do all that stuff women do before the wedding," he said and it didn't matter what kind of noise I made. "James Samuel has spoke," his pappy said as if that was it, no questions allowed.

But that didn't stop me. "Look at this place. There's too much to do for me to not be working with you." That was my first try followed by logical arguments, followed by tears. For all the good my protest did, I should have been in politics.

My poor students felt the depth of my irritation with reams of research papers, and cramming for test. They didn't get a break. I remember linen and kitchen showers, pretty hand made doilies and lace curtains and embroidered pillow cases. Mostly, I remember days of seconds, minutes, hours, sunrise and sunset and sleepless nights that passed slower than molasses drips of a freezing day in January. Mom Owen came every afternoon and started cooking and together we over fed exhausted men who sometimes fell asleep at the kitchen table.

The day came when I stood at our home site pinching myself. That awful creepy falling down spider infested weaving in the wind piece of junk was gone. In its place stood our home where you children were born and raised.

Our beautiful home was built by these men. Electric wires and outlets were ready before the WPA had poles down our road. Our wrap around porches and double fireplace came because they heard me wishing.

If this is a dream, don't wake me. I never want to know this man, this dream, this time, this love we share and all the wonder surrounding us is not real. So many of my someday dreams are becoming true. I love my downright "purty" house with its bedrooms waiting for babies. On the day you are born my darlings I will tell you more about our dreams for you. I could never write them as they keep growing. I promise the first words you will hear from me after I say your names and tell you I love you will be the wonderful stories.

By now three of you boys have figured out your middle names. Other than moonshine, my prayer is you will grow to be as wonderful and kind as Pete, Joe, and George. Somehow, the name Silent wouldn't work.

James Samuel and I have a home we will love forever, a home where we will raise you, our 12 children.

I thank God at least a million times a day.

Dreams and Work

My Darlings,

Other than a houseful of you, our most ambitious dream is buying the 100 acres between us and the boarding house and combining the farms. Our dream says someday the Owen Parker Farms will make the Covey Mac Pherson land holdings look like a kitchen garden. Someday, our farm will produce bumper crops. Our strawberries will sell at the Saint Louis Farmers Market. From far and near people will come to pick their own. Our apples, cherries, peaches and pears will be talk of the town. Someday, profit from fruit butters will pay your college tuition. Someday, our smoked hams will delight dignitaries, and our horses will run in lush green pastures.

Years of backbreaking work stretch ahead, but we're full of hope and dreams of our someday with you. Lord willing, these dreams will come true.

Jethro is becoming the worker I always knew he could be. Probably because two of James Samuel's sisters sweet talked him, but who cares why? It started one night after a family dinner with Annie and Maude sharing stories about canning time and turning the place into a factory. They start with May Strawberries, take a break, go into June peas and keep on canning until everything fit to eat in the garden, berry patch and orchard is down cellar. James Samuel said every year when they're done, they lie through their teeth and swear they'll never go through it again. Except for the third weekend in October when they pull out the brass kettles (not kettle, kettles) and make Apple Butter. He says back in his wild days that was purt near the only time he was tame as a kitten and doing his part. He peeled, he cut, he stirred, he stoked those big outdoor fires, did everything he could and loved every minute of it. Every year they finished the last quart of Apple Butter the week before they started the new batches, and were hungry and hankerin' for more by that third October weekend.

And they do the canning outdoors under shading trees! Owens men haul two great big six burner cook stoves from the storage shed to tables set up under the trees where everything waits. They say it's a production line and a science all rolled into one.

My brother, who dotes on being waited on, said he could hardly wait to help out. I nearly swooned but Maude and Annie acted like they'd expected his offer and gave him big hugs. All it takes to spur him on is hugs from pretty women. Come canning time, he'll be there every day.

Even though our boarding house cast iron cook stove was a fire breathing wood eating monster, we appreciated it during the cool times. But, let me tell you, when summer came and canning followed on its heels, I hated that thing. The heat was terrible. Momma heated wash water first and while she did laundry, I canned everything that wasn't nailed down. By July 100 or 1,000 degrees was the same to us and the heat filled the house. There was no escape from muggy Ozark heat outdoors or the fire breathing monster indoors. Our lot was to work in the heat all day and try to sleep at night in heat that wouldn't leave. Sometimes Jethro wiped straw and sawdust from a hunk of ice in our underground ice house, and put it in the front room window. He called it conditioned air. It didn't help as much as we liked to think it did. Now thinking about canning outdoors and escaping the house oven makes me feel spoiled

There I was concentrating on the future yet again! Do all brides jump from one happy dream to another? With a flick of my wrist I shall return to the present and tell you darlings about my trousseau and wedding gown. I won't be overly descriptive boys, as this is more for the girls. You may read if you dare.

Because setting up housekeeping is so expensive and also because this gown will be worn only once and then put away for you girls I decided to forgo store bought finery. My conscience had fits every time I tried on ready made gowns. True they were dreams of lace and seed pearls and satin. Also true, they cost more than a good mule. Thank goodness I saved my genuine imitation dime store pearls. They will be perfect with my gown.

That said, I will be ultra conservative and make my wedding gown from white voile on sale at 15 cents a yard. Fancy hand stitching momma taught goes into everything I sew for my wedding. I wish she were here to share my happiness.

Mom Owen and the girls are making my wedding night finery. I suggested a red flannel gown with lots of lace and they laughed fit to be tied. They said I'd heat up soon enough. Never mind what I said.

James Samuel and I will be married in one week. Seven days 189 hours. My darling children I love you with all my heart

My Wedding Day

My Darlings,

Today is my wedding day! Is this another of my dreams? Today is my wedding day. Did I really write that? Did I, Anna Augusta Verona Parker really write that? Yes! Yes! Yes! It is true. Today is my wedding day! Today I become Mrs. James Samuel Ernest Owen.

Weather report follows: It was beginning to look like we'd walk to church through mud puddles but the sky cleared to a soft powdery blue. It is an omen. On this day my painful past is over and my new life of happiness begins. Soon, my true love and I will be united forever. While the pastor says words over us we probably won't hear because we'll be drowning in each others eyes we will become one flesh. Husband and wife. Forever until our dying day, and then eternity.

Most importantly my darlings, you are no longer a dream. Your lives begin today. Or should I say tonight? Oh dear, never mind.

My darlings I will put the letters aside for a short time but as happiness grows, more will be written.

Six Months Later

My Darlings,

I once so faithful with details have waited six months to write. But, I am a newly wed and there are announcements requiring trumpeters and heralds. Since I don't see any crawling out of the woodwork, I'll give you a short version of the truth, the whole truth and nothing but the truth about my life as Mrs. James Samuel Ernest Owen. All six months of it.

Married life is more satisfying and wonderful than I ever dreamed.

The intimate things I wondered about and never had courage to talk about seem so natural and wonderful. I must boast just the tiniest bit.

Your father _my "professor"_ calls me a real quick learner and gives me a perfect report card. When I blush all over he pulls my nightgown off and says I'm the most beautiful hot house tomato he'd ever seen. By the way, my wedding night finery was nowhere close to red flannel, and that's all you need to know about that. (and yes, I'm blusing).

I think I'm traveling in that place called too much truth. I will tell you that during our honeymoon it was easier to stay indoors than go places. Never mind why. And I did enjoy breakfast in bed. I say enough and then keep on boasting. Seems I can't stop.

I've saved the most wonderful news for last. Rose Ellen you are on the way. James Samuel made sure of that on our wedding night. Several times. Not that I'm complaining! I asked my dear boy what if you were a James Samuel Junior and he just laughed He said he wants daughters and daughters, we would get.

Rose Ellen your daddy talks to you all the time. He kisses where you lay nestled and boasts you will be prettier than your momma. Then he says that would be impossible. Me pretty? Not now! I look like a pumpkin on stilts.

Sometimes, I have to laugh thinking how momma did her Christian duty and tried to tell me about men having their way. Would she know me now? Temptation to write more is being put to bed.

Small Stones

Is this a diary entry or another letter to our children? My only answer is heartache, and heartache can only question.

Momma never told me there could be that much pain or that it could go on for endless hours. Finally, I used my last ounce of strength and Rose Ellen was born. Dead. My baby was dead. Stillborn they called it.

I saw the look on Doctor Engels' face as he held her up and swatted her bottom. Then he suctioned her nose and moved her back and forth between basins of cold and warm water. He tried to breathe life into her.

I held her to my breast and begged her to breathe. She didn't move. Her eyes were never open. James Samuel walked the floor with her and cried and begged her to breathe.

Doctor Engels said she was too small. That can't be true. Rose Ellen was bigger than momma's doll size twins and they breathed and took nourishment for a week. I held Rose Ellen and traced her delicate white body with my fingers and kissed her pale cheeks while James Samuel cradled us and we cried together.

James Samuel left me holding her. As she lay in my arms, I could hear the almost soft tap of hammer against cedar as her father made Rose Ellen's coffin. It didn't take him very long. Yet, each time hammer hit nail and nail bit into wood, nails pierced my heart. Copper nails red cedar almost blood red. Small box. Together we lined her little cradle coffin with soft cotton batting and covered that with pearl white silk. Where she will lie forever looked like a sun kissed cloud.

Mom Owen and I bathed and powdered Rose Ellen and dressed her in her white christening gown. The only color around Rose Ellen is the pink rosebuds I embroidered on the gown. While I prayed for a miracle, Mom Owen rocked her and sang lullabies. Pop Owen took pictures of her and of us with Rose Ellen. He said it was so we'd never forget. I said, "as if we could," and Mom Owen told him to stop.

Rose Ellen is so beautiful. All white, dressed in white, soft red gold curls like a halo. There is nothing in heaven or on this earth that can hurt our baby. Nothing.

Doctor Engels said there was no law against our having a family cemetery. I told him I didn't care if there was. Why should she go to a town cemetery? People there didn't dream over her, did not love her, and had never held her. Rose Ellen belongs here at home.

Our cemetery will be out back near where the roses grow. She will lie there alone until her father and I join her.

My breast are swollen and leak. Is this also tears for Rose Ellen?

I can't write any more. I want my baby.

August 3, 1937. Elma Pauline lies beside her sister. Why?

July 1, 1938. Helene Bernice has joined them. I can't find God.

June 5, 1938. Mildred Louise is there. This time there was never a sick day. I sailed through this pregnancy, Labor was one push. But, she couldn't breathe. Four daughters in soft white christening gowns embroidered with pink roses. Lying in cradle coffins by the fence where the roses grow. James Samuel and I cling together, too tired of tears to cry, to heartbroken to pray. Are these letters to dead children who will never know our desperate longing?

Brother Jethro and Irene brought their two girls over. I held them and couldn't laugh or smile. Irene cooked supper and Jethro and James Samuel worked the woodlot. My dear boy Samuel always looks so beat down after they leave.

December 8, 1939. Barbara Anne lies with her four sisters. There are five small stones by the fence where the roses grow, each with a name and one date.

I have held and caressed, and dressed in white christening gowns five porcelain white daughters. Doctors Engels said he's consulted with doctors in Saint Louis and they agreed to disagree. They don't know,

July 8, 1940. This baby left me before we were sure I was pregnant. I had a cramp and passed a small blob without arms or legs. Then I started to hemorrhage. When Doctor Engels examined what would have been a baby he said the Lord had been merciful.

James Samuel said Doc Engels took care of the wee one. I felt so bad because all our babies have a name and a burial place and a stone. This small thing, this boy or girl has nothing but a place in our hearts. James Samuel says we can't forget how much Jesus loves our little ones.

Doctor Engels says I've used all my strength and we would never have our babies. He talked about an operation but I won't have it. They can't make me.

James Samuel is bent over like an old man. He cries when he looks at me and won't talk.

Jethro talks to him but if anything, James Samuel always looks worse when brother leaves

I have run out of tears. All I feel is this great empty ache like there's a hole in my heart. Days pass in a cloud.

Oh God! Oh God!

Our Daughter

Praise God. You live. You cry, You nurse. You move, and oh my goodness, how you wet your diapers.

I have held five silent babies to my breast and felt nothing but creeping cold taking them further from me. Now, I think *'this is what it is like: the warm squirming, the sound of your crying this tugging at my breast, this joy!*

When we touch your cheek, your little rosebud lips form into a soft baby smile. You are so happy when held and touched. Your daddy wanted to call you Janet. I thought of our first daughter and chose Ellen. So we made up your name. You are Jannelle. Beautiful perfect red headed always hungry Jannelle. Always loud Jannelle. Always wet Jannelle. Breathing. Alive! Jannelle. I love the music of your name. You are so short and plump; and have so much red hair I want to braid it.

Doctor Engels says he's never seen a cuter red head. He says with your red hair and brilliant green eyes, we'll have trouble with young men before we know it.

We wrap you in a soft blanket and just look at you lying between us in our bed. We spend every minute watching you breathe. My sweet boy watches the enthusiastic way you nurse and says you have his appetite. I know you will always be your daddy's girl.

It seemed he'd forgotten how to smile but you should see him when you wrap your little hand around his little finger. His face is a picture of pure contentment.

When Jethro, Irene and their three daughters visited, James Samuel said, "Jethro, what say you now?" I stared at the emotions on both faces and couldn't understand. Jethro didn't say a word. How strange. When our daughters were born dead Jethro could hardly wait to get James Samuel alone for a long talk. Now he can't even say congratulations! What ails that man?

Soon Jannelle your daddy and I will take you to the fence where the roses grow and introduce you to your sisters. You will know. They will know.

Doctor Engels says he'll never know for sure, but he and the doctors in Saint Louis think in some way my miscarriage helped him deliver a squalling baby. I told him we were just getting started.

Someday, I will record your ever move my miracle girl. Now, instead of reaching for pen and paper, I store memories and reach for sleep.

Beth Anne

My darlings,

The world is on the brink of war but that doesn't stop the rejoicing at our house. Jannelle woke from a deep sleep at 6:16 this morning the minute she hear your first cry Beth Anne. She was at my bedside before your cord was cut, and her alert eyes took it all in.

Jannelle the way you watch Beth Anne has convinced me that someday you will be a nurse. If your sister frowns in her sleep, or wakes and stares at you, you come for me or your daddy.

We watch the two of you together and wonder at the difference; short chunky Jannelle and long legged dark haired Beth Anne. "Your second model looks more like her daddy," Doc Engels said.

Bethie I stared into your green eyes and touched your dark hair and knew you, like your daddy, would always cling to me.

Jannelle as long as your life was on an even keel you were the model stay abed sleepy head. You fussed only if meals weren't ready on time and to refresh your memory that means if momma wasn't ready the bottle should be. Early on you had a way with that lower lip and crocodile tears.

Bethie my long legged slender doll you are the exact opposite. You were born with your eyes wide open and asking why? Your eyes question everything and rather than fuss, you look for answers. As you grow, I'll look back on our first talk and remember my predictions.

My someday wishes to record my daughters every moments are locked in my heart. When diapers become polishing rags your stories will be more than one line reminders jotted down in such a hurry.

Now, my darling daughters, you need to know that no matter what happens in our lives these are hours that bind us together. Your daddy and I will treasure this time forever.

Samantha Lynn

My darlings,

One year ago today Japanese planes bombed Pearl Harbor, Hawaii and. America was washed in tears and anger. Thousands of lives ended that terrible day. Thousands of homes were destroyed, millions of dreams ended. Within hours, American men, women, and might entered World War Two. The lives of everyone everywhere changed overnight.

Today, one year after the winds of war blew against our world we are rejoicing selfishly because you have joined our family Samantha Lynn.

At 8:15 this morning a bundle of contentment entered our lives when we heard your first melodious cry. I said melodious. Your cry was not the shrillness of a startled newborn, but that of a baby discovering wonder and love. It was, in a word, music.

What a world. We celebrate life while over the globe, men and machines of war destroy. Here, we celebrate. Heartbeats away from our haven, families mourn dead sons and daughters.

No one predicts what war will end tomorrow. But now, right here, we thank God for the safe delivery of our third beautiful daughter.

I wish you girls could remember your daddy on days like these. He tells everyone he feels like a king surrounded by a beautiful queen and three beautiful princesses. When Jethro is here he struts even more and Jethro sits and sulks. Sometimes I wonder even more about my brother.

Samantha Lynn your daddy and I know we've done it again. You not only don't look like your sisters you don't act like them either. Exhibit Number One: your red headed big sister Jannelle. Maybe I should describe her as your older sister as she's such a shrimp. When she doesn't get her way, her lower lip goes out in a pout and she turns on the water works. The few times she's not pouting, Jannelle is the delicate and somewhat self centered redhead. Quiet, but determined. She's a walking doll sized southern belle. Exhibit number two: Raven haired Beth Anne, head and shoulders taller than Jannelle, and the one who takes charge. I don't think there's a 'pity me' tear in her body. The looks she gives Jannelle when her waterworks come on! Priceless!

Now, we look at you my darling newborn. You radiate contentment. Smiles don't vanish when people look at you... Joy is 99 and 44 /100th percent of your makeup.

Sometimes, as I watch you breathe, my heart skips a beat. It's like I'm holding Rose Ellen again, begging her to breathe. Praise God, you do so without my prayers or pleading. Rose Ellen was so softly silent.

Samantha Lynn model baby or not, you add your share to the diaper pail. More on that later.

Once again I note the only upsetting thing in my life is no time to write your letters. Someday.

Five Months Later

My darlings,

It's a miracle! My daughters are napping and I am writing. My dear boy is in the barn. Dishes soak in the dishpan. Diapers need ironing. But it is quiet. I, therefore, am putting chores aside and taking time to write.

The world that shapes your future weeps. Destruction and death rule land and sea. In towns and villages with names I can't begin to pronounce, mothers watch helplessly as their children die of disease and starvation or worse yet have them torn from their arms and murdered while they're forced to watch. I wonder, do they wish then for revenge or for their own death? James Samuel says the mothers of Bethlehem are weeping again for their children.

My heart aches. I can't imagine the agony of parents in these far away places. Yes, we have suffered loss, we have cried unstoppable tears, our hearts have been torn apart but all our pain can't come close to this. My God! Their children are murdered and they can't stop the horror. What is so masterful about this race of Hitler's' that demands death of innocents? What are they taking from the future?

When I think about mothers with empty arms and broken hearts, I can't stop the tears. My mourning over five stillborn daughters is almost without meaning, yet I know God counts each tear.

My darlings we have always been a praying family, but when your father decided to join the fight for freedom, all I voiced was prayers. Morning, noon, and night, my prayers were selfish self centered and very unpatriotic. Thoughts off your growing up without him were unbearable.

Because other families face the same fear, I was able to wear a proud face. He never knew.

The recruiters said with his muscular build and strength he was a perfect physical specimen of American manhood. They'd make a sharpshooter out of him in no time, they said. After they examined his hearing they stamped 4-F on his papers and sent him home. When he proved his hearing was as good if not better than men with two good ears, they turned a deaf ear. They said all it would take for him to be in a real pickle was to loose hearing in his good ear.

On the warm February day he left, grass was greening and lilacs just bursting with impatience to show off. All I could think was we might never see him again. Jannelle you started bawling the minute he left and kept it up all day. Even when you ate. Chew, swallow, cry. Drink, cry. All day. You washed your face with tears. No matter what I said, you sobbed, you moaned, you cried for your daddy. After supper we bundled up and went to our favorite spot on the porch swing. I talked about your daddy. Jannelle you cried for your daddy. Samantha Lynn you slept in my arms. Beth Anne you put fingers in your ears snuggled up against me and did your best to ignore Jannelle's theatrics.

Bethie you were watching swallows heading toward the barns when you sat up straight and pointed toward the driveway. You said two of the most wonderful words I've ever heard when you said "Daddy home." Jannelle stopped crying, I stopped talking, and Samantha Lynn went on dreaming. Those of us awake sat staring like we were seeing a ghost. James Samuel came running toward us and we started toward him. By the grace of God, I didn't drop you Samantha Lynn. If your daddy hadn't moved fast enough you and I would have wound up crumpled.

He said other than coming home, the only good thing about being rejected was meeting a man from town with the same name. "We was sittin' there makin' idle talk about what heroes we was gonna be when they called out "McClain, James Samuel," I ran up to the desk to tell them they had the last name wrong and nearly tripped over this big fella. He says, "I'm James Samuel McClain," and I says "I'm James Samuel Owen."

Folks got a kick out of it, said havin' two men from the same town with the same name who'd never run into each other was good enough for Ripley's Believe It Or Not. I nearly told them why but didn't want to open that can of worms.

This other James Samuel said he knew how disappointed I was but he figured we could buy war bonds and help on the home front." Then James Samuel ran his fingers through his hair and my heart skipped a beat. What was he up to this time? I didn't have long to wait.

"Sweetheart I know you won't like me being away but four nights a week close on to dark, I'll patrol town with other air raid wardens. It's our responsibility to keep our home front safe from infiltrators and saboteur shenigans."

Beth Anne you stood there looking at Jannelle's tear streaked face and shaking your head. It was like you undertood. I felt like joining Jannelle's waterworks but he put a stop to that.

"Jannelle daddy is going to help keep us safe," he said. Little Nellie it must have been that tone because it worked with both of us. Your waterworks dried up and I hope they stay that way. Land sakes! I've never known a female to cry over every little thing the way you do.

When your daddy said we had to do our part to help American win the war for freedom and democracy, I remembered wondering long ago how our little bit of the Ozarks could do anything like that. Now that someday day was here.

And suddenly I knew something even more wonderful. It wasn't just our small part of America fighting for freedom, but men and women from other small towns and big cities, cowboys and fishermen, doctors and nurses, young boys just out of high school. Americans from sea to shining sea were united as one family. All Americans. For the first time, my tears were tears of thanksgiving and pride.

"We're the home front soldiers" James Samuel said. "At twilight, we patrol streets making sure homes have windows covered, stores are closed and street lights are off. Only emergency vehicles use the streets and with lights off, they barely crawl along. If enemy bombers make it across the ocean to bomb us, we ain't gonna make it easy."

This time my choice was to sit down or fall down. As a kitchen chair was closer I sat. Fast. Enemy bombers? Over America! Bombing Sainte Lillian's! My heart kicked in with a new rhythm. I called it fear. Then, once again I felt ashamed. What we were facing was if? Families in Great Britain and France and Poland and other places across the ocean lived with the reality of "When, what time today or tonight?"

James Samuel says night wardens have serious responsibilities. They carry walkie talkies and have special codes if they see suspicious people lurking in the shadows. I asked James Samuel what a suspicious looking person looked like and he said he hadn't seen one, but if he did, he would know right away.

Speaking of food-- I wasn't till now, rationing makes me really glad we live on a farm and that city folks have Victory Gardens. Even the President's wife has one on the White House lawn. Because the enemy sinks supply ships and because so much of our produce and material goes into the war effort, nearly everything we need is doled out by ration stamps and sugar books. We may fuss and groan, but for all the inconvenience, our skies are clear and we aren't starving.

All over America folks make do with patched tires and bailing wire quick fixes but we're lucky. On the farm we aren't on the alert for Nazis and we don't plow around bomb craters. American cities and roads need work but we're whole. Just like Aunt Vora said we need to count our blessings. I wonder how mothers who'll never see their sons and daughters again and how children will grow up without fathers fit in that picture. Is the death of their loved ones the price of our freedom?"

When James Samuel said because the enemy sinks our supply ships, we do without a lot of essentials; I asked if he remembered the Boston Tea Party. He said as he recalled, he wasn't invited. Like a good teacher, I said it takes a lot to keep Americans mad, but it was happening again. "No doubt in my mind, we'll win the war," I said. He laughed. I know once this war is over, I'll never drink a cup of chicory or Postum again.

Your daddy buys one Hershey's Chocolate Bar each week for you girls. Not one each. One bar. After supper he gives each of you a square. Jannelle said she should get Samantha Lynn's square because the baby doesn't have chewing teeth. Bethie broke the square into crumbs and showed that Samantha Lynn didn't need teeth to enjoy chocolate. True to form Jannelle's, lower lip went out. I said it seemed to me Jannelle would want the biggest slice of a split infinitive, and Jannelle held out her hand... to pout even more when all I put in it was a kiss.

All over America, communities support our troops. Church ladies tear and roll bed sheets into bandages. We bake cookies and fry donuts for train loads of soldiers passing through to and from Fort Custer training grounds in Battle Creek Michigan.

I'll never forget Bethie the way you stand so straight and tall and wave your little flag. I can't figure out if you're fascinated by men in uniform or so many different uniforms as we see train loads of Army brown, Navy Blue, Marines in some kind of green and Air Force men in blue every time we're downtown.

I remember one day a train load of Japanese prisoners rolled through town. Everyone was there, looking at them, and they were pressed against the windows staring at us. It didn't seem the train whistle penetrated the awful silence. It was so deep and...and...full of thoughts and memories: ours, and theirs. Marines so big they made the prisoners look like school boys were everywhere. The Marines carried big long barreled guns.

Here I am again, jumping from one subject to another. Seeing as how writing time is scarce as hen's teeth, when it comes what is in my thoughts goes on paper.

To return to the joy of mothering three wonderful, different as the seasons daughters: Nice weather, with the wash hung outdoors, our house looks wonderful. With a spell of bad weather, we're into a new phase of decorating as every room fills with baby laundry. Winter and early spring with the cook stove and King heater going things dry fast as they're hung. On hot muggy days a houseful of soggy laundry is enough to make a preacher cuss. Sometimes I want to cork your bottoms. There are so many diapers in my dreams, there's no longer room for my handsome prince. Oh, he's there somewhere, under a mound of diapers. There are always diapers to wash, dry and iron.

My wish is by the time you girls are mothers, some genius (a woman of course) will have come up with disposable diapers. Glory be! No baby poop to scrape. Fold the disposable, wipe the bottom and throw the mess away. Best of all, your hands won't be red and chapped. Lucky you, you'll have so much more time with your babies. And sleep. What ever that is. Naps I know. Deep sleep however?

True confession? There are days I feel like a limp dishrag. It's strange because I've always managed. Right now, I'm just worn out. There's so much to birthing and raising babies I wasn't prepared for. My forever ever after dreams didn't know a thing about buckets of dirty diapers, a messy house and sick babies. There are days Jannelle when you have a runny nose, Bethie you have a runny bottom and Samantha Lynn you have both and you all want momma. You don't want to take turns. You want momma. Once I threw up my arms and cried with you. Wouldn't you know your daddy walked in on us, took one look, slid down the wall and started bawling? It was so funny we all started laughing. Shame on me for complaining. Our life fills my heart.

Think I'll go to one of my favorites on the wishing list: A washer and dryer in the house. I'd design the washer to fill and empty itself. No more buckets of hot water to carry from the stove, no more wash water to dump outdoors. Nice clean clothes could go into the dryer and we could go about our business. Maybe have a cup of tea and watch the wonder of it all. Wash day could be any day of the week! –or night-- The only thing left would be folding and putting away. Unless they invent a folding putting away machine. Mrs. Englehardt says they already have. They're called kids.

Another? Wood fires are such a comfort in winter weather. But let summer come and the cook stove heats the entire house. How nice to have instant breakfast dinner and supper that wouldn't need heat. No, that wouldn't work around here... We couldn't make it without bacon and eggs and sweet potato pancakes. Not to forget our other staples like fried chicken and mashed potatoes and gravy. My dear boy couldn't last a week without his pineapple upside down cake. I fretted so when we couldn't get pineapple. Now James Samuel says our home canned peaches make the best upside down cake and after we win the war he might not want pineapple.

When I feel sad about what we don't have, James Samuel pulls a funny face to make me laugh and says "If wishes were pennies and heartaches were gold, what a party we could have."

Have I told you lately my darling daughters how much I love your wonderful handsome intelligent smart funny compassionate daddy?

Even though I've left so much out, this writing has made me feel much better. Now, dame duty calls and there's contentment in her voice.

I just gave this a quick read. Diapers? I had so much to write about and I wrote about diapers! I can hear you boys "That's a woman for you."

We Have a Son

My darlings,

You girls have a brother! James Samuel Ernest Owen Junior you are one week old today. Of course you will need at least two brothers. I promise to work on that..

Before I saw you my dear son I knew you were the image of your father. I told him that now that I have two of him to love I will be the parent with the Cheshire cat grin. I know our tears are over. I store the treasures of my growing family in my heart.

Not that I miss diapers, but with your sisters no longer wearing them, the clothes lines look almost empty when I hang up your daily laundry. Two more boys and the diapers will disappear.

Oh God!

As I was putting Jamie's brown shoes in the trunk, my fingers brushed the pillowcase holding my diary and I thought to write one final time.

Thank God some memories are written here. Your first smile my son. Your first laugh. Your first birthday cake when we had enough white sugar to make boiled icing, and the look on your face so smeared with cake and icing. The sparkle of your eyes. I sift your days like gold dust in my mind, and always treasure the joy you brought to our lives. You were a gift my son too soon taken away.

Time doesn't matter now. All I know is James Samuel and I had a son, our girls had a brother and begged for more just like him. Little Jamie was a beautiful baby, a beautiful little boy. His hair started red gold like mine but soon it was dark like his daddy's. His sparkling green eyes danced with merriment. He looked at his world and saw only good, and he shared that with us all of his days. His smile deepened his dimples and quickened our laughter. Even on the darkest drabbest days he was full to overflowing with love.

Two weeks to the day before he died, Jamie went outdoors with me to "help" hang the wash. I.e. hand me clothes pins, and other important things like rocks, and blades of grass.

I was reaching for a pillow slip when Jamie said "Look momma." He was standing on tiptoe in a beam of sunlight that enveloped him in a shimmering glow. I knelt for a hug and felt one of those mom awe moments as he opened his arms wide. My son, my little son smiled at me and said, "Jamie hug Jesus first momma."

Every morning after that Jamie and his sisters "hugged Jesus." "Lookit what God did all by Himself!" he said each evening as we watched twinkling stars from our porch swing. Little Jamie loved sunbeams and moonlight. Little Jamie loved.

Little Jamie was…. WAS…I don't like that word. I hate saying "My son was."

My son.

My little son.

Little shoes. Jamie's brown high tops are so small in my hands. I remember the clerk brought white Buster Brown high tops. Jamie shook his head and pointed at his daddy' shoes. His had to be like what his daddy wore on the farm. He was proud to be like his daddy. Young as he was,, he seemed to know so much.

What a picture it made when he stood by his daddy's side and mimicked his giant stride with his sturdy little legs. I close my eyes and see a big size 13 boot print and beside it, the soft small indent from Jamie's brown shoes. The light impression was not the length of my right hand. My two men were walking home from the barn to me.

Strong leather these shoes. I thought he'd wear them out but as I turned them in my hand they were almost like new; Just a few worn scuff marks on the sides and across the toes The right a bit more scuffed. I remember how Jamie…Oh God!

Brown shoes. A soft dark curl. Pictures. Memories. All that is left of my son. He was playing in the morning and died in my arms before sundown. Once again, I held one of my dead children near my heart.

He was so hot. James Samuel drove so fast that hills and curves and bushes on Maple Brook roads blurred into one. You girls were crying in the back seat

I held my son and prayed. Oh God how I prayed. But I knew when he took one last rattling breath and went limp. His body jerked once in my arms. His arms and legs flapped like he was a rag doll. James Samuel hit the brakes and we hadn't stopped before he was trying to breathe life into our son. He couldn't.

He's dead. James Samuel Ernest Owen the image of his father is dead. Writing my son is dead is one thing. Accepting it another. Doctor Engels tests weren't specific. His best guess is a brain hemorrhage. And we'll never know why

Now, near the fence where the roses grow there are six tiny graves. English Script on the arch above the wrought iron gate reads "Owen Family Cemetery.

After we buried Jamie, Grandma and Grandpa Owen placed a statue of Jesus holding a baby in the center. They chose grave sites near the babies. James Samuel's' brothers and sisters brought crushed white marble for paths. Now we all plan to be buried there. Someday. They said our babies wouldn't be alone in their sleep. Is that supposed to be comforting?

You girls deal with the loss of your brother in different ways. Beth Anne your grief is deep like mine. Jannelle you have not cried since Jamie died. You watch me and your daddy and say nothing. Not one word. Not one tear. When you play nurse with your dolls you tell them to not be afraid. You will make them not sick. And Samantha Lynn every day you promise to get all 'growd' up and have lots of boys. "I pwomis momma they won't go to heben till they're really really really real old."

Your daddy gave up telling you to stay away from Jamie's grave and put a little picket gate in the fence above the graves. If he thought you'd eventually stop playing there, it didn't work. You three sit above his grave and play with his little trucks and balls and talk to him. Each morning you remember to hug Jesus and Jamie.

Every minute, every hour, every day, my heart breaks so many times and in so many ways. I see Jamie's chair at the kitchen table and remember that each meal a different sister was by his side. His stuffed Teddy Bear and Raggedy Ann doll look lonely. Everything reminds me of my son.

If I. I keep repeating. If I. That morning if I had stopped washing dishes and took the time to measure him as he stood by their marking post. Maybe then. Maybe then I would have seen something wrong. Maybe then. Maybe. But I was so busy. So much to do before market day. I said "Jamie mommy is so busy now. We'll measure the four of you after supper." We didn't have supper.

God I hurt so bad there are times when I feel I can't take another breath.

My dearest James Samuel looks at me and turns away. His eyes are dry and hard. He won't cry. I can't

I wonder "How God? Why did you give him to us to take him away? What did we do wrong?" All I see is my son stumbling toward me, his arms outstretched, his face hot with sudden fever. And all I have are these little brown shoes, right shoe worn more than left, the memory of a perfect little boy and a coldness deep down inside. My heart feels made of flint

I have hope for my girls and determination to see life through. Now, I can't help but wonder when as a child I found comfort in someday dreams my heart knew what was coming.

My promise to write everything is broken. I can't, and I cannot tell you how I feel after so many dreams have died. I'll tuck this away with the pictures and all the memories. Because we have you my darling daughters, we will live

My remaining someday dream is that Bethie you will read my diary and understand the yearnings and heartache and somehow finish the story. Not your sisters. You alone can do this Beth Anne. Someday.

PART TWO

One

Mom picked the day Ralph and I left for Michigan to give me her unfinished diary and her plans for me to finish it. I knew she had a going away gift, but this? She had to be kidding. She wasn't.

I had to say no. I wanted to say no. I didn't want to remember pain. Patiently as possible, I tried to share my side of her story. "Mom I'm moving somewhere I've never lived to do things I've never done with people I don't know and you want me to do what? "Someday, not right away, but someday," she said. My opportunity to use the five W's and the elusive H were slim and none as she pulled me aside and put the small fading pillowcase in my hands. I felt something like a notebook.

"Do what?" and a few other words started in my brain but didn't pass my lips. She said, "This is my unfinished diary. Once you and that damn Yankee get me some grandbabies, you'll need to read it." My mouth opened again. Again she was quicker. "Once you've read it, put it away. But you can't forget it. Because someday you have to finish it." She didn't ask me if I would like to at least attempt the impossible or if I would think about doing so, she told me that someday I had to. Then she gave me time to talk, but all I could do was stutter. She wanted me to do what? I had to read it and put it away and remember what I read and someday finish it? Someday as in when, where, and my favorite question, why?

Ralph honking the car horn, leaning on it, blasting the air with it, waving me to hurry, family lined up to wave goodbye and she wanted me to…I stared into my mother's blue eyes. "Promise me Bethie. Promise me when you're older you'll use your memories and your life and finish my diary."

I found two W words; what? and why? Arm around my waist, whispering as we walked, she led me to my waiting husband. "Bethie don't tell your sisters I said this, but you and I, we're so much alike you're the only one that can." In a heartbeat, I remembered so many things; good and bad, things I did and didn't want to remember about our lives after little Jamie died. I knew two things; writing would bring it all back, and I didn't want to remember. Yet she was there, holding on to me, waiting for my promise.

She wanted me to dig up and face the forgotten years and finish her diary. Could I write the truth about her brother? Even when my sisters and I complained about his touching us she laughed it off. "Just playing," she said. Could I write that? Did she want me to remember that? Did she think I wanted to remember how dirty I felt when he tickled me?

And my pop, her "Dear Boy" was neither dear or boy, but a mean spirited angry sullen frustrated critical almost monster masquerading as a man. I knew she never stopped loving him or praying for him. How could I write that? And all the broken dreams? Were they supposed to be included?

"Someday daughter you will understand," she said, and her diary wrapped in an aging off-white unbleached Muslim pillowcase embroidered with pink rosebuds became mine, became our secret. I promised only because I had to and wondered why, and how, and when.

Mom read to me from her diary when my unborn baby came out of me in bits and pieces. Stories about my sisters and little Jamie filled our eyes with tears. Hers touched now fading blue ink on pages turning brittle and yellow and mine marked a secret place I knew I should visit someday. Not then, but someday. Rewrapped in the pink rosebud decorated pillowcase it went back to the trunk. Hidden in a far corner of a dark attic, it waited. Her need and my wonder nagged.

From time to time, I opened the trunk and read mom's diary. I stared at my long ago promise and wondered how? Wondered why? Wondered when? And, as time passed and understanding began, I started the long journey.

Growing up, my vivid dream life coupled with an overactive imagination helped me over a lot of rough spots. Tons of them as a matter of fact. So I couldn't sing or dance or draw anything resembling a straight line, a tree, a house, or a star. So what? I wrote about people that could. Mom said I was like her and like her I had to be careful about when and about whom I wrote. She said I shouldn't weave names of local people into my made up stories. Sometimes when I was mad at spiteful girls I wrote true stories for composition classes and got into trouble, and learned the hard way, but that was a long long long time ago.

My stories based loosely on dreams were a bonus in high school and college. Now, past the days of A's I don't have time to write about my dreams. Don't want to dream them, and don't want to remember them either. But, we're dealing with what I get, not what I want.

I remember crawling between cool sheets on my big bed that warm night and welcoming the warm embrace of deep sleep. Evaporating instantly: concerns about glad I married this man today, and tomorrow his morphing into a grouchy stranger; my kid's summer plans, and heart hurting worry about mom and pop.

This sleep brought the good darkness, complete no nonsense dream free darkness. Peaceful. I welcomed it. Sank into it, felt sure I'd have a dream free night. Wrong again.

My 'favorite' nightmare wrapped me like a spider wraps its prey. This clinging web stinking like damp mould covered my face, weighed my eyelids, blocked my nostrils, and almost sealed my lips. I breathed it, tasted it, and knew fear. Dark. It was horribly dark and I was weightless and floating

I was alone forced once again to relive the dream horror. Face to face again with hidden meanings in horrible dreams. Writhing unfinished shapes like broken promises ignored floated and danced and beckoned. Vivid colors; odd mixture of people, places, and things. Bitter followed sweet. Sometimes they touched like partners in a minuet before slowly drifting apart. They were vapor vanishing without wind leaving behind echoes of pain.

On schedule in my dream tape, my friends are talking about sex. Sometimes I think that's all they care about. I can't bring up religion, politics, literature or art without their adding sex. They say the world wouldn't exist without sex

Donna's voice. "How about Beth Anne? She says Ralph is man enough for her, she doesn't need fantasies."

In this dream, everything that is mine is always their ping pong game. From Donna to Mary Lou. "Maybe so, maybe not! Y'notice she looks... oh, I dunno, not happy, like she's shutting down. Y'think there's trouble in paradise?" I hear the melodious chime of wine glasses touching.

Voice of experience. "Maybe he's having a mid-life crisis. First thing they get a beer belly, and then they can't ...y'know." Big sigh of sympathy makes the circle.

"Let me tell ya, mid-life crisis or not, I wonder how she gets any sleep with that big thang beside her in bed." Questioning voice "You seem to know a lot about big thangs." Laughter. Innocence defense: "You ever see Ralph in a Speedo? Noises best identified as drooling. Again, I was ready to go into the dream and...And what? Kick butt! Pull hair! Who me, get what I want in real life or in dream land?

As predictable, as usual, as normal, my nightmare didn't stop there. It got worse. From a ringside seat I witnessed death and dying from every imaginable man made instrument of death in wars around the globe. Wars of past and future melded together. Scenes of unspeakable horror; and I could not escape. Always strong destroying the weak. Always, the innocent and defenseless who want nothing more than a good life suffer and die.

On a rocky hill, three crosses silhouette against a darkening sky. The central nude bleeding tortured victim finds strength to look heavenward and pray, "Father forgive them. They know not what they do."

Instant replay. All of it. Every sight, every sound. "Father forgive, forgive, forgive." Echoes. Silence. Silence meant that once again the dream was over. I told myself I was safe, that I could breathe again. But my lie to me didn't work. Questions came from a voice I never want to hear again, a voice I don't need to hear again because I will never forget it.

How could I understand Ralph's nightmares when he didn't talk about them? Once he said he had P.T. something but wouldn't say more. What could I do about Ralph's pain and buried childhood? For that matter, what could I do about my parent's world? My childhood? How could any one guess their reactions if all those so called goodies, those "this spanking hurts me more than it hurts you" lies from childhood were wrapped in a pretty box tied with a white satin ribbon and left at the door? Did this memory/soul searching mean I one again had to face the rape and murder of my best friend? Was this to include touchy feely tickly uncle Jethro, and always mad dear old pop? How about the people laughing at me in my pimply faced fat stage of gawky indecisive self conscious adolescence? Another twist to the nightmare screw; long buried memories crashed into one another in their hurry to haunt. "Enough! I've had enough! I think it, whisper it, scream it and this time break free. Wrapped in fear sweat, I fell into deeper darkness. Suddenly, mercifully, I was awake. My bed. My house. My time. Enough already! Questions, unwelcome dreams and promise to my mother met head on. This time, the promise won. It had to. But, I knew in order to finish this mosaic; I had to do it my way. Warts and all. What a combination; her diary, my memories and my life! My favorite question loomed. Continually topping the list and winner of the curiosity loving cup, the all around winner: "Why?"

Two

"Use your life" she said. "Use your memories" she said. "Finish my diary" she said. Well, at least it's a diagram.

O.k., we'll start with memories which had to begin with my first breath. I don't exactly remember that, but it's a given it happened and I told them I was ready and willing to embrace life. I remember sunlight on my face as I lay in the crib, suddenly not being able to stand upright under the kitchen table and absolutely hating cornmeal based pancakes. With or without honey, or extra butter, or lavish dollops of molasses. I hated them. And buttermilk. I wouldn't drink it, but no force on earth could keep me away from buttermilk pie or buttermilk biscuits.

Maybe for awhile I stopped storing memories…Maybe there was so much repetition. Whatever the reason I have jumbled images of the first years. It's like sometimes memories come in the window. Jannelle pouting, mom singing, daddy laughing, sunrise and sunset, snowflakes on my face, that sort of thing.

Some I kept. I never understood why mom said the three of us belonged on Arthur Godfrey's Talent Scouts. Jannelle and Samantha Lynn were talented enough to win, but all three of us! Like our mom, my sisters could play the piano and sing and they did at every opportunity. Whenever, wherever they had the chance they were on stage; school, church and the Gospel Barn, family reunions, and neighborhood parties. You name it, they were center stage. Me? It was my lot in life to be as unmusical as pop. Both of us were tone death and couldn't find middle C on the piano even if it was marked; simply because it didn't sound like middle anything.

Mom said I should not fret about minor things. She said my special talent was second sight. She said my dreams were insightful and deep, just like hers. She said this ability came from our Gaelic ancestors. She never said what good my talent would do on talent scouts, but she did say I was extra special. Me! I was special.

So I bragged to my sisters and our friends. Who became former friends and avoided me for a week. My sympathetic sisters said if momma was teaching pop to sing, she could do a better job with me because I was so much younger than our dear old dad. We thought he was old. He didn't. They said I could join them on stage at the Gospel Barn if... IF...and they took me off to our secret place in the sycamore grove to explain their hook, line, and sinker: IF... They said they would help me IF. IF I promised to never brag to our friends about second sight and knowing things other people didn't know ever again because they were tired of hearing me called a witch.

Me! A witch! I was too mad to cry, but by golly John if I were a witch what I wouldn't do to those snotty girls. First a big fire under a cauldron like Mr. Shakespeare's witches. Other than finding a big cauldron, my other problem was finding an eye of newt--whatever that was. If I could, I'd brew up something and make green puss drip from their noses and pig tails sprout through their dirty panties. I laugh at that memory.

We kept our word my sisters and me. The Owen Sisters duet became the Owen Sisters Trio. My special talent was turning pages on sheet music. Even then, Jannelle or Samantha Lynn had had to nudge me or give me a nod or something. Second sight didn't help a bit when the Owen Sisters Trio took center stage.

Jannelle was never known as plump. From day one she was fat. Roly poly cute as a button red headed and fat. She was, and is round from top to toe and wears roundness well. With her red hair and sparkling eyes, she's about the prettiest fat person I've ever seen. She drew boys to the house like honey draws flies.

Less popular girls decided to teach Jannelle a lesson. Oinking like pigs, they bumped into her in crowded hallways. She said nothing. Did nothing. Their next trick was tying a cowbell to her locker. Once again, they earned their least desired response. Jannelle yawned when they compared their 'figures' to her lack of one. Desperate for willing victims, they finally gave up.

Jannelle was and remains very serious and smart. Her dream of becoming a missionary crashed and burned when she learned missionaries were not needed in our comfortable Ozark hills and hollers. She was ten years old. She cried for a week and was so upset she couldn't eat.

When she recovered from the first major disappointment of her career oriented life she found new strength in over half of a three layer Duncan Hines Devils Food cake mom baked for a church bake sale. Mom was so relieved to see Jannelle back to normal, she baked another. For supper dessert, Jannelle was served one paper thin slice of the leftover cake and we got the rest. True to form, she pouted.

Jannelle eventually, like a good southern belle found strength to recover and researched limited careers available for the fairer sex. She never commented on the joys of being a beautician, work in the shoe factory, polishing secretarial skills or teaching. Though marriage and motherhood were not considered work, they were also a career choice. Jannelle was definitely interested in marriage, but babies were not part of her life plan.

The short list of glorious opportunities available for 'little women' in our world brought words from her mouth daddy said he never wanted to hear one of his ladies say again. So she did. I think that was the cause of her first real spanking. She milked for sympathy for over a week and then broke out in a rash. When her eyes were swollen shut, Mom let Jannelle know five dollar doctor visits for such a minor issue would not be repeated. Mom looked at her and said her famous end of argument statement. "I have spoke." Jannelle sulked. She said "I will eat but I will not cook. I will learn but I will not teach, I will dictate but not take dictation and if one more person tells me how much money their mothers make at the shoe factory, I will explode." That left nursing. She raised delicate eyebrows and said she might consider it. She definitely considered marriage and definitely decided against a family.

This brings us to Carl Marvin Mayfield, Jannell's true and devoted love. Jannelle picked her man when they were second graders. "Me and Marvin, we're engaged," she announced to a Sunday School assembly. Uncle Jethro slapped his knees and hooted. "Y' gonna get married cause you want to or you got to?"

Bees buzzing in through one open window paused in mid-flight and retreated. Babies stopped fussing. Grandma Knowles hymn book fell flat on the wood floor, and the sound of book hitting polished wood seemed louder than cannot fire in the suddenly quiet room. Eyes focused on Jannelle. The little red haired girl and her blond haired fiancé glared at tall- not quite ugly- Uncle Jethro. My sister made me proud. She said, "Uncle Jethro you have a habit of saying the dumbest things." Laughter and applause. But Jannelle being Jannelle never left a question unanswered. "We'll get married when we're good and ready and we ain't gonna cry over dead babies like momma and daddy did cause we ain't gonna have no babies.. Eight year old Carl Marvin said "Yes dear." To this day Marvin says "Yes, dear."

For years Sainte Lillian's gossip mill loved tossing them around. What they didn't love was Jannelle and Marvin eloping one Labor Day weekend. In church the following Sunday, Pastor Tom said his sermon could wait because he liked people paying attention.

Then, on behalf of Mr. and Mrs. Carl Marvin Mayfield, he invited everyone to a punch and cake reception in the church fellowship hall. Crude joke authors moaned longest and loudest. Translation: They mourned the reception buffet, the goulash and fried chicken, the meatballs and ham, the music and dancing. Even worse, there was just enough cake to go around. For the combined families, it was perfect

For Jannelle, dreams came true. She has Marvin, and even though missionary is not part of her job description as head county health nurse, she worked it in. She did double duty as nurse and missionary in territory where brave strong he men feared to go. She visited patients in homesteads off back county roads little more than gully saturated rock strewn dry creek beds. In these isolated country homes, Jannelle preached a strict and loving nursing gospel.

Following her childhood dream, Jannelle tied Jesus, soap and water together. "Jesus tells us to be good stewards. That means we gotta take care of things. Don't you know everything we call our own is really on loan from God? Her work and sermons combined converted old dyed in the wool never been in a church sinners and young sinners just getting their fires started. She said her Nobel Prize was patients following directions and turning their lives around.

Nothing stopped Jannelle. She forged swollen creeks rode old mules over roads too gully washed for her 4x4 and worked non-stop during flu epidemics. She's delivered breech babies, set broken bones, and pulled teeth. Once with nothing but years of observation to guide and a kitchen table as her operating table, she removed an inflamed appendix. She's seen the worst of the worst and nursed the impossible to health.

Our parents however were another picture. As they grew older, sicker, and more dependant, my nursing sister could not cope. When they were sick, she was sicker with head splitting migraines and dizzy spells.

Mom never said more than "Jannelle if it's not too much trouble..." before Jannelle had Samantha Lynn on the phone. Samantha Lynn would get the pet food, the groceries, the prescriptions. Jannelle barely had strength to carry tea cups to the sink what with her migraine coming on and all. Fortunately she always had strength to call Samantha Lynn. A family joke was "Jannelle does what for a living?" When mom and pop were hospitalized, I was the ace up her sleeve. She knew her Michigan Yankee turncoat sister would drop everything and charge to the rescue.

Supervised by phone, Samantha Lynn and I were the miracle workers and the cooks that had supper ready for Jannelle and "Yes dear." Migraine headache and fainting spells and vapors combined, Jannelle always had strength enough to show up for supper.

In a very round migraine suffering weepy feeling faint and getting the southern belle vapors when our parents were ill nutshell, that covers my big sister I love her, but I have memories of not liking her.

One more thing about cooking: Little sis and I are good cooks Inspired even. Grandma Parker's old English cookbook is the only one missing from our combined collection. Uncle Jethro "borrowed" it years ago and now it's lost. His big sigh is followed by a bigger lie. "I've looked everywheres and kaint find it: Old liar. Should I own that cookbook Samantha Lynn said she'd give me her farm in exchange. Not a postage stamp corner, but all of it: her ark full of animals, pasture lands, orchards, everything. Because I couldn't match that offer I decided should she claim it, my only recourse would be to steal it, run, and lie like Uncle Jethro...

If nothing else, dear uncle showed us sometimes a little old lie was better than glaring ugly truth. He was very good at it. We weren't, but we tried. We learned the hard way lying didn't work around mom and pop. Lying to them equaled sore bottoms and no dessert; double punishment as far as Jannelle was concerned:

Three

Together, Jannelle and I are first cousins to ever present prickly thorns on old fashioned wild rose bushes. Just like thorns, there are times you can't tell we're there ready to stir up trouble, and just like thorns, we never go away. On the other hand, our sister Samantha Lynn is the beautiful rose. The change to her contented childhood was a blossoming into full flower. The Ivory Snow baby, the precocious child, the teenager everyone in Sainte Lillian town, county and rural routes adored, now wears the glowing beauty of a statue carved from living marble.

Growing up in Sainte Lillian, we sisters were together all the time. The togetherness that identified us as "The Owens Girls" resulted in unending stuttering from home folks. When they saw us in our identical flour sack dresses, their eyes saw two dirty Cinderella's in rags and one radiantly beautiful princess in a gown of gossamer silk.

Honest Ozarkians never call skunk cabbage beautiful, or go out of their way to be cruel. They say what they see no apologies needed, and are very pleasant—purring even, when around untarnished natural beauty. That was Samantha Lynn. Like the brightest star, the perfect rose, the untarnished platinum encrusted diamond, our sister earned compliments and praise. When she was near, people smiled and forgot their in-laws, outlaws, toothaches, potholes and missed car payments.

It's easy to quote from memory. "Samantha Lynn Owen you are so beautiful. You glow. Your hair is just like your momma's, and shines like it's under a spotlight. You have the brightest bluest eyes, the most beautiful smile." The three of us stood under that shower of praise and smiled. They saw Samantha Lynn. They didn't see me and Jannelle, but we smiled and lapped it up anyway, because she was ours.

Recovered, they raked Jannelle and then me over the coals. Bless their hearts, they tried. While their lips worked to form compliments their eyes wondered how our parents buryin' all them babies could produce two lumps of coal and only one diamond. Their eyes back on Samantha Lynn said a perfectly formed diamond at that. Back to us and the eye question was "Why only one? It's a downright shame "their eyes said.

Jannelle and I knew more than anyone Samantha Lynn was perfect. We sure as shootin' couldn't get mad because folks agreed with out opinion. I think if people hadn't gushed over her, I would have kicked them. With our arms around Samantha Lynn and out best gap toothed smiles showing full approval, Jannelle and I agreed with their every compliment. We felt sorry for them because they could only stare at our treasure. We lived with her and knew how lucky we were.

With the wisdom of teenagers, Jannelle and I decided Samantha Lynn could become one of the most sought after models in America if not the whole wide world. We knew everyone in and around Sainte Lillian town, county and rural routes pinned their dreams on saying "I knew that purty little thang when she was just a youngun."

Jannelle and I knowing our baby sister wouldn't mind becoming rich and famous, and knowing full well we wouldn't mind the benefits did our best. Our Kodak pictures of Samantha Lynn in a swimming suit, dressed up for church, playing ball, and brushing her long shining hair went to modeling agencies in every major city. They wanted her. She laughed. Samantha Lynn was the only person in our universe not at all interested in her glorious glamorous money raking in world trotting future.

When she was ready, she and Mark Smith her fiancé since high school, had a quiet wedding in a white country church near their farm.

Surrounded by rolling acres, their big white farmhouse-- the one she would give me if I-- is filled with kids, cats and dogs. Their land is rolling hills and pleasant valleys, mist kissed in mornings, fog blanketed in autumn. It's alive with freshness in spring and burst with bounty of orchard fields and gardens at harvest. They named their home site Eden.

Samantha Lynn delivered three boys and three girls with a minimum of trouble. On Mark Junior's due date she walked up to the Maternity ward at Sainte Lillian's Hospital and, calm as you please, said "I'm having a baby."

Nurses glanced at her smiling face. "Yes, dear, you certainly are pregnant. Now be a good girl and come back when you're in labor." they said, and went back to work. Something in Samantha Lynn's voice when she said "Now"! made them run. They just made it into the delivery room. For her repeat performances, a wheelchair was waiting and the nursery was primed. We never heard stories of long hard labor.

It's also wonderful that though miles apart, her kids and mine are best friends. What I consider not praiseworthy is Samantha Lynn not having one stretch mark. Even worse, she still has the shape of an 18 year old. Nothing sags. I mean nothing. Top, mid-section or bottom.

With three big boned darlings to my credit I have more than enough stretch marks and pounds to go around, and like a good sister have offered to share. Both. Samantha Lynn hugs me and smiles her beautiful contented smile. "And you thought I'd be happy as a model," she said. "Rich model," I corrected looking at my callused hands.

Where Jannelle faded into helplessness with mom and pop, Samantha Lynn and her brood begged them to live at Eden. They refused. In their hearts and minds, mom and pop lived on sacred ground.

Four

A few more insights into both sisters before I move on: From day one, Jannelle stared straight ahead and saw what she wanted to see; her perfect daddy, with mom there to keep him that way. Of course he wasn't and she couldn't. Doing my duty, I spent years working on her warped vision. It's only by God's grace and mom's watching eyes, that she and I avoided knock down fights. Helpless around our aging parents, she reminded me of Ralph when the kids fell from bikes. They both called "Bethie! Help!"

Maybe in a hundred years I'll fault Samantha Lynn on something. Probably not. Not only that, she and Mark who, according to citizenry of Sainte Lillian looks more like Abraham Lincoln every day, are inseparable in thought, word and duty. Lucky sister. Luckier Mark. One of them is always a phone call away, willing to help. While I'm at it, lucky me!

Now since mom chose me to "use my memories and my life and finish her diary," it's time for more about me. To begin (again) not at the beginning, but at least to begin: Seems I've always been the one family, kith, kin neighbors and friends called know-it-all and bossy. Early on in our small world, it was "Watch out! Beth Anne looks mad. I told you we shouldn't call her a witch. Let's run." Later: "Here comes Beth Anne. She's always studying, we'll ask her." Even later: "Here comes Beth Anne. She writes for the school paper and knows all the jocks. We'll be her friends." Miraculously, we all survived.

I'm nearly as tall as Samantha Lynn and maybe 15 pounds lighter than Jannelle. Maybe. Our weight on Jannelle labels her fat. I'm tall, so skip that label. Whatever it means, I'm known as a "well built" woman. I'm three sizes away from the XXX's those horrible dress sizes without numbers.

O.k., o.k., it wouldn't hurt me to loose 20 pounds. I'm working on it, and have been for years. I loose it, I find it. Sometimes when it returns it brings a few friends. I'm not the gorgeous fat red head or the absolutely perfect coulda been rich model but what I lack in charm, and gorgeous red hair, I more than make up for in attitude.

Other good points? Early on I latched on to mom's example and gave my life to the Lord. I do not claim perfection, but at least I'm sane. Thank God.

Folks say my stubborn streak is like mom's. Good. I wouldn't trade it. From pop comes my long bones, dark hair and emerald eyes.. The rest of me is original, shaped and molded by time and circumstance.

Little sis and I are a lot alike but different. Older sis and I are different, but a lot alike. Disagreements aside, our relationship is both fun and frustrating and equals a bond held tighter than crazy glue could ever do. That's probably why I didn't smack Jannelle when she started her Southern Belle phony migraines acts. Predictably, they started with hand wringing and one of the following: "Oh deah, what shall I do?" Or, "I shall surely swoon. Or, "I must recline, I feel so faint." Before she read Gone With the Wind or saw the movie, my sister could out southern belle Scarlet O'Hara's aunt Pittypat. Her beloved "yes dear" husband as obedient as Uncle Peter fell for it every time. Why not Marvin, someone had to? The best part of her act was her habit of wrapping a gardenia scented tissue around the first two fingers of her right hand. Then delicately, like a proper southern lady, she'd discretely dab stray tears. She may have been close to fainting, but she never smudged her makeup. Now that's talent.

Jannelle adored her daddy from her first breath. By my seventh year, I gave up and said she could have him. I was mom's girl, hanging on to her uconditional love. Samantha Lynn loved them both. Completely. Thoroughly. No questions asked.

To the three of us, mom was mom and sometimes momma. Our father, however, was always and only daddy to Jannelle. Samantha Lynn and I called him pop and Samantha Lynn had a way of saying it that quieted many arguments. I promised myself I'd never call him daddy, because it sounded too loving and loving he wasn't. This man, dear boy or daddy or pop, hovered over us like a guardian junk yard dog. If we registered one degree above normal at our nightly temperature check, - nightly, as seven times a week all year long- he was on the phone and we were in quarantine. Like it or not and we didn't, we had daily doses of Cod Liver Oil. Stinking yeast cakes was his butter for our bread. After reading about a child choking on prunes, he insisted we chew our scrambled eggs at least 30 times. Mom called a halt before he added mashed potatoes and creamed peas. Pop had to know our friends, their parents, their religious beliefs their political standing, and authors of books in their bookcase. Strangers were taboo. We could not play in the rain, on hot muggy day, or during winter's fiercest cold. . We could never stay out after dark without our parents near. For years we took afternoon naps. He drove me nuts with his list of "don't do," so naturally I found ways to do the don'ts.

For a very long time I believed I was adopted and that someday my real daddy would kneel beside me, take my hand, look in my eyes and tell me he loved me. I yearned, I was hungry, and I was thirsty with the need to know my real daddy loved me.

When mom tended the graves of her babies, Jannelle was busy with pop, Samantha Lynn with her animals, and I was at her side witnessing silent tears. She whispered their names: "Rose Ellen, Elma Pauline, Helene Bernice, Mildred Louise," and "Barbara Anne." She never called my baby brother by his full name. She would whisper "Little Jamie," with so much grief I felt my own heart hurting. I wondered how she could cry over their graves as if each loss were fresh and then come back to us. She never explained; maybe because she couldn't, or perhaps because at that time I wouldn't understand. That comes with heartache and loss and then, that was not mine. That waited.

Five times mom held stillborn daughters to her heart. We had little Jamie four years. She was holding her little son in her arms as he took his least breath.

Ralph and I lost one baby. It started with an accident at school and the loss nearly killed me emotionally...and physically.

I'd volunteered for last recess playground duty on a beautiful afternoon. Test papers could wait. I wanted April. I remember breathing deep and thanking God for beauty of freshly washed sky and bouncy white clouds. Students ready for a long weekend were at full volume. Always so shy when caught unprepared in class they were ready for everything on the playground. I was smiling at the thought as I retrieved a soccer ball. I turned to remind my fourth graders for the ten thousandth time soccer balls and swings did not belong in the same area. "Someone could be hurt!" formed in my brain but didn't become voice.

Forever in my memory a sharp pain, a blinding flash of whiter than white light stretching like a tight rubber band. Then it broke and I was at the bottom of a cold black hole. Awareness brought pain and multicolored lights doing a psychedelic dance. Buzzing bees became screams from hysterical students crowded so close fresh air was a premium. Sound ebbed and flowed. Lights flashed on and off. Switch on; switch off, from light-- bright light to complete total darkness. The penumbra became a discotheque of red, green, and blue. This, in turn, became denim knees, bright plaid shirts, tear streaked faces and lips uttering almost recognizable sounds.

After an eternity, one calm adult voice came through the fog. My urge to tell her a few things about questions ending in o.k., was interrupted by a pressing need to spit out blood and chunks of teeth. They got the picture.

Emergency room doctors said. I had a mild concussion, beautiful black eyes, abrasions and bruises, and that I looked pretty good for a woman run over by a truck. If that was a joke, we didn't laugh. Then they emphasized "Stay awake. Have your husband and kids check you every hour." These critical instructions came only after they dosed me with enough pain meds to knock out a horse. It was really fun. All I wanted was sleep. My husband and kids would not let me sleep.

Eventually I was under the care of our family dentist, Doctor Willy B. Chewrit. Doctor Chewrit did what he could and forwarded my sore gums to oral surgeon Doctor Johnny Pullit. His job: cut out what was left. I was tempted to write surgically extract but the picture doesn't get any prettier. Doctor Pullit finished what the swing started. I was a maw of bleeding swollen sore gums. It was not beautiful. I couldn't teach, and I wouldn't leave the house for fear of scaring neighborhood kids. I hurt. I ate pain pills. For days. On that ridiculous pain scale of 1-10, mine was 20, and growing.

About a week later, agonizing abdominal cramps bent me double. Ralph said " "With all the pain meds you're on, you shouldn't feel anything." Doctor Claire Brygal Morgan said it wasn't appendicitis. "Probably nerves or pain meds messing with your gut," she said, and sent me home. By dawn's early light, I was bowed over and four inches shorter. I could not walk, talk, or think. Unfortunately, I could feel.

Ralph carried me into Doctor Morgan's office. This time she did a complete work up. No more of this "when I touch here does it hurt?", but blood work, urine, everything. Especially questions about my period which was two days late when the swinging swing brought me down. Questions about my period were not asked at the ER or by staff of dental and oral surgeon. As they were working on what they could see and not my reproductive organs they didn't ask. Or think to.

I was pregnant. Unknowingly, unexpectedly pregnant. We told Doctor Morgan she was wrong. We had not planned this baby. She told us things we didn't want to hear and called the hospital. According to Monopoly playing Doctor Morgan this was a "Go directly to jail and stay there" hospital stay. Don't go home, don't pack Bethie a bags, don't worry about the kids, GO!" We got the picture.

For three days IV's dripped into one arm and technicians took blood from the other. It felt like they took more than they gave. Doctors said they didn't know what effect drugs would have on the baby, but it was so early there was a good chance she'd be o.k. "Stay in bed. Let your body recover from the trauma."

I didn't want to her anything about drugs harming my baby. I wanted good news: cheerful news. I wanted a healthy baby.

Not even in my childhood double teamed with pneumonia and measles did I spend this much time in bed. I became a praying lying bedfast zombie. I slept the sleep of fear and exhaustion to wake exhausted and sleep again.

Mom took over. Every morning the kids spoon fed me scrambled eggs and cream of wheat laced with butter and honey. They brought me beautiful pictures of blue skies, flowers and a smiley faced sun. Perfume from moms world famous soup rich with cabbage, tomato, onion and peppers, sent me to a comfortable safe dreamland.

Ralph said we would name our baby Augusta Ruth after our mothers. "It's an old fashioned name, but strong and I like it," he said. I told Ralph she would be perfect. She would be beautiful. He told me I was right. We prayed a lot.

I fought for my baby. Nothing worked. I oozed dark thick blood if I moved the wrong way. Soon, there was no right way to move. I lied to myself, to Ralph, to my mother. Mom knew but I wouldn't accept her truth. I promised God everything.

In spite of my prayers, lies, and promises to God, Augusta Ruth came out of me in bloody yellow clumps that looked like chicken fat in the toilet bowl. I wanted to put the bloody chunks together and make my baby whole. I wanted to tell Augusta Ruth I was so sorry, so very sorry. There were clumps of what would never be Augusta Ruth floating in dark blood turning blue tinted toilet water purple.

Overcome with guilt and loss, I flushed them away. And flushed. And flushed. I watched the spiraling purple water take my baby down. What would never be Augusta Ruth went into a dark pit full of unthinkable sludge. Forever, she would lie under tons of soil and gravel in our septic tank. I sent tears after her and heard mom crying. I knew she was remembering.

Back to the hospital for a D&C. They wanted my womb clean. Were they kidding? Hadn't I flushed my baby and my wombs entire contents to the bottom of our septic tank? They said I was hysterical.

Three days later Ralph carried me into that silent empty place we called home. My eyes focused on a spot only I could see and both hands cupped protectively where Augusta Ruth was not.

Mom and I cried together as we read her diary. The hope and expectations and heartbreak over stillborn babies; the loss of my baby brother: all of it was yesterday to her. I remembered the way she was with us, and thought about my kids needing me. Was I near understanding her hidden meaning? I didn't ask her because then I couldn't stand the knowing.

She waited two weeks and one bright day packed her bags. "Maybe next year," I said, but she left and everything in my universe was wrapped in foggy darkness. Because my kids needed what was left of me, I functioned. Guilt whispered blame for a very long time.

Doctor Chewrit did an excellent job replacing my slightly crooked slightly yellow teeth with dentures of the same description. After all I went through he did that! I cried for a week.

One morning I woke surprised to have spent the night in a dream free deep non-threatening sleep that embraced me with compassion and forgiveness. Once again, my smile and laughter were real.

If Ralph found me staring off into nothing, he teased me with pithy sayings that would make a man laugh and a woman mad. Naturally, I chased him with a wooden spoon. The kids loved it. Their laughter brought the day I laughed at Ralph's corny jokes. One day I cleaned house. I tossed and scrubbed until I felt clean inside and my house didn't look like a misunderstood man, a woman fighting for sanity, three kids, three dogs, and three cats, had ever left a toe mark. My house was gloriously sparkling clean, organized to the last sock. Of course, it didn't last, but it was therapeutic.

Eventually I could flush the toilet without seeing clumps that looked like chicken fat but were really what was left of Augusta Ruth in dark red blood turning blue toilet water purple. It took a lot longer, but the day came when I held a newborn and tears didn't flow.

Five

Samantha Lynn and Jannelle grasped the truth that as different as men are, we can't live without them, and plucked their soul mates from the trees of home.

I looked at a lot of cute boys in grade school, but they weren't exatly right. My sisters said I'd wind up an old maid so I tried the dating scene in high school. One stood head and shoulders above the rest but when we graduated, his family sold everything down to the last rusty nail in the chicken coop, and bought citrus farms in Florida. In no time, they had so much money they couldn't spend it. When what's his name entered college he forgot me, and our letters full of promises. Distance made his heart grow fonder for a cute little blonde in her itsy bitsy teeny weenie polka dot bikini. She snatched him up faster than her daddy could say "shotgun wedding."

In teachers college when I wasn't attempting to learn the impossible-- understanding the adolescent-- I decide it was time for action. It didn't help that my friends and I were passionate pursuers of itsy bitsy teeny weensy age lines. True, lines visible only with a magnifying glass, but they were there! We had to act! Foolish romantic I, I knew what I wanted, and shed men of every shape and description like some folks shed dandruff.

Graduated, teacher certified, three of us at the ripe old unmarried age of twenty-one moved our search area far from Sainte Lillian's borders. Privately, we said we were shopping. "Operation Shopping" was carried out where variety was guaranteed when we became elementary teachers at a new school district near the U.S. Army's Fort Leonard Wood. Our home base was an adorable white bungalow with Periwinkle blue shutters, attached two and-a-half car garage, fenced in yard, three bedrooms one and-a half bathrooms, and everything else we needed except furniture. We learned quickly the benefit of living where transfers are a way of life and garage sales are sweet. Our best 'buy' was a free red leather couch by a curbside with a set of turquoise melamine thrown in for three dollars. . We settled in, school started, and we shopped.. Especially on weekends. Even without coupons or BOGO, bargains were everywhere.

Of course we were new to Army men, but long past being new to the ways of men. Stupid was not stamped on our foreheads. We knew some handsome hunks who said they were single weren't and some who said they were were interested only in back seat bingo. "Baby, I'll love you forever" said these smooth talkers as they attempted to convince us we wanted the little squirts they had to offer. We knew they called us "Baby" because after two beers they forgot our names. After all, in their bleary weary beer sedated minds "Baby" covered the basics.

We hunted...er ah shopped...wisely rejecting more than we cared to count, dated a few, compared notes and waited. Inevitably, destiny took over.

To help locals observe Veteran's Day, the fort's Community Relations Department arranged military drill presentations for local schools. After first hour assembly, each room was 'given' their very own hero for a day.

My fourth graders as do most young students, idolized men in uniform. They grew dizzy thinking about real soldiers eating in our school cafeteria, and spending the day in classrooms. Real soldiers! Not G.I Joe dolls on sale at the five and dime. "Real soldiers." If I heard that only once a minute something was wrong. They lived, breathed and talked real soldiers. Real soldiers that wore uniforms and medals and everything!

Everything was not defined, but it didn't need to be. "Everything" said in that breathless way, let imaginations run wild. Not only that, for one whole day, students could touch soldiers and talk to soldiers and ask all kinds of questions. About was it true their scrambled eggs were powder, and why did they march so much, and did they ever-ever-ever think kids like them could join the army and of course, my favorite question, "why?" followed by "do what?" Proper usage, of the term means "pardon me, please repeat." It is always politely spoken. "Do Whut?" On the other hand means trouble, tuck your tail in and run. When situations go from simmer to broil it's used a lot. That week, there were very few what's and no whuts.

Johnnie told Susie when him and his dad were downtown near some funny looking places with flashing lights and loud music shaking the building, they saw big men with armbands that read M.P. They used big sticks to break up a fight. Susie told the rest of the school. Big stick fever was contagious.

Thankful for opportunity to improve student behavior, I promoted myself to Superior Teacher General, and walked the halls with a ruler under my arm. For one week blue jeaned boys and girls were good soldiers. They saluted me, saluted one another, stood at attention and responded to orders with "Yes Mam! Superior General Owen Mam." Principle Merkle's office was student free the entire week.

The moving finger wrote and having writ, the stage was set. Actors assigned bit parts played them well. Eyes were rivited on the door. Silence was platable when Staff Sergeant Ralph George Brunswick, with the bearing and manner of a Spartan warrior marched into our room. This tall broad shouldered dark haired perfect specimen of American manhood saluted the flag, saluted the students, and saluted me. When I made sure he wasn't wearing a wedding ring and did not have a pale band where one belongs, he didn't stand a chance. To put it another way, Staff Sergeant Ralph George Brunswick was off the rack, rung up, bagged and out the door before he knew he was on sale.

My perceptive students looked at him looking at me and me looking at him and in one voice said, "Aaah." I smiled and worked at finding my voice, and was thankful I'd dressed for the hunt (kill?) in an A line black skirt, form fitting beige sweater and killer three inch shining black patent leather heels. I was so ready.

At our first pre-martial session with Pastor Poet, he and Ralph talked baseball for over 20 minutes. Baseball! Were they nuts? I was there to talk about life long commitment, and they talked about baseball. As mom would say, "That's a man for you!"

Pastor Poet cleared his throat, glanced at the wall clock and Ralph got the hint. Glory Hallelujah he swallowed bachelorhood and 'remembered' why we were there. Transition from man with a joke to real man with concerns took less than a heartbeat and more than a split second.

Ralph shared his anger about Uncle Jethro's broadcasting avenging angels would descend when his second favorite niece deserted her southern heritage and married a damn Yankee. Pastor Poet said "Pray about it Ralph."

One word question. "Pray?" Long pause, followed by two word question. "About Jethro?" Pause. Three word Question: "Everything he says?"

"You'll be in good company Ralph. Most Christians in Sainte Lillian's have that man on their prayer list."

With uncle out of the way, we moved to easier topics like faith in the Triune God, the meaning of salvation, the sanctity of marriage, sexual intimacy, and the raising of children. Ralph said he kinda liked the Old Testament guys having dumb blonde concubines as well as a wife or two.

I said I wondered how these great patriarchs liked it when they forgot wedding anniversaries. Ralph, smart man that he was, quickly changed the subject.

Ralph made sure Pastor Poet understood the word obey would not be in our vows. "Beth Anne and I are partners for life. We stand together, work together, make decisions together," he said. I was so proud of him.

Then the day! The glorious sun kissed day when Ralph and I stood hand in hand at the mahogany altar enhanced with yellow and white roses and lilacs. In the aura of candelabra candlelight, we promised to love, honor and cherish one another till death and then forever. Obey was not mentioned.

Our families became, and somehow remained best of friends. I told mom my married life would always be perfect. She sighed and hugged me.

Define death," I mumble when Ralph has another tantrum and my mind returns to that defining moment at the alter.: My groom so tall and handsome, me in my pure white size 11 gown, our eyes and hearts locked. We were alone in the world.

We were so young.

We were so innocent.

We had so much to learn.

Something like battle lines were drawn when Uncle Jethro edged closer in the receiving line. As he looked for a microphone to deliver the toast of the year, Uncle said "Spite of all I could do, Bethie married that damn Yankee."

Jannelle looked at me and winked. Out of town guest managed a nervous laugh Locals told him to shut his mouth. Slowly, dear uncle inched towards his second favorite niece and her damn Yankee husband.

Ralph said nothing, but I saw one of his slow smiles, the kind of deep knowing smile that made privates sweat.

In the good and wonderful days of childhood, before dirty old men were prosecuted for molesting, uncle was known as "Good old Uncle Jethro, the girl hugger." Women kept their defenseless daughters away. No matter how many times we told mom we didn't like his 'tickling', she said he didn't mean anything bad, it was just his way. On my wedding day, he was ready for one more time.

He stood in front of me, arms open. I backed away, and uncle said to Ralph's face "C'mon Bethie it's just for fun." My brand new husband grasped both of uncle's hands in his and bent the old hugger's fingers almost to the breaking point. Smiling Ralph was enjoying himself. Fun was no longer pasted on uncle's face.

My wonderful husband draped a muscular arm around uncle's shoulders and pulled him close in a 'loving' hug. Ralph looked happy. Uncle quickly learned what an entire town had not been able to teach. My hero. My husband. One and he same. And the best wedding reception ever. Honest!

Six

Our work paralleled. When I taught history to fourth graders, our topics were wars that shaped and kept America safe and the price of freedom. He taught young men how to pay that price. Army style.

From that perspective, our first year was a sad but sweet time. It was also for us a perfect year of love and discovery. On our weekend getaways to a lakeside cabin our perfect plans for a perfect life in the Ozarks were perfected. I would teach, he would build homes, our family would flourish. Four plus a few months and we'd be home free. Then the Army said, "Sergeant Brunswick pin on these gold bars, take your bride to Germany, train troops for a year and plan on another Nam tour. Your country needs you." Bonuses thick enough to buy us each a Mustang convertible sweetened the pot.

Germany. Main address: Close to the wonder and history of Europe. The British Isles called. Paris was a short ride through the Alps. Beaches of Normandy, battle fields and burial grounds of Belgium were weekend jaunts. Our dreams were full of tasting, seeing, and doing. German and French lessons were a must. Ralph chuckled, as I, in my mid-western slightly southern accent, practiced words and phrases I'd never heard for ordinary everyday items.

Easy to understand were words for mother, father, water, and hundreds more. But, "Langsam"? How in heaven's name could Langsam mean slow down? When it's time for our kids to stop we take the direct route. "Billy Bob and Jenny Sue slow down now y'hear." Emphasis of course is on the NOW! A German parent watching Eric and Helga running helter skelter would command "Langsam Eric. Langsam. Helga." While my fourth graders and I never understood how 'langsam' translated into "slow down," we had so much fun the end of school assembly was ours. Mothers provided American versions of cookies, cakes and candies representing Germany, France and Italy, and we "taught" our version of their languages. It was wonderful.

While I worked on that, Ralph worked on our future. Without consulting his 'partner for life, he told the army what to do with their bonuses. He was ten miles short of polite, and wasn't much better when he told me what "we" had decided. .

His D for decision day also marked the end of my school year. It was the last day to hug students who promised to remember me "forever n'ever." The last day to wipe glistening tears, the last day for discovery and laughter. It was at last time for my final walk around the empty room touching desks and remembering. Though I didn't know it then, this was also the last day I completely believed in Ralph.

At school, I wiped my last tear and hurried home where Ralph and our gloriously exciting adventurous dream come true future waited.

For a day of last, a first waited at home. Ralph was first home and looking smug. Our world radiated celebration! I bent to kiss him and he said...and something resembling my voice said "Ralph honey, don't tease me like that. You know how wonderful the next few years will be."

We aren't going," he said, and left me staring vacantly at broken dreams. Steaks charred. B&M Brick Oven Baked Beans burned through the pot. C.S. Lewis and Cathedrals joined broken dreams and burned beans. I blew my nose on hillside wineries along the river Rhine. Ralph didn't notice.

Overnight, I became a different wife. Less treasured, diminished somehow. I wore the role silently, wondering my favorite question.

Ralph, the man with a plan didn't waste a minute. Soon, we were headed to Michigan, his family construction business and opportunity spelled with credit cards and dollar signs. The finality of leaving the dreams Ralph and I built for the Ozarks took its time, but it sank in.

Mom gave me her diary the day we left. I gave her my promise, and this new, different, unplanned future to Ralph...my new...and different husband...

Ralph's family found us a fixer upper that would quickly became a tearer downer starter over, but we didn't know it then. Fortunately, it had acres of woodland and a nice old overgrown orchard. Everything else was my worst home sweet home nightmare. Grounds loaded with falling down buildings home to friendly bats, and mice and rats and who knew what else? House ready for major surgery and the septic tank covered with the greenest grass in three counties. Erma Bombeck would have loved it.

Ralph saw potential in every nook cranny and weed patch. The same potential keeping others away for a decade was ours for a song, a dance, and a humongous mortgage. Dad Brunswick helped bail us out (literally) after a three day downpour. He poked around for 15 minutes and said "Smarter to tear down and start over."

We parked the Brunswick family camper near the barn, set up the grill and worked our butts off. Ralph and a crew of Amish carpenters had the house livable in over a month, Dad Brunswick said hardware, furniture and flooring stores were fighting over which would name us customers of the year. "Not to despair, said I", as we moaned over bills. "There's always the lottery." Ralph didn't look up. "Think your mom would loan us a dollar?"

When the tenacled Octopus furnace was sold for scrap, Ralph explored the basement and discovered an old wine cellar. He said along with refinishing the basement, he'd tackle that wine cellar. It'll take a little work," he said. During my first Michigan winter, Ralph's time line became one of the world's biggest jokes. When winds blew blizzards and sleet and ice were diamonds on broken power lines, we worked so hard we never felt the cold. We worked when we should have been sleeping and sometime slept while working.

My one, and I promise, my only experience with glop men call mud came in our basement. Because young and innocents may sometime read these words, I shall deliberately omit any and all descriptive of this wonderful substance. Except for this: growing up on a farm, I knew mud. Trust me, grey glop does not look like, like feel like or behave like mud. Maybe men call glop mud because working with it makes them feel like little boys building mud forts. For weeks our routine was: slap it on, let it dry, sand, and start all over again. We had our own dust bowl not only in the basement but through the entire house.

Early spring brought my chance to play in real mud when Brunswick's gave us double French purple lilacs. I whined and begged from Brunswick relatives and neighbors within a 20 mile radius. Standing in line at Meijers didn't stop my hints to strangers. I posted "Wanted, anything that blossoms" at church and on bulletin boards. It worked. All sorts of things wound up in the driveway. Especially Hostas. The Missouri bred woman who thought she knew a lot about everything beautiful, blossoming and forever green wrinkled her nose and asked "What'sahosta? She learned. And stopped wrinkling her nose. Now she lobbies to have the Hosta and purple loosestrife on the state seal.

Neighbors loved our work, we loved the promise of year round beauty, and squirrels and chipmunks lovingly mapped the site of every planted bulb.

Ralph and I both loved my size12 jeans. Bonus, thanks to the furry map makers, every year my rear reduces a bit as bulbs are 'lovingly' replaced.

Ralph said the grape arbors were his. Brunswick Wine would make us famous. He'd use crates of cobalt blue long necked bottles from the old cellar, and our winery would start any day. While we waited, blue bottles wrapped in small white lights made wonderful Christmas decorations in every shining window. Juice, jelly, jam and grape pies weren't bad either.

Ralph had the arbors, I claimed the orchard. Ralph said he'd use it for firewood if it was too much work. Didn't happen. In bleak mid-winter my small orchard dreams of springtime's scented clouds. Summer growth promises delights in green, red, and yellow. Autumn brings our harvest of fruit and venison. Not Bambi! Venison. We provide for scavenging deer and each year one or two returns the compliment. Ralph? He who dared to say firewood? He can't make a day without our cinnamon/ nutmeg/ ginger/clove spiced apple butter. The year I spiced it with red pepper flakes he gave me his Good Conduct Medal.

During our first Michigan years, I was a good wife, following where Ralph led. If we disagreed I gave in a little here and a lot there and we worked whatever it was out to our 'mututal' satisfaction. (Read his not our) I began to feel put aside and my favorite question nagged. Why this? Why that? Why did he change our future without discussing it? I thought of my parents, the way they began; vowing as Ralph and I did a love that would last forever. Time and sorrow changed their dreams.

I wouldn't let our life mirror theirs. Yet slowly, little things began to erode my faith in dreams and promises. I told myself reality is one reason young lovers are blind. If they had an idea of what waited on life's discovery channel, they'd pack their bags and run.

Seven

Reality: The real world where dreams are remembered and packed away.

We grew, we changed. In many ways, I was the same, just wider by childbearing, and wiser through disappointment, pain and grief. Physically, Ralph's only difference is size; more, and hair, less. Lots less. It's his mental and emotional changes that have me stymied.

First the physical. To say he fills a doorway, or stands by our kids or plays with the dogs and looks big is not enough. In any doorway, Ralph's such a snug fit air and light somehow just manages to squeeze by. Kids, dogs, cats and little old ladies in tennis shoes crane their necks to look up at him.

More? Six foot six inch Ralph is nearly 300 pounds of muscle; BIG Bad John big, Paul Bunyan big. Read of a north woods lumberman, and think Ralph Brunswick: head high, feet firmly planted on mother earth, plaid shirt sleeves rolled over rippling muscles. Man in control.

Without speaking, Ralph gained respect from strangers and obedience from employees. Women Over 18 and past their century mark undressed him with their eyes. In public Ralph used size and humor to advantage, and was always the man in charge. One day he made the mistake of defining the initials C.M.F.I.C. on his desk name plate. I said "not tonight big guy." He slept on the couch. For a week. Women and kids in our combined families saw through his bluster and were the only ones to make "No" stick. We were the few and the proud.

Eating out, a glass of beer wouldn't do. Make it a pitcher and they'd better be damn sure it's ice cold. His salad greens hid under a foot of Thousand Island dressing. His T-bone? 16 ounces or more. His baked potato indecently lavished with three-- or if he was really hungry four or five dollops of sour cream and butter. Dessert? Chocolate covered cheese cake drizzled with caramel sauce, smothered in whipped topping and ground nuts was a good start. Three scoops of French Vanilla ice cream on the side helped. With Ralph "All you can eat" fish fry meant smelt. No fries. No slaw. Smelt! Fry cooks actually cried when waitresses called out "He's here!"

Having more maxed out credit cards than ten of my friends didn't stop "Charge it!" He loved spending, cursed the bills and the collectors and kept on spending. A Chrome and black Harley rested in the big barn beside the enormous boat the kids named Not a Canoe. Ham radio equipment and a top of the line photo lab took over the wine cellar.

I remembered bonfires at the lake and romantic music floating across the still waters. Johnny Mathis singing and Roger William's piano magic took us to another world. Our life was full of us, our dreams, our love and our tomorrows. Time came when I had trouble remembering the dreams. I woke to his piles of upside down turned around going places without me tomorrows and tried to not remember what I told mom. What I believed then.

On the positive side, Ralph and I parented three perfect kids. My take on their perfection: Sometimes they're perfectly wonderful, other times perfectly obnoxious; but, they are always perfect when they sleep. The three have nicknames used by the world, and nicknames used exclusively by their proud dad. Before passing out on the delivery room floor, he managed "Girl #1" for Mellie. Franklin Mac Duff became "Boy," and Mollie Kate, the little sweetie we were all guilty of spoiling became "Girl #2"

Mellshanna Priscilla Rose "Mellie" is a blue eyed strawberry blonde, long legged and bean pole skinny. We are a lot alike and share curiosities. Our favorite question is, of course, why?

Mac Duff aka "Boy," is one year, one day and 20 minutes younger than Mellie. Both answer to their full names only when troubles; low grades for example, or their grandma's use them. Otherwise, to quote Mellie, "Them there is fighting words." Mac Duff would make a great politician: President even. All charm, he lives to make people happy, and delights in smoothing troubled waters.

"Girl #2" Mollie Kate, has twinkling hazel green eyes, shining chestnut hair, and absolutely hates the 32 freckles dotting her peaches and cream completion. Only her dad is allowed to use a nickname. "I'm not Margaret! I'm Mollie. Not M-o-l-l-y, never with y but M-o-l-l-i-e with an i e, and don't try to call me Katherine or Catherine with a C., cause I won't answer.

I'm Mollie Kate. That's M-o-l-l-i-e K-a-t-e." She was little, she was loud, and make no mistake, she was Mollie Kate.

Her brother and sister's advice was to enjoy her youth. "You'll be grown up like us before you know it," they said. She looked at them, shook her head and left for the kitchen. Not to eat, to cook.

Mollie Kate "helped' me in the kitchen since she was old enough to figure out things that tasted very good came from there. Krazy Kake, a deep moist chocolate confection remained her specialty. Cleaning up after took awhile.

Ralph said the three were born with "Wonder what would happen if I itis." Most of the time, my perfect trio manages to behave…at least in public.

Noted for posterity is "That Easter Sunday, and the great pink jellybean debacle!" Easter Sunday. Day of reverent worship, fulfillment of the Christmas promise. The day of days.

Easter Sunday. Sanctuary, full of members, visitors and the three times a year worshippers. Organ music swelling. Whispers diminished. Beauty. Peace. All factors considered the bag of pink jelly beans Mollie Kate smuggled into the sanctuary had to split when both her brother and sister grabbed for it. Pink jelly beans had to fly and roll and slide across the sanctuary.

Beautiful scripture, Inspiring music and the promise of resurrection and redemption are expected and anticipated on Easter Sunday. A pink jelly bean shower however? It took one pink jelly bean to stop the music and everything else.

Grandmother Blanche seated with her beautiful daughter and her always (publicly and privately) perfectly behaved beautiful triplet daughters, took one pink projectile on the back of her neck. Shot from the baggie cannon, it hit hard. A terrorist hearing Grandmother B's anger would have turned tail and run.

My three prefect darlings looked completely innocent and were surprised with the congregation when three perfectly attired and always well mannered young ladies-- dressed alike in white dotted Swiss with beautiful red sashes tied precisely and perfectly at the waist,--spotted pink jelly beans."Pink jelly beans" triplet voices yelled as one. From side pews and balcony, kids caught pink jelly bean fever. They had to have pink jelly beans. They tromped on toes, crawled under pews, and cheered one another on.

My children, the only three not interested in pursuit of pink jelly beans, did not move an inch.

"Look what your three kids just started"! Ralph whispered.

I shot back "Be glad I didn't have a bag of jelly beans."

He started coughing.

Mollie Kate snuggled against me and, batted her twinkling eyes. "Honest mom. The devil made me do it."

I'm saving the video for my grandchildren.

Eight

Our first adoring looks at little bundles of burp did nothing to prepare us for becoming "My mom and dad can/will do that -whatever it was-parents." The kids didn't know we didn't have time, and we knew we didn't have the energy. I tried to beg off but it didn't work. They needed us. The kids learned promising seven dozen cupcakes for a next day party meant they helped, but that didn't stop the music. We learned we liked being heroes in their eyes, and got a kick out of students delighted with M&M decorated cupcakes. We ate a lot of hot dogs and pizza, shared sighs and laughter with other parents and managed to have fun.

When Ralph's moods began taking over, he told me and I quote, "Tell them I'm too friggin' busy for that crap." I told him he was no busier than normal. He came up with new combinations of excessive vulgarity aimed at their community spirit. I said, "Deliver that message yourself!" He didn't, and he didn't volunteer.

When the overworked committees wondered if maybe...and they stressed maybe as if that would goad Ralph into showing up, maybe I had time to find someone to fill his shoes I lied like an expert. "Ralph and I have been doing this for years. I can practically do it blindfolded." I knew it took quick minds, watching eyes unlimited energy to coach little league and T ball, arrange 4-H outings and work with scout troops, but why not try? So I compounded the lie. "With the school year winding down, it will be easy," I said.

It wasn't but with family honor at stake, I rewrote the super mom manual, did house work and laundry at midnight and gardens at dawn and dove in. I flunked little league. T-Ball was more my style. Little freckled faced wanna be home run sluggers were so cute.

Added bonus: the kids thought helping at T-Ball and church nursery was really cool. True they couldn't do more than field balls, or stack blocks at nursery, but it was a start. They worked wonders with blocks and balls in a church nursery overflowing with crying toddlers.

Middle School Band Trips require both bus driver and chaperone. From the squeaking clarinet section, Mellie and Mac Duff did it again. "My mom watched dad drive, she can drive if you want," they said. They quickly discovered I wouldn't drive a bus full of kids anywhere. I chaperoned when Ralph drove and kids behaved. Not perfectly, but they behaved. When not if, they got out of hand, all Ralph needed do was yell "Quiet!" Just once. It's the way he said it. When his chauffeuring duties were replaced by a diminutive father of nine, it took me five minutes to become chaperone from hell.

During away trips, students morphed into budding rock stars with too much time on hands that became very busy. When I wouldn't let them play doctor, they called me among other things "Nosey and rude." One little practicing sex pot said "My mom will beat you up if you don't leave us alone." Naturally, we went to her parents. Together. That was a lot of fun. Through 4-H vegetable and flower gardening and the "wabbit habit" and the myriad wonders of scouting, it didn't take me long to become one very tired super mom.

Ralph? Well, he still ate and slept at home. He was either angry with me or not, but always angry about something, and very verbal about whatever it was. Big mystery. Not to be discussed. He lost keys, ate too much, couldn't sleep, smashed his thumb. Those and ten thousand other things were always the result of my stupidity. Long and loud. Of course our fizzling sex life was, to quote "Your fault you stupid frigid…" end quote.

Marriage's worst scenario invaded my thoughts. Remembering Ralph's comments on dumb blonde concubines, I wondered. In increasingly awful nightmares the angry tirades of pop and Ralph became one and the same. I remembered mom "Finish my diary. Use your memories. Use your life. You'll understand." Yeah, someday, maybe.

I prayed, waited, tried talking to a stone wall and wondered why my marriage was stagnating in a dark hole called maybe. Maybe tomorrow or next week or next month it would be better. Maybe this was a bad dream. Maybe he would remember how once we were so happy. Maybe he would notice kids, cats, and dogs disappearing when he exploded. Maybe he would keep doctors appointments. Maybe I would forget his explosion when I made the first. "Woman I ain't the sick one," he yelled and, as he left every door slammed so hard I thought frames splintered.

The kids looked to me for answers I didn't have.

I re-read this and remembered too much pain and decided enough. There were better times.

Nine

My son knew we didn't want and I didn't need another dog. He and his sisters also knew a few other things like want has little to do with getting; and above all, their mom never refused one of their presents. Therefore, Superior German Shepherd Duffer became my official guard dog on Mother's Day.

Duffer's face with one tan ear permanently folded down, and one black ear always at rigid attention, is covered with a black mask. In his opinion, he is King of the hill, feller to be reckoned with, and absolute boss. Unchallenged leader. Ask Hookie, my king of the jungle cinnamon striped yellow cat pal, and it's another story entirely.

Duffer started out runt of the litter, but we fed him well. Size and volume were his advantage over Hookie, but that didn't faze my cat. He compensated with cat cunning, feline brains and speed. The way they played together reminded me of the kids.

Duffer acted like he sat at the feet of Jesus, and told Him not to worry, he King Duffer was guardian of the Brunswick world. Duffer complained if sunrise didn't meet his schedule. King of sheepdogs, Duffer, guarded, guided, and protected his three ornery two footed lambs. His morning herding got them to the school bus on time. Besides sleeping with one eye open during the day, his schedule included a late afternoon walk to the bus stop to bring them safely home. If said bus would be early, he knew it. Late, he knew it. He was Duffer.

One day, a long legged coal black not a speck of white anywhere Labrador retriever pup "followed Ralph home." Twenty miles, across three highways and the interstate, the pup followed him home. Miraculous. The little fella didn't sport one blister on his puppy pink paws. Ralph named him Abraham Lincoln. Mac Duff changed it to Tupid because the dog's favorite bedtime snack was panties. Boy or girl, he didn't care. Tossed toward but not in the dirty clothes hamper, they were his! Tupid stuck. Not so stupid, he tried blaming his pranks on Einstein Bear, my long eared liver and white Springer Spaniel, who never did anything wrong. If found with Mac Duff's socks and Mollie's panties in his mouth, Einey's sad crestfallen looks could convince a jury he was rescuing, and not guilty of snacking aforethought.

More than one cat? Of course. I've can't imagine a house with three dogs that didn't have the added excitement of three cats. If I could have kept dogs from eating panties and socks and puking on the carpet, and cats from chasing dogs, I'd say our four footed kids were nearly as perfect as the two footed ones they so zealously guarded and loved.

Of course we had fish. A nice big aquarium full. Long before Ralph's mood changes interrupted, the kids—three kid sized, one overgrown--, had a 50 gallon tank of finned friends. Guess who was in charge of fish feeding, house cleaning, fish ICU and burial. If you miss on the first four tries, keep guessing.

Ick struck and despite round the clock care was not cured. When the last floater floated up from deep blue waters, we conducted a very somber funeral service. Wearing Sunday best, the kids led assembled family and sympathetic friends to a rose garden three by three inch grave site.

Each child spoke eloquently on the merits of their dearly beloved finned friend, now robbed of his glorious future by unknown and dread disease. Ralph managed a reverent prayer. I borrowed from Jannelle and managetd to not smudge my makeup when I dabbed tears with a folded tissue. Unscented. Mac Duff blew a recognizable taps on his Boy Scout bugle. Dirt and gravel quickly filled the pint milk carton casket. It was a very sad funeral. One we will never forget.

Adjourned for a somber fish stick memorial dinner, I smeared the last sandwich with tartar sauce and dill relish before unloading both barrels. Combined, the petitioners stood as much chance as a swimmer going down for the fifth time in the middle of an ice cold gale. Without preamble, I said," There will be no more water living creatures in this house in a tank or jar, sink, bucket, bathtub or cute little bowl. Any and all creatures from river, lake, or deep dark sea including tuna, shark, lobster, clams smelt and shrimp will be baked, boiled, or fried." They tried tears. Tears didn't work. "No more fish. Not goldfish, poor cute little bluegill from the creek, not suckers, not first prize at the pet store, not exotic whatchamacallits, or," this directly to Ralph, "fish that follow you home. No More Fish!"

Attempting to convince me fish were absolutely essential for our happy household Ralph said two words. "But honey" Didn't work either.

The kids collective deep breath was as far as they got. Whatever they wanted to promise about that idyllic place called 'next time', was never known.

All of this: cats, dogs, fish, lizards with broken tails, baby birds fed with mashed worms, crippled crickets, and much more unwritten was before troubles multiplied like lemon drops and moved to the front burner.

To make life more challenging, dear old never changing Uncle Jethrow picked mealtimes to call about my parents. He called every day, every meal; including Sunday. Since he didn't have anything else to do, he slurped soup, chewed tough meat, and gulped his beverage of choice. Eventually, we learned to cover the phone with a pillow and yell "Is that so?" just to get it done.

His routine was easy to learn. Manners ignored, uncle gave the briefest nod to the kids and chewed and gulped his way into our hearts. From memory: "Slurp, gulp, pause, swallow. "I miss you Bethie. The kin miss you more every day. Hired help for your folks ain't worth a plug nickel. Things is behind." Pause to spit. Chewing something tough, turning old dentures into grinders. A three tiered swallow. I pictured partially chewed food working into his gullet and shook the thought away. Sound of knife and fork working on meat; pause, garbled words around grinding. "Your ma and pa need you here t'home in Lillian. Bethie you know you belong here to home in Lillian, and not up there in Yankee land." Chewing, chewing, and chewing. Swallow. Slurp. Gulp.

Once he swore Sainte Lillian's was the town's proper name and plain old Lillian would never leave his lips. "Won't let them hippie modernizers change it," he said. Now it's Lillian this and Lillian that like he's talking about a woman.

Because he feared Yankee germs would spread over the phone, uncle's conversations with Ralph were brief, to the point, and unchanging. "I'm a non-judgmental Southern gentleman Christian Ralph but I gotta tell ya Bethie sounds more like a Yankee every day. Doncha know you Yankees talk funny. Hit haint right. She needs to be with blood kin and helpin' take keer of her parents. Land sakes, with her sickly childhood and all, the way they kept her alive through that whoopin' cough and measles and nemounie she owes them that much." It didn't take long for uncle and Ralph to become partners in a mutual ignoring society. Ralph's angry eyes and hot breath always blasted me with scorn.

Once I tried "Honey don't you remember the way you shut him down on our wedding day? He needs to hear from you again." Ralph didn't return my smile because he didn't remember.

He was like pop, remembering every grievance stored over the years. I remembered mom, the way she held on to love. Blind love. Loyal. Was I supposed to be like her for sake of the kids?

Then a new and Ralph original twist to the screw. I learned to expect bouquets of yellow roses after his tantrums. Ralph exploded, stormed out, and next day, like rainbow after the rain, roses came. I put on the happy face my world expected until something broke inside. My award winning performance of contented wife took its last curtain call. I stopped lying to myself, stopped pushing his outburst aside as if they didn't matter, and stopped drawing parallels between my marriage and that of my parents. Vowing to be more than ready the next time Ralph's anger surfaced, I waited like a jumper poised to leap.

Once I reached that plateau, Ralph changed overnight. What the school committee needed he gave and more. Volunteer dad of the year was back Day after day with the kids, phone call after phone call from dear old uncle, Ralph was the man we loved; cheerful, happy, and helpful. My second sight told me to be prepared. I watched. I waited. My fine tuned nerves squeaked like they needed oiling, or changing, or both.

One winter night we collapsed in bed tired of bleak blahs and woke to sight, sound and color of spring. It came like an overdue love letter. Furnace off. Windows open. Lungs full of fresh clean air, air that smelled so good we feasted. Narcissi and dandelion competed. Soft blue sky, bird song and greening leaf were ours. Sweet violets of every violet color, crocus, daffodil and the dandiest lions we'd seen in ages were everywhere. Its Mellie's fault I'm partial to dandelions. She had just past the creeping stage the first time she ventured outdoors to bring me a fist full of beauty. Every year the fistful is bigger, and every bouquet signals a sweet sadness when she'll be too big or too busy. But not that year. The house was full of dandelions.

Fragile blossoms perfumed our orchards. Once again, lilac and roses were like little kids standing on tiptoe begging to be first chosen. Fields of grain and vegetable and flower gardens sprouted overnight.

For the first time in our recorded history, and our branch of Brunswick clan records everything including the first time Mellie uses Mac Duff's full name on New Years, we were too busy to keep track.

As days passed, I began to believe the Ralph I married was home to stay. There was champagne and roses on my pillow and sweet love in our big bed blanketed in moonlight. Treats for kids, dogs and cats were a constant. Plans for vacations and hobbies, grandiose plans for spending more money than we made in five years were common place. We all did it. We laughed a lot. As a family, we glowed.

Every day, every hour for those few beautiful weeks, even with the expected calls from dear old uncle, our life was a song. Our ever faithful old as dirt but still not leaking khaki green three rooms Coleman Tent went up near the creek. We grilled and reaped our harvest of spring. Often Ralph worked late and would have a late supper on the patio while we talked about everything. The kids accepted his late hours as they accepted everything he did and didn't. Blue skies or storm clouds, they adored him.

As a wonder filled spring day was slowly winding down, I thought the sun a show off as it took a slow walk into a long lasting rose tinted sunset. I remembered my long ago dream of Germany and reading such glorious sunsets were called Twilight of the Gods. What else? It was for me, the ending of a perfect day.

In the family room, P.J. Clad kids tossed popcorn to dogs, and dogs woofed them on. Ralph was heaven knew where on a job doing heaven knew what. I was in the kitchen browning ground chuck for chili—or spaghetti sauce; I wasn't sure but intent on working it into a slow cooker supper we all loved. Onions fresh garlic and peppers chopped that sort of thing. One second all was well with our world. Freeze the frame. Peace shattered...no worse than that; torn to bits, shredded and pulverized. The phone rang.

Ten

Family rule for kids, kith and kin: No phone calls after 10 p.m. even in summer. To be precise, the beautiful slate blue phone on the daffodil yellow wall above the soft orange cabinet top covering the purring dishwasher on my warmly tiled kitchen floor never rang that late. Never. Even obnoxious telemarketers calling from Timbuktu knew that rule. Yet this night, the phone rang. I let it ring, stared at it, swallowed fear, and let it ring.

Kid feet hit the stairs.

Kid ears heard my voice.

Kid feet reversed order of climb. As usual, Mollie Kate's pitter patter was sandwiched between clunk clunks. She was second in line behind brother, coming up second in line behind sister going down.

The phone rang. Shriller. Louder. Filling the house with noise.

"MooooMMMMM!" Stairway megaphone brought three kid voices wanting the irritating shrillness over. Dogs echoed with a high pitched storm warning siren whine. Smart cats yowled and ran for cover.

I turned the volume capable of alerting us in the back lot vegetable garden on low. Muted it even more with a pillow from the couch. I could hear it. They didn't need to. I added a folded blanket, but kept the noise.

"Here's Johnny" floated up the stairs. Kids cheered. "Johnny always puts me to sleep; but I'm not tired tonight."

"Franklin Mac Duff Brunswick!" Mellie's incensed voice flew up on wings of hurt girl pride.

"Don't do that teacher voice on me. I ain't done nothing wrong! And don't use my full name either Miss Mellshanna Priscilla Rose Brunswick."

"I know what you're planning Franklin Mac Duff Brunswick and I'm telling you if you steal my pillow tonight I'll pour ice water on your head. Get your own pillow." Pause of maybe thirty seconds while she thought it out. Then, deciding to not let him off easy, " Franklin Mac Duff Brunswick don't use my full name either!" War was brewing and Mollie Kate had enough. She laid down the law before the war of words advanced to full scale name calling and arm punching. "You two better be quiet or mommy will send us to bed right now without ice cream." Long pause as combatants considered. "Then definitively "I want my ice cream."

Losing ice cream was too dear a price to pay for sibling warfare. Without round table talks combatants shifted into cold war mode. I knew threatening postures, ugly face contests, and soft missiles that didn't go crash or bang filled the family room. *If only so simple a threat could work in the warring real world.*

End of musing. Back to reality. The phone rang...

If Ralph or Brunswick family members were in trouble, one of them would be at the door. If my sisters were hurt, their family would take care of it and call in the morning. Universal rule: do what has to be done first, talk later. I swallowed the knowing and let the phone ring

The phone rang. The phone rang. The phone rang.

I knew with the gut wrenching certainty that turns a world upside down this call was about mom and pop. And, whether dear old Uncle Jethro knew it or not, reality at long last had sped past his drama. I knew the wolf was real, hungry, and biting, and wanted to be talked out of the knowing.

My parents, two weak wrinkled old people were fading like last roses before a killing frost; becoming smaller, defenseless. My parents. My mom. The man I forced myself to call pop. Never mind what I wanted to call him. For mom's sake, he was "Pop." I stopped pretending to love him years ago, yet mom insisted they were one. She said love is eternal. She said over and over again that someday I would understand. I thought about them and about my marriage. Understand what? How far away is someday?

Year after year while her hope for him kept her alive, my love for her pulled me home.

Somehow, I knew this time it was both of them. I lectured myself. "Think about what they've been through. We're lucky they're alive" My lecture to me brushed aside heart attacks, cancer, cancer, cancer, arthritis, anemia, strokes, what the doctors said was pop's take on senility, chronic bronchitis and who knows what else. I had questions about senility that weren't answered. Maybe doctors didn't know or want me to know or didn't know how to deal with what they knew. "Needs to be watched all the time," they said and left me to wonder.

Over five hundred miles and uncounted unknowns from whatever was wrong, I pulled out the whole list of "things will be better tomorrow lies." My favorite top of the line lie: "I am Beth Anne. Once again, I'll work and a miracle will make them well and this time…this time, they will be happy," didn't do anything for me.

I wondered so many things and then asked myself why? Why wonder when I knew the answers. The unchanging truth? As they walked toward death that enormous grief, that heart shattering pain as fresh as the day Jamie died was the heartbeat of their life.

Still, my lovely slate blue phone shrilled, interrupting thoughts and hope. Wanting me. Waiting for me to hear what I didn't want to hear. Fumbling fingers touched, felt the smoothness, identified place for lips and ear. Not yet I couldn't. I wasn't ready. It could ring, call me, and nag but I could not, would not answer...

Chained against a cold rough wall of emotion, I prayed, pondered, and faced possibilities. Salty tears were acid on my face. Were they dying? Were they dead? Were they now suddenly and completely and forever dead? Whatever the answer, I wasn't ready.

The phone rang. Like a migraine, it was there to stay.

I keep mom's letters in Navy blue folders in my black walnut five shelf high kitchen bookcase. A quiet voice whispered there would be no more letters. As any sane woman would, I ignored it.

Tight. Binders were so wedged I was ready for a crowbar when the last in line surrendered. My final determined yank was so hard and the binders release so sudden, I landed on the floor. With an audible sigh that was more than rustling paper, remaining binders expanded like they'd been a fat man sucking in his gut as the last in a long line of bikini models sashayed by.

My treasured letters and I claimed the end chair at the big square oak dining table. Adding leaves seats the entire Brunswick family. Eventually, grandchildren will squeeze in. Now I sit alone, surrounded by yesterday. I *Smile to the non existent tuxedo clad waiter* standing in a halo of soft golden chandelier light. "No menu please. Just bring me a miracle."

The phone rang.

Eleven

I strained to read pale blue ink racing across pages of mom's letters. Like the light blue ink absorbed by thirsty paper, her life written with years of work, pain, and grief was being absorbed by time. I felt the weight of irreversible sadness.

Living in Michigan, my habit of reading and re-reading her letters kept her close and Sainte Lillian always familiar. Once again, I read her latest adventure at the IGA. A three -year-old escaped his mother's watching eyes as she strapped a crying baby into the cart seat. Every bit of boyhood mischief at his disposal, he became a three year old wrecking ball and turned into cascading dominos neatly stacked boxes of soup crackers and sugar coated kid cereals. Busy or pre-occupied, other shoppers either laughed or turned away.

"I had a choice: hold on to the cart, or try to corral a rambunctious boy. Old age won."

Had I skipped that? Worse, had I been so tuned to familiar kid noises and barking dogs that I laughed and went to the kids? Guilt! I was drowning in it.

My mom was never too busy. I remembered Freckled Frankie Freeman visiting on a summer Monday wash day. He sniffed the aroma of a tomato based cabbage laced soup, inhaled down to his toes and smiled. Before we knew it our house was the place to be on Monday.

Freckled Frankie brought our cousins. They told other kids bored with the fun of one too many back lot ballgames and too much fishing. They came, they sniffed and while my sisters and I hung shirts and pants on the clothes line, mom welcomed them with sugar cookies and ice cold lemonade. Was that extra work? Not then. She was mom doing what moms did and we were kids being kids. We played jacks and marbles near the open kitchen window, inhaling the wonderful aroma of simmering soup. Mom kept on working and never said she was too tired, never told the kids to play somewhere else, never refused refills.

I went back to her letter with a magnifying glass. She wrote of her dogs lined up under the picnic table as she cut a watermelon. Old Bodacious, his wide open jaws big enough to swallow half a melon was first in line. Next her collie Skipper wagging his golden tail expectantly, and last in line white as snow Spitz Pete, contentedly resting, his paws precisely aligned, his eyes never leaving the delicate operation. In memory, I was there under *Ozark only blue sky near the grey picnic table draped in sugar maple shade. Droplets of ice cold water slid down the round fat melon like they had all the time in the world. Obedient dogs knew the wait was worth it.*

I inhaled the sweet wet aroma that followed the first direct stab of her knife. With her, I saw succulent red fruit embedded with plump black seeds. Washed in guilt seconds before, now I was drooling.

The phone rang.

Another clue: The nursing home says they're sending your pop home for a short visit soon as they adjust his medication. I told them adjusted or not adjusted; I can't take care of him."

Like a drunk driver running from the long arm of the law, I'd ignored two flashing red lights. Drunk drivers and I have this in common; we ignore them, yet we know flashing red lights won't go away.

She wrote, "Two hours later, Jannelle brought him home. First thing, he had to have a laxative. Jannelle could do that for her daddy. Milk of Magnesia went in *one end and out the other.* Then she had a fit when I said I didn't have the strength to clean his mess. Jannelle said she felt a bad migraine coming on, but I didn't budge. I told her she was a nurse I wasn't her aide and since she knew to not give him a laxative she could take care of it. Bethie you should have heard her splutter. Funny now I think about it, I didn't hear another word about her headache." She who had never said "I can't," had filled a letter with it.

I retreated into the dark silent space where nothing interrupts: not fighting kids, barking dogs or Gabriel blowing that last longed for trumpet. I felt intense anger building for Jannelle, and covered my mouth with a clenched fist. I knew as good as it would make me feel, I didn't dare vent anger and frustration toward my big fat, dumb, blind, stupid sister.

Thin blue ink racing across pages, piling words on words on words, pulled me into my childhood. Once, we were a happy family. Mom sang all the time. Pop was always good for horseback rides around the house and big warm hugs. It was impossible to not love little Jamie with his beautiful eyes and happy smile. Young as we were, we girls knew the solid secure complete meaning of the word home. We knew home wasn't fancy toys and things because we didn't have fancy toys or things. We had rag dolls and wooden spoons and pans to form a marching band. We had a tire swing and kittens. And always parents full of love. We knew home was love because we were surrounded by it, deep in the middle of it, and complete.

Then one perfectly beautiful late spring afternoon, Jamie died. My little brother took nearly everything that made us so happy with him into the ground. Living wasn't much fun anymore.

Our life revolved around our farm, our beautiful full of promise farm. It managed to put food on the table, but little else. Pop sold enough to break even. No matter what they tried, at the last minute something went wrong. Profit from the pig auction was to be our salvation. I remember pop's promises and our excitement as he went to market. Forever etched in memory, the grey defeated look on his face when he came home. "Market fell," he said. Mom hid her face in her apron. We knew not to hope for bags of rock candy. Jannelle said it must have hit pretty hard to make her daddy look that hurt... I thought of mom who had never before hidden behind her apron.

At least we weren't alone. Fenced in by want, need, and make do, our community was like covered wagons circled against the unknown. Neighbor helped neighbor. Year after year in our small Ozark world, all of us; men, women and children held with tight fist to the hope of next year when our ship would come in. Our world changed, but pop didn't. When that long awaited ship neared shore under President Dwight David Eisenhower, pop had lost hope Everyone in the whole wide world with the exception of my pop, liked Ike. He'd looked at sunset for so many years he didn't recognize sunrise. I remember the cold harsh sound of his voice in argument with Uncle Jethro and their friends. He blamed a political economic system he didn't understand for problems his hard work couldn't solve.

He nursed and rehearsed deep seated resentment against everything that kept the poor man poor. He hated rich people. Not that we ever knew any, but in pop's eyes, if they bought a new car every two or three years, or went uptown to shop, or enjoyed vacations, they were rich. His brothers and sisters in Saint Louis who did all of these and joined a country club, miraculously missed his list.

One thing pop had plenty of, was answers. He said governments caused poverty. All politicians were cut from the same bolt of cloth, sewn together with gold thread, and would forever be rich money grubbing liars with no job skills. He believed rich men ran the world to start wars, talk, pose for pictures, travel and have big parties. "They believe poor people are poor because they're stupid and deserve it. Election time, that's the only time poor folks see politicians. Then, they're our best friends. Big liars! Why if they kept half their promises we'd be better off."

Once he got started on rich people he couldn't shut up. "Tax cuts and publicity, them's the main reason rich snobs do good works. They love applause, love dressin' up for fancy parties, love havin' their names put on hospitals and schools. Poor folks are lucky to get dogs named after em,' and for dang sure they don't get a dimes worth of attention when they die. Lemme prove it," he said, and turned to Sainte Lillian's weekly HELLO. First obituary, "Mrs. Margaret Hannibal Updyke Trowbridge, aged 85 years is survived by her last husband His honor Charles Finley Frankenfelter Trowbridge the Third and extended family. Mrs. Trowbridge lived a long and interesting life." His voice droned on and on about her schooling, travels, collection of antique jewelry, civic accomplishments, and surviving children, grandchildren, nieces, nephews and friends." I almost fell asleep.

Then he said, "And now to the obituary of our dearly departed Mr. Elmer Whitener. He looked over his reading glasses, cleared his throat and in less than 10 seconds read Mr. Whitener's life's story. "Mr. Elmer Whitener, age 86, met his loving Savior Sunday afternoon after a massive heart attack. He is survived by his loving wife of 60 years and 10 children. Burial will be Thursday noon, followed by a funeral dinner at Sainte Lillian's First Street Presbyterian Church.".

I snapped wide awake. If we had listen to all that stuff about some rich old lady we'd never heard of, I wanted to know more about Mr. Whitener's life. After all, we knew him enough to say hello and trick or treat at his house. "Pop, didn't Mr. Whitener have any civic accomplishments? Did he do anything except live, get married, have ten kids and die?" I wanted to know more.

Pop grinned and fluffed my hair. "Not according to the paper Bethie. They're both dead and buried, but even dead rich folk get better treatment and take up more room."

"Dead is dead ain't it pop?"

That's true Bethie, but there's cheap funeral wooden box poor folk dead, and rich folk solid mahogany caskets lined in silk coffin in an airtight box dead. They spend more on one funeral than we make in fifteen years."

Pop knew everything about infectious childhood disease. His remedy:" You girls don't have nothin' to do with foreign kids. The whole lot of them immigrants brings diseases we ain't even heard of. And don't you never play with kids you don't know, no tellin' what you'll bring home." Truth is measles, mumps, whooping cough and whatever else was in the air took up residence in every home.

No matter what he said, Jannelle believed her daddy. If he said the moon was made of green cheese, Jannelle wanted some on white bread with Miracle Whip and tomatoes. Samantha Lynn and-- I, with our pre-adolescent store of know everything itis, decided we'd question everything he said. We did until he said he'd never seen an honest politician. Since we'd never even seen a politician, we didn't know how to handle that one. Same goes for rich folks. Closest we came to that was a banker and a few doctors, but they weren't green or anything and always were nice to us.

When his tirades put churches and politicians in the same basket, mom said if we lived in China or Germany or Russia, pop could be shot for criticizing the government. Jannelle said her daddy was so brave. Not sure how close we were to those places; Samantha Lynn and I grabbed our dolls and hid under the kitchen table.

Ahh yes! The wonderful memories of childhood! Don't play it again Sam.

I asked mom why she put up with his angers. Her answer was always that look; the one that said she saw what I couldn't see, and remembered what I would never know. "Honor your father Bethie. Someday Bethie," she would say and brush my tears away. Someday what she never said, but she taught the three of us to lean on that one word promise. Mom answered so many of my questions with "someday" that my "someday dream" was someday, my daddy would tell me he loved me.

We girls were in high school when a speeding two door black truck paused at our driveway long enough for something small and whimpering to hit the gravel. Running after them, pop almost tripped over the little brown and white spotted pup.

Doc Seabaugh laughed when pop said the pup's name was Freckled Franky Freeman. "He'll never be as big as that name," Doc said, pop shortened it to Freckles. Freckles became a four footed Jannelle. Round and short, he followed pop everywhere. When pop whistled, Freckles danced. He would strut on his back legs then bow and wait for a treat (bologna please). Laughter returned to pop's eyes and optimism to our hearts.

About a year later, Freckles stopped eating, drinking and dancing. When pop buried him in the family graveyard, his laughter was buried under every shovelful of dirt falling on the small cedar coffin.

Mom understood.

I didn't.

She loved him

I wanted to. I wanted a happy family.

She remembered his laughter, kindness and compassionate heart.

"Stop wishing mom. Divorce him and get it done," I said after weeks of his unending explosions.

She whispered my name so it stood between us. She radiated hope, and I my usual two edged sword. Then, "Your pop and I love one another. In a small country church we promised to do so until death. I don't break promises to God."

"What about his promises mom?"

"Get me the bible Bethie."

"Don't preach mom. You know the Bible says each person is responsible for their own salvation?" This was one of the few times I knew I had the upper hand. After all, I studied psychology and behavioral science in college while earning a teaching degree; and her teaching certificate came from correspondence courses. I knew so much more than my mother! In a heartbeat she taught me how much I had to learn.

She quoted from memory, "Love bears all things, hopes all things, endures all things." She smiled. "As long as my dear boy is where I can reach him, my faith never wavers." She spoke of eternal love, and undying hope. Once again, she said "Someday Bethie."

My strong young hands complete with manicured nails, and her work worn blue veined hands became one as she folded them together. "Bethie darlin' before your father and I met, he gave up his wild ways and converted to Christianity. Now, it's like he's lost hope. He blames God for our losses: the babies, the farm, everything. I can't. Remember Bethie, God knows we'll weep for a night but He promises joy in the morning."

"Mom how long is the night?"

Her answer "As long as God says," was so full of faith it literally sent me to my knees.

I held her close as she had held me all those tearful growing up years ago and her voice whispered for me alone: "I know someday we'll be together and your pop will be whole and healthy again. Someday Bethie. Someday."

Tears overflowed her sad blue eyes as she turned away. Were they for me? For him? For all their losses?

This and more ran through my mind while the slate blue phone on the yellow wall above the now silent dishwasher rang and my senses begged for release. Release that would come only when I did the unbearable and answered. If not release, then at least an end to cruel wonder.

Was he dying? Or was he at long last dead without her long waited someday coming? Or, was it mom? Dread heavy and refusing to give me a moment's peace had run into a thick steel-lined with kryptonite wall. I was ready to quiet the invader of my shattered peace.

Twelve

Meathook, my cinnamon striped bobcat sized cat buddy claimed my lap. Living up to his name, he made lap taking an eye opening experience.

While flexing each feline muscle, Mr. Cat Universe managed to soften his cushion with claw work and curled into a striped yellow ball. With his signature amber "I love you" eye blinker; he let me know he knew love covers bumps, bruises and heartache. He purred "I'm here with you. We can handle this together."

When my phone completed the journey of a million fears and glued itself to my ear, Uncle Jethro pounced like hungry blue jay after a June bug.

"Beth Anne where at is your common sense at? You got me upset. My blood pressure kaint take hit. You know that there phone rang purt near seven minutes! And you know I know you're t'home this time of night!" That out of the way, three minutes of easy to ignore normal followed. Easy to unkink stiff neck and calm frantic thoughts. It may be bad, but not as bad as I thought.

Tired of ignoring him completely, I treated him to my version of normal and filled his breathless pauses with senseless babble. He didn't hear. I didn't care. He heard his voice, I heard mine. At least mine was funny.

His litany and my nonsense ended at the same time. He inhaled. I waited. Nothing happened. He gave up and did his best to whip me into submission. "You know your ma's been feelin' downright poorly?"

I gave him silence, the one thing he didn't want. It stretched while his prelude to more hawk and spit raspy breathing intensified.

According to him mom had been feeling poorly ever since I married the damned Yankee, deserted my Ozark heritage, and moved to Yankee land. Up North! Blue Belly Country! Since I wasn't holding the phone to hear nothing I said the sure fire Uncle Jethro blame starter. "Yes, uncle, I know."

It worked. He became the feral cat, and I the tame canary. He pounced. "Good Lord Bethie iffin you know she's done took a turn for the worst why am I on the phone?

I gasped. "Turn for the worst" was new.

While I stuttered, he reverted to normal and every disaster at Maple Brook Road since that there Eve and Adam thing was heaped on my uncaring shoulders. According to Uncle Jethro's rule book I owed him, our family, and the entire state of Missouri an apology for deserting them in their time of need. Did he care that he was ignored?

Our first years in Michigan Ralph and I dropped everything and broke speed limits racing to that beautiful house and the sick people on Maple Brook Road. Ralph's sympathy ran out in less than two years. He wouldn't go, didn't want me to go. Ralph said I wasn't needed there, it was just that old fool Uncle Jethro trying to get me back in the Ozarks. I told Ralph he always ran when his parents were sick. He said, "But they're right here Bethie." And I said "Miles? What's the matter with you Ralph? What difference can miles make? They are my parents." "Don't leave me," he said. His whining sounded worse than uncle Jethro. I didn't need that.

Substitute teachers took my classes, and I drove long dark roads alone. My mom needed me. Was cancer back? Was it her heart? With Jannelle's phone supervision, Samantha Lynn and I worked our miracle. Jannelle and "Yes Dear" were well enough to come for a home cooked supper every night.

In the early years, coming home to Ralph was honeymoon revisited. He forgave me for deserting him. I forgave him for forgiving me. Kiss, make up, and the beat went on. Comparing that time with the last dozen trips, it's like starting a story with "Long ago and far far away..."

Long ago and far far away does double duty because it also fits my life in Sainte Lillian. Michigan is home now. Ralph and I, our kids, our church family his family and our close friends are here. We have the hills and lakes and exuberantly sassy seasons. We have Mackinac Island. Not "Nack", but "Naw, as in Mackinaw." The kids put up with history as long as we include horseback rides and Mackinaw Island Fudge. Lots of it.

We have the great bear dunes, the Soo locks and pine forest. No other state has our Youpers. Tony the Tiger lives in Battle Creek. The Republican Party was born in Jackson, home also to Coney Dogs and slam dunk Civil War reenactments at the Cascades. Where else but Jackson can a person soak in the breathtaking beauty of Ella Sharp Park, and read the prose of Jill Cline and the wry humor of Brad Flory in the Citizen Patriot? Where other than Michigan can a person visit Hell and Paradise the same day and send postcards home to prove it?. Michigan is home and Missouri a kaleidoscope of memories.

Uncle Jethro's whining, and complaining, hawking and spitting invaded. It was past time to call his bluff. "If you can't tell me why you called," big pause before, clearing my throat in exact imitation of his habit, "let me talk to Aunt Irene."

My mistake. He revived. Wonder of wonders, the old coot stopped blaming me for everything. Now I was really scared.

"Well, me and the wife we came down for a visit and there she was layin' down lookin' downright peaked. "She didn't feel like eatin, didn't want nothin' no food, no drink, no company. Now I think about hit, she's been offin her feed and hain't felt too pert fer a couple months. Samantha Lynn takes her to the doctor. She stocks up on pills and and stuff to perk up her appetite. Nothin' seems to be workin'.""

I wasted my breath but said it anyway, "She has to take it first," I knew mom put her meds aside for a real emergency. As dear old uncle was ignoring me again, my brain opened memory storage. *How many times had I counted bottles of half used antibiotics, unopened vitamins, pain pills she wouldn't take because of warnings on the label? I read them and questioned: "Mom are you pregnant? "Haven't been exposed lately," she said. I paused dramatically, "Are you planning to be?" She snorted and did her very best to change the subject.*

Uncle's voice came loud and clear. "She said when she feels strong enough to open a can of chicken noodle soup or cook a TV dinner, or make a bologna and Velveta sandwich It tuckers her out so she kaint find the strength to eat. Even a bit of toast with Elderberry jelly makes her want to throw up. Irene got her to take dry toast with a few sips of tea and honey then we took her to the E.R. That there nurse took one look and we didn't wait no time a' tall, went right back we did.

That there young doc he up and examined her real fast; heart, lungs and blood pressure and all that stuff. Woulda done a urine but she couldn't pee. Doc wanted her admitted then and there. She flat out refused, said she had to take care of her cats and dogs and make sure James Samuel knew he shouldn't come home."

Something beating between my chest and feet weighed a ton. How could a heart feel that heavy?

Now that he had me, he hit hard. Your ma's sayin' she's not goin' nowheres till you and the kids get here to take care of her. Wife's' doin' her best to talk sense, but it don't do no good. She just turns away." He waited. Silence, his favorite enemy stretched.

"You hear what I'm sayin' Bethie?

Quiet as he wasn't half of Sainte Lillian heard. Only TV blaring The Tonight Show kept my kids from hearing. He didn't want an answer. For the first time, I gave him what he wanted. Naturally, he didn't like it.

Deep breath, raspy breathing. Bragging. "Me and Irene, we got ourselves another grand. Cute little gal." Complaining: Your sisters been to the Grand Ole Opre and campin' in them Smokies for purt near two, goin' on three weeks, so nobody checked on that cleanin' woman."

Short break. Peaceful silence. Long mournful sound. "That's all hit took fer her to slack off." nose blowing "Land sakes, the way you gals pay thru the nose you should be in control. Ain't you been tellin' her what's what?" Back to normal. Troubles were my fault again. Funny sounds, like clacking of denture castanets. More long mournful sighs. "Sink full of dirty dishes. Oh my God! Maggots! Beth Anne you get down here this instant and clean this up!"

Uncle knew I'd jump on my magic carpet, buckle up, zoom over Michigan hills and Indiana and Illinois flat land, skim over Old Muddy, ride the Ozark hill wind, brake at Maple Brook Road and take charge. I wondered if five minutes would be too much time.

Remembering my upbringting, I sent "Do Whut?" full volume into his ear. No mistake, he heard. One word covered disbelief, questioned his sanity, and gave us both breathing time.

While he recovered, the black spear point of our big grandfather clock second hand completed its circle and started another. Tick tock at a time, it moved closer to circle three. Tick tock, tick tock and Meathook music filled the room. Bad as the news and the deep and dark unknown were, I pictured him staring at the phone and fought laughter.

Almost back to normal. "Wait a minute! Hits rice! This pause stretched longer than the others before the gate opened and he was off and running. "Well, hit shorely looked like maggots! Lord have mercy this house is a sight. Winders kivered with streaks like the dogs' been lickin' em. Them there starched Priscilla curtains Anna takes such pride in is hangin' limp and filthy. And the bathrooms! You wouldn't believe the stink and mould. There's so much dust under them beds a feller could plant a garden. And that's jist indoors. Outside all them gardens your pappy took sech good keer of air sech a sight hits a wonder folks haint talking.'

When true sadness filled his voice, I almost dredged up a smidgen of sympathy for the old conniver. "Where your baby sisters and little Jamie air I kaint tell you how poor white trash hit looks. You know your momma set some store on keepin' them graves clean and purty. Now they're covered with crab grass and thistle and weeds air jest chokin' out them little markers. Kain't hardly read no names." I knew he was foraging in his back pocket for his red handkerchief. It was back there somewhere, under the pen knife and spare change, Juicy Fruit gum and his plug of Red Man.. He dug and grunted. Silence grow and found another memory: *Mom on her knees caring for her dead babies.*

I thought about Ralph. To deliberately censor him, I more or less quote: "That hillbilly crap gets deeper and deeper. I pictured his red face and bulging eyes and shut that out. Maybe, maybe this time. Enough! Ralph came later. Back to uncle. I cut him off in mid-complaint. "I need to talk to mom," I said, my voice harsh, commanding. It worked.

His footsteps faded into nothing. Finally, as nerve wrenching as nails across a chalkboard, uncle drug the phone across the scared maple leaf table. He panted for breath. He hawked and spat. When he ran out of stall tactics, his weary voice reported, "She says she's too weak to come to the phone. She kain't hardly talk what with a bad breathin' spell and all. Bethie she don't look that good a-tall. I don't like this."

I'm hours and miles away. My thoughts were a tangled net blown helter skelter in a strong clinging damp wind.

Uncle tried to cover other voices. Now what?

Like a small child he whispered "Jannelle just brung your dad home. Says her and Marvin went to visit soon as they got back from Tennessee. Said the nursing home had him dressed and out the door in ten minutes, they want him to spend a few days at home, and before the month is out Anna's gotta find another place. They can't handle the way his mind don't work and him running away. Said they're plum tard out chasin' him down. Your sister's grinnin' her haid off. Fer a nurse she hain't got a lick of smarts far as he's concerned. To top it off, she's plumb blind about your mammy. Jist told her she needed to get up and fix him some soup.

And your pappy! Heck fire Bethie! Never thought I'd say this about him, but he haint the man he used to was. His mind plum wanders all over the place.

Coming from uncle, winner of the golden ring on the carousel of dumb, that was better than good. Fortunately for both of us, his mouth took over.

Jist now Janneelle stood in front of your ma stuck out her lower lip purt near a mile and told her if she tried harder, her daddy would be happier."

Jumbled thoughts: I'm hours away. Mom can't breathe. Pop home, Jannelle blind as a bat and causing trouble, the house a disaster area. Unspeakable the best description for what was once a showcase of yard and family cemetery. Maggots. Nursing home tired of pop. Specific battling unspecific. Above all, the need for me to make it all better.

One thing for sure, butts needed kicking, and my first target was her royal roundness, daddy centered, first, last and foremost daddy indulging sister. It's a miracle she found time for "Yes Dear," and nursing.

Uncle's voice shredded my thoughts. "What? I kain't hear you?

"Because I didn't say anything," I said.

"Not you Bethie. They're callin' me!"

Again, the familiar phone drop, tattoo, silence and scratching. I knew what he'd say, said it with him. Bethie she wants you to come home." It ricocheted in my brain, chipping away bits and pieces of me and mine and what we needed to keep peace.

I looked down at her letter. "We've called you home many times because the doctors said your pop was on his last legs. He's proved them wrong. Now that he's getting over this last stroke he's as strong willed as ever and if possible, physically stronger. He tries to mow the nursing home yard, gets up early to hoe their garden and halfway through forgets what he's doing and wanders off. Even though harvest is months away, He's ready to help Wilbur Head and Dick Brown in the fields. We knew to expect changes but his mind puts two and two together and comes up with "It takes 22 apples to bake a pickle pie." It's easier to laugh than to reason with him, but even then we have to be careful. He still gets mad at the drop of a hat and sometimes our laughter sets him off. Seems there's no medicine can help and we have to accept the way he is. We don't plan to call you home any time soon Bethie. We manage."

The promise was not 12 days old. She had to know as she was writing their downward spiral was picking up speed.

The only indicator uncle was still on the line was harsh post asthmatic breathing. It cut across my "what if's?" and "How will Ralph react this time thoughts. I was trapped in a cage while a family of gawkers waited to "ooh" and "Aah," and throw peanuts for my performance.

Numbed to the core, knowing I had yet to face Ralph, I said what had to be said. Plus a little. "Tell mom if she wants me to come home to get her butt back to the hospital. I followed that with our unwritten but clearly understandable code meaning among other things. "No argument tolerated." She gives you any sass tell her Bethie has spoke."

Uncle dropped the phone again. Poor phone. Poor scarred maple table top. Poor ear and shattered nerves.

Normal every night sounds floated up from the red and brown brick family room. Duffer seldom missed popcorn, snapping up what was tossed for Tupid and Einstein Bear. Kids thought it hilarious. Tupid and the pup moaned displeasure while Duffer woofed for more. Kid and dog noises faded as TV commercial megaphoned listeners to reach out and touch someone.

My plan exactly. When uncle did a three peat phone drag, he got it first. He was expecting me to pack kids and bags and be on the next flight. He heard "Tell Jannelle she has two choices: Either take pop home with her or back to the nursing home. Now! He choked on a wad of self assurance.

Beautiful!

"Put her on if you can't do it." He recognized authority. I heard Jannelle shriek and pop complaining. He wanted his supper. He wanted his woman to get up and take care of him. He wanted a warm bath and bed. He wanted to stay home. Nearly 11 p.m., and he wanted.

'Uncle Jethro tell the old man I don't give a damn what he wants." Uncle did it word for word. After all the theatrics, my ears were left in peace. Momentarily.

Bless her delicate heart, Jannelle found strength enough to come to the phone. Poor sis. Her whining, her migraine and how cruel I was to her daddy, how all he needed was time at home and all mom needed was to try harder did nothing to win her case but was more than enough to fuel my anger.

This caged animal roared.

Thirteen

Laughter that said they weren't sure, but because everyone laughed at Johnny Carson maybe they'd better, floated up the stairs. On second thought, a pillow fight would win over Johnny any day. I heard the first solid whacks. Then Mollie Kate said" Ice Cream." Pillow fight? Ridiculous idea when pitted against the thought planted in steaming minds of no bedtime chocolate covered ice cream hyper-sweet energy boost. In the instantaneous pause as big sister and brother calmed, I counted heartbeats as seconds. A given, before one thousand and thirty, I would hear more from our little manager.

She was getting better. I made it to five when Mollie Kate's sugar coated voice floated up carpeted stairs. "Mommie dear our tummies are starving for ice cream right now." Nightly, Mollie Kate, my sweet child with an unquenchable sweet tooth leads very willing brother and sister to cavity land.

Home made so thick it was never poured but had to be scooped chocolate sauce followed the tub of French Vanilla to the counter. Fruit and nut toppings and, three cans of genuine imitation whipped cream followed. Note three cans. Not one, one wouldn't last a day. Not two, two wouldn't do. Our specialty called for three cans. Initials of proud owners are in permanent marker on each can. War erupts if Franklin Mac Duff "accidentally" uses whipped topping with Mellie's initials in azure blue. If she 'accidentally' touches his initialed in khaki green, it's much worse. Mollie Kate never worries. She claims her pink initialed and pink ribboned can first.

I called "Mollie Kate dear…" stretching dear into a very longdearrrrrrrr
Get yourself in gear and lead your brother and sister to the kitchen. My
voice was in the "I have spoke" mode and they knew it well.

Mac Duff grinned. "Yippee and yahoo, we're going to grandma and
grandpa's house." His grin faded. "We've gotta be back in time for Scout
camp." Scout camp and everything that smacked of outdoor adventure was
bread and butter to this wanna be Green Beret. Perfection sleeping in leaky
tents, hiking in poison ivy flea and tick infested woods and spotting wild
and wooly critters. Ground hogs and opossums and maybe even a bear.
Maybe not a bear, but they dreamed big. A camp out was ultra successful
if they braved high winds and thunder storms. Ambrosia was foil wrapped
potatoes, burned to charcoal perfection under red campfire coals. The
worse their adventures seemed to civilized moms, the "more better" it was
to his scout troop.

Missing the County Fair in Mellie's opinion one of the main reasons to
celebrate summer, was something else. "Grilled Polish sausage, humongous
scoops of ice cream, Frish Fries, Pizza, and Lemonade made while you
wait, Ferris wheels, rides! Displays! Blue ribbons! Recognition! And you,
Franklin Mac Duff Brunswick are worried you'll miss smelly old scout
camp! She sneered. She wasn't finished

"Mellshanna Priscilla Rose Brunswick I told you a thousand times
already today don't use my full name and whatever you do, don't insult
scout camp!"

My throat clearing sounded nothing at all like the offerings of
emotionally impaired conniving uncle Jethro, but as my hands were on a
tub of ice cream, it worked.

Mellie knew when to back down. "Sorry Mac Duff," she said in kid
speak. As every mother knows, kid speak never contains emotions the
words express. As every mother does when winning half the battle, I let it
slide. Besides, by this time, the four of us needed ice cream. Desperately.

Mollie Kate rolled her big hazel brown eyes. "Scout camp can't be
as 'citing as that nest of snakes we killed at Grandma Irene's creek last
summer."

I shrieked "Snakes! What snakes? "Even though I'd grown up in snake
territory Missouri Ozarks, I hate snakes. All snakes, snakes in the reptile
house at the Saint Louis Zoo, little bitty emerald green grass snakes,
blue racers or mouse eating whatevers, I hate them! Water Moccasin,
Cottonmouth and rattlers tipped the top of my most dreaded. Grandma
Irene's tree lined sluggish creek draws them like ice cream draws my kids.
How many snakes make that nest? 10? 12? More? Not that it mattered. I
hate snakes.

"Now you've done it!" Big brother looked at little sister like he was ready to punch her but this time, Mellie saved the day. "We helped Grandma Irene kill a bunch of water moccasins and cottonmouth at the creek. Near where those old tree roots are. Y'know the place? (I knew the place) "She had us promise to not tell you. Besides mom we knew you'd beat our butts if we went in the creek."

Creek. Snakes. Horrible memory. Once again, I felt the dry summer Saturday heat, saw the cloud free sky, heard the babble of happy voices. About 200 of Franky Freeman's closest friends and a passel of relatives gathered at the park for his farewell party. Freckled Franky would uphold the honor and glorious reputation of Sainte Lillian Sojers as a member of the famous WW11 liberators of Europe, the 82nd Airborne. Not a man, woman or child in Sainte Lillian town, county and rural route missed feeling very very proud of Freckled Franky Freeman.

If that wasn't enough rumors had it --he was head over heels madly in love totally and absolutely gone over Aunt Millie's middle sister. Known all her life as "sister" because that's what her big sister always called her and because she didn't want anyone to know she had seven or eight or was that eight or nine names on her birth certificate? The funny part: Freckled Franky Freeman only had six between his first and last name. Their mom talked about it a lot. Mrs. Freeman said she used all the names she liked just to be double sure she wouldn't have to raise another red headed son. Millie's momma said she was in a real pickle when she come up pregnant cause she thought she'd used all the purty names. Then she come up with Millicent. Millicent said that was an o.k. name but Millie was easier to remember. Sister said she just might give her kids- if she ever had kids- Initials and skip names completely. Freckled Franky Freeman said he was kinda partial to all his names and would use them for their sons. Sister said "Not that many boys," and then blushed and hid her face.

"Good luck Freckled Franky" was spelled out in bright gold against a long Khaki banner hung across the park entrance. Red, white, and blue balloons were everywhere. Sainte Lillian's High School band marched all over, playin' request. Even Polkas and Elvis Pressley and Little Richard. Folks danced wherever the ground was flat enough. It was wonderfully loud and exciting! Freckle Franky's pa made sure there were pony rides for kids, volleyball tournaments for teens, and horseshoes and lawn tennis, and for them brave enough a watermelon eating contest. Loaded picnic tables bulged.

Clear as day, I could see Cousin Millie, arms loaded with a mesh bag of volleyballs start across the low water bridge. Then the overfull bag spewed balls into the murky water. Millie went after the volleyballs. Screams.

Freeze frame. People everywhere instantly upright and still. Ear piercing screams silenced the band. Mothers grabbed kids. Millie running from the water. People running towards her. Snakes, awful slimy snakes on her arms and legs, and their heads…striking her over and over and over.

Mom grabbed me at the first scream, but couldn't hold me. I broke free and ran to help Millie. All I thought about was my cousin. All I heard was her screams. None of us were fast enough.

There was poison enough for Millie and her best friend Billy Joe who tried to save her. I saw him kiss her hand and the way her hand went up and brushed his face. Millie told her family she heard beautiful bells. Screams and prayers blended together as they died. As Billy Joe took his last breath his arms kept Millie from falling onto the gravel.

Thank God I had happy memories. I loved the Gospel barn. Every weekend April through October church choirs from all over southeastern Missouri sang their hearts out. . Folks said angels crowded the bleachers to hear the soprano soloist from the Patton Presbyterian Church.

And the Widow's Walk atop the courthouse: Thanksgiving to New Years, church loud speakers gifted the town with Christmas music, and families lined up to climb the winding stairs because music under twinkling stars was pure magic. Mom said she felt closer to her babies in heaven.

One Christmas Eve, a town drunk tapped her shoulder polite like. She turned; he exhaled, and using his best manners, said, "Miz Owen I'm shore happy about you and your little angels. Plum warms my heart. Now me and the fellers here," and he pointed to a bewhiskered group behind us, "Me and the fellers shore do find that there Christmas music plum heaven like. Yessir, plum heaven like." Later mom said his breath was strong enough to make her tipsy and pop said he watched them follow blinking lights to their favorite watering hole.

Mellie watching color return to my face could tell I was almost back to normal..

"Honest mom. Grandma Irene's snakes weren't that big a deal. She told daddy and he said he'd tell you later."

I had to laugh. Ralph would tell me on my deathbed or 99th birthday whichever came first, but not when the kids were still home. Funny, how killing snakes and hunting never bothered him. Yet, this big strong man was all too happy to let me handle routine ordinary emergencies: kids hit by balls, or falls from bikes. Always, he'd turn green and hurry away when barn cats died crossing the road. Other than the fish demise and funeral, cost of living experiences guaranteed Ralph would do his disappearing act.

"No snakes this time momma, I promise," Mollie Kate said. "Beside we got more 'portant things to do. Grandma teached me about homemade ice cream."

"She didn't teached, she taughikated."

Mellie rolled her eyes. "Mother, these children are just too much. Perhaps we could teach them proper usage of the English language before they gradiate kinneygartden?"

As is my habit in ticklish times, I dropped to my knees, raised arms heavenward and thanked the Good Lord "fer givin' me such a passle of alert smart younguns. That they're intelligent too is a mighty fine bonus," I added.

We talked what if's while I overfilled huge bowls with-sorry kids- store bought- French Vanilla. They topped my fattening fudge with fruit and nuts of choosing and always, their own genuine imitation whipped cream, and three big red maraschino cherries. Six eyes told me I was the best mom in the world.

I took my overloaded bowl topped with the remaining cherries to the patio and looked into yesterday. There were times I needed tears but for reasons known only to God I held on to grief and hurt. Burying our Tiger cat was different because we didn't bury a cat. He came with us from the Ozarks little more than a purr and handful of grey striped fluff and he took over. He was by right of possession, property guardian, king of the hill, and eventually baby guardian. When he died we didn't bury a cat, we buried a best friend and it hurt down deep where innocence is stored.

My thoughts scanned the years. Lost opportunities, lost jobs, lost direction, dying pets, dying baby, not enough money and too much month. Broken dreams. Aching hearts. Unshed tears. I lost myself in the silence of the night.

Fourteen

Memories washed me. When pop came in from the barn he'd hold little Jamie and Samantha Lynn on his lap kiss mom, scooch over so Jannelle could snuggle and say "Sing my songs love. She could make it through "Come Angel Band," and "Will there be any Stars in my Crown?" When he started singing "Just as I am" with her, Jannelle jumped out of character and hushed him with fingers over his mouth. We had to hear mom sing.

Looking into a sky full of twinkling diamonds on this summer night, I could hear mom singing Stephen Foster's Stars of the Summer Night... My almost tuneful alto joined her clear soprano and my vision blurred. She sang that song the night before my brother died. It took her a long time to sing again.

I begged God." Don't take her! I'm not ready. I've waited so long to see her happy again. I want. I want. I want. God don't you know how I fear for her? Do you understand why I can't pray for pop? Why do you want me to love him? You know Jannelle adores him and Samantha Lynn ignores his moods and bad habits that drive me insane. Two out of three is pretty good isn't it?

My prayers were like a landfill of discarded wonder, bouncing from the needs of my parents to Ralph and his angers and all that lay between. Was I ready to find if this present pleasant Ralph was real? Or was my husband wearing another mask? The sensible me ordered the lost in what if me to pack. I pulled suitcases from storage, left one for each kid, and aimed essentials at mine.

Voice of son greeting father. Father response. Heavy footsteps nailing the stairs. The cold biting anger I didn't want. "How bad is it this time?" He stood, muscled arms crossed over expanding girth, fire in his eyes.

"I won't know until we get there," I said and read him and had my answer. He inhaled, and I cut him off. I remembered telling mom when it came to soft answers turning away Ralph's wrath, volume was more important than words. The kids didn't hear, but Ralph with his face inches from mine got every word. Low voice. Controlled. Cold. Ice. Brittle like it would break if it went past his ears. I told him exactly what to do with his temper. The depth of my pain met the heat of his anger head on. He backed down. Wise woman I, I let him speak first.

Much better. He sounded almost like the Ralph I needed. "Boy gives me the news he might not get to scout camp then Girl One and Girl Two tell me your mother is dying. Again!" That word held a lifetime of resentment and brought anger hot and fast like lightening in a sudden summer storm.

AWOL my tender loving husband. His bulging eyes bored through me bleeding my strength. His breath fast and hard like he'd run a mile uphill in blazing heat. His face into mine, his words granit hard. "Now you're heading to that shit hole, and you tell me you…don't…know?" Each word was drawn out like he was talking to a thing far beneath his level of superior intelligence.

On this day, fresh from uncle's sneak attack, I was more than ready for my Damn Yankee. Surrender was not my game plan. Poor Ralph. He started "It's the same old thing. They'll work you nearly to death like that winter when you had pneumonia. Your lazy assed sisters can take ca…" He didn't finish. Control. I had it. Sufficient to say as I used more than enough of his favorite expressions, he deflated. I checked twice to be sure he was breathing.

Uncle Jethro was ready with more criticisms until he heard Ralph's voice. Then all we heard was his breathing because Damn Yankees don't deserve nothin' good, not even "good mornin', good evenin' or good night." Wasn't his fault, it was therin' count of how them damn Yankees acted in that civil war burnin' through Georgia and all. If that wasn't enough to frost his rebel heart, the damn Yankee his second favorite niece married was trying to talk to him. He remembered that reception line. Lord knows, his heart didn't warm up none when that damn Yankee nearly broke his hand. Honest to God, all he wanted then was a little fun ticklin' Bethie. Just like he usta. Wouldn't hurt her none.

All we heard from uncle was "Ralph I kain't unnerstan a word yer sayin'." Before Ralph could do an unheard of Yankee thing and retreat, I took the phone. In a voice dripping gardenia blossom honeysuckle gentility, I insulted uncle's manners, and especially the lack thereof. It worked.

"Bethie it waran't but minutes after we talked she had another spell. That there ambulance better get here. Anna can hardly take breath."

Ralph asked "Did she feed and water her damn dogs and cats?"

"Jannelle couldn't, she had a migraine coming on," uncle said and then remembered he'd answered Ralph. Who did what was left out. I repeated and uncle worked his way around the mine field. "Well, yes, but hit plum wore her out."

I ignored Ralph. My voice traveled the miles and dear old uncle heard what he needed. It was like promising a child reward for good behavior. Then, Ralph issued orders and disconnected. "That'll teach the old bastard," he said.

A transformed Ralph shooed the kids thru bowl rinsing and tooth brushing and sent them to bed. He walked me into the shower, shampooed my hair, wrapped me in a big warm towel and carried me to bed. After massaging my aching body with perfumed lotion he began to love me. Sweet, and tender, and long. When he wanted to be, Ralph was the perfect lover. And he wanted to be. Again.

Long after his deep even breathing told me he slept, I lay wide awake staring into the night. Sorting memories. Making plans. Following the usual pattern, made plans would be modified yet I plan for it is a foundation for action. We had so much to do and so little time

Fifteen

Sleep; blissful and dream free held me for less than a minute before my sheet was pulled back. Cool air did not revive me. Satisfying sex was wonderful, but this was ridiculous. "Not again Ralph!" I mumbled and was ready to kick him out of bed when the warm nose in my face was followed by Duffer's doggie breath. Full force.

More from memory than sight I followed my guide dog. His routine: lead me to each door where he would sniff, give me a long searching look, and eventually return to his side of Mac Duff's bed.

As usual, I'm not able to walk away from sleeping kids. So much of who we are is reflected in each child. Generations of inbred habits are in the things they say and do, the way they look at life. I marvel at the repetive cycle of heritage and hope and discovery.

My son in his khaki Army green room, with camouflage bedding and wild jungle wallpaper, sleeps with a red Gideon Bible swiped from a motel and his water pistol under his pillow. When pistol and Bible shared the same place, the Bible cover became streaked with water stains that resembled tears streaking a sunburned face. I marvel at the growth of my son whose feet now stretch the length of my size nine running shoes. He towers over the grandmother who used his name for silly songs as she rocked him to sleep. I knew one touch, one light kiss and he would wake ready to talk for hours.

Standing in the doorway of Mellie's moonlit azure blue room, I watched her turn and stretch. Mellie smiled as I moved her red gold sun kissed hair from her face. This is our song. My lips brushed her cheek softly. A do not disturb this sleeping beauty kiss but I kiss her because she is mine, because I love her; this growing beauty that daily is contradiction and affirmation.

In her pink room: "I want everything pink because pink is my favorite color," Mollie Kate sleeps on her back. Her arms open as if she is running to me. Sheepy, her white sheep with the crooked pink ear and satin pink bow tie and pink eyes is tucked under her chin on the pink pillowcase. Solid sleeper of the three, she never remembers Duffer's bed check or my kiss. Nor is she aware her boy growing into man brother has this evening lined his favorite stuffed toys under her window. I wondered why and let it slide.

Kneeling in my room I looked above the dark humpbacked silhouette of our patch of earth until all that filled my eyes was the starlit night. Mellie told us when we saw twinkling stars our eye sight traveled millions of miles. Twinkling stars, millions of miles away yet so easy to see. But, seeing into the long line of tomorrows? I stared into the stars and lost myself in musing.

God created and called that which was eternal and more or less predictable, very good. Eventually God created families which are supposed to be good.

Geography and centuries aside, continuously reproducing family units follow the sometime patterns of good, bad, or indifferent before they become dust. Our earth bound body feeds on the need to live, love, and procreate. In our allotted time span we choose between heaven and hell, and then, death and facing for the first time the true meaning of eternity.

My messed up dream was begging for attention. I tried: We're so predictable. Why don't we learn, pass the test and move on to things greater and grander than senseless wars? Century after century blind sided by greed humanity follows the same path. How many times must a child die before we get it right? Why are humans so determined to destroy? If we possess the intelligence we brag about, why don't we show it?

Long minutes of lostness passed before I realized it wasn't helping. Resigned, I thought three cheers for tradition, the key to survival. Wait! Could it be tradition is the key to detruction?

Then and there, I needed three things: Answers -to life's questions-, Understanding-- - my kids I can handle, it's my husband driving me nuts - and above all, the ability to stop thinking so much. Make that four. Desperately needed was something more than claws of fear arching from the depths of my hurting heart.

I claimed bed and pillow as the first glow of sunrise peeked over the horizon. Sleep claimed me; strong rock solid sleep. Five minutes or five hours, as long as it lasted, it was wonderful.

Bedlam in the guise of my two and four footed menagerie marched into my bedroom. Why were they insisting I'd overslept? Why did they wake me when I'd just fallen asleep? "Why?" is always one of the hardest questions to answer and I didn't want answers. I wanted sleep.

"Go away! Loving super mom lips formed words dried vocal chords couldn't voice. Not that three kids, three dogs and three cats all talking, woofing and meowing on one loud note (identified as hunger) would have heard or obeyed.

Then urgently, the intense voice of our manager Mollie Kate. "He's not being fair. Last night when I gave brother my biggest best blue marble the one that's darker than night but still blue---you know the one mommie?" (I didn't have a clue) Seeing my almost open eyes aimed in her direction she tripped over her tongue. "When Johnny came on Mac Duff said he'd be my best buddy forever if I gave it to him. So I did. Now he says he won't make cinnamon toast and that's what best buddies are supposed to do! Mommie will you make him keep his promise?" Big sigh, close to a sob.

Cool, calm, collected Mellie took over. "Really mother! These kids! Why can't the younger generation behave? Must they always be so noisy?"

Mac Duff to his own defense. "Why do girls remember every thing they're promised?"

I was awake enough to control laughter. In asking, my son joined the ranks of every man--living, dead, or out there somewhere waiting to be born that begs the answer: why do men promise if they don't mean it?"

Mac Duff on a roll: "Why does Mellie need quiet? We're hungry mom. We want pizza for breakfast not cinnamon toast. Pizza's much more nutritious and just because we overslept doesn't mean we can't have pizza." Ice cream last night made us hungry. We're starving. Besides, we know Mollie Kate makes a mean cinnamon toast." He grinned an all male smug know everything grin.

Loving the sound of home on a summer morning, I was making sense of my sons all male logic until I examined the forbidden under any circumstance word "overslept."

Mellie did it again."Motherr, why did you sleep so late?""

"The question should be "what are you doing up so early? I just got to bed."

"Motherrrr, look at the clock?" I did and called it a liar. Even on normal days, there's too much to do and this definitely was not a normal day.

They wanted food, not excuses, denial, or a clock busted for lying. Three voices in concert told me it was a beautiful day. Six hands did their best to pull me from bed. Mellie said "Dad baked some Pillsbury cinnamon rolls and…" ah ha, that' solves the Mollie Kate mystery. Mac Duff and Mollie Kate: "Mom we gotta have pizza." ."

Before my third mug of coffee, three left over meat and everything edible including a ton of mushrooms and green peppers crowded the oven. Mac Duff's, as usual, sported extra onion and green pepper. The girls: light on onion heavy on mushrooms. All had thick with double cheese in common. Kitchen perfume was rich and inspirational, and made us ready for everything, which is what we got.

Four hours later and major work out of the way; I left kids to their packing and picked our first strawberries. Red, ripe, sweet strawberries I didn't see because my mother's hands were in the way. Succulent red berries plunked into pails. As I crawled down straw padded rows, all I saw was my mother's hands, slender fingers so pail, veins thick and blue, and her lips and flesh under her nails, always so blue. Once, I thought her 'blue blood' meant we weren't always dirt poor.

As the last berries went into the freezer, Ralph came home with bags of burgers, fries, and shakes. He told the kids to enjoy a picnic at the creek because we had to talk. I said, "While we're away don't pickle everything and watch the hot sauce." He said "Stay home and help me." I glared. "Don't go there," I said, and whatever he was going to add to the stewing pot was cut short by my blue friend on the kitchen wall.

Doctor Brian Jolly Junior was on the bad news good news wagon. Good: You and Jethro saved her life. Bad: "When she arrived, she was almost comatose." Good: "We've drained fluid from her lungs and have her stabilized." Bad: "Beth Anne we've just touched the tip of this ice berg." I wanted more good. He gave a little: "No sign of recurring cancer."

I thought of her 20 year old invasive breast cancer surgery that left parchment skin over bone. Consulting doctors at her bedside cleared their throats, looked directly at me and said she had five years at best. Said it like they were talking about someone not there, like they'd given up. To make sure I understood, they looked down at their small supposedly drugged patient and shook their heads. One after another, signing her death warrant. . Mom snorted "That's the best you can do?" Within six weeks she was back with her students and her columns in the Sainte Lillian's paper never missed a deadline.

In the days when the dreaded "C" word was locked in the closet, mom wasn't secretive. She talked about cancer, wrote about cancer, and brought it into the light of day. "With help from the Good Lord a person makes the best of what they get," she wrote. Self pity was not her style.

154

Doctor Jolly drew me back. "Beth Anne her heart is too big and tired." He paused. Would my asking for information I didn't have help?"

I didn't have questions I had facts. "Her heart has always been too big," I said, because I remembered mom first up, last to bed, always working, helping everyone. Weeks later I learned he meant something different. Then, I didn't know to ask. Should have. Didn't.

He'd ordered tests; her red blood cell count wasn't up to seven after one transfusion. His "I don't know" responses belonged on a stuck recording. He said, "Too early to commit to diagnosis or prognosis, but we have a very sick lady."

Ralph took over. You've said she's stabilized. What good would it do for Bethie to race down there for God knows how long when you've got her on the mend?" And his favorite word, loaded with contempt. "Again! I'm damn sick and tired of this. Bethie's lazy assed sisters can carry the ball for a change."

Doctor Jolly knew Ralph and wasn't in the mood to waste time. In a voice sharp as a surgeon's scalpel, he said, "Mr. Brunswick, (Not Ralph... Mr. Brunswick) "I'm working with a very sick lady who needs all the help and support she can get to pull through. And that includes Bethe and the kids. I am not a marriage counselor. I will not arbitrate a family dispute" Mad man Ralph slammed my beautiful slate blue phone in its cradle, and was on fire again. Hotter than ever.

Unmasked, my true love turned to me. He gave it his best shot, but other than the usual criticisms of my "Lard assed sisters," his attack was everything selfish, self serving, lewd and vulgar.

This thing in Ralph's skin that looked like Ralph and used Ralph's voice, tried to melt me with his eyes. Then, casually, it prospected the caverns of its nose with a pick ax forefinger. Examining the nuggets mined as if they were gold, it –this Ralph thing--- flicked them toward my freshly scrubbed floor.

Then, the man I had promised to love through everything until death, forced me against the wall. With his face inches away he spat more anger and hatred.

Leaning weakly where his salvo left me, I was alert enough to recognize the loud growl of his Harley. I knew he'd ride for hours over country roads. And I was thankful, that I his newly crowned "worthless hunk of shit," was still alive. I could breathe. That meant I could work.

I wanted the kids. Needed them desperately. Just to see them, to hold them to know something good was left of him. But I knew they didn't need what was left of me. I was so glad they were outdoors. So glad they were spared.

Sixteen

When girl voice said "Gosh mom you're so pale," my relationship to Uncle Jethro kicked in. In less than a millisecond I morphed into the biggest liar either side of the Potomac. "Headache kids, really big headache. Stress and all that," They believed and followed with "Where's dad?"

That was harder, but I was ready. Why couldn't I give them the truth? Wanted to, just once I really wanted to, but this was so easy because they'd heard the phone. "Called back to the job. He's gonna be out late. One of those construction emergencies." I scratched my head. "Oh yeah, I think he said wall problems, something like that." Well, there had been a big problem by a kitchen wall. It was the best I could do. The girls said "not again!" and went about their work. Mac Duff stood back watching me. He turned away when my eyes found his. I said "Son?" "Gotta finish packin' mom," he said in a stuffy voice that told me his allergies were kicking in. Kinda early, but who knew about allergies? Mentally, I added Benadryl to the list of must have kid meds.

We loaded the van. The kids wolfed nightly ice cream, showered, dressed for travel and crawled into bed. "Honest mom we're too excited to sleep. We might as well stay up." Excitement lasted nine minutes 35 seconds.

Fueling up for the journey, I forced down one mug after another of double strength high lead dark roast. At least it smelled good brewing. Drinking? Well, even with all the help sweetener and creamer could give it... never mind. Ralph's morning supply of donuts and long johns kept the coffee down. Besides, greasy sugar coated chocolate filled pastries and caffeine provided energy and I needed all that I could get.

I had to hear moms voice. Yet, guilt and fear told me this time I'd listened to Ralph, and waited too long. It was my fault just like dear old uncle said. Finally, on a sugar/caffeine high laced with fear sweat and pounding heart, I found less courage than the cowardly lion, but courage enough to call.

She picked up before as the first ring echoed the hall. The voice in my ear was strong and healthy.

"Mom?" I wanted it to be mom, was so afraid it wasn't mom.

"You were expecting the mayor?"

I said "mom" again and her laughter flowed. "That Damn Yankee giving you trouble?"

I knew if she knew it would kill her. She heard: "Mother!" seasoned with the perfect amount of shock.

It worked. Humor intact, she parried my questions with fact "These smart young doctors sure ain't in a hurry. It's like I've had this before and got it againitis. Makes me real proud of the medical profession but we gotta remember they just practice medicine." We both laughed at her favorite doctor joke. "My personal diagnosis is old age, plumtiredoutitis." Slowly, the laughter faded.

"Bethie darlin' I know I promised this call wouldn't come but this spell hit way too fast. No matter what kind of fuss that damn Yankee makes I need you. You tell him for me that I have spoke." I laughed because she expected it and skipped telling her my truth, that the thought of Ralph— the thought of my saying anything to Ralph made me want to scream or vomit or both.

At least "We don't know, but get here fast," was familiar. We talked about everything she loved until we ran out of words. We whispered prayers and said goodnight one more time. It hurt so much when I thought this could be the last time.

Before Ralph's hog roared into the driveway, I showered and downed another pot of coffee strong enough to kink my hair. As he got gear together, I herded almost awake kids into the waiting van. Mac Duff yawned and mumbled he "was glad we were so quiet we didn't wake dad."

Quiet? We're never quiet when we leave, but there was no sense in pointing that out. Van headlights picked out a waving giant in the front door with three sad faced dogs pressed against his legs. My focus shifted to their sad eyes asking why they were left behind.

Before we hit the highway the kids were into their pillows. It was me, my thoughts, the dark night and the hum of tires across a lonely stretch of road. My job whether I was up to it or not, was to navigate dark- winding-empty-isolated two lane Michigan roads en route to the Interstate. Van headlights pulled us through a dark lonely tunnel of night. Either side of the road, tall waving trees formed an almost perfect canopy.

I wished for auto pilot; set it, forget it, and let the van drive itself. If only! Yet, for the next 10 to 12 hours I had to stay awake and alert. Forget the wild life on these lonely dark country roads. Deer, coons and serpentine possums are nothing when stacked against the long arm of the law. Men in blue snuggle down in patrol cars with one eye asleep and another on the radar, just waiting. Their favorite game: "Gotcha!" I was ready for them on this dark night with dark thoughts fueled by caffeine alertness and a sugar high.

With nothing else to do, I played pick a worry. Would the nerve wracked driver of this van speeding into the unknown choose troubles in the rear view mirror, or those waiting ahead? Prince or the tiger?

Sounds of entire audience inhaling, a thousand drum's beating tattoo. Time standing in a vacuum. Decisions, decisions. Drum roll: the scoreboard reads "Troubles O." And the winner is the hidden ingredient: Memories that make me proud of my Ozark roots. Bad and good all mixed up together. Just like real life. Me and memories, all alone in the moonlight. Two hours passed, then three. I knew Sainte Lillian to be as close to utopia as any equal sized town in the states could be. As long as I didn't tell Ralph.

Ralph's face inches from mine. I wanted the last 36 plus hours with Ralph out of my mind. I wanted 36 hour amnesia... That wish took me to the beginning of my life history. Me? Get what I want?

My hands shook as my mind toyed with my world favorite troubled trio. Regardless of my brain drain, a paramount truth smacked me in the face. Shaking hands do not belong on the steering wheel of a van careening down a dark freeway at 100 mph! Kids and cops didn't catch me. Time to breathe. Next step: Count my blessings? At least the damn Yankee wasn't there.

Time to put mom and pop up front... All the he said, she said they said stories brought a few decisions closer, I knew Jannelle would fight, but her dear daddy had to have 24 hour care. Even if I wanted to do it, I wouldn't. And as much as she wanted to, she couldn't force that on me.

On to mom. With so much unknown, what waited loomed dark and lonely.Worse, much as I wanted this time I couldn't plan ahead. But I could worry. I'm good at worry. I'm president for life of this worry club.

Did they expect me, their favorite miracle worker to do it all? I turned cold at the thought. Exits back to predictable good old mad today glad tomorrow Ralph almost felt my screeching tires. On second thought, whatever waited ahead couldn't be as bad as the confused hurting mess left behind.

Searching for answers to the unanswerable, gave me miles of nothing. I thought nothing, felt nothing. Tires hummed over grey asphalt patched with fresh black tar/gravel-- or whatever road crews use to patch pot holes. Headlights wakened dusty roadside greenery seconds before darkness returned its sleep. Raccoon eyes glowed eerily red in golden headlights. One was too many and the road edge held way too many blood smeared tire marked gray possum bodies. Why do possums cross the road? To die trying. There a beautiful red and white collie, lying on its side, feet curled up as if asleep: then, near a barn a mangled calico cat. I mourned because sleeping kids couldn't.

At times scrub brush and fledgling trees bowed to a passing something stronger than wind. Tall grasses waved. Were things going bump in the night real? Were fanged monsters robed in black roaming? Does Bigfoot wait for darkness? Are Lions and Tigers and Bears up and about not to mention alligators and dinosaurs? Who knew what mysteries this night held?

An enormous fast moving furry fanged creature materialized. Trees trembled and tried to blow him away. He cursed. He threatened. Pedal pushed metal. Closed in on ninety before my foot eased. Got away with 100 once won't try that again! He can get close but he can't get in. Not now! What then?

The great sister mystery? Take Jannelle, somebody please take Jannelle (couldn't' resist). Just like Monday night football, nothing changes with instant replay. Jannelle never carried the ball made a field goal or a touchdown. She warmed the bench delicately dabbing her eyes with gardenia scented tissue and never, smeared her mascara or makeup. Talk about talent! Talk about skill! She has the moves down.

Jannelle went back to the penalty box surrounded by a ten mile wide ten mile high barbed wire fence. Lying for the umpteenth time I promised myself since she was outa sight, she was outa mind She looked lonely, like she needed company. Ahh yes, what's his name back there in Michigan? There's a real odd couple! I laughed at the thought.

Could I think about my beautiful wonderful eternally contented baby sister Samantha Lynn without turning green with envy? At least green is my favorite color. The question almost tops how love and envy can live in the same heart.

Keeping van on road and kids safe required eliminating the following topics : What's going on with Christianity, what's his name, my wonderful sisters, our delightful parents, politics and politicians, war, famine, pestilence, disease, art, literature, world travel, market prices of grain, Oil by the barrel or cup? General Motors, Mac Donald aircraft and wars, rumors of wars, and a few hundred others. Good! Now that I've exhausted my field of interest.

Woops, shouldn't use the 'e' word. Also to avoid: words that reflect emotions like angry, confused, desperate, despondent, depressed and hurt. Above all, must avoid the stewpot of downright mad. My mission whether I accepted it or not; staying out of the ditch, keeping, the kids alive and well, and while I'm at it, the world safe for democracy. Finding the miracle chapter in my Super Mom manual would have been a bonus.

Once again, the furry humanoid invaded. Ambushed in the narrow pass, a dramatic instant replay aimed at my heart. I don't know how sports casters do that, but I know Ralph. He was there. The lens of my mind focused on his bulging eyes. Avalanche boulders of emotion shattered pieces of my resolve. He was full blown and full volume. So much for fences!

Caffeine flavored bitter gall rose in my throat. My mind screamed for release. My heart said "easier thought than done." Other times replayed. Overdue for his yearly physical, he screamed. "Woman!" Not "Beth Anne" or "Bethie," not even "Big Butt," but "Woman! I ain't the sick one." "Woman" spittle on his lip, delivered with explosive force. Always, the look full of hate and scorn, the look reserved for a child molester caught in unspeakable acts. Enough! No! Not enough! More than enough! Time to wake the kids.

Seventeen

Ralph strained his eyes watching the van's red tail lights fade into nothing. Still he stood staring at where they had been; wishing he could call them back, wishing he could erase yesterday. He knew remorse and wishing didn't do a damn thing to bring them back or ease his pain, but he kept it up until he was covered in cold sweat.

He survived a childhood filled with bullies until he grew bigger and meaner. They learned. He made damn sure they learned. Scars from Nam proved he'd been shot so full of holes they had telegrams ready to send his family. Medics gave up. He didn't. He fought back from Nam and from more than his share of other crap. Sometimes he was so full of deep down gut pain all he had left was fight. He fought all of his life, and all of his life, he won. He had medals. People respected him. He was the problem solving man. Big man. Can do man!

This was different. He couldn't blame bullies or his dad or Nam or any other crap. The way he hurt Bethie was the mother of all pain. It hit everywhere. Hot coals would have been kinder. He'd never forget the look on her face when he backed her against the kitchen wall. Was she afraid? Had she passed pissed off? Was she so tired of him she didn't give a damn? The way she looked through him, her eyes said all that and more. Oh God! Her eyes said all that and more.

His kids. How could he let them go? Guilt slapped, nagged, and shamed him.

Now, he couldn't make it better. They were gone, on the way to friggin' Sainte Lillian. Stressed and tired as Bethie was, if they died in an accident, and he never saw them again, how could he stand it? They would never know how much he cared, how sorry he was.

It wasn't his fault. He'd wanted to explain, and slip the kids a coupla dollars but didn't get a chance. Wasn't his fault they left so quick, like she'd been waiting for him. Bethie looked right through him like he wasn't there. The kids didn't see him or notice the dogs. His wife. His kids. His life.

They walked out on him because of those phony old fools in that friggin' fallin' down house on friggin' Maple Brook Road in friggin' Sainte Lillian.

Never mind what that smart assed doctor said. He knew it was the same friggin' story. "Hurry Bethie! Get here before they die. Hurry. Hurry. They're dying!" Like hell they were. Not a damn thing wrong with either of them a good kick in the ass wouldn't cure. Yeah, they're old and rusty and falling apart like their old Allis Chalmers tractor. So what? Everything wears out. Old machinery, old furniture, old things and old people rust out, fall apart and wind up in the dump or grave yard. Same thing.

Did they expect his Bethie to order new parts from the Sears catalogue, rub off the rust and give them a grease job? Sometimes twice, three times a year she had to perform some frigid' miracle. He was sick of it.

Why couldn't Bethie see the same friggin' pattern, and leave them alone? Their good time and their useful time was long past finished. Now was their dying time. Why couldn't she just let them do it?

Ralph knew his home was the only one in the world with five seasons. The damned fifth, the Season of Disaster came whenever his friggin' in-laws wound up in the hospital. When it came… spring, summer, fall or winter, Bethie had to drop everything and race to the rescue. She did before the kids came, when she was pregnant, when the kids wore Pampers, when they were in school and his mom moved in to take care of them and keep house. Every friggin' time one of them old farts knocked at death's door, his Bethie made damn sure that door never opened. It wasn't her job. She was his. Not theirs. Why couldn't that damn family of hers understand how much he needed her?

Pacing the floor, cursing, Ralph ran into a stone wall of hated self doubt. Was he wrong? Nahh! No friggin' way. He was never wrong…but, the little old bat couldn't fake cancer or a weak heart. She wasn't that tall to begin with. Now arthritis was takin' over. Seemed like she was shorter every year.

Thoughts of his mother-in-law just tall enough for her feet to touch the ground, faded. Ralph's mind went to his tall wife and her beautiful long legs. He loved her legs. How the hell did long legs like hers come out of a woman as small as her mother? For seconds all Ralph saw was Bethie's long sculpted legs.

That sure as hell didn't help. Back to the old bat. How about that time she came down with bronchitis? That was a good one. Not a clue the night before. Up till midnight whopping his ass game after game of checkers, and laughing her fool head off every time she cleared the board. Six hours later she woke the whole house coughing her lungs up. Harsh cough. Hurt to hear it. His joke about her midnight hours and hillbilly hangover didn't get past his brain before she spat out a wad of bloody yellow mucus. He almost puked. Bethie had to calm him before they left for the E.R. Maybe they thought he was chicken, but he didn't give a damn. He couldn't handle that crap. Not even when the kids were sick. It always surprised him he nursed Bethie when she lost their baby. But that was different, hell of a lot different than the old woman dying…again….

If ever a man belonged in the looney bin, it was the old fart. He'd say the diverticulitis was tearin' up his gut. It was killin' him. Soon as the old woman spoon fed him corn meal mush laced with sorghum molasses, he'd be at the table. That phony worked his knife and fork like he had 40 plus acres to plow with a mule so old he had to push it along the furrows. True, he'd had a mild heart attack or two and a coupla minor strokes but, so what? Ingrown toenails caused him more trouble. It was frickin' funny watching him scan newspapers and watch TV for reports on disastrous diseases. Ten miles, ten counties, ten states or ten countries away didn't matter. He'd sniff the wind like a starving man sniffing KFC, and in a day or two be in the E.R. The old fart spent more time with doctors in a month than most red blooded men did in a year or two---or three. Ralph laughed. Just like the old bat, the old fart always got better!

Yet it never failed. Whenever they were called, Bethie and her saintly sisters performed their miracle cure and kept cold death away.

Jannelle? Yeah right! Dumb bitch was useless! How the hell could she nurse sick people all over Sainte Lillian County and not take care of her own parents? Hell! Bees made her faint.

Samantha Lynn the beautiful couldn't chase death away by herself. She could do and do and do, but the friggin' miracles wouldn't happen without Bethie. She had to be there and lay her hands on everything and mumble prayers and work her ass off.

Hell, they didn't need Bethie. Lard Ass and Wonder woman lived close enough. His Bethie should be taking care of him. Her duties as his wife and mother of his kids didn't include mission impossible. What in God's name was wrong with her?

Ralph paced. He couldn't. He wouldn't. He refused to admit it, but buried deep inside with his secrets, he hurt with the loneliness of a soul eternally alone in hell. He ached for Bethie and his kids. Would they believe if he told them? Especially the kids, the way he yelled. It wouldn't be manly to tell them he missed their noise and laughter. He ached for the sight of them when Boy teased Girl One and Girl Two. And Boy and Girl One ganging up on Girl Two about her being so young and inexperienced. Then there was the Easter Sunday with Jelly beans., and that stupid fish funeral. Ralph wiped blurred eyes. More than anything, he missed the five of them together. The completeness when they were together.

He could see her face wash with shock if he ever tried to tell her. As if, he heard in that slight soft southern accent all the years in Michigan hadn't erased: "O.k., Ralph darling stop sugar coatin'. What did you buy this time?"

His dad never showed love like that, and for damn sure he never let his mother get away with anything. He was in charge at home, with her and with his brothers, and on the job. Do and don't do came out of his mouth and the doin' and the dontin' were law. All those years of watching his dad taught Ralph about men and women.

The way his dad watched him lately, not saying anything just watching, made Ralph sure the family knew he'd been too soft with Bethie. What else could it be?

As head of the house, as husband and father it was his job------ No! Hold on a friggin' minute. This was more than a job. On the job, a man clocks in does his eight; if he's lucky a little overtime at time and a half, and clocks out. Bein' man of the house ain't no friggin' job. It's a 24 seven 365 days a year responsibility. He was Head Mother Fricker in Charge. Bethie made him say frick and frickin' and fricker. Even with her away, he couldn't stop saying it. Hold on! Real men said what they wanted. If there was one real man in this world, Ralph saw his face every morning in the mirror. By God, he'd use any word he wanted. He did. Cats and dogs heard him first, and then he covered every room and every object. Bed, book, and candle, bathrooms, and medicine cabinets, towel racks and toilet seats, soup and soup pots window shades and window panes, they all got it. Until he looked at Bethie's bedside Bible. Then like a madman he ran through the house opening windows and lighting scented candles. A hot shower didn't wash away the shame. But it didn't stop him either. At 4:30 in the morning, Ralph inhaled a pitcher of Miller's doctored the dog's water dish with a shot or two and let them help him finish a ring bologna and box of Hi-Ho's crackers spread thick with Schuler's Bar cheese. After he lit a smuggled Cuban the dogs let him know they needed fresh air. Damn dogs, he didn't smell anything. Wait, maybe they did it, way they were scratching their noses and whining.

He turned them free in the back yard and decided things were gonna change. It was his right to keep a tight reign. Just like his dad said, women were best in bed, cookin', cleanin,' barefoot and pregnant.

Bethie said his dad was a big joker, and more than slightly chauvinistic. She said his mom did what she pleased. Sure, now him and his brothers had families of their own, she could join the flower society and tutor at the elementary school. But by God when the house was full of boys, she toed the mark. The old man got what he wanted for supper. She kept the house spotless, even ironed his bed sheets and underwear. She made damn sure me and the boys were full of "Yes sir!" and "Right away sir!" when he was around.

Bethie said if he wanted his sheets and jockey shorts ironed, he could do it. To make sure he understood she hadn't signed on as his personal servant, she said if he made messes, he cleaned up! She wasn't into pickin' up after a grown man. The one time he said her cookin' wasn't as good as his moms, he learned it was a lot better than cold corn flakes laced with horseradish spiced shrimp sauce. Give him credit though, he asked for seconds. Bethie laughed till they both cried.

And the kids. Well, they were kids. Good kids. Maybe they didn't snap to attention when he was around, but they looked up to him and minded pretty good. Sometime? No, most of the time.

It wasn't just Bethie though. Just like her, his brother's wives acted like they don't need no man bossing them around. Well that was over! The entire Brunswick family was gonna be the way it was supposed to be with men in charge! Frickin' right! That damn women's liberation did it. Like his dad and the men at the coffee manor said, women want to wear the pants. Not his Bethie! He wouldn't allow it!

His wife promised God in front of over 200 witnesses she would love, honor and cherish him. Some promise! Look at her now! On the road to friggin' Sainte Lillian in friggin' hillbilly Missouri to love, honor and cherish and obey every whim of her friggin' phony parents.

Ralph decided "friggin'" sounded better. Even though changing the pronunciation didn't change the meaning, it just made him feel more civilized; cleaner somehow. Then he wondered if scented candles made the house smell better, and a second later cursed himself for bein' a stupid idiot. As if friggin' swearin' could dirty a house. He whacked himself in the forehead and got another pitcher of Miller's, this time to drink from the pitcher like a real man. Who the hell needed a glass? He burped on the wings of a scent he couldn't blame on the dogs. Hell, that one beat his father in law's best effort by a mile. Ralph was the man! For another three minutes.

Ralph knew with gut tearing certainty his old bat of a mother-in-law had a rich farmer waitin' to keep Bethie and his kids down there. He panicked. He couldn't live without her or his kids. He had to plan. He was good at fixing things. He knew what to do. First off, he'd have candy and balloons waiting for the kids in the old bat's hospital room. Then his master stroke. Ma Brown could order yellow roses from the Saint Louis Flower Exchange. Three, four, five, six dozen. What the hell if he couldn't afford it? Credit cards work. Bethie was a sucker for yellow roses.

And he'd been a sucker for Ma Brown every since him and Bethie got married. That old black lady could look right through a person and know what they needed. She did it to him first thing. They took to each other like sweet butter to warm biscuits and they'd been friends every since. Soon as he could every visit, he'd be hanging out with Ma Brown, just to be there and talk. He loved her start up story, the way she skipped hurtful things and brought out the good, the way her deep brown eyes looked into his soul and made him feel understood and loved.

"Was the summer of the terrible tornado. Way too much grief to talk about, so I won't. This white gal Melanie Morrison...Melanie Levine now. Called her white gal or white child then, now I calls her Honey Lamb...anyways she was in a heap of trouble and needed to see my son John somethin' fierce. She kept knockin' on doors till she wound up to my place. We had us a great big talk. And I ain't gonna tell you what about, so don't ask. Well sir I'll tell ya, she up and noticed all my purty African Violets and gloxinia and peonies and all, and started talkin' about how her momma surely wished she could do what I did but her momma could do what I couldn't with fancy arrangements and she thought it'd be nice if we got together cause Saint Lillian surely needed a florist. Me and Margaret Morrison talked it out, and our only problem was namin' the place. We didn't want to call it The Flower Shop or anything that common. We tossed names around for two weeks when Honey Lamb and her brothers came up with Mo Browns. Mo for Morrison, Brown for yours truly. Mo Brown's fit like a glove. That's my story and I'm stickin' to it," she said and hard as he tried to get more out of her, she did.

Bethie filled in the blanks. Good Lord! How could she love a town that full of evil? Still, he wished he could see his only true friend in Sainte Lillian. Best he could do was one phone call and a weeks worth of profit.

He knew Bethie and yellow roses! Let those beer drinkin' up past their boot tops in cow shit hick farmers top that! Good feelings lasted maybe a minute before fear delivered a knock out punch! Panicked, he looked for his kids in cold quiet empty rooms, and hurt even more. It was like they were dead and he was forced to remember everything he could have done, should have done, didn't. It hurt, hurt like hell.

How the hell did I get in here? He asked as he stood where Bethie always dished up her bowls of homemade soups and spaghetti and stews. He could see her as she was every year at Easter. His hand ached for the feel of hers as they clasped hands and bowed heads for grace. The way she smiled, the way she prayed. Once or twice his folks felt duty bound to say the blessing. Starting with world hunger and wars, they prayed like they were out of practice. They named every country where kids didn't get three square a day, worked into wars and rumors of wars, earthquakes, drought and flooding and then really got going on the state of the economy, their business their neighbors business and potholes. Sometimes they even blessed the food... which by that time was cold; wilt on the salad and grease on the gravy. When Bethie prayed surrounded by a hungry family, it took her two minutes max and she covered all the bases. Best of all kids didn't go to sleep and the food was hot! One time when his dad cleared his throat to pray Mac Duff spoke up. "Momma pray now grandpa, you pray before dessert, he said and laughter rippled around the table

"Why?" he cried to the night and the night had no answer

Ralph's bare right foot stabbed a popcorn kernel. He cursed, and then retrieved it to rub it like a good luck charm. Boy always sat there. Had he touched this kernel?

Ralph did another circuit. He looked again at empty beds and wished again each child was there safely sleeping. In Boy's room, Ralph bent to smooth the bedspread and was surprised he couldn't focus through free flowing tears. On his second attempt, his hand connected with Boy's Gideon Bible. He hugged it to his heart and paced and cursed and doubted.

Sunrise. Dogs and cats lined up wanting food. What the hell?

Eighteen

They slept while I conquered bumps, turns, hills and potholes and mused and remembered mom telling me "In all things be thankful" and wondered how, and worried and sometimes sent groans to God that passed for prayers.

Once or twice Mellie loosed a long rattling snore, the snore we've learned to hate, because it warns of coming ear infections. The only good thing, since I'm desperately looking for good things, we're experts handling ear infections.

Our favorite truck stop at Tecumseh and countless other neon flashing-billboard invitations to pull over, waste money and rest were ancient history, nothing more than blinks in the night. Now we were miles away from Ralph, equal distant miles away from the unknown.

Elvis and "You ain't nothin' but a hound dawg," worked wonders. Sleepers rubbed bleary eyes, and the first sound out of my three darlings, "Are we there yet?" was chased away by Mellie's "I've got to pee and right now." Mac Duff said if she were only a boy, she could pee out the window. Mollie Kate swatted him. He yelled "Mom, they're picking on me!" I love the sounds of morning. We pulled into a Mac Donald's--- gas station with barely a minute to spare. Mellie ran.

I put Elvis to bed and enjoyed my morning trio. Noisy. Hungry. Fussing over which was in charge of specific junk foods. Decided: If Mellie got the Pringles, she couldn't handle the corn chips. Mac Duff had full reign on pickles and chocolate chip cookies and Mollie Kate controlled Coke and corn chips. Beautiful noise that chased dark thoughts and that forbidden 'e' word away. I said to me, "You dumbie! Why didn't you spare yourself and wake them sooner?"

Sunrise tiptoed softly, like a new mother going into the nursery to treasure the wonder of her sleeping baby. Mother Nature's first light bathed our world in soft rose mauve and showcased mid-America's forest and fields. I knew Ralph would have stopped the van and used a roll of film. "Leave Ralph out of this," I said to me.

At last, my love hate relationship with the Indianapolis Freeway was over. This rubbed raw of emotions day, I delighted in venting discontent on this stretch of dangerous road. This time there were only three detours, and by actual count she said- lying again- three thousand thirty three and one half gardens of ever blooming orange cones. Thank God I wasn't driving through one of the famous Indiana rainstorms, or on roads slick with black ice. Early morning commuter traffic on a dry Indiana Morning is all I can handle. Even then, keeping up with Indy 500 wanna be's pushed petal to the metal.

Knock knock jokes-- the sillier the better were next . After thirty miles and three kids doing their best to get the orange who? punch line, I gave them the grand slam finish. "Aren't you glad I didn't say banana?"

They booed and glared and I was queen of the road. Then, it was their turn. Translated: "Get even with mom." My wait was short.

Mac duff did his with "if there have to be stop signs why aren't there go signs? And why do maps have north south, east and west? Wouldn't up down right and left be easier?" He held us spellbound before Mellie had enough and gave her opinion of men with flat butts. Board butts are so boring," she said and laughed at her own wit. Mollie Kate topped them both. "Mommie darling," she said in that I want ice cream voice---and then paused for her brother's whisper ---pause, pause, pause----But brother what does it mean?" "Never mind just do it," he said and she, obedient, did not give me "I scream you scream we all scream for ice cream." Her sweet voice asked "Mommie, when a person pleasures themselves does that mean they're sneaking ice cream?"

I wasn't over Mellie's fascination with male butts, and now this! I managed a very weak "What else could it mean?" and vowed to speak facts of wife to my less than brilliant husband. Then," Speaking of ice cream kids we're eating the miles." I was thoroughly booed for a least 20 miles.

Mac Duff was first by a split second to spot the Meramac Caverns sign on the big red barn and once again regaled us with his version of Mellie shedding pink panties and peeing on Meramac Caverns floor. "In front of God and everybody," he said, laughing his way through the tingling tale. Mollie Kate said she didn't care what he said, it didn't happen because she can't remember. She knows she'd remember her sister peeing on a cavern floor and in case it was true, were her panties really pink? Pink being her favorite color. Mac Duff said "Women!" Three of us laughed.

I, the driver, and supreme person in charge of this trio of wishful thinkers moaning over every lost fast food exit, was wide awake. Kids made sure I stayed that way and did their best to convince me we could afford a dollar. Apiece. Or two. Make that three.

When I didn't give in to their desperate pleas, three starving kids dove into a cooler full of delicious all American bologna and cheese sandwiches. Mac Duff layered a sandwich with Pringles, pickles and chocolate chip cookies, and grossed out his sisters. Mellie said "Men!"

In spite of their best efforts, it happened. The beautiful homeward bound road blurred. Cars, trucks, busses, horse drawn carriages, cowboys on horseback and flying saucers didn't exist. I saw road. Grey black road and white lines that meant something, I wasn't sure but since there was no road behind them, I knew to stay inside the lines. That funny colored road and white lines and yellow lines turned into a ribbon flying up to slap my face. I fought to keep them alive.

Sighting the narrow steel girdled bridge over the Mississippi River, was enough to put me on full alert. I have an intense dislike for that bridge. For all bridges. So what if this particular bridge was older than dirt and historic? That it survived storms and gully washing floods and suicide by car and barges hitting girders was insignificant. All I cared about was getting off, way off, as fast as possible. Given opportunity, I would race flashing police car lights, ear splitting sirens, tanks, and helicopters just to get off. I wanted terra firma, the firma the terra the better.

"Bridge fear is some kind of phobia" I said to me. My little voice said "alright already, be responsible! Pick a phobia." Ahh! Something to do besides twist the steering wheel into macaroni! It wasn't agro phobia that's fear of spiders which I've more or less conquered. Neither was it sickofmadallthetimehusbandtheunknownwaitingwithmomandpoppphobia. I decided "Troll Phobia" covered my fear to a T. "Don't be grim, I said to me" and laughed like a ninny. The kids, busy counting barges and paddle wheelers and wishing Tom Sawyer and Huckleberry Finn were around, so they could have real fun, didn't notice.

Knowing my duty, I did it and nipped adventures on the big muddy in the bud. "Gator gars big enough to bite off your arm, and big poisonous snakes." "Mom said the S word!" Mellie whispered and they became motionless, and watched me. It was very quiet. For a long time.

Missouri! I was safely home to family, the rolling Ozark hills, long hot days and star bright nights. Home where my insatiable curiosities and all those 'wonderful' memories mom so wanted me to use began. Home, where problems ignored, remains the warp and woof of my identity. Ready or not, and I was not, I was home.

Every mile brought us closer. Fatigue faded. There, the hills of home breathtakingly beautiful every season. In soft spring the hills are ladies dressed for spring dances. They seduce in full blown Ozark summer, sass gloriously in autumn, and in winter, dream in a wonderland framed in pristine ice.

There, green valleys where spring fed creeks flourish and newborn calves, lambs and foals find delight in fields. There, peach, apple and pears grow in roadside orchards. Hillsides covered with grape vines support winery rumors. There, alongside narrow gravel roads where cars and trucks yield right of way to combines and tractors, are fields of corn, alfalfa and soybeans. We crest a hill and are awed by a new wonder, acres of golden yellow sunflowers stretching to the horizon. Van Gogh brilliant beauty.

Narrow roads, hills and curves. Always a part of memories, of home. Hayrides on moonlit nights, full moon glow on fields, crackling fire for wiener roast on creek banks. Home. I was almost home. Good memories. Mom would be pleased.

Then, red gravel one lane Maple Brook Road bordered with maple and a few scraggly peely bark sycamores Tall and skinny, these looked like they knew they didn't belong, but they had roots and were there to stay. This is my road, this Maple Brook road. I want it to deny progress and always be country road narrow blessed with steep curves and low water bridges. Maple Brook Road requires...and at least in my memory, is driven with respectful caution.

Story has it the closest folks around here came to a wreck was years ago on a dark cold windy Halloween night. Plum perfect fer ghosts and haints to go a roamin'. That there moanin' wind was blowin' fleecy clouds way too close to earth. Bare bones skeleton branches on oak and maple was clackin' like a witches laugh, and that there Halloween moon put an eerie glow over purt near everything. Driving home from the Robinsons party the Rogers boys noticed right off chills just racin' up and down their spines. Downright spooky night they said and they just wanted to get home from the party, maybe get a pot of hot cocoa and get warm.

Next thing you know, they crested a hill and had to take to the ditch because comin' right at them the scariest sight they'd ever seen. Scared the hard cider right out of them, they said. Wet their britches they said. Good thing they weren't goin' more than twenty...well, maybe a little faster. They said they were drivin' careful like count of that hard cider they drunk way too much of, so they was able to take corrective action. They went smack dab into the ditch they did and that there big blood wild eyed foamin' at the mouth red stallion just missed their car. Purt near skeered them senseless to think about it, they said.

They said that there gigantic fire breathin' red horse chargin' at them down the middle of Maple Brook Road was the biggest thing they ever seed, twice the size of Pete Parkers old red bull they said. And everbody knowed that there red bull was not only big but the meanest critter in the county of Saint Lillian, state of Missouri U.S. of A.

They wound up walkin' two miles down that lonely shadow filled wind bitin' road back to Robinson's Party. Harold's pa, incidentally the county wide brewer of really good hard cider, pulled their car outa the ditch. He was as serious as a heart attack when he told folks them there horse shoe marks were unbelievable. "Biggest he'd ever seen his entire life," he said. "Pity getting that car outa the ditch erased them," he said. The Rogers boys said after that, they'd surely drink their hard cider when they were t'home and definitely not drive down Maple Brook Road on a cold, dark, eerie wind whipped Halloween night. That there story made a real impression on Saint Lillian's younguns. Fer shure.

Seconds after I reminded the kids we did not, do not and will never speed on Maple Brook Road a speeding convertible of teenagers nearly forced us into the roadside ditch. (I could hear Ralph) Mac Duff asked if he'd get a merit badge if he didn't wave at them the way they waved at us.

I managed "No, but glad you didn't," and warned the kids to stay off the road as once again, we were edged to the side. We had no way of knowing this simple country road would become the site of heartbreak that would affect the entire community. At that minute, rude drivers were just a bump at the end of our long journey.

At last, the farm before my parents; the pink farm home where Freckled Franky Freeman and his five freckled faced red headed brothers grew to handsome manhood. All American into everything boys, folks considered it miraculous all the Freeman boys grew up.

My kids loved Freckled Franky Freeman stories and the pink farm almost as much as they loved Freckled Franky Freeman and his mother's Pink Door Café. There, steaming homemade chicken noodle soup thick with broth and home made noodles (plain or laced with pepper and poultry seasoning) is served in large white bowls. There Saturday's Blue Plate Special—meat loaf, mashed potatoes and gravy and green peas with a side of Waldorf salad--is served on blue plates. Any other color is against the rules. Once a cook was fired for trying it.

Red road gravel sent little welcome back pings against the van. Little pings made little dents, something else to make Ralph happy. Before Ralph invaded full force, I pushed him aside. Thank the Good Lord, this time the pushing was almost as easy as ignoring the bathroom scale. Underscore almost and add almost home. Worries nagging echoes joined Ralph and the bathroom scale.

Now the kids weren't bugging me to speed. Slowly, like we were walking on egg shells, we approached the last hairpin curve. Each of my smart and intelligent trio tuning into yet another of their "I'm gonna be first" contest, swore they would be first to spot the lilac lined driveway, the big white house, the red barns, the three big dogs. Especially the three big dogs. They needed dogs.

After the farewell that wasn't from Ralph, after countless miles and ten thousand "Are we there yet?" And "I've got to pee and I mean right now," After all the wondering, I was home. Somehow being home was all that mattered.

Nineteen

Three 'e' words: exhaled, energy, exhaustion. I exhaled, ran out of energy, and was up to my nose in exhaustion. My brain worked enough to tell me to get busy. I ignored it, and sat quieter than a little church mouse and as frozen in place as the statue outside the Saint Louis Art Museum. Big man on a big horse. That's all I remember. Life support was on automatic. Jumbled together images were like watching the flickering screen of a very old home movie. Like kids waiting to be chosen at a back lot ball game, memories jumped and waved and begged to be chosen. "Pick me! No pick me! Memory A argued with memory B "You were first last time, now it's my turn!" Chunks of memories C through Z jumped and cried and begged.

Doors opened and closed. Mom called us to supper. The wonderful inviting aroma of freshly baked bread and simmering soup followed her voice.

There, Jannelle in her usual place, waiting for her daddy to come in from the barn. There, Samantha Lynn at her bedroom window calling her dogs.

Another memory on instant replay. Ralph shouting: "Snap out of it woman you know damn good and well you can't go home again. And I shot back to this visible only to me person "You idiot! You never spent enough time with your mother to know what its like." Good old Ralph was down for the count. Bye-bye Ralph.

Minutes before my now mute trio made enough noise to put the county on alert. Poor darlings, their reality and my memories weren't in the same universe.

Mellie pointed to her favorite rose arbor almost overpowered by wild grape vines and…was that poison ivy? Mollie Kate found voice enough to stutter, and Mac Duff, ignoring what could be repaired, reworked and replaced jumped from the van to call his second favorite three dogs.

Baying and barking ended my home movie. Kids and dogs collided in the exuberance known only by kids that love dogs and dogs that know they're loved; fleas, doggy breath and all.

While pop's American Eskimo Pete, and Mom's collie Skipper wagged and woofed up a dust storm Bodacious waited his turn and used a hind paw big as a saucer to scratch his newest itch. In doggy lineage this Bodacious is 3,000 grandson 7,000 times removed--or something like that--- of the original Bodacious a cross between every dog roaming the Ozarks since the time of Adam or Noah. I never get that straight either, but he comes from a long line of huge. Definitely, his appetite is bodacious, his feet are bodacious, his shedding of dark grey-brown-white Brillo pad coarse hair is bodacious, and his bodacious bark, while guaranteeing homeland security defies description. He's not big, he's bodacious.

Three dogs fit. Nothing else did, and everything we saw added to confusion and some kind of deep inner hurt.

Three hours later when we crowded into mom's hospital room, we learned our education was just beginning. Swallowed by bed sheets and a soft blue spread, was the smallest woman I've ever seen. It was like her head was above water and her body was less than a ripple on a smooth surface. Yet this frail woman sounded like my mom. She had mom's blue eyes. She had mom's voice. Who was she? The robust slightly overweight woman we hugged at Thanksgiving now didn't look much bigger than Mollie Kate. Days ago, Jannelle said she'd be better if she tried harder. Samantha Lynn said she didn't know what to think because when they left for vacation mom was o.k., she'd never seen anything like this and mom sure was breathing funny. Uncle Jethro said a lot and so did Doctor Jolly but not one of them told me I'd have to look twice before I found her. There was a small ripple under a bed sheet, but it was her never changing voice that convinced me we were in the right room.

Kids got over it first and ran to her.

Mac Duff asked if her goatee was real.

Mellie and Mollie Kate together: "Eeew, gramma you got whiskers!"

Mom said "Bethie darling you know you've probably inherited a gene for cancer and arthritis. I figured that was enough, so doing my duty as a good mom, I kept chin whiskers a secret long as I could. Besides, my momma died way too young to sprout the dad gummed things, so maybe …" she let the wish slide as the kids reacted.

Mac Duff said "Mom's gonna get whiskers?" He looked at his sisters and true to the spirit of sibling rivalry, "Mellie and Mollie Kate will get whiskers!"

"At least we won't be bowling balls" Mellie said and Mollie Kate did an absolute perfect imitation of her aunt Jannelle. Her lower lip went out a mile and big fat tears made her eyes glow.

Mom rolled her eyes. "You kids keep that up, and you'll be standing in the corner." She tried to move her arm. I pushed it down and tweezed evidence of what waited for me and my sisters 30 years down the road. We needed a razor but tweezers worked.

The kids stood like meek lambs, eyes on their shoes. Three quiet kids. Wondering what they had done wrong. Feeling misunderstood, picked on, and innocent. But quiet.

Mom mumbled and grumbled and put on a show for the kids. They perked up and cheered me on. "Get em mom." "Don't let her have more whiskers than grandpa." "Don't worry Grandma; I'll give you a merit badge for bravery."

My troubled mind, removed from this happy family scene, brought Ralph back. I wanted to shout "Ralph you jerk! You were so wrong! My mother is dying."

Then denial kicked in. True, death was closer, but not today. Not next week. Not next month. I slammed the door so fast and hard on reality, it took weeks to resurface.

Finally able to reach for the kids, she caressed each face, lingering seconds longer with my son as she does with Samantha Lynn's boys. Sis and I knew she was remembering Jamie. The boys didn't, and didn't need to and took the extra attention as their just due.

"Grandma you and Grandma Brunswick are the only people who say my name right." Mac Duff turned to his sisters. "Now listen to Grandma and maybe you'll get it."." He smiled that smug boy growing into man sure of himself smile.

"Anything to make you happy Franklin Mac Duff darlin'," she said

"No way will we call him darling" two sister voices sounded as one and the room filled with laughter.

Mom agreed to plans for home made ice cream, wiener roast on the creek bank and fishing at Lake Sa Ho Li. She wanted what they wanted and they would do it, see it, and taste it she said, as soon as her strength came back.

The kids knew that to be a promise on hold. They had to know when it would come back. Mollie Kate asked where her strength went to and why she let it get away. No answer was their answer. Before more of their how's and why's she pointed to a corner filled with a big red recliner. Earlier I told you kids you'd have to stand in the corner. Want to do it now?"

"Grandma!" From three innocent voices.

"Tell you what, when we go fishin,' let's use some of the suckers your dad sent for bait."

All eyes followed her skin on bone pointing finger. Hidden by the red recliner, the corner was stacked full of balloons and enormous swirl carnival sized suckers.

"Bethie the next time I talk to your damn Yankee I'm gonna make sure he learns my grandkids have names and not numbers. Explaining him to the staff plum wore me out. His Girl One, Boy One, Girl Two stuff has to end! Not only that, he didn't send me one little sucker!" She did a Jannelle pout. I had enough sense to grin but not enough presence of mind to comment stuck as I was on her saying she'd explained Ralph to the staff. How? I wanted to know how. Better yet, I wanted to hear that one. Yes, mother, please explain Ralph.

Ralph! She brought Ralph into the room. His most recent explosion replayed. Word for word, accusation for accusation, vulgarity for...

"Forget it Bethie" my heart urged and my mind flicked the off switch. Again. This time it worked perfectly.

Kids went for their treats. My smile came: not for their pleasure, but at the thought of turning Ralph off. What fun!

Mellie said, "Hold out your hands and close your eyes mom." I tried. The hard part was staying upright. Darkness, sneaking in a lullaby had closed my eyes.

"Knock Knock."

I snapped awake.

"Keep them closed mom."

I obeyed, and staggered, and self inflicted pinches kept me in the game.

First Mellshanna, then Franklin Mac duff Darlin,' and then Mollie Kate more than ready with the punch line.

I knew this was pay back for the orange joke. Also, as I was the only super mom they owned, I might as well enjoy myself.

I was allowed to ask "Chocolate who?" one more time.

"Covered," Mac Duff said.

Urge to ask chocolate covered what? ignored, I obeyed the knock knock rule book. "Chocolate covered who?" I asked dramatically, as if the answer would save Democracy from Democrats.

"Chocolate Covered Cherries!" Mellie squealed in delight. "Daddy thinks of everything," she said.

My outstretched arms were filled with boxes of candy and half a dozen cans of my favorite instant coffee Café Vienna. I grinned to please them and mentally added at least another fifty to my tally. Exhaustion short circuited my math.

Kid's worried looks stopped my marathon praise of their generous thoughtful loving wonderful father. Could I in my desire to show appreciation have overplayed my role? Was it intentional? Of course it was. The way nurses kept peeking in, I knew that Sainte Lillian's main topic for the next week would be the generous heart of Bethie's tall handsome mother-in-law adoring Yankee. "Dollars will get you donuts" as somebody somewhere once said, I knew that miles away, Ralph was basking in the glow of public applause.

As candy syrup hit my taste buds, a screaming miniature Ralph perched on my shoulder. Forty plus hours ago were all mine. "Bethie I'm washing my hands of the whole damn mess in that hell hole I'm sick and tired of it. Sick and tired, sick and tired, sick and tired."

The off button didn't work. Inches away, I saw his face complete with bulging eyes, three triangulated blackheads on his right cheek, and white nose hairs needing scissors. For me and me alone, my best beloved screamed: "They'll work you to death and what do I get out of it?" He didn't want an answer. He told me and more. "I'll get a dead wife. I don't need a dead wife. Why can't them fool hillbillies think about how I feel? I'm friggin'over it. I refuse to spend another dime on that old bat." There was more. Too much more. They couldn't see or hear Ralph. They didn't need to see me throw up. I made the bathroom just in time. Cold water felt good on my flushed face, and short circuited my unwelcome visitor.

Mom insisted the kids call their daddy. They looked to me. "Sure, mom, as long as they call collect we don't need to add to your bill, I said," and whispered under my breath "Big spender add another ten bucks to what you absolutely friggin' won't spend on the friggin' old bat"

The kids had to tell everything about our wonderful fun filled trip. Mac Duff ordered another merit badge because he was first to spot the Merrimac Caverns barn sign. Mellie told him about Mac Duff's new chocolate chip, pickle, Pringle, bologna sandwich. Mollie Kate said she counted ten hundred whiskers on her grandma's chin. Since it was mom's phone it was her turn. She did her best to laugh at Ralph's special brand of corny jokes. Too soon, the black phone rested in my hand. It felt like burning coals. I held it with two fingers and managed "Hi." His booming voice filled the room. He missed his kids. He was glad the treats were a success. He was overjoyed to hear his favorite mother-in-law was doing so much better." Just for me one word that changed his voice to disgust. "Again."

Another opportunity to rejoice at my relationship to Uncle Jethro didn't slip by. "Oh darn, we were cut off," I lied, and I knew Ralph heard. Instantly, the instrument of my torture returned to its silent cradle.

The kids busy adding fuel for visits to the dentist, didn't notice. Sick as she was, mom was not eating candy, or blind, or deaf. Her eyes said she knew. My eyes told her she had a clue. A microscopically small Clue. Her eyebrows shot up. Even smaller my eyes said.

Before she could worm her way into it, the kids and I were heading to the Pink Door Cafe for supper. "Then to bed," I said and this time she read my exhaustion. As we backed out the door, I saw the worry frown between her eyes, winked, shrugged the universal woman "you know how men are" shrug, and let kid energy draw me away. Nearly a half century later, my face found a pillow. Tired as it was, my stressed out brain did not let the stretched passed its limits body find sleep. I watched the bedside clock move from 10 p.m., through 11, into midnight.

Mac Duff's raced to the ringing phone. His excited voice cut through my grogginess. "Guess what dad? No, skip it. You'd never get this one so I'll tell ya'. Soon as we could, me and the girls brushed the dogs. Yeah, dad, that's right. I got the girls organized and we got it done. Let me tell ya, they were full of burs and dirt and you wouldn't believe how bad they stunk.You know dad since I'm not home you have to brush the fellas. Did you? What? C'mon dad no jokes. Dad you think I'll get a merit badge? You want me to do what? You want mom to kill me?" He laughed a strong boy laugh.

I thought I knew and then knew I knew. "Dad you had me sing that scout song to mom when I was younger and didn't know no better. I'm not gonna go through that again. Mom might be asleep but she'd wake up. You know she would.

I said "Say goodnight son," as Ralph's voice floated over the miles. "Be prepared, that's the Boy Scout marching song. Be prepared as through life...

I hissed "Now!"

Mac Duff effectively muted the remaining lines with a shouted good night and laughing scurried back to bed.

My lullaby the voice of my best beloved "Hell hole. Damn old woman. Work you to death. What about me? What about me? What about me? The needle stuck and his eyes bulged as he covered me with pellets of spit spite.

Poor pillows pounded and bunched over my face to mute moaning. Poor bed sheets twisted and tortured. Sleep. Where was sleep? The kids sleeping at least half the trip away, found more without Johnny or ice cream. And I, on edge for over 40 hours, felt every cell in my body begging for a release that could be found only in a quiet deep dark place without memories or dreams.

Wide awake, I wiped tears and stared out the big window to a sky full of millions of miles away stars of summer. Missouri Ozark sky bright with twinkling diamonds after a hot clear summer day took me back to other times, other people, other dreams.

Without effort, I remembered nights under these same watching stars. Stars my mother knew by name and place season after season.

My father's voice and my mother's singing were there on the wind. The years of growing danced before my eyes. It was all there; seasons, people, the lush beauty of cloud capped green hills and valleys thick with fog in early morning. I always wondered if God's first garden was as beautiful as our Missouri Ozarks. Then Ralph's voice came and echoes bounced over and over and over.

If I knew anything it was this truth, absolutely and positively, sleep would not come the whole night through. Suddenly, I couldn't find millions of miles away starlight in the intense darkness. It wasn't strong arms, but at least it held me.

Twenty

One week later we waved goodbye to the clan from a renovated home site. Our labor of love gave Sainte Lillian something else to talk about and was worth a feature spread in the weekly paper.

Mom was on the mend and nursing homes complaints about pop were way down. We expected routine to kick in. I told myself two more weeks, two-and-a-half at most, and we could pack the van and head back across the bridge I love to hate, wend our way past Indianapolis and be home. Our home. Michigan.

Thrilled they would be celebrities, the kids saw routine as a big problem. They begged "Promise we won't go home till we get hundreds of copies of the story."

"Hundreds! Surely you jest, why do you need hundreds?"

Mac Duff gave his dad's response. "My name ain't Shirley and I don't joke."

Mellie pleaded their case. "Motherrrrrr long drawn out 'r' again, hands on hips as she stared up at me. "This is the first time ever, in our whole lives we've been important news. We're y'know, like famous and everything. We have to take copies to church youth group and then to school and the neighborhood and all our Yankee cousins and sign them and everything." Jannelle hooted. "Back home less than 10 days and she's talkin' about her Yankee cousins."

Mollie Kate stressing the importance of this momentous event as if their life span had passed 100 years echoed Mellie's, "Ever in our whole lives."

"We'll do our best," I said. What else could I tell them when the wish of my heart was sidelined by nagging worry? Mom should be much better, instead of so listless and frail. She reminded me of a rag doll. All I could think about pop was he was so…so… not normal. Because there was no way around it, I lied to myself again. I said to me, "this time our miracle is slower, but it's working."

However, the homesite was another story. The house, outbuildings, gardens and yard were shining like a roll of new silver dollars.

Mark, "Yes Dear," and the boys re-graveled the driveway and made "doube dang sure" potholes didn't stand a chance. Mark said he did it to keep Ralph happy. Then he slipped the reporter a crisp twenty to guarantee she'd quote him. Mark said his Yankee brother-in-law's fits about Missouri potholes were out of line. He said he personally knew potholes in Michigan were big enough to swaller a horse. The down home sharp as a tack reporter laughed at Mark and said some of his language wasn't fittin', but she'd be happy to clean it up a bit and oblige. Smart girl, she kept the twenty.

For days my sisters and I talked about everything except mom and pop. We'd get to the bolted door and then, by mutual unspoken agreement, change the subject. Our secret thoughts and worries were question marks hovering overhead like hungry vultures. Out of the blue questions about pop, worry over mom would swoop, peck, and fly away unsatisfied.

We knew how to do everything around the home place; paint, scrub, disinfect, clean, and restore lawn and gardens. We could solve world hunger, end war, stop abortions and oust crooked politicians, but we could not discuss mom and pop. We told the kids they would be well. We didn't tell them we didn't know what to do or how to deal with little sick people so unlike our parents.

Mid-morning the day they left for home, my sisters and I pretended we were grown up and had tea in the living room. Samantha Lynn poured mint tea from mom's favorite blue Wedgwood tea pot. "One lump or two, she asked passing my cup to Jannelle. "One and a drop of cream please," I said politely. We were so proper we had linen napkins on our laps and apple scones from mom's favorite recipe on our plates.

I waited for my sisters to say something. They waited for me. We each waited for the other to clear foggy air. Like polite stranger, we made polite stranger talk. We covered weather, flowers, and the juicy who said what about whom in town. We giggled at the thought of Sally Cronkite-Bush naming her identical twins De'Javan and De'Javal. We sipped tea politely and enjoyed our scones. We said "My, how the kids are growing." We agreed they were so cute together.

We talked a lot. Nothing new, even when we disagree, we talk. This time, when we should have talked about mom and pop and let everything else slide, they slid and we talked about everything else. Judging by our laughter, mom, pop, Uncle Jethro and what's his name in Yankee land didn't exist. We cleared our throats every time their names came close. We cleared our throats a lot.

I couldn't take it. I said, "This is taking a little longer, because they're older. Nothing but a minor setback. Every day they look better." It worked for maybe three point ten seconds.

Samantha Lynn gave me a searching look and turned away. Her silence fueled my fears.

Jannelle didn't want to talk about them or hear anything about them. Her tears started and she dug for another gardenia scented tissue.

I tried again, "We can't not talk about them." My sisters chose to glare at me. I changed to "We have to talk." Samantha Lynn smiled one of her soft smiles, a smile that said she couldn't talk, but she could listen. Jannelle wadded her scented tissue and reached for another. They looked to me waiting. Why always me?

"Can we talk about what we've always thought, the way we felt years and years ago?" They didn't say yes or no. They didn't say anything. I tried. "Remember, how we always knew they would never grow old and helpless? Remember how strong they were, how they could do anything?" they didn't tell me to shut up. They remembered.

I focused on mom. "She's not supposed to be hunched over and weak. She looks like she's been washed in bleach and hung out to drip dry. They keep saying her heart's too big but we know that. Why do they make that such an issue?"

Jannelle looked like she wanted to say something, but the moment passed. They wanted more from me, but I was empty.

We sipped our tea and stared into memories. Each our own. We knew the mom held in our hearts was not this little thing a strong wind could topple.

I waited on my sisters to say something bright and hopeful. I waited on them to say anything. My nurse sister with a head full of medical knowledge didn't. My optimistic hard working gentle sister didn't. We looked everywhere, at the floor, the ceiling, through the shining windows graced with starched Priscillas, at the dogs chasing kids chasing balls, but not at one another. Not at the truth.

Pop wasn't any easier. For all his faults, ignored as usual by Jannelle, we couldn't fit the puzzle pieces together and find the man we remembered.

Our pop was always strong, hearty, and opinionated. Given the chance, he'd argue with the devil and Saint Peter at the same time.

Every Saturday morning with his cronies at the country store he was with politicians as Uncle Jethro was with me, blaming them for everything. Pop preached to the choir about money hungry crooked good for nothing politicians. His cronies knew it. They believed it. Their hard scrabble lives proved it. When pop preached "Amen's" filled the air.

He had to have a good side. Where in our memories was it hiding? Thinking his anger took the shine from sunlight, I stared at my sisters.

Jannelle stuck up for her hero. "Daddy sure was patient with mom and her singing lessons." Trust Jannelle. Her daddy was patient with mom, never the other way around.

I thought how he loved his grandkids. That was good. But who didn't love them? Couldn't one of us come up with a good memory about pop? *I tried food.* "Pop's favorite meal was food." Jannelle actually laughed. "Lots of it, but he could really dig into corn bread and great northern beans cooked with onions and ham, and if mom didn't bake at least one pineapple upside down cake a week, you'd think the world was ending." Samantha Lynn added "Sweet potato pancakes covered with sorghum and always a side of home fries." My turn again. "Remember how he took mom to the Audubon every year anniversary of their first date? How she said he said snails weren't snails but escargot, and how she said a snail was a snail was a snail. It was like putting pearls on a sow and calling her a princess. Remember on our 12th birthday we had to get dressed up and go there and eat them?" Samantha Lynn turned pale, I grimaced and Jannelle licked her lips. "Delicious," she said. That was it! We were doing much better.

We took a giant step onto safer ground and compared this pop with the man we remembered. He didn't wander into territory-- or talk to people we couldn't see. He never drooled. Our pop, the original bathe and change twice a day man never looked like, or shuffled like a derelict. These days, derelicts looked better. Jannelle said sometimes her daddy smelled like he was rotting from the inside out. From Jannelle, that was too much truth. Silence long and thick came as Samantha Lynn stared at me and Jannelle took her good old sweet gardenia scented tissue time to crawl from her self dug ditch.

I said "Little Freckles," but that didn't help. Our silence didn't stop me from thinking their dying in their sleep would be the ideal solution. That was too wishy-washy. I got very specific. Not tomorrow or the next day or next week, but now, while we were together. Now, before they got sicker and our lives became even more complicated.

Then the phone rang; loud, shrill, and demanding. It rang and my hard heart broke. Pieces of it landed somewhere between my stomach and toes with the force of a hardball hit with a home run destiny. The room, my sisters, my tea cup and saucer, dessert plate; everything blurred. How the fragile china made it safely to the coffee table will forever remain a mystery.

In the seconds it took to reach the phone my prayer was anything but groans. I told God I was tired and confused and scared. I reminded him neither I nor my sisters knew which way to turn or what to do. Then, I reminded God we weren't ready to see either of them lowered into deep rocky red Missouri Ozark soil. After telling God everything He already knew, I started begging.

It was a wrong number, but since Odessa of Plaid sister fame had me on the phone she wanted to talk anyway. For her sake, we didn't.

Twenty-One

Good news, we "Yankees" were almost adjusted to our up too early-- to bed too late routine, and ready for a day off. No house, yard, or garden work allowed. In fact, if nursing home and hospital staff couldn't manage without us for a day, they were in trouble. This was our day. "Anything goes," I said to the kids.

"Define anything motherrrrr" They were all ears and hanging on to every word.

Sparing them down home humor, I grinned and winked. "Anything my darlings cannot include the four letter word beginning with 'w' and ending in 'k.' To further clarify," I said, and that's as far as I got.

Mollie Kate shrieked. "Work, we're gonna work! That's all we do around here. I'm tired of work!"

Her older and wiser brother and sister scribbled the alphabet and showed her that particular dreaded and deservedly hated dirty word was the one thing we would not do. Mac Duff spelled it out. "Knowing mom we'll do a W with an a and l and k at the end, but not even a hint of an o or an r. No sir baby sister! We're gonna have 6-21-14." Into the game now, Mollie Kate was plum tickled by the idea. She sang "Fun-fun- fun till daddy takes the T-bird away."

Five minutes, give or take, we'd have been out of there and missed everything.

Then the phone, my very best non-friend, did it again. Feet said "run." Brain said "answer it." Three dogs tired of the incessant ringing as I howled as kids laughed. Neither made enough noise to still the darn thing.

I managed five giant steps before Bodacious cut me off. Moving gigantic dog became gigantic rock; fortunately, a soft furry rock. Big furry dog and I rolled in the grass. First to recover, Bodacious put his face in mine and moaned in true doggy sympathy. The kids roared with laughter. I giggled and wished for Ralph and his every present camera. Big bad mad Ralph on mute for two weeks was back full force. Good old Ralph; always there when I didn't need him, never there when I did.

Phone, what phone? Ralph? What was a Ralph? Questions became vapor when Mo Brown's beauteous van decaled with purt near every flowering plant known to humankind roared into the driveway. Shades of red, yellow, orange and loud purple flowers I'd never heard of decorated every inch. Guaranteed, it would never be mistaken for an ordinary run of the mill van. P.T., Ma-Browns third youngest -to my knowledge- of 14 grandsons jumped out before the last ping of gravel pinged its doors. "Miss Bethie betcha didn't know I'm almost old enough to drive."

"Almost?"

"That's surely right Miz Bethie. Next week come Monday first thing... well, not exactly first thing, the suns gotta rise and folks has to eat first and Gramma and Miz Morrison has to open the shop and all, but first thing after that, I'd say somewheres about 9 or 9:30 dependin' on how Gramma's arthritis is botherin' her, me and her, we're goin' to the Secretary of State's Office down there in the courthouse...la, ain't you proud of that courthouse?... and she's gonna sign a buncha papers and we're gonna get me a special drivin' permit thang. Sure hope it's purty. I don't want no special permit thang unless it's downright purty I prefers green but grandma says I should hesh and take it even ifin' its pink. Me, take anything pink? I'm, sproutin' up too bein' a full growed man. Men and pink don't go nowheres together."

Audacious boy insulting pink! Mollie Kate tried to declare war, but with P.T., she couldn't charge, she had to take cover.

"Me and gramma, we done got it worked out, long as I gots an adult with me, I can drive anywheres less there's an emergency special delivery like this un here. Then she puts my guardian angel in the passenger seat and lets me drive. Gramma said next week was just a few hours away, and she shore didn't want these here yallar roses to wilt none so me and my angel, we're right here makin' a special delivery. I ask how come she didn't put Jesus in the passenger seat and she said he has enough to do without takin' me on." He took a deep breath.

I managed a very weak "Oh my!" The kids didn't have that much time. P.T. didn't notice. "Miz Bethie you looked so surprised to see me I reckon you didn't get gramma's call. Iffin my showin' up unexpected like gave you a fright, I shorely am sorry I gots to pologize."

Mac Duff managed a short version of my misadventure. Something like "Phone, ran, tripped" if that much.

"Miz Bethie I'm thankin' the Good Lord you didn't get hurt none but surely sorry you took a fall! What a morning! Seems like all I'm doin' is pologizin.' I'm downright sorry for that!"

Mellie and Mollie Kate found voice. "Do what?"

P.T. grinned. "Anyways, I'se so glad to see y'all, I nearly forgot what brung me here. Miz Bethie that Yankee man of yours shore must love you lots.!"

Opened double doors released cascading bouquets of yellow roses. They tumbled like dozens of raw eggs from a broken crate. The cascade grew and spread side to side. Free at last. They were free at last.

I lost count. True: breathtakingly beautiful. Also true: Ralph maxed out his credit cards. Then I realized Ralph had advanced to step three. Step One: guilt. Step Two, self doubt. Step Three: make it all better. The warm up was goodies for the kids, and the candy and coffee. Then with Ma Brown's help, he'd arranged this overabundance. I wanted to run and hide somewhere; anywhere trouble free, safe and cool and comforting.

Michigan gal friends always envied my roses. Big Ralph was "Soo romantic. Soooo sweet, soooo thoughtful. Their husbands should take lessons and shower them with roses and candy. They wished they were married to a big handsome man. (emphasis on big). I gave up. "Girls you need the rest of the story."

Their looks said I'd gripe if hung with a gold rope. They needed, but didn't want or get the rest of the story. Probably a good thing as they wouldn't have believed it anyway. Soooooo sorry girls.

I wanted to douse Ralph's "Make everything better" offering with gasoline and have the world's biggest rose fire. Once the wind blew away rose dust it would be like they never were. But I had to think of the kids. Wonder of wonders I knew what to do. "P.T., y'know what?"

Surprising us, P.T. waited quietly. The kids stopped counting. Eyes like spotlights focused on me. I smiled, and without a hint of my need to barf, shared my plan to cheer hospital patients

"But mommmmm" came from three voices. "I didn't say all." They backed down but still looked hurt. I was ready.

"You kids think how selfish I'd be keeping these beautiful roses when they could do so much good at the hospital. You know your grandma loves yellow roses much as I do." "Yeah," three voices said. Then Mellie caught the fever. "We always talk to that old man across the hall, and there's Miss

Robbie." They stopped frowning and my big finish turned the tide. "P. T., here's the important part. You must tell every patient, visitor, new parent, nurse, aide, doctor, technician, cook office worker and custodian that Mellie, Mac Duff's and Mollie Kate's dad sent the roses from Michigan because he cares so much.

For the first time since he'd discovered words could either charm--or exhaust-- P.T., was speechless. His big brown eyes went back and forth from me to the kids back and forth, back and forth before shifting and locking on the roses. Then quietly, "Miz Bethie that there's a passel of roses. Grammy took forever getting 'em from the Saint Louis Flower Exchange cause your Yankee wouldn't settle for nothin' but yaller roses." Voice returning to normal "Grammy tried to get a few white and pink ones, told him it'd take awhile to make 'em all yeller but he didn't keer. He said he didn't want no white rose or pink rose or red rose or peace rose, or purple rose either for that matter."

P.T. paused long enough to scratch his head. "That bothered me some Miz Bethie. Honest Injun Miz Bethie does they really make a purple rose? I shore ain't never heard of no purple rose Miz Bethie. That man of yours sure is a caution Miz Bethie."

"What's a caution mom?

"Mellie answered, "I'm not sure, but from the size of P.T.'s grin, it must be o.k."

Mollie Kate managed to open her mouth. A fully recharged P.T. cut her off. "Don't get me wrong Miz Bethie. I think you're doin' a mighty fine thing. And for sure, I don't mind deliverin' roses to sick folk. Fact is, I'd be some proud to do it. When I tell Grammy I took them sick folk roses and prayed with 'em, she'll be right pleased. Count of how she's plum set in me takin' up preachin'.' She might even give me the cash money raise I've been askin' for."

He laughed. "Y'know, that there raise is a doubt. I'm thinkin' a real serious one. Every single time I asks Grammy how come she only wants to pay me one whole dollar stead of a dollar fifty an hour for deliverin', she gives me one of them there looks all you ladies is good at givin'. Then she follers that by askin' if I think all that food I eat and clothes I wear done grows on trees." P.T. shook his head as if understanding women, especially his Grammy was too hard a chore.

I jumped in before he exhaled. I said "Yes! Deliver them now," and would have said more but Mac Duff was busy cheering his dad.

"If dad was a scout, he'd get a merit badge because helping sick people is something we do." The girls beamed. My trio was ready with "Motherrrrr, are we having fun yet?"

With all but one small arrangement of nauseatingly lovely yellow roses reloaded in the splendiferous van, we followed P.T. from the driveway. He cut off at Fourth Street and we headed into town.

First stop, Big Pa Donzee's Wild West themed drug store, where our memories and reality were identical. Mollie Kate's stuffed bear stood exactly where she remembered, guarding magazines and pain pills. Above the soda counter, the long mirror of legend gleamed. Was it really and truly from a saloon in Dodge City Kansas? Had women from the Temperance society really took lye soap and scrub brushes and scrubbed away a picture of a purt near necked woman? The mirror's origin covered two paragraphs of the historical society pamphlet without mention of a necked lady or women with scrub brushes. Still the story lived on. Maybe because the big ruckus over men sharing facts of life with their sons under that mirror was true and the story had to live? Families know, but they ain't sayin.' Our favorite cowboy murals covered every wall. Every visit we stare at lonesome cowboys roundin' up little doggies or hunkered around a campfire. We always promise that someday, we'll pack our bags, go west, and camp under jillions of stars too bright and beautiful to count.

Cherry cokes, fifteen cents during my teen years, were now a quarter and the sign posted last Thanksgiving, said that price would go up "any day now." We weren't worried. Wild bunch that we were, we alternated between dipping French Fries in Cherry Coke and catsup.

We used hours to visit every favorite nook, cranny, old grandpa and granny in Sainte Lillian and spent way too much time in the museum. When we're surrounded by what was it's always easy to forget things we absolutely need do; like buy gas and shop at the IGA. We forced ourselves away.

Surrounded by paper bags of groceries, stretched out and relaxing their 'dogs" the kids peppered me with questions. In no particular order, I heard: "Mom I'm glad we saw the Plaid sisters again. They know so much stuff. Member Thanksgiving when we talked to them and dad said they were old biddies? What's a biddy, and why do they talk so much? Is that what a biddy does mom? Honestly! Boys! Mother explained that biddies are old chickens too tough to eat and too old to lay eggs so they walk around the chicken yard clucking chicken crossed the road jokes. Honestly, don't your remember important stuff? And, mom, if you let them tell us about the two headed kitten that nursed with both heads, why won't you let them tell us the whole tornado story? It's history ain't it? And don't cross your eyes motherrrr you know what we mean; the stuff you keep the Plaid sisters from talking about. Every time they get close you look at us and they go on to something else. Anyway, Franklin Mac Duff that Biddy stuff ain't as interesting as the story about Jane used to be Winter's problem in high school. Sometimes I wonder if we'll

Mom make her stop using my full name. When you got chips, you two missed the really good stuff about the double wedding when Melanie Morrison married that Jewish lawyer and Jane married Melanie's old boyfriend George Clayton. Motherrrr wasn't it so funny when Mrs. Brown got embarrassed about admitting she drank wine at the wedding and then Mac Duff tried to make her feel better by telling her our daddy grows grapes to make wine? Oh Motherrr, I wanted so bad to laugh at the way her face changed. Oh mother, it's so heavenly that Jane and George are going to have a baby and we get to help make decorations for the baby shower? I just love doing things like that. With the baby due in about eight weeks, we really have to get busy. I'll bake cakes motherrrr. Everyone loves my Krazy Kakes and I'll help make decorations too. We're really going to have a lot more 6-21-14." Silence sudden and deep. Then three voices with one message. "Mom we can't go home now."

It was almost the end of a perfect day. And for my dear older sister, almost is as good as it got.

Twenty-Two

My favorite If I's include: If I had spent five minutes more at the IGA, If I had not listened to the kids and for the first and last time driven Maple Brook Road like a moonshiner running from revenuers, If I had not... Naturally, the wondering If I's lead to conclusions: then I, then Jannelle, then we, then Mom and pop, and on into infinity.

Fortunately, we used those five minutes recklessly, but as it turned out wisely. We didn't miss Janelle's planned exit. She did.

When she called the house and found us out, Jannelle tuned in to her version of 6-21-14, delivered her packages, and was heading home to "Yes Dear." She was so proud she couldn't wait another minute to share her exciting news.

Her daddy was happy now because he and momma were home together the way he wanted. Deep down in her heart, she knew Bethie and the kids would be as happy--- if not more so.

Jannelle's eyes misted as she thought how her unselfish act would spare Bethie daily trips to hospital and nursing home. She could see Bethie's smile; and the kids. Oh my! Thinking about their excitement made her heart swell with contentment. She pulled a gardenia scented tissue from her ever ready supply. Genteel way in play, she dabbed her eyes without smudging mascara or make up.

As we neared the house, the kids were poking around in grocery bags. Mac Duff grumbled, "Who in their right mind eats Grits, Okra and Collard Greens." "Mom does," a sister said and another resigned sister voice added... "You know every time we're here we've gotta eat that stuff at least once. Mom says it's a good cultural experience." Mac Duff said

"Oh yeah!" and decided to slink down until I could just see the top of his head in the rear view mirror.

Digesting the impact of their once again becoming sacrificial lambs for southern cooking, brought momentary gloom. Maybe they thought about Southern fried chicken, because the mood changed.

When I turned into the circular driveway, Mac Duff perked up. "When grandpa and grandma come home, we're goin' fishin'. He says he won't go, but I have a plan, and it's gonna work." Hungry girls drooled over thoughts of their grandma's strawberry shortcake and homemade hand churned ice cream. Mellie said grandma had to help her with knitting and Mollie Kate said "I'm gonna tell grandma I need different needles. Maybe if she…"

Fishful thinking and knitting needles vanished into thin air as Mac Duff shouted in a tone both question and incredulous statement, "Grandpa! Grandma!" His voice faded to a whisper.

Caught in the moment, he ran toward them before the last bit of red gravel did its denting best against the van door. Then he froze in mid stride and did a slow turn. Without music, my son became a graceful music box dancer... On one revolution he stared at me, and then in a slow graceful spin he revolved to stare at two little old people.

Separated, she snug in her hospital bed, he secure and protected in the nursing home, they were still grandma and grandpa. Together, who were they?

I wanted to run back to big grouchy dependable Ralph; sometimes glad, sometimes bad, but manageable Ralph. He was alive. He was breathing. But were they, this very old almost unrecognizable couple standing by the door?

I had waited for this moment with the anticipation of a child waiting for 'the gift' on Christmas morning. Now, two frail old imposters stood where my mom and pop always stood. They were good, able to mimic my parents, with arms opened in welcome. I blinked. Two arms were open. The other two were stretched wedding bands keeping them upright. I wanted my parents, the parents of my memories and my dreams, not this, not these, not them.

Jannelle, bless her overly filled with denial heart, couldn't see the reality the kids and I faced head on. Jannelle saw her beloved daddy home with his bride where she could care for him. They would be so happy. Samantha Lynn and her family would help and she and Marvin would be worry free and available for supper. Once again, life at Maple Brook Road was perfect for Jannelle.

According to her script, the kids and I would walk in on mom and daddy having tea in the kitchen. After laughter and hugs and everyone talking at once, the day would fade into a perfect golden sunset. Everything washed in gold the way she liked it. Her problem was two fold; we got there before she left, and mom and pop followed her out. She had specifically told them to wait and surprise Bethie and the kids. Why hadn't they listened? What could she do? Fortunately, her migraine kicked in.

Each holding onto the other, mom and pop looked like they might withstand winds no stronger than two mph. My parents, the whole, hale, healthy parents who always welcomed us were now like shrunken apples on a winter worn tree. "Better call the old biddies and spread the news," I said. Mac Duff said "Mom!" But he knew.

Was this little bent thing my mother? I blinked three times. The urge to turn away and look for my mom was so strong.

And pop? This skin over bone caricature wasn't my muscular pop. His loosely fitting pants and shirt made him look like a straw starved scarecrow. Exposed flesh resembled fading speckled leather tossed aside to rot in the changing seasons.

"Jannelle, I said, and what I wanted to add had to wait. I had to think of them --whoever they were-- and my kids.

Instantly defensive, Jannelle charged full mouth ahead, and proved she was Uncle Jethro's favorite niece. "How could you spoil my surprise? Her lower lip quivered, and tears threatened. As her blubbering started before we were together five minutes, I knew this to be a new record in our book of sisters.

I spat questions so fast she could only blink. "Did you talk to Samantha Lynn? Did you ask if we could do this? What about the doctors? What do you think is next?" She backed up at that one. How dare I ask her that? She knew I knew what she knew would happen. Routine would kick in. Just like always.

Definitely tissue time. She didn't need comfort. She needed slapping. But, much as I wanted to, I couldn't. Besides it would be unjenteel of me to knock sense into aunt Pittypat. And I had to think of the kids. The old people. Whoever they were.

"Bethie and you kids, we're not going to stand here all day." I didn't see mom in that poor little body, but I knew her unchanging voice. By force of will, my fist unclenched one finger at a time. Fingers became part of hands, arms moved ready as a unit to hug the masquerading couple.

The wrinkled old man assigned the role of my pop bowed and offered his arm to the frail lady who had mom's voice. "My bride," he said.

She placed her pale blue veined hand on his arm. "Dear boy," she said.

Jannelle whispered "Listen to him Bethie"

"Listen to what?"

"Bethie this is so cute. Stop asking questions for once in your life and listen. He's been singing to her all afternoon.

I opened my mouth, looked at my misty eyed sister-- shut my mouth, turned toward them, and stopped pretending.

Pop caressed mom's white curls with a shaking hand. Her arm moved slowly like she needed extra strength to raise it to touch his face. Jannelle, my kids and I were silent members of a very small audience, as we heard pop's recognizable completely in tune solo.

"Silver threads among the gold.

Darling you are growing old.

But my darling you will be

Ever fair and young to me."

"Dear boy" mom said in a voice that was almost young.

Together they walked across the concrete porch.

Did Jannelle see their feet not leaving the pavement? Could she hear the soft sound of dry leaves in a chill wind as their slippers traveled the years? Why did I ask myself these questions?

Jannelle saw what she wanted to see. She was Mollie Kate playing with her Barbie and Ken dolls. "They're so cute" Mollie Kate said when she dressed Barbie in a red strapless formal, Ken in a black Tuxedo.

They're so cute" Jannelle said.

"Cute?" Was she nuts? These little things doing their best to greet us were so old, so sick, and so weak I couldn't bear to watch. My best effort combined a pasted on smile and eyes focused somewhere over their heads. Blue shutters, Navy blue shingles, soft blue white sky turning into evening registered. They didn't. They were not cute. They were anything but cute. They were, but how could they be my parents.

My eyes rested on the porch. There, marks on the concrete made over countless summers with hammer and ice pick when we mangled blocks of ice into chips small enough to fit around the ice cream freezer drum. Marks made so long ago visible now only to the knowing eye. I knew. It was easier focusing on fading marks than on old fading parents. It hurt to know marks in concrete and the mishmash of good and bad memories were made so long ago.

There, shading maple trees so small when planted. Little trees then now grown tall and branched out. Different. Like me and my sisters. And they who nurtured daughters and trees were now shrinking and fading.

I had to force myself to watch. Together, they smiled at me and my three big healthy kids. I almost felt frail arms embracing me, the short breath expelled from blue lips on my cheek.

Pop smelled. And it wasn't body odor or after shave lotion. I sniffed again this time deeper and longer. Bourbon?

"Jannelle?" I said. Once more her name was enough.

She was too pleased with herself to lie. "Good Kentucky bourbon. Really old. Cost an arm and a leg. Daddy said it smelled almost as good as shine and would make him feel better. Bethie he even talked mom and me into a toddy. We sat at the table and chatted while he cut lemons and played bartender. He was so cute."

She couldn't shut up. Everything her daddy did was so cute. He bowed, it was cute. He draped a dishtowel over his arm when he served them. It was so cute. Everything he did was so cute. Was she nuts or blind or both? Barbie Doll cute was not part of this picture. Was there an off chance she wanted me to tell her exactly what to do with cute?

More bragging. "You know how daddy likes BBQ at The Pig?" The whole town knew that. Did she want an answer? Finally, she made eye contact.

"Yes." One word came from my tight lips. Satisfied, she took her tongue out of the page and continued her cute story. "He bought us lunch there. He ate two spicy pork sandwiches with extra hot sauce a double cole slaw and baked beans and spiced up the beans with three packs of Louisiana hot sauce. Then he up and ordered a double on French Fries and Onion rings. I couldn't believe he had room for anything else, but you know daddy and food."

"Jannelle there's not a person in Saint Lillian: town, county or rural routes that doesn't know pop and food," I said. This time she caught the sarcasm and put her cute story of her cute daddy and momma's cute reunion on hold long enough to glare.

That done, her cute story continued. She was so proud of her daddy. "Seemed like he started on the left side of their menu and worked his way to the dessert side. He polished off a strawberry sundae with a double dip on berries and whipped cream. He was grinning like a little boy. You should have been there Bethie."

My hands clenched into nails biting flesh fist. "Don't you dare tell me that was cute," I said.

She was using so much energy wiping her eyes her usual cautious genteel way, she didn't hear my threat. Implied or otherwise, I wasn't sure what I'd have done anyway, and fortunately, "cute" didn't leave her mouth.

It gets better Bethie. You know how picky mom's been about her food lately…well, that didn't stop him. He ordered her bbq beef, slaw and fries and a banana milkshake and she ate everything. Even slurped the last of the shake like a little kid. She said everything was perfect. I know with their appetites and you and the kids doing for them they'll be better in no time."

Jannelle was so pleased with herself and so out of touch. I was torn. Should I say, or should I do what was playing in my mind. Fortunately, the county jail wasn't that inviting. Had to think of the kids, had to think of mom and pop.

She knew pop had diverticulitis, that spicy food gave him cramps and diarrhea. And he topped that off with strawberries? What was she thinking? Better yet, had she stopped to think? Over the years, we lost track of emergency runs to the hospital because he wouldn't stop eating strawberries. He would scream with pain, cry worse than a woman in labor and, soon as he was better, give strawberries another chance. Did she know or care what the good old down home greasy cooking and that wonderful whiskey would do once it mixed with their meds?

The kids waited at my side. Truth hurt more by the second. Their old formula: grandma and grandpa get bad sick, we come, they get all better, wasn't in place. They knew there would be no trips to the Saint Louis Zoo, no picnics at Elephant Rocks, and no fishing at Lake Sa Ho Li. Yet, they held on to hope. Always before, we'd worked miracles. Their eyes begged for reassurance we would do it again. Funny, how sun bright sky can make eyes mist.

Their grandparents moved from our hugs in a slow bent over creep a learning to crawl baby could best. "Dry leaves that before the wild hurricane fly," I said to the wind.

I grabbed for good times like a drowning swimmer grabs at a helping hand, and held them close, and released them with a mournful sigh. Now was the time to put yesterday away.

Pop escorted mom to the chaise like a Grand Duke escorting his Duchess. He covered her legs with a soft yellow afghan, and did little touchy things that spoke of love and assured comfort. Mom patted his cheek. "My dear boy," she said.

Jannelle looked at me with raised eyebrows. Thank the Lord she didn't say cute.

Our small not real talk ended when pop bent to kiss mom's hand. A loud noise like a bursting balloon produced the fermented odor of everything he'd eaten in three days. Low to the ground summer wind became instantly overripe.

One was never enough for pop. His encore performance lasted longer. Mom said "My Dear Boy!" It was the closest I'd ever heard her come to swearing.

Jannelle gasped, inhaled, and turned a shade of yellow green. She knew. "Bethie I've got another migraine coming on. I must get home to Marvin."

Cute was gone on the wind, and with it. Poor sis. She thought her headache was bad then, what would she think in half an hour? Another of my dumb questions but this time I had the answer. Usual for Jannelle was going to change. Put another way, it was Jannelle's time to listen.

She read my face and knew what was coming. Tears welled. Another gardenia scented tissue magically appeared and true to her delicate feminine pattern, she avoided the ultimate disaster of smeared mascara or makeup.

I snarled "Turn off the tears," and with a good strong sisterly hug, I drug her closer to mom and pop. Slowly. Rib nudges our parents couldn't see worked wonders. Jannelle tried gasping and dragging her feet. She didn't want to go there, not where the air was so---so indelicate. She didn't have a choice.

Sister to sister whispers: "I can't stand that smell. Stop pushing me."

"Jannelle this is just the beginning. Take a deep breath darlin' you started this and you're gonna finish it."

Tears in her voice. "Bethie Marvin needs me. I can't stay."

"I'll handle him Jannelle. Now you need to pull on your nursing gloves and clean up what you started. Then dear sister make plans for the middle of the night because you're gonna be here when pop's high wears off." She glared. "And for a long time after," I said and meant it.

She tried to faint. I pinched her. She couldn't swoon and cry 'ouch' at the same time.

"Take another deep breath Jannelle." We both turned green, but that didn't stop me. "Will pop walk away during the night? Will mom have another bad breathing spell? Got your plans made sis?"

Jannelle didn't want my 'rude' questions. She wanted her way because after all, she always had her way. Tears always worked before and she kept a ready supply for emergencies. "Honestly, Bethie" (muted sobs) you don't understand. I had no other choice. (Dramatic brave try at stopping tears). "Really I didn't. The nursing home staff said they had enough to do without chasing down an old man day and night. They said I had to bring him home today. Not tomorrow Bethie! Today!" (Strong nurse reverting to helpless victimized female) "I felt so helpless, and I knew he'd be so happy at home. They had him packed and us out of there in twenty minutes. Daddy said with you and the kids here we could spring momma from the hospital. Honestly Bethie you should have been there when he said "spring momma" He sounded like Edward G. Robinson. He was so"... "Whatever you do, don't say cute Jannelle." She heard the cold Yankee tone in my voice and stuttered. "Well, he was so dramatic, so gallant," she said and watched my reaction. I stared her down and waited.

"Nurses tried to stop us at the hospital, but mom signed herself out. Then daddy said we had to celebrate at The Pig. After that we went to Tom's for the whiskey and, and, and, well, here we are." She wiped her eyes and smiled through her tears, and delivered her guaranteed winning grand finale. "Bethie daddy didn't mean to do that. You can take care of it. You and the kids have handled them before. It's not like you'll be alone. Samantha Lynn's near, and Marvin and I will check every evening and weekends." To make sure she knew I knew her intent, I translated. "That means you'll be here for supper, and a fast exit before we do dishes or you get another migraine."

"Bethie," she sobbed helplessly and managed to pull another tissue and do that thing again. "I know you didn't mean to sound mean. I know you understand. Now I really have to go home to Marvin."

With one breath Jannelle told me the way it was. Of course medication, what if anything doctors said and other 'minor' details were left out. She couldn't bear that. She knew when she told me I'd tell Samantha Lynn and overnight all of heaven and Sainte Lillian would know. She couldn't bear that! She'd done her part, now it was time for me to take over, and clean up her mess and time for her to go home to Marvin. Dear "Yes dear," was worried to death. He needed her.

I tried to not breathe and failed. The kids were doing their best to move down wind while Jannelle was doing her best to leave me with what she started Poor sis. Sister to sister close, we walked away from out watching parents. Jannelle convinced she'd won again was ready for another grand exit. She pulled keys from her jeans pocket.

I, knowing truth was about to smack her between the eyes and set me free, said "Not this time Jannelle."

It was her turn for the fish out of water act. Her keys flew to Mac Duff before she could blink. After one questioning look, he flashed an understanding grin. "Can't catch me," he challenged his sisters. They escaped on winged feet.

I remembered mom's letter. Now was my turn to tell Jannelle no. Only I wouldn't be gentle. To keep kids and parents out of hearing distance, Jannelle and I took a little walk. The "Damn Yankee" in me took over. Ralph would have been so proud.

Twenty-Three

Why had he lost track of time? How many days did he hurry home expecting them there? Where were his kids? How many night had he stared at Bethie's side of the bed? Hell! There was no need to count hours and days, he knew what she was up to! By now Bethie'd hooked up with her old boyfriend, good old Sheriff Hale or Fail or was it Jail? Yeah, good old sheriff Jail. He knew they were poisoning his kids against him.

Last few times he'd called Boy the kid could hardly talk. Hell, it was only midnight—maybe a couple hours past. Boy said he'd been sitting by the phone reading the Bible and musta dozed off. Sounded like he could hardly stay awake. Ralph knew for a fact he hadn't heard right. His Boy reading the Bible that time of night! No way! Why the hell would the kid do that?

He read the Bible on Sunday when Pastor John used his deep commanding preacher voice and said "Turn in your Bible to…" such and such a place. Boy did it for him because he was quicker at the kind of stuff. But his Boy readin' that holier than thou crap on his own at that hour! Hell no!

Maybe he was. Lately, Boy cut him off as he shared jokes from guys at the sports bar. Kid said he liked good jokes, but all that sex and cussin' wasn't funny." You and mom are raising us to be Christians; we're going to church and all." Ralph didn't get a chance to ask what "all" meant, because the kid jumped into stories about Sainte Lillian Free Methodist youth pastors Howie and Cartier starting a youth Bible Quiz group. "We're doing a whathamacallit dad." Long pause. Ralph had no idea. Boy replaced whatchamacallit with view. "You know, some kind of view."

Ralph bit. "Preview?" "No dad that's not it." Another pause longer than the first. "Well, maybe, kinda sorta." "Review?" "No dad. Put your thinkin' cap on. Wait! I've got it. Kinda like an introduction. Yeah!" Overview! That's what they call it. Like they hold the Bible up and shake out the gooder parts. Get it?"

Ralph's laughter built inside. That Boy. His Boy!

The more Boy talked Bible, the more Ralph tuned out. He wondered if he'd know his son when they came home from that God forsaken hick hillbilly town. The kid didn't talk fishing, or merit badges, or complain about his sisters. It was Bible this, and Bible that. Soon we're gonna study the book of John. That's in the New Testament case you forgot. Our youth pastors say that's the best book to start serious reading. I hope we'll do Bible Quiz at home. Dad y'know what? You gotta read this New Testament."

"What do you mean in case I forgot? Doncha remember Matthew, Mark, Luke and John, everybody quick get their hard hats on? Are you telling me that hillbilly New Testament is different than ours? And while I'm asking, did you buy yourself a coupla youth pastors?"

"C'mon dad! Stop the corny jokes. Pastor Howie says we gotta carry the Bible lessons in our minds ready to use like a flashlight in the dark. He says the Bible's the best guide book ever."

Kid sounded like he'd been given a million bucks. What's your problem son? You're acting like it's a friggin' sin to laugh".

"Dad if you listen, I'll tell you. You gonna listen?"

Ralph doubted any answer would please the kid so he waited. Words poured into his burning ear. "When we read to think about good things, I asked if jokes were good. I told one of yours that you like, you know, the one about the old log inn. They looked kinda funny and got quiet. Then Pastor Cartier said when jokes didn't have swear words or put down other people or make sex sound dirty they were fine. He said to look for sit-ua-tio-nal comedy."

Ralph knew and was damn sure Boy knew a good joke had to be spiced with vulgarity. After all, that's the only kind he told. He ignored the latest mini-sermon on his multiple mistakes and wrongs, and focused on Boy breaking down words. Was he turning into another windbag like Jethro?

Boy's voice again, word together. ""Situational! That's it! Pastor Howie said with all its bumps and bruises life can be really funny even hilarious. I know I said hilarious right dad so don't fuss at me for not choppin' it up first."

Fighting laughter, Ralph coughed. It was the best he could do.

"Pastor Howie said life has lots of funny stuff and re-runs of Red Skeleton and I Love Lucy are full of situational comedy. Pastor Howie said if God didn't love laughter, he wouldn't have created puppies and kittens. Good thing God did dad.—Puppies and kittens I mean--cause we ain't got time for TV, and grandma's dogs sure make us laugh. When Bodacious chases his tail he gets so dizzy he falls over. Then skipper and Pete tackle him. Grandpa says it's like having a houseful of rambunctious boys. What's rambunctious mean dad?"

Ralph gave up and their laughter joined. He missed his chance to define rambunctious whatever the hell it was. He knew he could come up with something if Boy went back to it...like a kid being like a ram bucking into things. Might work, anyway, it put ram and bucking together.

"Dad, you laughed about the dogs, and nothing I said was dirty. I'm tired of dirty jokes. They're more mean than funny. I don't know why you laugh.

Ralph shouted his anger but Boy talked him down. "Other than not liking it dad, you know I'm a scout and a Christian and we don't talk dirty. Jesus didn't. Not ever dad. Not one time. Even when they beat him up, He didn't."

Boy sounded near tears. "Dad sometimes you sound like you don't respect women." Then he launched into his version of front page news. "My mom is a lady. My sisters are little ladies and my aunts and both my Grammies are ladies too. Just Grammies are older, but the same thing. Dad, all the ladies we know aren't like your jokes."

Pissed him off. Who the hell the kid think he was? His own son telling him what to and what not to say, and acting like his mother and all the women they knew were goodie two shoes saints.

If the kid wanted a sermon, he'd give him one on back talk. It wasn't the first time he'd yelled into a dead phone. One night he forgot he was talking about Bethie and made a side comment. Money? Big boobs? Wide ass? He didn't remember and it didn't mean anything. It was just man talk, the way real men talk

That was another time boy got real quiet. Ralph heard him breathing, choked up like he was holding in tears. Boys don't cry. His opportunity to tell Boy his dad wouldn't let him cry escaped when the years disappeared.

He was waiting to cross the street coming home from school. Best Buddy, his yellow tiger cat waited on the porch railing just like always. He spotted Ralph and ran to him just like always. Three years of always ended.

This time Best Buddy didn't run into Ralph's arms, but under the front tires of a speeding green coupe. Ralph was close enough to hear the last sound Best Buddy ever made; a strange garbled cry full of pain. He was spun around like a toy and spat out directly in line for the back tire. The car didn't stop.

Ralph dropped everything: report cards, notes to parents, and homework, and screamed so loud his mom ran from back of the house. He scooped Best Buddy in his arms and ran indoors. He didn't know blood covered his hands and shirt and bits of Best Buddy, fur and bone and flesh stained his new jeans. He only knew Best Buddy was hurt bad and they had to save him. His dad fixed things. He could fix Best Buddy.

Dad took one look and said the cat was dead. His voice was like Best Buddy didn't matter, like he didn't sleep on his pillow every night or share his breakfast scrambled eggs or sit on his lap and purr when he worked long division. His dad grabbed Best Buddy and wrapped him in the Sunday Funnies and threw him in the trash. Ralph remembered Best Buddy's blood turned Prince Valiant and Peanuts dark red. Then his dad shook him till his head hurt and said words he'd never forget. Words that had the habit of sneaking up on him at the damnedest times. He could hear his dad's voice, the cold anger of it. "For God's sake, doncha know real boys don't cry over dead cats! Stop your god danged bawlin' and change your crappy clothes."

For the first time ever, his mother stood up to the old man. She took Best Buddy out of the bloody funnies and swaddled him in a brand new white bath towel. All they saw was the tip of one blood smeared ear. Ralph took a wet wash rag and tried to wipe blood away, but it just stained Best Buddies ear darker, kinda takin' the yellow away, turning it brown red.

Best Buddy's coffin was one of his dads big work boot boxes. Before they taped the lid on, they covered him with yellow and white roses until all they could see was yellow and white stripes soft and beautiful just like Best Buddy.

Him and mom dug the grave together while the old man stood at the back window watchin, not sayin' a word, just watchin.' Mom said Best Buddy would be happy by the lilac bushes because he loved to lie in the sun and watch everything; clouds and birds and grasses waving in the wind. When they finally finished the last shovelful of dirt and patted it down smooth, mom grabbed him, held him tight and cried like her heart was broke. Ralph remembered holding on to her like she was his only lifeline. Finally, he hurt so much inside, much as he wanted to, he couldn't cry no more. Even the hell of Nam, the smoke and screams and stench of death didn't erase the memory of Best Buddy's death.

Boy's voice brought Ralph back." Dad I know when you talk about women you're talking about mom. You sound mad, like you did before we left. You told her she didn't have crap for brains when it came to time or family or money. But dad you didn't say crap. You used the 's' word. You said a lot of mean dirty things."

Ralph had enough. He was raising his son to be a man's man, not some lilly livered pussy. "Listen smart ass I know more about women than you'll ever know. I've had more women than…" Boy's voice clear and sharp cut him off "What does that mean dad?"

Ralph cursed under his breath, and lied his way out "I meant to say military experience and all, I know more about women than most men in friggin' hillbilly Sainte Lillian-- including your youth pastors—and he said that mean and slow, insulting the pastors as much as he dared-- will ever know. That's all." Before Boy questioned, "you better listen to me kid. You can bet your merit badges I'm a world class expert on women."

Boy got loud like he didn't care if he woke every friggin' fool in Sainte Lillian. "Uncle Mark and Marvin and Sheriff Hale and our youth pastors treat women the way they like to be treated. Dad you know the Sherriff's name is Hale so don't make a joke about that either. Another thing, his family is just like ours, just turned around."

Pissed as he was Ralph bit. "Like us but turned around? What the hell is that supposed to mean?"

Boy stopped shouting. "Think dad. There's a tall handsome dad but not as tall and handsome as you, a beautiful mom, but not as beautiful as mom, and instead of two girls and one boy, they've got two boys and one girl. Get it dad? Turned around." Boy laughed at his own genius. "Dad, that Sheila is kinda pretty." Ralph noticed the change in his sons' voice and felt a twinge of sadness His boy was growing up and they weren't together. "Dad you gotta hear this! Sheriff Hale's family had us over for a cookout. They had special wheelchairs for grandma and grandpa and dad you won't believe this, but I took grandpa fishin' off their boat dock. Dad I took grandpa fishin.' He caught a turtle!"

Boys prattling went up in smoke. He didn't remember that Grandpa and Boy fishing together was one of his son's life long dreams. He didn't care if the old fart caught a fish or a snappin' turtle. Explosive spittle sprayed the wall.

"Your mother dated that upstanding citizen. I remember the way he melted when she looked at him. Oh Yeah, I remember. He's suckin' up, that mother frickin' sonnabitch probably got you thinkin' he needs a merit badge.

Calm as you please, Boy said "You know I love you dad, but right now I'm havin' trouble with the respect part. I got to go." How many times had he heard that dark buzz? What the hell was wrong with that kid?

In his bedroom, Ralph dumped a full pillowcase of letters on the bed. In a lazy take all day slide, sealed letters found the carpeted floor. Ralph stared, seeing, not seeing white envelopes against brown work boots on the shadow green carpet.

Boy always asked why he didn't answer their letters and he always lied about being too busy. Boy said every night the whole family had devotions; Bible reading and discussion and prayer. "Then, dad we write to you. Every night I write what me and the girls do and they write their side of It."

Boy said family. Hell, they weren't family without him. Lost in thought, Ralph forgot to make his I'm not listening to this crap but make noises to make you think I am sounds, and Boy threw him a ringer. "You think me and the girls are doin' a good job helpin' out dad?"

Thinking fast, he awarded three merit badges apiece. Silence made him sweat. Then, "Considerin' the suckers and balloons, three might be enough. Just make mine the biggest because I scoop poop for three dogs."

Ralph's attempt to hide laughter made Boy panic. "Come on dad! I'm earning them. All by himself Bodacious makes more poop than our three dogs at home Even on Sunday!

Ralph groaned. Would Boy paint word pictures as his mother and grandma did. Would he include color, size, and odor? Wait a minute, it couldn't be all bad. Hell, if Boy talked about dog poop it was a good sign he wasn't all churchified!

"I'm tellin' you dad if we didn't stop that dog he'd eat a 20 pound sack of dog chow every day. And since I'm the apprentice man around here --mom done told me what that means dad-- I'm in charge of scoopin' that stuff and cleanin' the yard every day. Grandpa likes to walk all over the yard and one day when he was actin' weird he played with some. You shoulda heard Auntie Nellie yell. Bodacious is getting over an itch sorta like the mange. Grandpa said to mix sulphur with slab bacon grease and smear that on his hot spots. Problem is we only eat bacon on Sunday and then not as much as we want because of grandpa and grandma's diet. Mom said I should use olive oil and that dog licks it off like he's part Italian. But it's workin' dad. Only problem is Bodacious poops more. Dad did I say sulphur or sulfa? I don't remember, but it's yellow and it stinks. Dad I hope you're cleaning up after our dogs. I don't want to come home to a yard full of dog poop. Dad don't tell me you're too busy." His groan was pure boy agony.

This time Ralph didn't stop his laughter. "What kind of a dad do you think I am anyway?" Boy's voice, pure and clean. "Why, dad when you're not mad all the time, you're the best." Ralph choked. Hell, he wasn't mad all the time. Hell no! Stalling to clear his mind, Ralph cleared his throat and realized he sounded like dear old jackass Jethro.

Time to change the subject. Conversational like without a hint of sarcasm or anger, he said," The way you kids help must give your mom time to relax and run around."

Ralph found out he had a lot to learn." Dad are you serious? Mom's running around alright. She starts before sunrise and runs till past midnight. She takes grandma to the doctor every other day, and shops and cleans and cooks and takes us kids places. Last week Mellie had another of her bad ear infections. Mom took her to the ER at midnight and purt near didn't stop all day. How's that for runnin' around dad? Don't you read our letters?"

"Purt near! Don't use any hillbilly talk on me Boy," Ralph said but Boy was a far from ending his lesson.

"Yeah dad! When mom was running around in the garden, she found a cucumber patch. She's making your favorite pickles from Grandma Irene's recipe. The house smells like spicy pickle juice. Me and grandpa love it." A sudden intake of breath. "Dad don't tell mom I told you, they're a special surprise." He was so tempted to ask how the hell he could tell Bethie anything when he never talked to her, but Boy didn't give him time.

"I know you won't believe this dad, but mom has Auntie Nellie taking care of grandpa. She says he's worse than a houseful of kids. You shoulda heard mom lay down the law the day Aunt Nellie brought grandma and grandpa home. Aunt Nelly thought she was gonna surprise us. Honest dad she's the one that got surprised!

Also dad"…" Long pause for emphasis. Ralph had to admit the kid was good. "While mom's running around"…accent on running around… Mom pays their bills, does their banking, gets their medicine and takes care of everything else. Y'know what we had to do last week dad right in the middle of a big laundry? Well, I'll tell ya. We had to take wet clothes out of the washer, stack everything in wash tubs and drain the washer… one cup at a time dad… Betcha you never did that dad. And then we got this plug of something that looked worse than dog poop out of the hose and put the machine back together. Course then we had to change our clothes and mop the floor but we got 'er done. Funny thing dad, mom said that was a lot of fun. Y'think she was kidding?

Ralph knew to not bite.

"Then yesterday me and mom changed a flat on the van. Harold Robinson at the garage said to tell you he fixed up that flat so you'll never know it was. He said you weren't supposed to worry.

Oh yeah dad! Mom runs around a lot!"

Didn't the kid know when enough was?

Ralph stared at the pile of letters. Anger took over. He remembered full moon summer nights at their lakeside cabin. Water wore a silver blue sheen and lazy ripples lapped the shore. He could see their stone bordered fire pit, the red orange flames as they flickered and danced. He could smell pine scented air.

And her lips feather light as she snuggled into his shoulder and whispered in his ear. "Sweetheart it's so quiet we must be the only people awake in the world, yet creatures of the night are talking." He laughed. "Yeah, lions and tigers and drunks on skid row."

"Darlin' if you want magic, you have to listen: not to the noise, but to the quiet. Then as they lay bathed in moon glow, she whispered night secrets, and hypnotized him with her emerald eyes. Now was she whispering the same lies to old boyfriends? Thoughts about Bethie with other men tore his guts.

This crap about her parents had to be a lie. Hell, they'd been good as dead so many times he'd lost count.

Darkness. All around him darkness until his thoughts about Bethie faded and he was back with the last time he'd talked with Boy. Now it was like the kid was next to him. "Dad maybe I'm not interested in a career in construction. Y'know why dad? Well, I'll tell ya. The more I hang out with our youth pastors and Sheriff Hale, the more I think about becoming a pastor or working in law enforcement or both! How bout that dad? Can't you see me wearing a uniform and preachin'? That way dad I could be like them and always helping people. Ain't that great?

He didn't give Boy a damn thing, not one "yeah," or "say it again slowly," or Uncle Jethro sized throat clearing." This time, he hung up first. Maybe boys don't cry, but Ralph discovered grown men do.

Boy's voice wouldn't leave his mind. "Dad you gotta read the New Testament. Them two Corinthians and James and John and Romans are so cool. Revelation will scare the pants right off ya and make you really really glad Jesus took all our sins to the cross. Honest Dad!"

"Son I'm a hammer and nails man, I saw what I see. Get it?" Time was boy'd have laughed himself silly. Not this time. Another good joke slid into oblivion. He couldn't take the hurt of Boy not laughing.

First Bethie and her family stuffing him with the Bible and now his own son. Bet your sweet ass he believed in God. With a world full of evidence, he'd be a fool to not. Fact of the matter, we wouldn't know the difference between good and evil, and sure as hell wouldn't know about the devil if God didn't exist. But for God's sake did he have to hear it all the time? Can't a man be a man without looking over his shoulder scared to death he'd just sent his soul to hell?

This stuff about being born again and washed in the Blood of the Lamb. Washed in blood! He'd seen enough men washed in blood, seen them hosed down and white like they'd been bleached. Hell! Every friggin' person on this earth was born washed in blood. And their baby that died, nothing but flesh drowned in blood.

Bethie did her best to explain. What she didn't know was her words washed over him, not into him the way she intended. She said Old Testament sacrifices rams and lambs and bulls and pigeons and what not were sacrificed as atonement for sins, and they did it all the time. He remembered the smell of blood and burning flesh and paled.

Bethie reached out and touched his arm and smiled. She said "Then Jesus Came and daily sacrifices ended because He was the Lamb of God; the perfect and final sacrifice. He willingly shed his blood and took on the sins of all humanity. From then, until forever, all a person need do to be saved was believe and accept Jesus in their life. "Saved from what?" he asked. Before she could turn to verses in Matthew, he said he was a honest hard working man, never cheated nobody, and the good stuff he did guaranteed he was a Christian. She gave him one of those looks and said "Now Ralph honey...." and she went on and on and on. He pretended to listen and promised to think and pray and escaped. Sometimes he prayed. Sometimes he thought. Sometimes it was like he was being pulled apart

Ralph looked at Bethie's NIV Bible. Its red silk marker with her name embossed in gold letters was somewhere in the New Testament. He found it in Romans Eight and read verses she claimed as her own. Something about the love of God. Seeing, not seeing, he stared at the open Bible.

Twenty-Four

Collard Greens, batter dipped pork steak fried up nice and crisp, fried potatoes loaded with onion and smothered with pepper gravy and a great chunk of butter drippin' cornbread filled his plate. Mac Duff gave the Plaid sisters a pathetic pleading look, turned it toward me and his sisters, and sighed long and dramatically. Then like a good scout facing untold dangers, my brave son dug in.

Determined to win a merit badge for bravery above and beyond the call of duty, he complimented the beaming sisters. "Them there were the best collards I ever ate."

Mellie rewarded him with her version of the mom stare. "Franklin Mac Duff Brunswick, seein' as how they're the first…" In deep water after committing two all but unpardonable sins against her brother, Mellie didn't get to the third. It was lost in "Ooohmommm!" as her brother's right foot connected with her left shin.

Mollie Kate, not interested in their same old same old, wiped buttermilk from her upper lip and reached for more cornbread. She knew cornbread. She told the Plaids' theirs would be as good as her mom's if they'd add a little sugar and a pinch more salt.

I decided to let my perfect darlings crawl from their hole and busied myself with more collards. Chopped and cooked with bacon they were absolutely delicious.

"I declare to goodness, Bethie's boy Mac Duff had seconds on everything cept the pork steak and he ate half of a third. I'm tellin' you he's got his grandpa's appetite. The way he dug into them collards makes me wonder if Bethie's been feeding them kids right," said the Plaids to the Brown family. The Browns; man, woman and six kids did their duty. Up to the minute news went fence row to fence row. Duty called and the neighborhood and church family answered. Spurred into acts of exemplary culinary heroism, my son ate more greens than Popeye ever dreamed of, or ate. Every red blood American male or female under the age of 110 knows Popeye dreamed and ate a lot.

Mom begged off crowding around the dining room table. "Easier for all of you if I eat in my chair," she said. If her empty plates were an indicator, her appetite, other than for dessert, was every bit as good as pops. Every night as we enjoyed dessert in the living room she complained: "I can't eat another bite! My slacks are so tight they'll split." They laughed politely and raised eyebrows toward me. One raised eyebrow too many clicked. Stooping near her chair for an imaginary crumb, I saw-- if anything-- that her slacks were looser. Her compliments to the cooks cut off my "But, mom!"

I stopped halfway between interrupting and insisting she have dessert and thought how lately my straight talking mom sounded like a politickin' Democrat. Bianca Pegorer heard her lasagna was perfectly Italian. "Just the right amount of garlic and I adored the additional basil and oregano." Miz Brown's Chicken and Dumplings "would win the cook off." Pinkie Finn's Tuna Noodle Casserole "Had to have fresh tuna and home made Noodles," she said. Quoting her, quoting her, "I've never in my life tasted better. Your adding peas was a stroke of genius, the casserole was so colorful." Shy Pinkie Finn, who made her casserole at the last minute, wasn't about to say she used canned Albacore tuna and added two whole bags of frozen peas when she ran short on packaged noodles. Pinkie lived off that praise for a week.

With "nothing else to do," I put on an invisible cap and trench coat, chewed on an equally invisible pipe stem and became the female Sherlock Holmes. Elementary, my dear Watson. I watched mom's eyes on her friends. When they raved over Mollie Kate's moist rich Krazy Kake, she licked her lips. They sipped tea, she swallowed. Add: loose slacks, fatter dog, clean napkins, and plates and silverware all so clean it seemed a shame to waste soap and water, and I knew. I steamed. I stewed, I paced. I planned and, I kicked myself because I dressed her every day and was too focused on doing it to see what was literally under my nose.

During breakfast, Mac Duff donned my invisible detective gear. Pictures shot with our Polaroid instamatic proved that after two bites she fed everything to Skipper. No wonder she looked paler and weaker. No wonder her cutlery was so clean. No wonder Skipper's belly looked like a balloon. Next wonder: did she take her meds or flush them down the toilet?

My knees buckled as I realized what she was doing. I came so very close to breaking every plate and bowl Skipper had washed, and even closer to screaming in mom's face.

The kids didn't wait on what I wanted. Pictures in hand, Mac Duff stood in front of her. "Grandma, we caught you and you're under arrest." "Grandma me and Mollie Kate get up early to cook breakfast for you and you feed it to skipper!? How could you?" Mellie swiped tears away with the back of her crumb dotted right hand. I knew she'd never imitate Jannelle.

Mac Duff couldn't resist. He started with "Wellll," but when I walked in the famous mom stare worked and commentary on his sister's cooking ended.

Mom tried. Her pale blue veined hands reached for mine. Hers cold; so cold and lifeless. Small wrinkles of flaccid blue white flesh followed my fingers trying to massage warmth and life. Sluggish flesh dotted with freckle size age spots moved after, not under my fingers. First left, then right. slowly left, slowly right. Tired flesh. Blue. Cold.

These hands guided me and my sisters and little Jamie as we took our first steps; were comfort when we fell. Once warm and active, they directed our lives, and we were the song she sang. Now, there was no more music. Her red rimmed eyes spoke depression and defeat.

Then from her pale blue lips a voice I'd never heard before, a sad defeated voice. "Bethie I try to eat but after a bite or two, I get so nauseous. I can't. I'm tired. I'm worn out, and I'm not any good here. I want to be with my babies." Her white curl capped head rested somewhere above her chest. She looked away.

"Grandma" three voices said together. One word half sob, half plea, 100% love brought her back. There was hope in her voice as she spoke our names.

I said, "First we talk to Doctor Jolly."

"No more pills," she said.

"Then you will follow his diet and do everything he recommends. And, if he gives you more pills…" The mom stare worked on her too.

Three voices, equal intensity, equal determination "Yeah grandma!"

I talked food. "Remember scones, how we three girls sat at the kitchen table and cut raisins into tiny pieces. Remember Jannelle tried to eat half of every raisin she cut? Remember dicing apples and mixing them with our raisins and how Jannelle wanted more cinnamon and sugar."

She smiled. I should have stopped there, but since she wanted memories, I gave them to her. And went too far remembering: baskets of food at picnics, family reunions, with the whole family singing their hearts out. I gave her memories of harvest meals with tables overloaded with home fried chicken, pot roast and stews. Not one cake or pie but two or three or more and nothing left over at days end. I remembered birthday parties with her beautiful white cakes on tiered cake stands, and wiener roast on the creek bank. Memories supposed to make her feel better worked on me but not on her. Mom knew what was had been good, and that it wouldn't be again. It hurt. Through tight lips she whispered. "I can't do it Bethie. Just leave me alone."

I thought a lot of things. All I did was ask Jannelle to pack mom's bag for the hospital. "Doctor Jolly will have a room and IV's ready soon as I get off the phone" I said. For once in her life, Jannelle didn't argue. She raced for the bedroom. We heard the suitcase snapping shut before mom faced with the end all two choices, chose wisely, and surrendered.

We started with tapioca pudding and egg custard and moved into other favorites. Mrs. Freeman's world famous Chicken Noodle Soup topped the list. A kid, a dish, and a spoonful of pudding or soup or ice cream were ready whenever she opened her mouth. She complained "I'm not a Thanksgiving turkey, stop stuffing me." Two days later, with the long missing twinkle back in her eyes, 'if you must feed me, give me more than a spoonful." Skipper lost his dishwashing job and eventually his round belly. The kids earned so many merit badges they collected IOU's.

When the Plaid sisters brought supper again, she wanted a larger slice of cake. "We'll send Mac duff down cellar for the ice cream freezer tomorrow" she said. " Mollie Kate sang "6-18-21," and did a victory dance. The Plaids said that looked like fun and formed a conga line. These old ladies who blushed when admitting they'd tasted wine at Melanie's wedding weren't the least bit shy with high kicks. Pop whistled and applauded.

We lost track of time. Michigan was somewhere over there. We weren't sure, but knew it was….somewhere. When the kids stopped talking about going home I didn't use energy to mark the calendar. Naps came at traffic lights, and in Doctor Jolly's office. Mom's calls in the night kept deep sleep away but that was o.k., because the few times I fell into that dark hole, mad man Ralph was there. Cursing and screaming, he held his 357 on the dogs. Daymares and nightmares became one and the same, and mad man Ralph was there. Always.

Who, me, complain? No way! Compared to Jannelle, I had it easy. Jannelle had her daddy. I made sure she was totally responsible for this little old man who quote, "Looked so cute with mom. She, who always told mom to"try harder," earned her doctorate in that specialty from the university of the same name. Jannelle had her daddy.

To my Southern Belle sister, life with daddy wasn't funny. For me, it was better than a blender of I love Lucy, Red Skelton and TheThree Stooges. If something could go wrong, Murphy 's Law kicked in three times a minute. All Jannelle could do was...try harder. Watching her reaction was like watching clouds on a storm filled sun shadowed day. Mom said she liked my laughter, especially during early mornings as I watched Jannelle and her daddy do breakfast. Different men disguised as Jannell's daddy always sat in his chair. Man one was a hard working farmer at harvest time, eating twice-three times-- of everything in sight. Number two was precise and mannerly as a king, and number three, a dependent old infant smearing food in his hair. Jannelle had her daddy.

Pop loved country roads. Long lonely walks were his night time specialty. After his first adventure Jannelle put a recliner by his bedroom door. She slept, she snored, and her daddy tiptoed away. She fought back and tied silver bells around his ankles. They'll keep lions and tigers and bears away daddy...AND"-- her big sell-- "Things that go bump in the night!" He remembered his little girl Nellie always afraid of night sounds and his trick with silver bells and laughed. She slept confident bells would wake her. She snored. She lost.

Her daddy tiptoed past, and once free to roam used them as insurance against creatures of the night. He never remembered why police brought him home, and couldn't understand why Jannelle, his little girl who had never ever questioned anything he said or did, developed the habit of lecturing and yelling.

He hated bathing until Jannelle convinced him bathing got rid of bugs and germs. That worked for a week, and then Jannelle learned she had to...try harder. Pop decided cleanliness was what she wanted; he'd give it to her. He'd sit fully clothed in a tub of lukewarm water. She learned the hard way to check bathrooms first and more than once caught him just in time. Jannelle had her daddy.

The day she asked Mollie Kate's help in baking a Krazy Kake, I found enough voice to splutter something like "Jannelle! You, you..." and words failed. Each afternoon when her daddy napped Jannelle took over the kitchen. She loved it. I loved her breakfast blueberry Krazy Kake with streusel toppings

We worked, watched, and waited for the day we'd announce to the world our miracle was working. And we waited. Days of forward steps came slowly. Mom grew strong enough to visit the graves of her babies.

Pop spent more quality time with her and the kids. Small victories kept us hoping. Hope aside, truth was they kept on draining our strength.

On the bright side in a routine with few bright spots, Uncle Jethro kept his hands to himself and never 'tickled' me or my girls. Because I vowed my girls would never be alone with him, Mac Duff earned extra merit badges by supervising their time together. If Uncle Jethro got 'that' look in his eye and said "Mollie Kate, let's go down cellar for canned peaches," Mac Duff, Mellie, grandpa and Jannelle tagged along. Eventually, dear old uncle got my message. He didn't like it, and I didn't care.

Twenty-Five

Sunrise: One of those shrug my shoulders and get busier mornings. From the kitchen window, we watched the yellow orange fireball sun sip night damp in its walk across the lawn.

The kids pointed out a good sized dew wet brown rabbit doing its hip hop pause to nibble at clover blossoms waltz. Mollie Kate wanted to take him/her (she wasn't sure so she said Peter or Petunia) a carrot. Mellie said she knew "the cute wittle wabbit" wanted lettuce. Mac Duff said they couldn't catch that fur ball he'd send the dogs.

Jannelle said it would be a cold day in January before she let him send three vicious dogs after a poor defenseless bunny.

Mellie asked "Where did grandma and grandpa get vicious dogs."

Pop said he wouldn't mind a dish of rabbit stew.

Mom said rabbit stew with biscuits and gravy sounded real good, especially if we added lots of carrots and potatoes. Maybe a turnip or two.

Mollie Kate out shouted her brother and sister. "Grandma! Grandpa! How could you?

I love the sounds of home in the morning.

Jannelle smiled and handed me my first jolt of caffeine. I tasted before wondering if she brewed it and then looked into her grinning face. Perfect cakes, perfect casseroles, and now ladies and gentlemen, perfect coffee. Had we created an over achiever?

Mom looked at the phone, checked the kitchen clock, and reminded the girls she was cut off salt but her favorite doctor hadn't said a word about sugar. "More brown sugar in my Cream of Wheat girls. Every one of my

215

dentures is a sweet tooth." They giggled. She laughed. She kept her eyes on the phone.

Mom inhaled coffee and breakfast perfume and smiled contentedly. "Morning always smells like home," she said as I poured second cups. Together we said "extra cream and sugar."

Seconds before its shrill irritating ring made us jump, she said, "Bethie, the phone's for you."

Young Doctor Jolly didn't sound jolly. His strained voice put my senses on high alert. As if each word hurt his vocal cords, he said, "Samantha Lynn will be there soon. You and Jannelle need to get ready.

Always capable in unusual circumstances, I said a brilliant "Do what?"

He told me. When and where. He left out why. I stared at a silent phone and turned toward my family.

Mom went on with her breakfast plans. "More cinnamon and sugar on my toast if you puhlease. Speaking of sweet teeth, when Mark and your cousins get here"---My opened mouth didn't pass the w of "what" as in "WHAT?" Mom gave me that look, and my lips locked--- "You kids stay out of his way and work on Jane's shower decorations, and when we get back we'll make ice cream." They cheered. Once again Mollie Kate led the kids in her dance. Jannelle's shoulders slumped.

Sherlock Holmes went back to work. Mom knew Samantha Lynn's brood was coming. She knew not only when the phone would ring but that it was for me. Partially elementary my dear Watson: She was behind it. Whatever it was.

Before I could say "That was Doctor Jolly, and he wants…" mom said "It don't matter if he wants us at 8 or purt near 8 because he's never on time." The next hour was a blur, but we were purt near on time. Then, nearly hypnotized by the tick tock and glide of the golden minute hand on his big brown wall clock, we waited. My sisters and I watched our mother leaf through a year old Life magazine.

"Tick tock" went the big clock as the arrow hands slid slower than sands in an hourglass, slower than a cold snail, slower than ice melts at the South Pole. Well, maybe not that slow; but slow. "Tick tock." Dull, routine, commonplace. First "tick," then "tock." Would the world end if tock came before tick? Tock tick, tock tick, tock tick, tock tick. Back to tick tock, tick tock, tick tock. Urge to scream. We watched the door. We watched the clock arrows not do much of anything. Time was so heavy.

To be polite, we took tiny sips of the Jolly trademark strong brew that was supposed to be coffee. Extra cream and sugar didn't help. How could it? Who ever heard of sugar and cream improving crank shaft oil? Jannelle even though she hadn't been there in months sniffed out and passed around a blue and white tin of shortbread cookies.

"Tick tock."

Padded chairs that were supposed to be comfortable were not.

"Tick tock."

My sisters, tired of door watching, strong coffee and sweet cookies, admired Doctor Jolly's remodeled office. His cherry wood desk loaded with gold framed photographs of parents, brothers, sisters, wife, four kids and three golden retrievers drew appreciative "Ooh's!" and "Ahhs!

I heard the clock. I heard the clock. I heard the clock. "Tick tock.

"Tick tock, tick tock. Should I break it or stop it?

My sisters didn't know about Doctor Jolly's habit of humming as he read mom's charts; or that for the past two weeks all he did was make that tuneless noise. I questioned. He ignored me. Nothing new there. One time we hummed along. He didn't notice. Mom and I fancied ourselves "hummmm" translators. One meant repeating blood work. Two, head scratching and a medication change. Three hums long and drawn out (till I wondered if he had super capacity lungs) followed by head scratching and long searching looks at mom, made me want to run. Lately, humms and scratching were so close together I wondered if he would have voice or scalp left.

Sisters, momma, clock, closed door, bad coffee, too tense to nap. Read. I could read. Lovely, a National Geographic full color spread of lions chowing down on fresh bloody zebra meat. Gag! Blood red teeth above black and white blood smeared Zebra flank...Back to safety of "tick tock, tick tock, tick tock tick tock tick tock tick tock....." My head drooped and Ralph was there again with his 357. A new twist this time, he was looking down at a pile of letters.

"Tick tock." Opening door. In a few minutes, I wanted both Ralph and my dear companions tick and tock and cojoined twins tock and tick back.

Another first: instead of perching on his desk top like a bird ready for flight, Doctor Jolly sank into his beautiful brown leather Father's Day chair. For a split second, his face wore a look of contentment. It disappeared. He leaned forward, looked at us, and said nothing; no jokes, or questions about pop and the kids. Nothing. In the silence storm clouds gathered. Where was tock and tick when I needed them?

I was wet with fear sweat. The same kind of sweat that drenched me as a child walking down a long hot street to the dentist office. Dental visits were my hell on earth, and there was no way out. Abscesses had to be lanced. Cavities had to be filled. Beloved family dentist didn't believe in pain killers. Why should he, he didn't feel anything?

Once again, I didn't have a choice. I knew there would be nothing to dull the pain.

Time stood silent in the silent room as we waited for a silent doctor to speak. I didn't hear the clock, I didn't hear our breathing. I stared down a long tunnel at a doctor looking at us with eyes that said he didn't want to be there.

Finally mom had enough. "My girls need to hear it from you. Tell them."

Six eyes held the same wonder. We took our time about it, but finally, in perfect birth order, "Tell us what?"

The doctor of many "hummmm's" didn't. He had a new routine. Clearing his throat, he ran a shaking finger around his suddenly too tight white shirt collar. Finally, "Miss Anna are you absolutely certain this is necessary. New medication comes out nearly every day."

Mom's blue eyes were a shaft of determination. "I'm tired of being a pin cushion. I'm tired of x-rays and test results that don't change and all those dad burned pills! Tell them." she said.

He did.

I'll take the dentist any day.

Doctor Jolly's voice dry and factual. "On top of everything Miss Anna's been through: loss of the babies, cancer, heart attacks all the years of bronchitis and pneumonia, she's running out of strength. Her body is wearing out." His tight shirt collar got in the way.

Mom cleared her throat. Doctor Jolly stuttered.

Mom: "Oh for goodness sake, you'd think a doctor could do his job! He's trying to tell you I'm dying and there's nothing we can do about it."

As far as tick and tock and tock and tick were concerned, time stood still in the small room. My sisters and I looked around the room. There, the doctor, there pearl grey walls, there soft light filtered through a rose tinted window, and there, hunched over in a chair our dying mother. Our no two ways or three lies about it, our soon to be dead mom. Not passed away, not gone to the other side. Dead. Not breathing, not alive. Dead. Decomposing. A memory from childhood: Kids singing "The worms crawl in the worms crawl out. The worms play pinochle on my snout." That kind of dead. Forever.

We'd worked and waited and lied to ourselves. Her recovery was taking longer

because she was older, because she was this and that, because stress and worry about pop had side tracked her. "She's not as young as she used to be," we said. "It'll just take longer," we said, and sometimes we believed it because we had been, were and would always be miracle working sisters.

Slowly, our long list of lies and hope crumpled. Harder to see, harder still to accept, but our time of miracles was over. Together my sisters and I stared at truth and didn't know what to do with it. In our weeks of work and prayer and lies we had spread in Sainte Lillian the truth faced us: mom was not better. She tried and it didn't work. Now she was too tired to pretend, and of holding on to the remaining threads of her life just to please us.

At home, and everywhere in her shrinking world, she sat hunched over, and looked too tired to correct her posture or take a deep breath. She spent most of the day under grandkid power in her wheelchair. She slept curled into a little ball and sometimes her smile was the same sweet smile we saw when she spoke of her babies and her mother. Did she dream of them?

If over twenty years ago we'd wondered what could be worse when oncologist said she'd be lucky to live five years, we now had the answer. Then she told her cancer doctors to stand back and see what God would do. Now? Now she was ready.

Doctor Jolly found his voice. "It's everything, but overall, it's her heart."

I remembered the long ago phone call when he said her heart was too big. Was this what he meant? I talked to nurses and technicians and they all spoke of her big tired heart. I thought one thing, they meant another and Jannelle, who should have helped with this, was so lost in denial, she didn't. Then I thought of my personal misdiagnoses Emphysema, (she had this way of gasping)—or depression (that had to be true that was true, I knew it) --- and some kind of anemia (she'd been through that once and he said her red blood cell count was too low) Now he said it was all her heart. Everything wrong with mom was centered in her heart. Her big tired heart.

"Heal it," I said, and wondered why a man of multiple degrees hadn't come up with such a simple logical solution.

Doctor Jolly didn't bother with medical terms we wouldn't understand or sympathetic double speak or those stunningly brilliant things TV doctors do to cure every disease under the sun in one hour--- less--- if we count commercials. Above all, he didn't take time to dumbfound us with his intelligence or expansive vocabulary. Simply and sadly, he said "Can't." Not: "I can't." Just "can't." End of story. Translated, there was no need for us to mortgage the farm. This one word meant only an act of God could change the irreversible fact our mother was dying. "It's just a matter of time." he said. One of us asked "How do you measure time?" Once again his brilliance was a dim light in a quiet room. He didn't know. He said he'd learned long ago to not guess or predict.

A steady stream of tears marked Samantha Lynn's ivory cheeks and aged her ten years. Jannelle found her nurse voice and said aloud what she'd suspected and kept to herself for weeks. "Last stage congestive heart failure?"

"Yes," He said. "I want Miss Anna in the hospital. She wants to be home. This is her choice and much as I don't like it, I'll support her every step of the way." The door opened and with a soft swish closed, and we were alone.

We sat in the office lined with filing cabinets, pictures, walls full of diplomas and certificates and books everywhere, and breathed. That's all. In went the good air out went the bad air." Tick tock, tick tock, tick tock," louder every second, and faster, because now each tick, each tock measured her remaining life span. Tick and tock had never been so loud.

Mom said, "Girls I don't know what to do."

"We know," we said because we not only didn't know what to do or say, but how we would face all the unknown hours. How many hours? Days? Weeks?

"Girls I'm worried about your father." Minutes ago we heard her death sentence, and her focus was pop. Without looking at my sisters, I knew this was one of the few times we were on the same page.

Jannelle offered her magic formula. Mom said "Sweet little Nellie," and waited as she had when childish Jannelle stomped her feet and demanded the impossible. Jannelle's surrender was one soft sob.

Mom's voice clear and strong. "Nursing homes don't want your father because he runs from them to be with me. That's all he wants, and I want to help him….somehow."

"Bethie you remember the talk we had before you married your damn Yankee and you asked me why I stuck with your dad when he was so difficult."

"Yes," I said and remembered difficult was ten miles short of the names I'd called him.

"I told you then that I loved him. I love him Bethie. Do you remember the rest?"

A blurred memory, but a memory to the rescue. "You promised God you would be together, that you would pray and you knew someday he'd come back to God?" Big question in my voice. Long pause as my sisters watched and waited. "Tick tock tick tock tick tock" fading, becoming nothing in the small room...

"Girls when your dad's with me we read the Bible and pray together. He identifies with Job's suffering. Last week he told me brother Jethro was his version of Job's so called comforters. When our babies were stillborn, he and Jethro would go to the woodlot and Jethro told him God was paying him back for his wild life. Jethro did his best to convince him our babies died because of his sins." She fought tears and we heard her whisper "All these years, and he never told me." She took a sip of lukewarm coffee and grimaced. "Needs more cream and sugar," she said, and we grinned. We were afraid to speak, to think, to act. Not that long ago, I'd wanted to smack her. Now that I wanted to hold her, I couldn't move.

Her voice again, each word on a soft whisper of a breath. "He thought Jethro was right.."

Her eyes held us, but she was seeing pop and that day, and the long held guilt and reliving the squeezing pain in her heart. I knew heart pain.

My sisters squirmed in their chairs, but I could not move. Mom's pain, my pain—different, but the same. I was able to take her pale cold hand. She looked up.

"Sorry girls, I was… well, never mind"

"I know, I really know," I said

Soft and caressing her fingers that patted my hand. "Yes, Bethie I knew you'd understand," she said.

My sister's eyes bored holes through me but I ignored them. Their questions were only questions, and not important.

We drew closer to mom. "My dear boy and I cried together for the first time since little Jamie died. When we ran out of tears, he said he felt for the second time in his adult life that he was washed clean and born again. His pain and guilt were washed away by the Blood of the Lamb. He truly was a sinner saved by grace.

As one, we reached for her. To her, our tears were another chapter in her book of daughters.

Her voice grew stronger. "I heard him tell our grandsons he was looking forward to being with Jesus and our babies in our heavenly home". She smiled. "Bethie just think what would have happened to his soul if I'd quit and walked away."

I didn't think about pop because my tears were for Ralph, my Ralph who was back in my heart and there to stay.

Mom' sigh was long, drawn out "Girls I know what a trial he can be."

Jannelle reverted to type to defend her daddy. "He is not!" she said and the defiant lower lip in use since childhood was in action.

What Samantha Lynn wanted to say she covered with a cough, but I didn't have a cough or sneeze on standby. Naturally, I went full bore. "If changing your daddy's diapers is not a trial, you need your head examined."

While we three glared, mom used her famous stare. It worked, even at our age.

"Girls your father and I love one another."

Jannelle and I together: "We know, Mom but."

"Don't yeah but me girls."

Maybe Jannelle wanted to throw in another try harder, but all my 'yeah but' amounted to was he had a weird way of showing love. *"Just like Ralph,"* my mind said

Mom wanted us to listen. "I said love. Our love matured through sorrow. Maybe someday Jannelle and Samantha Lynn you'll face your own trials and understand." In the silence I thought about my dream, the three crosses, the echoing "forgive," and realized mom knew, and that somehow, in some way I had to share secrets with my sisters. They looked at me. "Later," I whispered.

Mom's voice: "I've learned life gets in the way of someday happy ever after dreams but life is better because it's real."

I looked at my sisters, looked at mom and said "What she said covers it" and determined that for the time being, that was all they needed. "We know," I said, hoping for the three of us this wasn't an Uncle Jethro sized lie. Considering the weight of the day, we understood as much as we were capable. .

"I've watched you girls and know you can't take much more. Besides, Bethie's Damn Yankee is having fits." She almost laughed. "Again." I grinned. My sisters were clueless, but mom knew, and proved she was in charge. "Because we both need round the clock care, I think we should move to a nursing home. As for this," she paused met our eyes "He doesn't need to know everything."

Jannelle exploded. "No!"

"Little Nellie." Her voice was the same as it was a lifetime ago.

"Little Nellie you must be patient. I'll tell your daddy it's only temporary. We have to move in now and get into the routine and all that pamperin.' When he gets antsy, I'll tell him we'll be home come springtime. All he needs to know is that we'll be together. Time'll take care of the rest."

Time. How much time? She stared truth in the eye and came up with a whopper that made Uncle Jethro sound like an amateur. What chilled me to the bone was the three letter word now. Whatever it meant to us as individuals, collectively, "Now" was the imperative.

"He won't go" said Jannelle who knew that next to God she understood her daddy better than anyone.

"Nellie you've been daddy's girl since you were born. You need to remember I've had him wrapped around my heart quite a bit longer."

Jannelle dug in her heels. She tried again, and threw in a threat she knew would win her case. "He'll get so upset he'll have another stroke." Louder than words, her smirk said, "There, let mom top that."

In the balance one man, two women who loved him dearly. A world and a lifetime of difference. "Trust me," mom said

Twenty-Six

Pop said, "I won't go."

Jannelle said "I told you so."

Mom said "Dear boy, I will miss you. Promise me you'll visit every day."

Pop said "What?"

Mom smiled and patted his cheek.

Pop found his voice. "Will we take our own furniture? You know I love my bed and green recliner. How soon before we leave?"

When Jannelle found her southern belle knees, I made sure she folded into the nearest chair. Her "Did I hear what I heard?" was not at all Jannellish.

Mom said "Sweet Nellie it's knowing not only when to try harder, but how."

Samantha Lynn read promises from the Resting Oaks Brochure, She passed around pictures: spacious rooms, a foyer complete with stone fireplace and grand piano, neatly dressed and smiling residents, and attractive attendants. Pop drooled over pictures of the buffet, and said he'd go pack.

Jannelle finished her fainting spell. Dramatically; right hand over her heart, left across her pale brow. Samantha Lynn and I found release in laughter until we were reduced to helpless giggles. We needed it considering everything, and for once everything didn't include the many moods of my damn Yankee.

Pop's daily changes were all for the better. To keep him happy, we said yes to everything he wanted. Jannelle was first up. "Resting Oaks has everything except a good sized vegetable garden. There's enough room on that south lawn to plant everything a body needs to make it through the winter. I'll get the men organized and we'll plan, plant and harvest. Yes sir, I can hardly wait!" Big smile, floor pacing, seed catalogues pulled from cabinet drawers.

"Good idea daddy. Whatever you plan, make sure you have a good sized plot of sweet potatoes."

To Samantha Lynn: "All I saw in that brochure was pictures of shrubbery and a few scrawny Iris near the big house. Didn't see no terracing, or flower beds or rose gardens. Lotta work to do. You think I could take care of that?"

"Best idea you've had all day pop! You could start right away. You know how Iris rhizomes rot. You'll have to thin and transplant, then get daffodil and tulips planted and stake out plots for spring planting. We could get some Lilac settings ready for spring, and I know you'll find room for a rock garden and moss rose."

Pop touched her hand ever so lightly, patting it in an old familiar way. Then he turned to me. "You girls are too agreeable. Tell you what Bethie, soon as we get settled in, I'll take your mom fishing to Lake Sa- Ho-Li and later we'll go dancing."

I jumped on the pleasing pop bandwagon. "As long as it's not rock and roll music pop! You and mom are so cute together when you waltz." I bit my tongue. Had I said cute? Then reality hit. "Hey, pop wait a minute! The only time you've ever gone fishing was when Mac Duff had you in the wheelchair at Sheriff Hales"

His laughter was that of a younger freer man. "Gotcha!"

"Sure did pop!" Three sheepish voices joined in the laughter.

"Y'all come on down to Resting Oaks. Get a tour. Have a meal on us." boomed a very friendly deep basso voice on the phone.

"Sixteen of us?"

"Absolutely no problem. We want the entire family to be happy."

Y'all come on down. Breakfast y'say? Perfect. Don't be shy, and whatever you do, bring your appetites."

Shy is the last thing we'd be when faced with a breakfast buffet loaded with goodies we never had time to cook. Once the kids stopped staring, they kept cooks busy filling two inch serving pans of sausage, bacon and pancakes. Our men ate like they were starving. Mom said "Restricted diet? I don't think so," and ate twice her usual servings. We sisters, following our eat till we drop plan, nibbled at everything. Multiple times. Just like pop, I went for the fried potatoes and pepper gravy. Knowing someone else did all the work made me feel fat cat in the sunshine good. I was head over heels ready to move in myself in love with wonderful graceful perfect Resting Oaks. Hilltop view of Ozark hills said we were close to heaven.

With the kids adopted by lonely grandparents for rousing games of checkers, we overfed and very comfy adults greeted the administrator. Quick as a Tinker Belle wink, we were first name friendly. While Billy Bob John led us through the usual weather talk, Marvin, Mark and pop helped themselves to pastry. To be polite mom, my sisters and I accepted coffee served in gold rimmed china cups. Billy Joe John instructed the server "Miss Anna likes extra cream and sugar."

How did he know that? Content after a tour that reminded me of a four star hotel and a wonderful breakfast, now sipping perfect coffee I decided to wonder but not ask what else he knew. This time, I would follow the urging of my sisters and keep my mouth shut. I would sit demurely like a lady, cross my legs at the ankle, smile sweetly, and be charming. Everything was wonderful. For two more seconds.

Air started leaking from the balloon when pop tired of small talk, stirred his coffee, looked around and said. "Dang nice place you've got here. How much?"

His three daughters did the fish out of water act. Not in birth order, but all together, like lake trout after a fat worm.

Mom touched his arm. "Dear boy!" she said.

Marvin said "Good question pops." Mark grabbed another pastry, checked the selection on the tray and took three more chocolate covered crème filled Long Johns.

While it lasted, we on the distaff side were snug in fantasy land; pleased with everything, and loving Resting Oaks. To our men however, our fantasy land was as alien as are carburetors and transmissions to women in charge of shopping, laundry, kitchens and kids bruised knees.

Pop helped himself to a sugar glazed donut, looked our new best friend Billy Joe John in the eye, and asked the same question in the same dry voice. Somehow, someway, pop was back and in full battle gear. I recognized his declaration of war.

Our larger than life overgrown well fed host settled back in his king sized red leather swivel chair. I blinked. Was he towering over us? Was something in the coffee? Sherlock Holmes was reborn. I snooped. With his oversized chair centered on a foot high dais, what else could he do but tower over us? I gawked like a kid on a first time Natural Science Museum visit. And swallowed. Twice. Fantasy land was fading and I didn't want it to go. It had been so long since I'd been a charming guest I wasn't ready to give up.

No matter what he did or said, my neck couldn't take looking up at good old friendly as close kin Billy Joe John.

Wearing cat stalking canary smile, our host pounced. He talked money. A lot of money. All of us together didn't have that kind of money. I could see Good old Ralph's bulging eyes when I confessed I'd signed away our vacation savings, grocery money, tithe, gifts to charity, utility bills and the kid's college funds. My defense: "Oh darlin' Resting Oaks was wonderful. I had to do it for mom and pop."

My promise to my sisters broke into tiny pieces as my voice went off the scale. In fact, I shrieked "You want how much! For each!" Demure gone. Definitely unladylike.

Billy Joe John lowered his eyes, searched the room, passed ever so quickly over me and kept on travelin'.

He spoke slowly. Were cue cards on the back wall guiding him through this 'delicate' procedure? "Show real concern for the old folks. Frown when the family asks questions, smile when they react."And the cautionary reminder in large black letters, "Watch that right eyebrow Billy Joe John!"

"We must make sacrifices to give our parents the best care, and that is what Resting Oaks prides itself on doing." From numb lips my sisters said "Of course Billy Joe John."

Not me. I said, Are your parent's residents?" Again my voice lacked ladylike modulations.

Billy Joe John, like all domineering men ignored me.

Did he say we should sell the farm? No, that wasn't it. He advised our deeding it to Resting Oaks. It would stay in the family till mom and pop "passed on." His voice so understanding, his eyes resting above our heads like he could see the pearly gates. After that "sad day", they would develop the property. Development decisions would be made at a "more appropriate time," he said with just the right hint of sadness in his voice.

I wanted to know what they'd do at the "appropriate time." I wanted to know why he wanted everything they'd spent a lifetime creating. I wanted to know a lot more 'indelicate' inappropriate unladylike things. And I was geared to ask

The voice again, almost hissing. "I assume their Medicare co-pay is met for the year?" If this pompous jerk knew about mom's coffee, why was he assuming something one look at these sick old people would tell a small child? Something resembling an answer floated by. Frog after fly, he got it. .

"The good news is once you deed the property, you'll not have to worry about money for…" he really looked at them then. Calculator eyes blinked…

once, twice, three times. He smiled a benign smile and generously gave them at least three more years. *My mind swirled. We sign, mom and pop move in. She dies in a month or less. Pop won't last long without her. Resting Oaks wins? Billy Joe John, the only person in the room with time to spare, waited.*

Mark, first to breathe normally, wrapped donuts and chocolate covered custard filled long johns in a soft white Resting Oaks linen napkin. Marvin didn't wait for Jannelle to give him the nod. He filled another napkin. Billy Joe John did his best to not look upset. It wasn't good enough. I wondered how he'd react if I'd tuck the beautiful porcelain Resting Oaks serving tray under my shirtfront. Silly me. But the thought brought a grin to my frozen face. "Take that you big jerk!"

Billy Joe John waited. Because we didn't want Billy Joe John to think our momma had raised us wrong, my sisters and I said nothing, did nothing.

With a tee time and a cute blonde waiting, Billy Joe John forgot the cue cards and put an edge to his voice. "We're agreed? Of course, after the-- ahh shall we say estimated time"--- Billy Joe John gave his version of an understanding how difficult this is for you smile, and tiger after meat, almost made eye contact. Eye contact was easier when he was stalking money.

One look in mom and pop's eyes when I took their coffee cups told me they hadn't heard much after "deed the farm."

Was mom, silently saying farewell to her babies? Did pop remember the long ago yesterday he, Silent George and the twins conspired to surprise her?

Their lives -- our lives started on the Maple Brook Road farm. We were part of that rocky soil; of countless sunrise and sunsets, of laughter and tears. Now big overbearing Billy Joe John who knew more than he needed to know about us wanted it. Worse, he had to know his time frame was a stretch. His bottom line: they were dying; they might as well die in more luxury than they'd ever known.

Again the voice after money. "If In the event of a longer residency here or unexpected emergencies" I shot him a look that said "Hey B.J.J.,-- I didn't know there were any other kind--- He read my eyes, frowned and brushed it aside

He almost looked at mom. Looked as in seeing her as a real person for the first time. "We would require you Anna, and you James Samuel to sign over your Social Security earnings, and your daughters to cover the remaining balance."

He waited.

So did we. Whatever he wanted, required, or wished on a star for, he wasn't about to get from us.

He took a leisurely pull from a tall crystal glass of ice water. Neat little beads on the glass seemed hesitant about sliding onto the polished desk top. Did they dare? Would he let that happen?

Tired of our silence, Billy Joe John shifted to Jannelle and Marvin. "Jannelle should your sisters be unable to meet their obligation, as older sister, the agreement dictates you would have full responsibility."

Jannelle came out of her trance and blinked. A very ungenteel utterance from my southern bell sister followed. "Do whut? Emphasis on the "U".

Her turn to be ignored. "Of course the amount would then depend upon how you ladies decide to meet their other needs, and the allowance you give your parents.

Samantha Lynn said "Allowance? We give them an allowance!"

I thought: Billy Joe John you are an idiot! We want them to have the world! What we don't want is you and your ridiculous price tag.

Couldn't he read our glazed eyes? Didn't he know we were Christians in the Coliseum staring at attacking lions, afraid to breathe?

He pulled one sheet of thick off white paper from the single folder aligned neatly against the blotter on his desk. "This is the contract we ask all family members to sign." As I was seated nearer his throne, he held the paper at my eye level. I saw a large sheltering oak tree, its branches spread over embossed gold letterhead. Weight of the single sheet of paper drug his hand down as I read the last three words of their mission statement: "Because We Care!"

Secure in his role, Billy Joe John positioned the paper for one of us to rise approach his throne and humbly seal their doom. A gasping softness as we fought for air was not as loud as the sound of thick paper circumventing the width of his desk.

Billy Joe John showed his perfect white teeth. and offered a fat gold pen to each of us in turn.

He was ready with more assurance. "Of course the Owen Family cemetery will not be disturbed for another 50 years or,"…again, the brilliance of white teeth "Until you've all passed on."

Pop gave me one long look. I opened my mouth, determined to get past the lump in my throat. "It's o.k., Bethie, I've got this one," he said. Mom's Dear Boy said "Go to hell several times and in more ways than I knew possible. He started with "You pompous ass!" and it got spicier.

He told the blue suited white faced administrator exactly what he could do with Resting Oaks including the exact portion of his lower body to stuff with papers that would not have our signatures. Almost as an afterthought, he recommended the fat gold pen be used to assist the paper in reaching its proper destination… "Way up."

"Dear boy!" mom said.

Samantha Lynn applauded.

Jannelle, still speechless and having no way to show her genteel side, glared. Not at all politely.

My reaction? "Way to go daddy," I said, and Jannelle said "What did you call him?" and her daddy smiled and winked. I couldn't stop grinning.

Mark, knowing we had a long ride home, decided to save wait staff work of clearing the tray and claimed remaining sweet rolls.

I knew mom was proud of her daughters as we made rounds thanking cooks and staff for the delicious breakfast and the enlightening tour. For once Jannelle didn't tell me to hush when I expressed our "undying gratitude, amazement, and pleasure, and promised we had memories we'd treasure forever." In fact she had to pinch me to get me to quit. Delicious Krispy Kremes rather than excessive exclamations kept our jaws busy all the way home.

Jannelle registered our parents at every private nursing home. They said they would welcome them when beds became available. "After the funerals," Jannelle translated.

Days drug. Days became a drug. One weary work filled day followed another down a long endless road.

In my 'spare time,' I envied Scarlett the luxury of thinking about Rhett tomorrow. Ralph was on my mind all the time. I called his family. His brothers said he was fine, busy, taking care of business. His mom was too busy crying to lie. Finally I called good old hometown downtown Sheriff Lew the one man with know how and ability to locate missing persons. As Ralph was sharing morning donuts with him, he didn't' have far to go. When Lew choked out my name, Ralph's cursing made my nightmare come alive.

My mom was dying, my pop didn't know it, my husband was …was what? My kids, my sisters; the list went on and on. I stared at a blank wall.

Twenty-Seven

Uncle Jethro said a friend of a friend said "Quiet Rest" was the perfect answer. "Got there myself iffin I had to," he said. When we pulled into a weed infested pot hole filled yard, my first thought was uncle would fit right in.

Pop, the old man who walked with a limp, actually jumped from the van to rehang a fading sign above the flapping hole filled rusting screen door. "Ain't no way I'm taking my bride into that hell hole!"

Jannelle and mom, identical twins when it came to social justice, gave him a withering look, and said, "We have to look into this." Pop groaned. Years of experience schooled him in what was coming.

Before the administrator found us, we'd wheeled mom down narrow hallways, peeked into overcrowded cluttered rooms, stinking bathrooms and a kitchen so filthy the stench made me gag.

A tall fat man with a grease soiled ketchup smeared napkin tucked into his unbuttoned shirt corralled us. His eyes accused us of invading his sanctuary. "Snoops, get the hell out of here!" his eyes said. We smiled and introduced ourselves and –more or less- forced him into a small corner office that smelled almost as bad as the kitchen.

As he'd forgone the pleasure of name sharing, I wondered what pop would call him. I knew that wouldn't work. I settled on Mr. Knuks (skunk backwards)

Standing at a scarred dirty undersized steel grey-green left over Army surplus desk, Mr. Knuks glared. Doing our best to breathe, we dusted off the old style wood slat funeral home chairs and waited. "Might as well get it over with," Knuks eyes said. His bowels seconded the motion.

We needed help. We needed air. He didn't care.

Our 'host' squeezed into a chair big enough for Mollie Kate and a teddy bear. I was back at the science fair---"Gee, mom! Did you see that?

With a dying gasp, the chair added a stronger moldy scent to a room full of oxygen unworthy of the name...

A monotone voice came from above the napkin? "You have toured the facility?" Fortunately we were not offered refreshments. He had this in common with good old Billy Joe John; he was taking our measure and sharpening his claws.

Pop didn't get a chance. Jannelle, seasoned, experienced, and a graduate of the University of Trying Harder, was on him faster than a blue jay after a June bug. Putting it my way but nicely, my big sister was becoming a very good Yankee.

She said two words: "We have." Then she loosed both barrels. "I am appalled. The entire facility reeks of urine and feces. There is no clean air. Unwashed residents in dirty clothing are tied with filthy rags to their equally filthy wheel chairs. Every room is a pigsty! Your exit doors are not lighted and are locked...not with a simple chain, but padlocked! This entire building is a fire hazard!"

Mom pointed at Jannelle. "Who is that?" she whispered. I rubbed my eyes. This warrior in Jannelle's flesh was still there, and from all indicators she was just getting started.

Jannelle consulted her list. I had been so busy staying alive I didn't know she had a list that filled pages. "Each room has unmade and sometimes soiled beds. Hallways are full of garbage bags. Showers and bathrooms reek of mould. Unwashed dishes, pots, pans and utensils are stacked on the kitchen floor. Deep sinks are full of greasy water, and the exhaust system is broken. Your kitchen reeks of old grease, stale food and garbage, and is a breeding ground for vermin, roaches, and disease."

You forgot the flies," was the best I could do. Recovering from sister shock, Samantha Lynn managed "It looks like a month of rotting garbage piled by the dumpster."

"Coons were enjoying a buffet," mom said in a voice that made a lie of her weakness.

Our smelly host shifted his bulk and a fresh supply of foul body odor filled the room. Defiantly, "Lady, you're sure as hell out of line!" Then he got really rude!

"Time was, old folks died off. Now, miracle drugs make sure their hearts beat and that they piss and crap. Not in the toilet. In diapers. Course with all these drugs, their minds don't work. Uncle Sam says they're alive. Hell! How can they call dried out shells alive?"

He was talking about my parents. Worse, they knew it. Then he shifted blame. "Families should live together like they did fifty some years ago, sons and daughters taking care of the old folks. That don't happen no more. Kids leave home and part time jobs leave them too much month and not enough money. They can't help. It's all down hill. Old folks get sick, they can't manage and they're dumped bag and baggage on people like me! You sound so snotty about the wheelchairs. Well let me tell you little lady…" He glared daggers at Jannelle… "It ain't pretty, but it's better than broken bones.

His pity party went on and on. He couldn't help it if work wasn't done, he couldn't blame workers for quitting, and he didn't have enough money, so what if garbage piled up? To quote him exactly, "By God my residents have clean asses!"

What he wanted from us was out there somewhere in left field and we weren't searching for it. What he got was a full dose of Jannelle unleashed. Was it my imagination, or did she become taller while Mr. Knuks deflated like a leaking balloon? Understatement of the year follows: this was getting very interesting.

Her voice was a double edged sword. "Your excuses for the appalling conditions are unacceptable. " He managed to open his mouth. "I am a county health nurse and"… she waved her notebook. "I have a list of violations that will have inspectors here by mid-afternoon. Unless you're a miracle worker, I absolutely guarantee you will be shut down! Furthermore, if we find one resident suffering from malnutrition or bed sores, I'll personally see you prosecuted.

For the first time in weeks, mom sat erect. She said she had writing to do, and needed to get busy. The reeking of mould air was electrified; charged with something it had needed for a long time; determination and energy.

Jannelle pointed to the Sainte Lillian's HELLO the only clean paper on his desk top. "My mother", she said and winked at mom, "is the most popular newspaper columnist in the Ozarks. I guarantee she will have a cover story in this week's paper. And my pictures will illustrate everything she writes." Talk about a popped balloon. The stripes on Mr. Knuks back quivered as we watched.

I found myself really proud of this person masquerading as my sister. Samantha Lynn and mom and pop and I couldn't stop grinning.

Jannelle sweetly asked permission to use his office phone and history was made. I heard the story then silence, then: "Yes your honor, that's correct, your honor, I know just the place your honor." By court order all residents were transferred gratis to Resting Oaks. His honor judge Carl

Mayfield Senior, (also known as Grandpa to "Yes Dear") officiated at the ribbon cutting of Resting Oaks new wing. He welcomed each resident and then spent a very very long time explaining the facts of life, civic duty and Masonry to Billy Joe John.

It was the first time in 20 years mom's column earned a front page spread (continued on pages three and seven), and the first time in history the paper did a second printing.

Jannelle's plans were approved and Quiet Rest was renamed Hope House. That Jannelle would become the new administrator was not an accident. At long last she and her true life mission embraced.

Our parents said they were tired of looking, and would be the first new residents at Hope House. Reenergized, mom regained strength and pop caught her renewed optimism. Every afternoon, friends came over to work on the baby shower. With Mollie Kate helping her grandma, the last loops went into pink and blue baby blankets. Mom said one blanket was the right color and the second could wait a year or two. Mollie Kate said it wouldn't hurt a boy to have a pink blanket (Pink being her favorite color) or a girl to have blue because Mellie had a blue room and she was purt near perfect. Mac Duff was so busy helping his grandpa work on garden and landscaping plans for Hope House, he said nothing.

Pop whistled off key but somehow tuneful old favorites like Turkey in the Straw and Vinegar Works, and continued to treat mom like they were newlyweds. They glowed.

Another miracle: Pop gave up his night trips. His seat at the corner store was dusted off and each evening he played checkers with the kids. Tall tales of his adventurous Tom Sawyer days brought much needed laughter. There were more and bigger rattlesnakes in the burlap bag every time Mac Duff convinced him to tell the story." Grandpa did your mom cook them?" Mac Duff asked and pop winked.

I hissed "Mac Duff you will not!" Young boy man learning and old man remembering shared laughter.

Doctor Jolly stopped humming and scratching his head. He said they were both walking miracles and if this kept up the kids and I could head home to Michigan in a week or two.

Home to Michigan. Home to Ralph. Brunswick men said Ralph was taking care of business. Their advice: "Stop worrying." Yet another example of typical male logic kept me laughing most of the day. For all the good it did, my home phone rang off the hook day and night.

Mac Duff was full of late night phone call stories about his dad doing this, his dad doing that, his dad going fishing, playing with the dogs. Stories grew until my trying to make life easier for his mom son overplayed his role. His whoppers became higher, wider and deeper than anything we'd ever heard from Uncle Jethro. Enough was enough.

I called a halt. Torn between sharing his hurt and keeping it to himself my son was in a real pickle. In a habit he'd picked up from his grandpa, he rubbed his hands through his hair. Like his dad, he tried to change the subject. Jokes fell flat. Then he sighed like the world's weight was his alone to carry, and slumped at the table. The look on his face redefined misery.

"I'm waiting son."

Like his grandma, he tried one more time, and told his shirt collar, "It's our secret, mine and dad's."

My hand closed over his clenched fist. Mac Duff let out a big sigh and pulled out the serious stuff. "Pinkie swear and promise you won't tell nobody else?"

"Cross my heart and hope to die." From Mellie and Mollie Kate's "Or get run over by a garbage truck" made their promise officially official.

Mac Duff needed more. "Put your hands where I can see. I don't want no crossed fingers so you can blab at school."

" Mac Duff! We don't blab!" Motherrrrr tell him we don't blab. Does he think we're stupid or something?"

In times like these, I'm so very grateful for the Sainte Lillian mom stare. Peace and what passed for order restored, Mac Duff told us more than we needed to know and, much more than he needed to carry alone.

For the second time in my life, I had no words to comfort a hurting child. A newer larger nameless dread rested on my shoulders, and whispered fears.

Twenty-Eight

Ralph knew he was the man! Day after day, seven days a week, he did it all: roofing, siding, dry walls, electrical, plumbing. Sunrise to past sunset, it was his ball and his game, his rules; no talk, no breaks.

If he slept more than two hours, dreams from hell took over. Work kept the thick grey damp fog away. Every night, he brushed the dogs because he'd promised Boy. When he brushed them Boy was there. They talked scouting, fishing, and baseball. By God, that kid had a way with words. Boy always made him feel good. Sometimes when the kid prattled on he remembered his own dad, the man he'd wanted to look up to and love more than anything. Ralph vowed he'd never be like that cold old man.

It was the day again. He was hurrying home from school. Best Buddy was on the porch railing waiting for him just like always. Just like always, he started running, but this time wasn't just like always. A green Coupe: Dodge, Plymouth, DeSoTo? He didn't remember but it was green, deep dark green. He remembered green. It was green... It turned the corner and sped down the street. He couldn't. He wouldn't remember. His dad washing and washing and washing his hands, his mom crying, Prince Valiant and Charlie Brown covered in blood. God! That pain still tore his guts.

He couldn't stop the echoes. First Best buddy, then Grandpa Joe, then buddies in Nam blown to bits washed in blood and gore. And more. So much more. Remembering brought the fog. More every day, He had to keep it away. He hated it, feared it, and ran from it.

Work. He had to work. Work kept it away. Pre-sunrise till dark he was on the job. Then home. He had to do Bethie's canning and freezing.

Nothing, not even her slimy okra escaped. He painted walls, laid new carpet washed imaginary dirt from shining windows, cleaned frig, range, freezers, and scrubbed bathrooms that never had a chance to earn a water stain. Now, with extra time staring him in the face, he changed oil on his Chevy truck, and sharpened lawn mower blades. He stared at his callused palms and fingers stained from work, grease and oil. That's all it took for the damned fog to come back. It was everywhere; so thick he couldn't tell dog from door, bed from bench.

He tried to run but it was so thick and powerful he could only move like a puppet under control of a drunken puppeteer. Strings pulled his limbs into chopping movements; right leg, then left, right, left. Ralph lost count. Nothing mattered. He body slammed into his black gun safe so hard it shoulda cold cocked him. Shoulda, didn't. He didn't feel anything.

Blank mind. No memories. No thoughts. Numb. Now his only movements were involuntary: Heart. Lungs. Ralph heard his heart; loud, fast, strong. Like a coal powered railroad engine pullin' pig iron up a steep incline. "Chug, chug chugchugchug." He felt the creeping fog's cold dampness and waited.

Ralph's right arm jerked from shoulder, to elbow, to wrist. His clenched fist opened slowly. And even slower his wooden fingers closed around the dial, finding their numbers, the days of their lives. They clicked in order, and a hollow sound echoed through the big empty house.

Audience and puppet combined, Ralph watched his every move. His big hands easily claimed the black leather case home to his Smith and Wesson 357 Magnum. Of all the guns in the safe, the single and double shot over and under, his deer rifle, his kids target shooting twenty two, and his colt revolvers, this was his favorite. Had been for years. He loved that gun like a real man loved his woman. Like Bethie, it was beautiful. Like Bethie, it belonged to him.

For years Bethie'd watched him drool and dream over this beauty. Secretly, she filled Miracle Whip jars with every spare nickel, dime, quarter and dollar. This blue steel beauty became his first of September present when she was pregnant with Girl One. It was supposed to be for Christmas, she said, but she couldn't wait.

First thing they were out back by the old barn target range. "Twist your arm, just a little, keep your wrist steady, keep a firm grip, and squeeze nice and easy. Whatever you do, don't jerk." He said. She tried. She said that much power scared her. She said much as the shotguns bruised her shoulder, they were kinder. But Bethie shot his gun because he wanted her to. Good thing I didn't let you teach my recruits. You can't hit the side of a red barn," he said, and they laughed.

Then without aiming, he showed her how to shoot. It was one Bull's eye after another each bullet in the same spot and hay bales torn apart in the barn. Bethie said thinking about what one of those could do to a person made her sick. He knew what they could do. He held her and promised her that would never happen. Now, he thought about that promise.

Ralph looked at his gun. He felt less like a puppet, more like a man. Grey thick fog shimmered away. He felt alive. He loved that gun, the look of it, the solid weight, the rich manly smell, and especially, its power. One bullet anywhere near a vital organ could blast anything to hell. This gun, his pride and joy always lay in steel gray beauty on soft blue velvet in a locked black case. It was safely hidden in plain sight because he alone had the combination.

This was his gun He wiped grease and oil on his jeans and pulled it almost reverently from its resting place. Overpowering, the scent of powder and gun oil. Slowly he loaded it with six copper cased snub nosed beauties: each with enough power to penetrate sheets of steel.

Ralph called the dogs. "Sit," he commanded and obediently they sat in a row, oldest to youngest, tails wagging, tongues drooling. Expecting a treat were they?

"Not this time boys."

So they could taste approaching death, Ralph forced the barrel past resistant teeth into each mouth. They whined and quivered. First Duffer, then Tupid, and Bethie's new pup, Einstein Bear. They shook with nameless dread, and ammonia rich urine ran down their shaking legs, soaking the bedroom carpet.

Ralph didn't see, hear, or smell. Was it yesterday? The day Boy convinced him the perfect Mother's Day gift was definitely not just the climbing white and yellow old fashioned rose bushes. "They're great, dad," he said, "But what mom really needs is a good guard dog." Ralph said "No way!" and Boy sealed the deal "Just think dad when you're at work and us kids aren't around you won't have to worry cause we'll know mom's safe and protected and stuff."

His Boy knew the exact location down to the back yard dog pen where a litter of seven week old German Shepherd pups were old enough to face the big wide world. Smart kid, his Boy. He'd planned everything.

There they were, him and his three excited kids the Saturday before Mother's Day. Boy hunkered down in the scratched bare of grass earth by the wire pen and talked to the pups. Best friend to best friend talk like he did so long ago with Best Buddy. Watching his son hurt but he watched. The pups busy chewing on a blue jean leg knotted together pull toy growled and ignored him. Happy puppy growls and little tails wags made such a perfect picture Ralph wish he'd brought the Nikon.

Boy's voice pulled frisky pups ears up and growls down. They looked up and all but one decided pullin' and growlin' was more fun. The small one with the black up ear and tan down ear trotted to the fence plopped down on his black and tan hind legs and looked at Boy. Up ear and down ear and drinking puppy eyes took it all in. He understood. Another pup ambled over, did that funny puppy splay sit and scratched in the direction of an ear with a hind leg. He lasted about half way through Boy's second sentence.

"Now I know we're taking you away from your mom and your family but you're old enough to go and sides, we've got a ready made family for you. You'll get two sisters and me and a mom and a dad and you've never had a dad."

The little flop eared would be guardian of all that was dear to Boy stared long and intently, as if reading the future. "Don't worry about leaving your mom," Boy said when flop ears whined and looked toward her. Boy stuck two fingers through the fence so the pup could get a good idea of his new family smell. Like he knew what was expected, the pup gave Boy's fingers a good sniff and lick. "You're gonna get a real good mom, and she'll love you so much you won't miss your own mom." Little flop ear gave his best try at a growl and Boy did his best at acting afraid, and backed up. "Well, maybe you will at first, but everything will be fine," he said.

Ralph knowing it was decision making time tested his son. "Boy you don't want to give your mom a one up ear one down ear guard dog. And, he ain't the best looking one in the litter either. Look at his uneven black and tan marking. To top it off the damn pup's the runt of the litter."

Girl One and Girl Two looked at their dad, their brother and the pup now looking at their dad with the same damn look he'd just had with the gun in his mouth. Long ago, and minutes ago, his brown eyes held a question, a statement, a wonder too deep for words.

Ralph forced himself back to the good memory; the good day.

Boy stuck up for his choice and then and there he got the kid started on merit badges. Ralph said, "You made the best choice, taking pity on the smallest pup, the one nobody else would want. I'm gonna make you a merit badge."

"What's that dad?"

"It's like a medal. Scouts earn them for doing good deeds."

Instant sell. Course the girls got in on it too and they all had to learn merit badges weren't earned for makin' beds or carryin' out the trash. Somehow, that never stopped them from askin'.

Ralph forced memories away. The gun was in his hand, dogs at his feet shivering' like they'd been hit with a blast of frigid arctic air.

Ralph pictured skull bones and brains splattered over the friggin' room. Blood, fur, bone, lifeless dogs stinking' before they were found. Thought about the cats. God! About the only part left whole would be their tails.

Back to Mother's Day. Bethie took one look at the little thing definitely missing his mother and not the least bit shy in telling his new world about it. She scooped him out of the basket, kissed his little pink nose and nestled him over her heart. Next thing they knew, he peed on her blouse, gave a big sigh and went to sleep. Bethie didn't fuss, she said "Poor little feller," and let him sleep. Later, she said Flop Ear wasn't a decent name for a guard dog and since Boy picked him out she'd name him Duffer, sort of after him. The girls loved it. Told their brother to remember not to bark when they called the pup. He wanted to know if not smacking them would earn him a merit badge.

Next thing Ralph knew, Boy baptized Duffer. He said when Duffer died he wanted him waiting for his mom in heaven, cause she'd be there in a hundred years or so. He wanted them to be together for ever n' ever."

After that every pet was baptized. Fish missed out and only because they couldn't figure out how. Were they supposed to use dirt since fish lived in water? Would fish stay alive long enough to be baptized? If not what? Questions floated for weeks before they gave up.

While Bethie watched each ceremony, he was busy with cameras recording family history. Now these pictures rested on the bedroom fireplace mantle, like anchors marking family milestones. Ralph stared long and hard and found his heart swelling with pride. He loved his kids, was so proud of them.

The heavy 357 seemed heavier by the minute. His hand and arm cramped. For damn sure this gun was almost as heavy as it was powerful. He knew if he fired once he wouldn't stop. Ralph wiped dog spit onto his grease stained jeans and put the cold barrel to his forehead. Heavy. It was so damn heavy the weight pulled his hand down, the gun away from his head. He turned and found his eyes on Bethie's Bible.

He heard Boys voice. "Have you ever read the New Testament dad? Have you?"

Ralph gave a sound more animal misery than human and walked on shaking legs to Bethie's bedside table.

Why did she spend so much time reading it? Why did she always find answers to questions he couldn't even think to ask? And if the Bible was that great, why did she spend as much time reading those little footnotes and checking every damn reference and her concordance as she did reading the Bible? Seemed like every night she would say something like "Honey! Listen to this," and she'd read wordy explanations from footnotes about politics and murder and sin and crap like that. Hell, sin was sin far as he was concerned. Why all this crap that she threw in? The kids were fascinated with facts about Bible times when people didn't have radio TV and baseball and Mac Donalds. It never ceased to amaze him that the human race survived when they didn't have a clue about aspirin or Hungry Man TV Dinners, Monday Night football, outboard motors, or KFC. To name just a few.

Ralph knew he wasn't a dumb ass. When Bethie pulled that "Honey did you know this and that about Bible times" on him the first time he said "How about that Bethie, people sure have come a long way. Just think they used to kill with the sword. Now we have atomic bombs and threat of nuclear war. We eat better, know more, live longer and kill faster. Ain't humanity great?" He never went that route again. Now when she started with "Honey did you?" he'd change the subject, make a joke and get away. He was good at it.

And why the hell does she read the Bible every day? Sometimes twice. Wasn't reading it once every now and then enough? And for the past year or so, why was she so deep in study about forgiveness and love? Then there's the red silk marker with her name in gold letters stuck permanent like in Romans Chapter eight. Every day she went back to verses she'd highlighted and underlined? When he got up enough nerve to ask, she said they were her verses. When he said "Like private property that you don't want to share?" What she said to that bit of logic burned his ears. Then she started reading them to him every day until they were practically embedded in his brain: Tired as he was, he remembered they said nothing in, on, or around heaven and earth and hell itself could take the love of God away. Not even death. So he could kill himself and God would still love him? Well, the Bible said so, but it didn't say what kind of love. Something told Ralph it wasn't the kind of love that said "Come on in" when he knocked at heaven's door. Without knowing how he knew, Ralph realized that if he killed himself, he'd be on a slide going straight down into fire. And there was God, still loving him, crying with heartbreak kind of like his mom did when Best Buddy died. Was that another reason Bethie read the Bible and talked to God every day?

Because he knew deep inside God was real and was up there, out there, somewhere "close as a breath away" Bethie always said, Ralph's knees gave out and he collapsed on the yellow and white bedspread. Bethie's NIV Bible in his right hand, his cherished gun in the left.

Ralph looked up and out the big bedroom window into the full moonlit night. Peaceful night. Calm. "God if you're really interested in me—help me! Talk to me!"

Bible and gun, Bible or gun? Ralph clicked safety on and dropped his beautiful gun on the yellow and white bedspread. Not thinking to check for grease or remnant dog spit, he dropped it like it was hot, hell fire hot and looked at his hand. Burning. His hand felt like he'd pulled it out of flames. A cold chill shook his body. He looked again at the gun, double checked the safety. Not if, but when it went off, it wasn't going to be a friggin' accident.

Like they knew the crisis was over, three dogs suddenly stopped shaking and walked to his side.

Ralph leafed through the Bible. Something...not a voice the dogs could hear, but a voice in his head, told him to stop. A quiet yet commanding voice, that said clear as a bell "Stop! Read this!" His fingers marked 1 Corinthians chapter 13. "13 ain't no lucky number," he said and tried to turn the page. Tried again. The flimsy onion skin paper wouldn't move. Flimsy paper was another thing that bothered Ralph. If the Bible was supposed to be read so much and used as a guide book and all that crap, why wasn't it printed on manly paper? Paper a man could get a grip on without being scared he'd tear it to shreds? Ralph wanted to ask, but that voice only he could hear told him to save it for later.

"God you're supposed to talk to me. Is this it sticking' pages together?" Then the voice in his head; quiet, patient, insistent, urging him to read.

Ralph knew hairs on the back of his neck stood at "Ready for Inspection Sir!" rigid attention. He looked around the room, at the dogs, and finally down at the Bible and read aloud, "If I speak with the tongues of men and of angels and have not love, I am only a resounding gong or a clanging cymbal."

Ralph knew cymbals. Who the hell didn't? Damned noise makers never let his sleep through one of the kids band concerts. He'd be slinking' down in his seat trying to shut out the racket passed off as music when that crash louder than thunder jarred him wide awake. Friggin' cymbals weren't good for nothing' else.

He felt a prick of conscience. "All right, all right, maybe I'm like that, Makin' a lot of noise. Now and then."

"That doesn't answer my question God!" Had he shouted?

He heard: "Keep reading Ralph. He looked around. Ignored the voice. Again: "Read Ralph."

He jumped as if vaccinated with a needle big enough to put down a horse. "Better read," he mumbled. As members of a respectful congregation should, three dogs settled down to listen.

When Bethie's cat Meathook crawled from under the bed and claimed his lap, Ralph barely registered sharp needle pricks. Time was he'd have cussed the damn cat and his sharp claws and if Bethie was out of the room, sent him flyin'. Not to hurt him, just to let him know that he, Ralph George Brunswick was boss. Not that the damn cat ever got the message but sometimes, it made him feel better.

Ralph read "If I have the gift of prophecy and can fathom all mysteries and all knowledge, and if I have faith that can move mountains but have not love, I am nothing."

"Fathom all mysteries? Hell! He didn't understand women and far as he was concerned, women were the biggest mystery in the universe. Mechanical, electrical, building, blueprints, changing seasons, wars, all that was easy. But women!

And who other than women has the gift of prophecy? They know when kids are gonn do stuff before the kids think about it, when things are gonna happen and what people will say. That has to be prophecy. Who the hell understands women?

He knew he was off track. It wasn't but a week or two ago that Boy told him to stop making jokes about important stuff. For damn sure the kid would think this was very important. Boy's voice came clear in his mind, like he was right there at his side. He broke into a cold sweat and looked around. He missed them, the sight and sound of them, he wanted them at his side but want didn't b ring them. He focused on their pictures. Remembering. Finally, his eyes returned to the Bible and rested on words about faith moving mountains. Get real! What kind of faith can move mountains? What kind of mountain? A real rock, stone, tree, waterfall cougars, bears, squirrels and deer and all their blood and crap mountain or a crap load of problems mountain? There was a crap load of difference between the two.

Because he'd had enough of Meathook's needle sharp claws, but wasn't in the mood to toss him, Ralph inched himself slowly and carefully towards Bethie's bedside lamp. "If I give all I possess to the poor and surrender my body to the flames but have not love, I am nothing."

Ralph groaned. How was he supposed to understand? This time when the voice said "Keep reading Ralph," his eyes flew to the printed word.

"Love is patient. Love is kind. It does not envy. It does not boast. It is not proud.

It is not rude. It is not self seeking. It is not easily angered. It keeps no record of wrongs." He had to admit this time around Bethie'd really exploded. He'd pissed her off and goaded her before till she cut him a new ass, but before times were nothing like this one. The ways she went off, fire was in her eyes and her nose was blowin' smoke. She was like a pressure cooker blowin' its top.

The voice: "Answer this one off the top of your head. Who would you say is sometimes rude or self seeking? Who keeps records of wrongs and is easily angered?" Ralph looked blank. "Hell," he muttered, "I don't keep no records, not my fault those idiots piss me off." Speaking of, he was sick and tired of all this self seeking crap. Crap. Crap. Crap.

His mind raced. Maybe his usual way of changing subjects would work this time. "Hey you keep telling me to read. I'm ready."

Voice. Softer, yet somehow firmer, more commanding. "I have eternity to wait for your answer Ralph. You don't have that much time to give it."

Ralph laughed aloud. He appreciated a sense of humor. Now it was time to read. He tried, but the print blurred.

"Ralph." His name spoken so softly and with so much love and patience he couldn't turn or run.

Surrender began. Me! I envy. I boast. I'm proud. I keep records on every mean sonabitch. Truth is, I'm probably the meanest sona…"The soft voice whispering his name wouldn't let him finish.

"Ralph."

He refused to think, speak, or answer. Yet the voice persisted. The soft comforting understanding voice.

In spite of his resolve, shouted: "What? I came to you for help and you give me this! What do you want from me?

"Ralph you who are so loved, why do you fear love?"

Ralph's eyes cleared as words moved from the page directly into his mind and heart.

"Love does not delight in evil but rejoices with the truth. It always protects, it always trust, always hopes, always perseveres. Love never fails." Echoes in the room. Never fails. Never ever fails. Love is patient. Love is kind. Love never fails.

Somehow, he didn't know how, the Bible was open to Psalm 23. "The Lord is My Shepherd." Ralph knew about sheep and shepherds. Sheep followed the shepherd's voice. They knew it, they trusted it. He'd heard Bethie say they were all like sheep and Jesus was their shepherd. Hell, he wasn't no sheep. Holy crap! There was the L word again. Goodness and love will follow you all the days of your life."

He was sick of that word. With all his strength, he slammed the bible onto the floor. Instead of laying flat, it opened and pages moved as if directed by an unseen hand. He had no choice but to retrieve the Bible. But he did choose to not read were his hand rested.

Finally, without urging from his inner voice, he read from Numbers 14, verse 18. "The Lord is slow to anger abounding in love and forgiving sins and rebellion."

Ralph began a blind random search. He read Psalm 91, verse 14. "Satisfy us in the morning with your unfailing love.

To the waiting dogs, he promised "I'll find something in this book that doesn't talk about the consequences of not loving, the rewards of loving or just plain love."

Duffer cocked his head the exact way he did the first time Boy talked to him and made a noise that sounded so much like "No," that Ralph Jumped. "Damn dog! Don't tell me Bethie has you reading the Bible!" Duffer growled a low in his throat don't mess with me growl.

Ralph took the hint. He fanned pages, and opened and closed the Bible a dozen times before slamming it shut, closing his eyes and opening it with a harsh jerk.

Convinced he'd won, he gave Duffer a triumphant look. Duffer held his gaze.

Damn, when would he ever learn he couldn't outstare dog or cat? Duffer won. Again. Ralph looked at the open Bible and read aloud: "John Chapter Three, Verse 18. "For God so loved the world that he gave His only begotten son that whosoever believes in Him should not perish but have everlasting life."

Ralph did not know how long he sat bathed in truth. When he looked up, there were no questions or doubts troubling his soul. He grabbed Bethie's concordance and reference books and read through the night. After talking with Pastor Marl, he slept 12 hours.

Twenty Nine

Our fears, needs, work, prayers, all that circled our wagons against disaster at Maple Brook Road, ended. Everything that consumed our thoughts and energies and ran rough shod over our private personal don't think about anything else but us and what we're going through was over. Faster than air escapes a pin pricked balloon, everything around us changed. Suddenly we didn't matter that much anymore; to ourselves, or to Sainte Lillian town, county and rural routes.

It was five years, give or take a week or two since Suzanne Faye Ward said she'd never talk to the snotty Venable women again in her entire life and she didn't care if they were second cousins. Quicker than wind blowing' up a dust storm, Elvira June heard what else that Ward woman said. She let it be known if her sister Pat weren't with her in church she'd pull that woman's bleached blonde hair out. "Down past the dark grey roots," she said Being a good Christian and all, she bit her tongue to keep from saying in public exactly what that snooty pretentious Ward so called lady could do with her uppity airs. But she hinted enough and sighed enough and looked hurt enough till most folks knew she meant it. Cause they knew when Elvira June got mad she stayed that way. Permanent like.

Now, in this need, Elvira June and Suzanne Faye met at the church alter and fell sobbing into one another's arms. Times like these, family needed family, needed to reach out and feel life and remember the wonder of love.

Small groups of men, shopkeepers and factory workers, doctors and policemen met for breakfast at Miz Freeman's Pink Door Café. Eggs and grits turned funny lookin' and cold on their plates. Bill Mayhew got plum tired of the quiet gloom. He looked at his food and said he'd never thought grits could look like that. Here most of his life he'd been eatin' em, but lookin' at that congealed mound maybe he wouldn't touch them no more ever again. "No siree Bob, I mean it," he said. Douglass Campbell sure as shootin' not wantin' silence to come back and make the place any gloomier nudged his friend in the ribs. "That's cause you always put a pound of butter and half a bottle of hot sauce on the dad blamed things. No wonder you don't know what grits look like seein' as how it's the first time you've seen em without your fixins."

Nobody else said anything. In fact, they acted like they wished Bill and Douglass would just shut up. So they did. As individuals, or groups of two, three, four or more, men sat and stared off somewhere, not really seeing anything, just staring. Not even drinking coffee that lost steam and turned cold.

Kids didn't need to hear "Now quiet down y'hear!" or to be told to bring bikes off the sidewalk, eat their oatmeal or wash behind their ears.

Day and night in Sainte Lillian, grief was a palatable thing.

The familiar old black crow, so old it was showing gray wing tips, flew past the front porch of the country store. As usual, it settled on the nearest telephone pole. Its beady eyes focused on the unusually quiet group of overall blue chambray shirt clad men on the long wooden bench. "C'mon old feller y' need t'get your donut," Gabby said as he tossed a chocolate covered Wing Ding toward the pole. Old crow didn't budge. Maybe it wasn't hungry, or maybe he wanted a Krispy Kreme and knew a Wing Ding when he saw one.

On the porch, old comrades echoed voices on the wind.

"Dad blamed shame, dyin'thataway."

Jane and George were tickled pink about the baby. Hear tell soon as they got results, he was struttin' like a Tom turkey. Doncha know he nearly went broke handin' out them fancy ceegars wrapped in pink crinkly cellophane paper.

Didn't rile him none at all when folks teased him about waitin' till the baby came. Said he was getting in practice, decidin' if the overhand was better than the slow pitch or should he just pull em out of his pocket. Said he had serious decisions to make. And when some said he'd feel funny if he had to trade em in for blue, he just laughed em off. Said he was getting' himself a daughter.

"Soon as Jane heard what he was up to she had t-shirts made with one of them big arrows pointin' down to the biggest bluest letters they could find sayin' "This is a Boy." Then doncha know her folks and his folks said they'd have a 50-50 raffle to make it more interestin' Jane's folks said they'd go for a girl and George's folks the boy." Solda lotta tickets too. Me, I only bought five…each." Smiles, not laughter as each man pulled tickets from overall pockets.

"Pray to God Jane and George never knew what happened."

Silence settled like a wet towel. Samuel Benable, old Gabby and the fellas stretched arthritic overall clad legs and shared a chaw of Red Man.

Eyes open, they saw nothing. Time was nothing. Individual thoughts were wanderers with no road map or place in mind to rest.

None of them thought to bring up weather, or stupid politicians or the Cards. Sides, times like these, they didn't need to talk much. Just bein' together 'bout covered all the bases.

Gabby, duty bound to live up to his name, got them started. "Reckon they mighta had a glimmer before that truck full of drunks hit em head on?"

It was one of them there questions didn't need talkin' about cause they shared the same wonder, the same hope they had not. How could they seen it, goin' over that big double S curve on Maple Brook Road.?

Samuel kept it goin'. "Maybe. Maybe not. Hope not."

"Yessir!" Meaning agreement, end of discussion, meaning a lot of things, came from Bill Robinson who punctuated his feelings with a dead center stream of mahogany colored Red Man juice into the rusty well spit into Maxwell House can.

Once talk started it had to wear out. "That their car. Lorda Mercy, iffin you didn't know it was Ira Levine's old red Thunderbird, you'd have two chances –slim, and none—to come right out and say what it wuz. Like it was…oh, I dunno, like it went through a compactor or sumpin."

"What kinda thang is that Gabby?"

"They're gret big machines that makes big cars and trucks and sech into square boxes. Big old magnet thang grabs em, drops em into this big box lookin' thang…only it ain't no box. Somethin' brings the sides together and it squeezes until what comes out don't look like a car or whatever went in.

"Car! Car!' The old crow's voice cut across theirs.

Gabby threw another Wing Ding in its direction. "Well with this here car it's more like the front got put in that there machine. The back cut off the way it was didn't have a chanct to get itself compacted. And them baby things fresh from the shower was scattered everywhere. Purty little hand knit shawls and blankets and sech like. Blood stained and all, ain't nobody gonna use them."

"Story is Beth Anne and Miz Owen and Beth Anne's kids were carryin' shower stuff that didn't fit in Winter's truck and coulda got kilt themselves."

"Yeaup." Was a quartet of single word agreement.

"Doncha know they saw it all.?" Beth Anne says the noise sticks with her. Like an explosion keeps your ears ringing', she says. Didn't hear no screams. Then there was moans and her mom prayin, and her kids scared nearly to death yellin' and all."

Silence. Tears washed creases on aged weather worn flesh.

Historian to the core, Samuel spoke in a voice choked with tears of remembrance. "That Clayton family's had more'n its share of this here kind of grief. Hasn't been that long ago that Claire and Bill Clayton and their little gal died. Same day too, just like…" his voice faded.

"Seems there's a little gal growin up name of Mary Claire."

"Yeah, the Levine baby. That there Ira Levine up and adopted her soon as him and Melanie got hitched."

They knew Gabby had the whole story and they knew since he'd up and started this here conversation such a time as this was their best bet of gettin' the whole dad blamed story. Eyes on him, they waited.

"That's another story," Gabby said, and they inched forward on the old bench. Wanting. Waiting.

Gabby gave a long mournful sigh. He was always careful to agree with what they knew but that was it. Years after the tornado they kept tryin' to worm the Gibson story out of him. They should know by now he was like a sleeping dog on this here story. Best to let Gabby and that ole dog be. The old crow flew toward the second wing ding changed its mind mid flight, and went back to its roost. Just like the expectant men, watching it was, and waiting.

Bill Robinson, brother-in-law to Olathe of Plaid sisters fame, decided to try again. It'd sure be a feather in his cap and worth a pecan pie or two if he learnt something new. Downright hungry for pecan pie as he was, he cleared his throat.

"The wife told me she heard that those two couples…you know, Ira and Melanie and George and Jane had this agreement that ifin anything permanent like happened, the others would raise the kid. Y'know, Jane and George raise Melanie and Ira's Mary Claire, and iffin it were the other way around Melanie and Ira would take over with Thomas. Got it all legal like cause that Ira Levine is one smart lawyer. Sharp as a tack with that legal stuff he is."

He waited. A stray breeze blew dust devils across the parking lot. The watching crow tried to call its mate but lost heart. His beady eyes closed and his head drew in.

The fellas knew Bill's way of buildin' up, getting things outa people. They knew he'd finish up. Maybe this time they'd get the whole story. Bill took his time cause time was the only thing he had plenty of. He wadded his chaw in a napkin, popped the cap of his Royal Crown Cola, and tossed cap and chaw into the nearby trash can. He rinsed the tobacco with a good swig, and sent another perfect shot into the can. He wanted to know. He'd waited long enough.

"Just the other day, I was deliverin' chicken feed out to Ma Gibson's Home. First thing I knew a passel of little blond haired blue eyed fellers came runnin' out to help. Never seen em all together like that before. They coulda been triplets. Thomas Winter Clayton, that youngun of Janes looks like em too.

He waited. Not one voice told him to hush. "Seems I recollect m'wife tellin' me she heard direct from the mouth of Nurse Gibson she up and adopted three little fellers in memory of her son Tommy. Seems purty far fetched to me. Course I'm just a country farmer. I don't know nothin' about such stuff." There he'd given it his best shot. It was up to Gabby.

"That's the ever lovin truth!" Just the way Gabby said it told them Bill Robinson didn't have a clue. Gabby took time to unkink his stretched legs and pulled his hat over his eyes.

The men knew he knew. They also knew all of Bill's talkin' and their questions and wonder, didn't do a bit of good. Gabby shook his head.

"Been telling you fellers for years to not try and get me talkin' about that there time. Looks to me like you'd get around to listenin' one of these days. Somethings is best left alone. The past is done past, and fer shure, Melanie' choice won't ever get writ up in the Sainte Lillian history books."

"You're right Gabby but doncha know we got ourselves curious wimmen folk so we sure as shootin' gotta keep on tryin'." Six men agreed with head shakes and a period of long brooding silence.

That left Bill more determined than ever to get that pecan pie. Olathe needed some new tidbit to pass on. "So whatcha think gonna happen to them drunks that done kilt them? Raised eyebrows, mouths opened, but he didn't give them a chance. "No Sir! I ain't callin' this no accident. They was drunker than skunks, they was speeedin', and Jane and George and the baby is dead cause of it.

Eyes turned to Gabby. His lips didn't open, so Samuel, thinkin' this was a safe question, stepped to the plate. "Y mean once they get out of intensive care…if they get out. Hear tell one of them kain't even breathe on his own. And the other two all busted up no tellin' what'll happen."

Wasn't much for Bill, but worth somethin'. Word dry, the men sat chewing. The graying old crow, tired of silence, spread its big wings and flew away.

Talk, rumor, tears, all over town.

For once, truth and rumor were on the same page. Mom and the kids and I were laughing about the shower, glad it was such fun. Mom said "The way she looks, that baby could come any time." "I get to hold her first,"Mellie said. And her brother said "Not if it's a boy and Jane said she's having a boy"… and then we crested the hill and then and then…

Everything followed me room to room, thought after thought. First the visual, without sound. The head on collision of truck and convertible. No sound for maybe a second, maybe two. Then it came, grating, ripping, loud and rough, and the explosion. Filling air around us. Pieces of car and truck flying up and out and around, hitting roadway and roadside, shredding tree leaves. Shards of glass glistened in bright sunlight. One perfectly round band new B.F. Goodrich white sidewall tire rolled as if pushed by unseen hands. One tire.

Mom's prayers were drowned by screaming kids. They could not, would not go where I had to go. They had to run back to Mrs. Brown's house and call 911. "Don't look back, run!" Scream all you want, but run. And stay there!" Imperative they stay in that little white house where there was no blood and gore and horror. Mom had to stay in the van. If there was life to save, it was up to me.. I stumbled across and around shards of glass and twisted metal and found Jane. Pale white, bled dry. So fast. Blood. So much blood. Cut from her forehead all the way down. And her baby. Dead. And George. Headless George. I tried. I couldn't put them together. One man lay in the red gravel road like he was asleep on a feather bed, knees pulled up, hands tucked under his chin, still as you please. His breath was a long slow rattle. Dark blood seeped from his nose and ears. Somehow I pulled two nearly dead men from the cab of the burning truck. Beer bottles, Whiskey bottles. Fire. Black smoke. Flies. Suddenly, everywhere, buzzing big flies, and a sticky almost sweet smell hanging heavy in hot muggy air.

Doctor Jolly said it was bad enough mom had to witness the accident he would not give her permission to attend the funeral. "Miss Anna temps are in the 90's. The church'll be packed. Are you trying to kill yourself?"

She didn't say anything. He stared into her determined blue eyes and once again, the mom stare worked. "Very well, but you absolutely must not attend the graveside service," he lectured with full authority of his doctor voice.

He was with her and pop through it all including the graveside service. At the funeral in our packed s.r.o. church, tear stained eyes seldom left pictures topping twin sealed caskets: Jane and George in their wedding pictures. Jane pregnant and George with his box of ceegars. Caskets closed because all they could do was sew them together.

They said Jane went head first through the windshield and glass and steel cut her open clean as a butcher's knife.

Now, the baby she never saw or held in her arms lay in her arms wrapped in a soft pink blanket. Girl it was, just like George wanted.

I remember Mac Duff refusing to go to a "girlie thing," and George saying "Fine, more cake and ice cream for me." Mac Duff reversing gears, "well, maybe I'll try it" and then racing George for the door.

Mac Duff learned Sainte Lillian's menfolk have a habit of showin' up for baby showers. Course they're kinda bashful about it and sit in the background, but they don't fool nobody. Once the women finish their oohin' and aawin', work scarred hands are surprisingly gentle handling bonnets and booties.

Jane passed out blue cellophane wrapped cigars. George walked behind her with pink. Later, as they packed smaller gifts in the back seat of their convertible, I had the oddest feeling; time was running out like sand in an hourglass.

Looking over assorted gifts supposedly essential for newborns, I laughed. "Hey kids, you turned our pretty good without any of this stuff," I said. Drawn to red and black blocks and balls my girls said "Didja ever think how much better we'd be if we'd had them?" "You couldn't be any better," I said meaning it. They beamed.

Soon to be grandparents said they'd join us to help unload as soon as decorations were stored and the reception room cleaned. I stood in the parking lot remembering my showers and thinking about the long road ahead for Jane and George. Jane gave her parents one last happy hug, and then they took the lead down Maple Brook Road.

Mac Duff's sisters teased him when he said showers weren't all that bad as long as there was plenty of cake, ice cream and punch. Laughter. It was good to remember the laughter.

The hill. My slow driving on the scenic route I loved put us at the end of Jane and George's dust cloud. "Step on it mom. Catch up!" I topped the hill and the double S curve, and...and...and... nightmares and horror merged piling sight and sound into one long memory...

Each day automatic pilot guided me through kid care, washing and ironing and cleaning and warming food people dropped off. And all the time, I watched my mother. I watched my father and sisters watch my mother. And somehow, I managed to hold my children, breathe, and drink coffee.

Somehow, somewhere in that time, reality forced me to admit our prayed for miracle had worn itself out. How could she be any smaller, any weaker, this mother of mine?

Oxygen whispered from a bedside tank. IV's kept her hydrated and mildly sedated. Doctor Jolly was there twice, sometimes three times a day. Once he said, "I want her in the hospital immediately."

My sisters and I said yes. Mom said "No," and we jumped. Her weak but determined voice "Not this time. You're a good doctor and good friend Brian but there's nothing more to do. I'm going to die at home with my babies around me."

From her bedside, pop said "If she wants to die here at home, she will" I wondered how long he'd known, wondered so much.

My sisters and I reached for one another. I looked at mom and pop and broke free and ran. Mom whispered "Let her go."

The grove of sycamores lining the creek bank welcomed me as they had since childhood. Once again, I cried until there were no tears and then I threw up. Everything, including pain and denial.

"Mom."

Mac Duff called three times before I turned.

"Mom you know how much me and the girls miss dad?"

"Me too," I said and in spite of heart pain knew it was true.

"When we were sittin' with grandma the other day we thought she was sleepin' and we talked about that stuff I told you."

His voice cracked. "Yes, son," I said and wished with all my heart he'd spared her. Wished, but didn't tell him.

His voice cleared. Grandma told us to stop worrying about him. She said her and grandpa spends lots of time talking to Jesus about dad and Jesus told her it would be all right. Ain't that neat mom?" Hope in his eyes.

"Neat, real neat," I said and we shared a big hug and walked together back to the waiting.

In spite of all the unknowns, the dreams, the fears, I ached with want for my husband. My good loving Ralph. The only one I ever wanted.

What I got was a houseful of Samantha Lynn's family and Marvin. Simple equation. More work. Needed now! My place in the big back bedroom went to nine kids. Sleeping bags, pallets on the floor, changing beds every night, unsupervised pillow fights, way too much ice cream. They needed time away from parents and serious adults. They needed time to talk and be kids.

The clock ticked. Mom grew weaker. Her dying was a slow thing, gradual, soft. Minutes became hours, days, a week. While we counted each breath, the second week began.

Hers was a slow releasing that kept us watching. We did not want her to be alone when death came.

Her breathing became slower, if possible more shallow. Pop was always by her side. While the family jostled for places at the table or carried meals to the shaded picnic table, pop carried trays to her. Countless times every day with a patience I had never seen, he fed mom Mrs. Freemans Chicken Noodle Soup, her favorite tapioca pudding crumbs of Mollie Kate's Krazy Kake and anything else she wanted, including her coffee, laced to perfection with extra cream and sugar. One teaspoonful at a time. Slowly. Lovingly.

She kept her eyes riveted on his face. She was happiest when he spoke of their baby daughters and little Jamie. He told her they were not lying near the fence where the roses grow, but with Jesus in Heaven waiting for her.

She silenced his talk of angry years with a finger over his lips. When he cried she brushed his tears away. "You're my dearest dear boy," she said.

Once she woke from a nap singing. Pop's voice was drowned in tears when he started to sing with her. She paused and reached for his hand and my sisters and I sang for them. To them. For the first time. For the last time.

> " Just as I am without one plea
> But that Thy blood was shed for me
> And that Thou bid'st me come to Thee
> O Lamb of God, I come! I come!"

We were strong on the first verse. Jannell's voice became almost a whisper on the second, leaving a teary voiced duet on the second.

> *"Just as I am but waiting not*
> To rid my soul of one dark blot,
> To Thee whose blood can cleanse each spot
> O Lamb of God, I come! I come!"

Mom and pop were smiling, their lips forming words their voices were too weak to utter. Somehow, Jannelle found her voice and we harmonized to finish the third. I remember the look in pop's eyes when I took the lead.

"Just as I am, though tossed about
With many a conflict, many a doubt,
Fightings and fears within, with-out,
O Lamb of God I come! I come!"

"Bethie! Your momma taught the both of us to sing. Your voice is beautiful, he said." His praise was music to my ears; for the first time, and the only time.

Thirty

Tuesday, week two. Uncle Jethro pleasant and mannerly for weeks, spent the morning. Maybe his third cup of coffee wasn't strong enough, or the sugar cookies weren't sweet enough; whatever the reason, the familiar Jethro surfaced. All you need dear sister is to make up your mind you ain't gonna give up and get outa that there bed."

His mouth was still open, and more brotherly advice was waiting in the wings. Fingers like steel claws dug into his upper arms and a very strong jerk pulled him from the chair. Two old men locked in battle as pop and Uncle stood face to face. "Tell my wife you'll see her later," pop ordered..

Uncle Jethro dug in his heels. "I been watchin' her layin' around and the lot of you doin' nothin' fer quite a spell, and I kaint take it no more. I'm telling you iffin I talk serious like to her for a few more minutes, she'll get outa that there bed."

Determined claws dug deeper, and suddenly uncle faced reality. Pop said "Now." Uncle Jethrow found the strength to surrender and pop escorted him from the room. Or bounced. I prefer bounced.

I stood by the front door holding it and my mouth wide open. Pop wasn't finished. "My wife is dying and she will die in peace. If you can't understand that, don't come back," he said and raised a foot as if he wanted to hasten dear uncle's exit.

I tried to cheer. I wanted to applaud. I did nothing but stare at pop. He winked, and would never know how long I'd waited for him to stand up to dear old uncle Jethro.

Wednesday, mom's breathing slowed and she wasn't as alert. She still loved the rich inviting perfume of perking coffee, and whispered "Extra cream and sugar."

Ladies from mom's church circle were there every day with prayer vigils. With the Plaid sisters official seal on Miz Owen bein' on her deathbed, the house became as busy as Grand Central station.

Friends brought food and with a buffet of down home country cookin' set up in the dining room we were busier than the Pink door Café.

Countless witnesses to mom's passing stood around her bed. They held her hand, prayed with her, hugged pop, and left to check out the buffet and make room for more.

I remember the laughter as stories were told about a mother I never knew. One afternoon two big men I'd never seen knocked at the door. They looked twice as old as mom. We're the Mouser boys." One said and my eyebrows went up. Well, years ago when Miz Anna Taught at Carver Creek School we were boys," the other said, and I had to laugh. "We jest wanted to tell her how we remember them years. She was some kind of teacher that's fer shore. Never let our fist fights get in the way of her lessons. More'n onct she busted up our up fights at that there school. She said she was there to teach not to referee our squabbles but since there warn't nobody else to do it she reckoned she was more'n up to it. We shorely didn't stand a chanct when she was riled. A reglar tonarde she was even iffin we was two, three times her size. Yessir-e-Bob she could take the rag offin the bush anytime." Laughter tears. Sad tears. Tears of remembrance.

Mollie Kate's Krazy Kake and Mellie's tea were always ready, and Mac Duff surprised everyone with dishwashing skills. It was definitely merit badge time for my three kids.

My sisters and I split nights into three shifts. My pillows were at her bedside from midnight until the rooster crowed. I kept watch while my sisers pretended to sleep. Pop, his tired green eyes never leaving her face on one side of he bed, I the other near the door.

I sifted yesterdays. Birthday cakes on tall crystal stands, daffodils in springtime, the breathtaking joy of Easter Sunrise Service on bluffs above the river. As first rays of sun illuminated the congregation, trumpeters gave all their strength to the Hallelujah Chorus. I remembered the joy on mom's face.

I remembered family laughter, family tears. For the first time in years I held my baby brother in my heart. I remembered his smile, his laughter, the way he held out his arms to hug Jesus. Sweet sadness was my blanket. I wept silently for my lost unborn baby, and for sisters I never knew. Would they have been like me, or Samantha Lynn, or Jannelle? Would they love mom as we did? Would we as a family have known contentment? I felt the weight of all our losses; for bruised hope, for unknown tomorrows with Ralph. My head slipped forward on the blue and pink double wedding ring bedspread covering her still form. And both arms reached out to touch her. My mother. So tiny.

I was moving. Effortlessly. Strong arms held me. Knowing I was dreaming, I welcomed the dream. I had wanted my gentle Ralph- needed him so desperately; if this soul searing strength sapping exhaustion brought him to me, I did not have or want strength to deny or to fight.

I was asleep. Deep, restful invigorating sleep. My husband was bringing me coffee. All the horror, the sadness had been just another of my bad dreams. It had to have been. That meant Jane and George and the baby weren't dead. That meant mom wasn't dying. That meant Ralph. Ralph. I heard his voice. I heard my children laughing. My sisters. My sisters? They weren't at my house.

I sat upright and pushed sleep away. Yet, Ralph was there, holding me.

Was this Ralph? Who was this gentle man with the soft voice and comforting arms?

Pop was at the bedroom door. "Come now!" he said. Not to me, but to all of us.

Doctor Jolly came in the front door as we rounded the corner into mom's room.

"Her mom and the babies are with her," pop said.

Mom saw what we could not see. She was singing a lullaby to her babies.

I spoke her name and she said "Bethie you and that damn Yankee get over here."

My reply was a barely audible croak, noise without meaning.

"Daughter don't make me say it again," she said and then to Ralph, "I have spoke."

In the crowded bedroom in what had to be her last moments, I had the urge to laugh. So I did. So did we all. The room filled with laughter.

Ralph and I knelt beside her bed and she placed his hands over mine. I turned to stare at him and looked into the most peaceful eyes I've ever seen. His anger, his fears, his confused self was gone and replaced by this answer to prayers, this miracle.

We strained to hear her faltering voice. "Tell...my funeral..." she managed. "Promise." He said "Yes, mom," and began sobbing. We had cried together over our baby, but in our years together he had never mourned like this. Mom patted his cheek. "Your damn Yankee finally knows what it means to be washed in the Blood of the Lamb ," she whispered.

We had time to kiss her goodbye. Time for Pastor Carl Clayton to give her communion. And to lead us in reciting the 23rd Psalm. Then sunrise filled the room. Mom was smiling. I've never seen such a beautiful smile.

There wasn't much to do. Her favorite pink chiffon gown with the old fashioned lace collar hung in her closet. Underneath in a tissue lined box, a pair of never worn pink satin slippers. Years ago she had us promise to put them in her casket someday… Maybe the undertakers won't put them on, but come judgment morning, I'm going to." she said. Made sense to us then.

Now we were dealing with the first awful aching sense of loss. Mom was there. She wasn't there.

I knelt to hold her hand. So warm. Long slender fingers that played the piano braided my hair, made birthday cakes, caressed my newborn babies with tenderness only a grandmother knows Hands that became weak, and shaking, hands that minutes ago had strength to place mine and Ralph's together. *Without being told I knew she had been waiting for him.* Soft, the sound of our mourning.

Pop asked us to leave. They did. I couldn't. A bony hand cupped my face and I looked up. My real daddy said "Bethie you know I love you. Now, kiss your mom goodnight and let me have time alone with my wife."

We were emerald eyes to emerald eyes. He smiled. Love and peace and understanding were in his smile. My real daddy told me he loved me. It took a second of time to erase a lifetime of pain.

They were alone for over an hour before the hearse came. Two white uniformed men with a stretcher found them together in her rocking chair. Pop had wrapped her in a soft lavender blanket and was singing their song. So softly.The men went to lift her.

Pop told them to stand aside. "I carried my bride her into this house for the first time on our wedding day. I'll carry her out now."

Doctor Jolly said "Mr. Owen, I wouldn't advise…" and said nothing more as pop rose almost effortlessly.

He carried mom through every room. Upstairs and down. Rooms where dreams began. The big kitchen where an electric range had years ago replaced the wood burning cook stove. When winters blew cold they talked about how they missed biscuits going in one side of the oven and coming out golden brown on the other before bacon and eggs were ready. They never spoke lovingly of that hot monster in summer.

He paused at the scarred maple kitchen table and looked lovingly at her chair. Every step he was talking to her. Softly, almost a whisper as if he didn't want to disturb her sleep. He carried her outdoors so they could take in the glorious sun filled morning; greenness of grass and trees, the just turning into day blue sky, soft cooing of mourning doves, the sweet peppery perfume of roses. He spoke about everything she loved.

We formed a silent procession. My sisters and I as close as we dared. Ralph with one arm around me, the other around Uncle Jethro. I blinked twice. His arm didn't move. Uncle wasn't fighting. Mellie, Mac Duff his grammie's Franklin Mac Duff Darlin' and Mollie Kate were with us. Samantha Lynn, Mark, their six kids, Jannelle and Marvin; all of us watching. Lost in this newfound sadness, understanding but not understanding.

In the cemetery, pop paused by each small stone to whisper names: "Rose Ellen, Helene Bernice, Elma Pauline, Mildred Louise, Barbara Anne." He took another step and his voice was filled with unbelievable joy. He knelt. "Oh, my dear our son! Our little Jamie! Our little boy!" His voice was so filled with wonder.

His final breath was released in one long sigh. Holding his bride close to his heart, he too was smiling.

*   *   *

My Kids are grown and gone. Mellie is a Social worker and writes scripts for popular TV dramas. She's very good. We expect her name in lights someday soon. Mac Duff followed his dream and as an Army Chaplain, travels the world. Somehow he's always involved in building projects. Mollie Kate teaches Home Economics at a local high school and owns the Krazy Kake franchise, famous for anything chocolate.

About Ralph: He enrolled in a Christian college shortly after our return to Michigan. During a summer break from Seminary, he organized and led a mission trip to a 3rd world country. There he designed and supervised the building of churches a school and a hospital. One evening after a hard day in the back country, he walked from camp to sit on a hillside and video the sunset. His last words were "Bethie I feel so much peace it's like I can reach beyond the sunset and walk with God." The official report stated he placed the camera in a small rock crevice and jumped down a few feet. They said the explosion rocked the camp site. They sent his camera home and buried the bloody boot where they found it.

Someday my dearest. Someday.

Mollie Kate's Krazy Kake

My mom said someday she would write about the summer grandma and grandpa died and she wanted me to write my Krazy Kake recipe for the book. I waited a year to do it. Rememberin' that summer and the last time me and grandma made ice cream together hurts awful bad. I miss my grandma.

Here's the way to make my Krazy Kake.

Heat oven to 350 degrees. Don't wait till the last minute to turn it on. The oven has to be good and hot before you put the cake in.

THEN
Sift into 9x13 ungreased cake pan 3 cups white flour, 2 cups granulated sugar, 2 teaspoons baking soda, one third cup cocoa and 1 teaspoon salt. Sift it a couple times to get it all mixed up nice. Uniform lookin' momma calls it. Smooth it out real nice.

THEN
Make three holes in the mix. Pour three fourth cup of oil (I use Crisco, use any kind you like) in one hole, 3 tablespoons cider vinegar (that's the brown kind) in another and 2 tablespoons vanilla in the last one. (I don't think olive oil would work, but try it if you want).

THEN
Pour two cups of water over that. Here comes the hard part. You gotta use forks and stir it real slow. It takes a really long time but you can't beat this cake in a mixer or use a spoon. You gotta be patient. My mom says it's a good way to learn patience and the cake is worth the eating. And when

I say a long time, it's like this. When you're stirring and you think you're done, you've just started. It takes a long time. Make sure you don't let Kake batter stick to sides of the pan. It just makes a mess that way and you don't want a mess. You want every bite of Krazy Kake you can get.

THEN
Put the cake pan in the heated oven for 35 to 40 minutes and pull it out. When it's all cool, put anything on top you like but we like butter cream frosting.

Mom said I could write what Auntie Nellie did when I taught her how to cook: which was really funny because she's so much older than me. But anyway, when grandma and grandpa were dying, I got her in the kitchen and got her started on desserts. Auntie Nellie loves desserts. She experimented. She dredged blueberries in sugar and cinnamon and flour. Dredge means you mix dry stuff together and then roll fruit or whatever in it to get it all covered so the fruit won't just sink to the bottom of the pan.

THEN
You mix the dredged stuff careful like in the batter. No dumping allowed. Auntie Nellie made a streusel topping out of butter, sugar, cinnamon and flour and sprinkled it on the batter before she put it in the oven. Momma loved it. So did grandma and grandpa. Mac Duff wouldn't eat it because it had berries but Mellie did and Mellie got auntie Nellie to do the same thing with apples. Grandpa said "who'd ever think blueberries or apples could taste so good all covered with chocolate?" Grandma got her to use two bottles of maraschino cherries. That cake turned out to be better than chocolate covered cherries. Oh, I almost forgot. She drained the cherries and let them sit on a paper towel awhile before she dredged them and put them in. She measured space between cherries with the bottom of a teaspoon so there were lots of them. This time the icing was white. This was soooo good.

There's lots of other things to do with that recipe but Auntie Jannelle says someday we're going into business and I can't share all our secrets.

I left out the best part. That's eating it.

My mom just read this. She said I forgot to add Auntie Nellie Kept telling me cleanliness was next to Godliness and made me clean up everything before—BEFORE-- and after we baked a cake. Mom thinks I forgot. I just didn't want to remember all that cleaning.

*   *   *

DEPRESSION CAKE

Heat oven to 350

Mix together two cups brown sugar; 2 cups hot water; 2 teaspoons lard (or vegetable shortening); 1 box raisins, 1 teaspoon salt, 1 teaspoon cinnamon, 1 teaspoon cloves. Boil for five minutes after it starts to bubble.

Get this cold. Not warm. Cold.

THEN add 3 cups flour and 1 teaspoon baking soda dissolved in a couple teaspoons of hot water. Mix it real good and bake in a greased and floured tube cake for about one hour at 350 to 375 degrees.

Don't have to be frosted but can if you want. It's a heavy dark cake that sticks to your ribs.

The Roofers

In the Missouri Ozark foothills, especially around the peaceful Mississippi River town of Sainte Lillian, where me and my famly's lived purt near forever, folks has always been agreeable and more or less easy goin'. Just seemed natural like considerin' the pleasant climate and all. Got lotsa things to tell you about us, so might as well get started with the basics.

Boys and girls in Saint Lillian grew up doin' the usual things, and fooled around awhile. Some went away to school and came home doctors, lawyers, teachers, things like that, but eventually them that did and them that didn't got tired of foolin' around, got married, settled down and bred a new batch of agreeable folk. Always, every generation boys and girls went away to war. More boys than girls mind ya, but girls went too. Patriotic as folks is around Sainte Lillian it was jest natural. Sometimes these "sojers"--No matter which branch of service they jined- weuns lumped em all together as sojers-- came back home and did what everybody else did. Iffin a feller brought home a German or Japanese or Korean or French or English or Hula dancing wife, it didn't matter none. They belonged. Sometimes though our sojers didn't come home 'tall 'cept in sealed coffins. And folks has to believe it's their own son or brother or father. Kaint look. Ain't allowed. Sometimes nothin' but dog tags and bloody letters came home. Those there heroes ifin they hadn't done it afore never got the chanct to marry or breed a new batch of agreeable folks.

Some Sainte Lillian younguns managed to breed before marryin,' others bred with more-n-one partner but the end result was always a batch of agreeable folk. And somethin' else really important, no matter who they were, how they got there or where they lived, 99 and 99 100% of Sainte

Lillian folks were in church every Sunday morning. Ceptin those of the Jewish persuasion. Seems they had to worship on a Friday. Sundown Friday to Sundown Saturday seems it was. You can betcha though there is more places to worship in Sainte Lillian than gas stations, and there was one of them on purt near every other corner downtown. Fellers jumpin' around all over the place pumpin' gas, checkin' tires, washin' windows. Anyways, all our places of worship are nice tidy buildings. Catholics have what they call Masses; not only on Sunday but every dad gummed day. Take communion and everythin.' And Boy Howdee, you ain't seen nothing till you see one of their Midnight Masses on Christmas Eve. Goose pimple stuff. Then there's Free Methodist and the other kind of Methodist that must charge for religion cause they jest called themselves Methodist, and two or three different kind of Baptist. As I recklect Catholics and Lutherans both have prayers books and rituals- And I know for sure them Lutherans and Episcopalians have the loudest dad gummed organs you'd ever want to hear. Dog my cats, I donno why they calls that stuff music! Gives a feller a headache. There's a bunch weuns call the Hoot and Holler born again back woods tell it like it is bretheren. They'se got all kinds of weird ideas, and I ain't even goin' into any of that stuff. Hit jist ain't right with the good book. I tell ya, if all that ain't enuf for the average ordinary sinner, revivalist tents spring up with the dandelions and other weeds north and south side of town round mid-March. They keep on preachin' hell fire and damnation till frost hits come October. Yessir, we's a churched people. Preachers take turns at the Sainte Lillian County Jail. Every month a different preacher, priest, rabbi, pastor, er brother takes over duties at Sainte Lillian's hospital. Made it a mite difficult for a Baptist preacher or Jewish Rabbi to administer last rites or prayers for believers not of their persuasion doncha know, but the all round prayer book always worked in a pinch. Besides, by that time the dyin' don't see that clear anyways. They hear purty good though. That's the important part. Faith takes over. Like I said, folks went to church. Not goin' was worse than not salutin' the flag and definitely much worse than kickin' a dog. As I see it, some folks actually did attend church to worship while others went just to be agreeable cause after all, that's the Sainte Lillian way.

. Now that I got that outa the way, I gotta tell a story about folks other than town folk factory workers and farmers. Which is what I started to do anyways, but I had to get that er first part done first though come to think about it I didn't say much about factory workers or farmers and purty little about town folk, what I done did was cover the mood of our town. That's the important thing...

What I want to talk about is folks that ain't like the rest of us. Bein' as how I'm kinda the keep track person, not the historian like that Benable fella, I writes stuff down. Seemed like a good idea to get this here story on paper. Especially since it involves one of my favorite nieces Beth Anne. She's the one up and married a Yankee and moved to Michigan and I kain't hardly stand thinking about it since there was so many fellers around here interested in her.

Anyway, these other Sainte Lillian folks lived in what I called a world within a world. Kinda clever don't ya think? Batches of 'em lived near old muddy Mississippi or as we used to say Big M two straight humpback humpback, one straight double p, i.- spread out along the railroad tracks. Like I said, they ain't like the rest of us. They is just plum different. That's the best way to describe 'em, plum different. Now I ain't sayin' they is stupid, just different. They could walk the walk and talk the talk and be polite as you please cause public manners is pretty much the same doncha know? Wasn't the speakin' though, it was--- well, I might as well say it. It was like this. If they get close enough to talk to town folk, the talkin'gets purty short. Especially in summer. And it's even worse in dog days. These here folks man, woman and child was bornd allergic to soap and water. Hit's shorely a lot easier to converse with them after frost hit and before spring warmed up things doncha knows? Rest of us folks weren't rude or nothin' like completely ignorin' them during the hot spells, but ever body was awful busy on them hot muggy days. Polite and all, still couldn't manage much more than a "how do" before hurryin' off.

These soap and water phobic folks was o.k., in my book. Fact is one of them Hardgrass boys---Tom it was, had his eyes on Beth Anne when they was in High school. I told her about hit and she gave me one of them looks and didn't say nothing,' no sir not a dad gummed word. Seemed like she gave me a lot of them looks after she growd up some and I wanted to tickle her. Her sisters too matter of fact. Now that I'm on the subject, lotsa women around these parts keep givin' me those looks and watchin' me around their gals... Sure riles me some. I'd like to know what's the matter with a little ticklin?'

Anyways like I *said*, this whole batch of folks lived close to the river and not too far from the railroad tracks. River gave fish and all kinds of game. Railroad tracks gave coal and what'nall. Folks'd be surprised. Money even. Beverages of the spirited kind, all kinds of clothes. Why one of the Crandall girls even got herself a husband. Walkin' all by her lonesome one spring day came on this feller sittin' there. He looked at her, she looked at him they both looked like they liked what they seed and she took him home. Nice lookin feller, given to snuff. He shorely did enjoy a Saturday night bath which was a new idea to the Crandalls. But like I said he was a nice enough feller. And when he played the banjer. Boy Howdee!

Crandalls and all them folk didn't care much for work or drawin reg'lr paychecks. They said life was too short for that. Men folk made do with part time jobs. There was food stamps and hand outs from churches and the Salvation Army. Families got by. Kids got free lunch at school and school kept them outa sight for awhile. School bullies didn't bother them none. Need be, ary one of these here boys or girls could whop a bully one arm tied behind their backs and blindfolded to boot. Said the bullies didn't smell right. Learnin' wasn't much but now and then one of them younguns wound up real smart and made everybody proud. Got a doctor outa there, a lawyer, factory foreman, nurses and teachers, things like that. Lotsa young fellers jined the Army and stuck it out. Got all kinds of trainin' three squares a day, free medical, travel everywheres and money to send home and hep out.

Women folk stayed pretty much t' home havin babies every year. Them that don't get wore out with the doin' of it, live long enough to see grands and greats keepin' family traditions alive.

Then there's the more or less professional workers comin' outa the flats. That's where the Hardgrass boys come in. They was up and comin' that's for shore. Banker Bill Wendom said Tom, Dick, and Harry Hardgrass was the first real entrepreneurs he'd seen or heard tell of comin' out of the flats. Made the boys right proud. Not that they knew for sure what that big word meant, but by dab, they had their own business and they was proud of it. Worked real hard at it for a year or two. Made good money. Coulda done that expandin' thing, hirin' folks on and all but hit was too much work and taxes and all doncha know? Folks spoke good things about their work too..

Bein' that big word started one day when they cut crost' the junk yard headin' for their favorite fishin' hole down river. Tom spied the old bus first, remembered ridin' it many a school day, how he liked sittin' there in the back seat, not mindin' the potholes or creeks it crossed. He liked that there old bus and before he knew what he was doin' or for sure why, they owned it. Had to get two old mules to pull it home and then it went in the old barn with their pappy's roofin' buckets, brushes, ladders, hammers and other truck. One thing led to another; the next thing you knowd they cut her up. Made themselves a truck bed outa the back and their own private camper t' the front. Kinda close quarters and all. Two by fours covered with cork board covered with green linoleum from their mammy's kitchen floor made their camper bed. Tom said he was shore his mammy wouldn't mind none. Dick said seein' as how she'd been dead and buried awhile probably not. Baby Harry rememberin' his purty momma didn't say nothin' just blew his nose on his red bandana. Anyways, they fixed it up real nice with bunk beds and a camp stove and porta potty, and then got to work on the outside.

Tom said he wanted to keep it school bus yeller. Dick said Red would get more attention. Harry was all for green. Tom made sure they left his yeller hood alone. They got her all painted up red and green leavin' the hood yeller and then wrote in big black letters down both sides "ROOFERS WE FIX WHAT STORMS TEARS UP.

Growed up on fat back, greens, beans and cornbread, Tom, Dick and Harry was good sized boys. Their mammy'd liked to boast they was twice the size of other creek bottom men and that was before they growed some more. But bein' overgrowed didn't stop them none. No siree Bob! Them Hardgrass boys could shimmy up on a roof, shed limbs, rotton boards and loose shingles and get them roofs fixed in no time. For quite a few years they was honest workers, but that got tiresome. Specially when they started workin' down in the boot heel. Then one thing leadin' to another, they took side trips to Arkansas and Kentucky back ridge country and into the flat lands near river bottom Illinois. They learnt real quick that old folks were too trustin'. It didn't bother them boys none to do shoddy work and ride off into the sunset with hardly earned money in their pockets.

But I gotta honestly say bein' truthful and all, I didn't know they was runnin' afowl of the law. All I knowed was every time I seen Tom he asked about Beth Anne. Had it bad fer her after all them years.

Come the summer my sister Anna and her old man James Samuel Owen was dyin' and Beth Anne and her kids came down for the long haul. Same summer the Hardgrass boys came t'home after bein' out of state for ever so long.. Talk was they was comfortable rich and didn't need to work much no more so I figured hit'd be a good time fer Tom to hook up with Beth Anne, try his luck again, y'know what I mean?

The boys laid back for awhile and when nothin' much came of rumors about trouble outa state, they got busy again. Usually, they was purty good about it. Most of the time almost honest. Close enough to get by anyways, Cause these was home folks they was workin' for and they didn't have no choice. Course now and then they coulda cheated, cause they didn't know no old arthritic farmer able to crawl up on his roof and check er out anyway but they were more-or-less honest. They was like this: Roofs around town needed work they got their money's worth. Outside town on them farms where roads was little more than a dry krik bed t'was another story... They got a real kick outa them old farmers blessin' their hearts and thankin' them fer savin' them so much money. Tom said he'd plum got tired of feelin' guilty about rippin' em off but if they was that dumb they deserved it. By dab. "Amen!" said Dick and Harry.

So when I ran into em at the country store I sent em to Anna and James Samuel's place, didn't tell Beth Anne about it or nothing, wanted it to be a big surprise. Was alright, but not the way I figered.

Tom said they was parked neath the big old maple trees lookin' over the house when the next thang he knew, he heard the purtiest voice like it were plum floatin' over the barkin' of old Bodatious.

My goodness," it said. If it ain't the Hardgrass boys." It said "Now Bodacious that's no way to treat old friends, you aughta be ashamed of yourself." And that old dog that'd been jumpin' on the cab and barkin' his fool haid off took one look at her and laid down and surrendered. Calm as you please.

Dick glared. Harry stuttered and Tom grinned all over his face. "Dog my cats if it ain't Beth Anne Owen…er, I mean Brunswick less you gave up on that Yankee and came back home took up your rightful name." Well sir, she laughed fit to be tied at that one.

"You fellers lookin for work?" she asked innocent like and Tom he up and says "Well, matter of fact, we talked to your pappy bout a month ago about that there roof. We inspected it right good and found some bad boards, and loose shingles jest waitin t' take off in the next big wind. We was supposed to be back week or so ago but got so busy we're jist getting here.

"That so," she said.

Your pappy said ifin he wasn't here one of you gals would pay and he'd get back to ya… Seein' as how youns are kinda special we cut the price to four hundred." "That so?" she said.

Somehow or other before Beth Anne came up with another of her "that so's?" they got outa that cab and started off loadin'. That was o.k. with the Dick and Harry. Shore Tom was stuck on her. Always had been, but they didn't see nothin' to like in her uppity ways. They wanted to get busy. While Tom stood around like a lovesick hound dawg, Harry took over. "Tell ya what Beth Anne, you just stand aside there and watch us experts. We'll get er done in no time, save your folks thousands of dollars with our work." Harry moved his chaw of Red Man to his left cheek and spat a mahogany stream of juice into the Kentucky blue grass. The grass kinda curlin up and dyin' didn't surprise him none. Seemed Kentucky Blue jist didn't take to juice like their own yard full of crab grass and nettles.

"That so." Beth Anne done and went and said it again and Dick and Harry didn't like it 'tall. They started walkin' towards her, stompin' the grass and all, flexin' their muscles, stuff like that. "That's fer sure so," said

Harry and the next thing they knowed, that there Beth Anne was throwin' her head back and laffin.

Later on she said she was plum scared wonderin' what they was up to, wishin' she had a knight in shinin' armour or the Lone Ranger to ride to her rescue but she said she told herself she could handle three down home boys easier than she could handle her Yankee.

"If y'all think you're getting up on that hot roof without having some refreshments, you've got another think comin," she said and jist then her three kids came runnin outa' the house. My youngest great niece-- Mollie Kate her name is --sashayed right up to them and waved this here chocolate cake under their noses. "It's my special cake and it's just loaded with butter cream frosting," she said. Then this long legged long haired thang--- that 's Mellshana, my first great niece,--- lookin' like her mammy did all them years ago, walked by with a tray full of glasses loaded with ice and the biggest dag gummed pitcher they's ever seed. "Sweet Tea, puhlease tell me hits Sweet tea Missie" Tom said and Mellshanna looked at him and laffed jest like her mammy. "Is there any other kind?" Then my great Nephew Mac Duff Franklin, no, that's wrong he's' Franklin Mac Duff the spittin' image of his pappy, came by and asked "Y'all like sugar cookies?"

Givin' Beth Anne's kids three of the Ozarks most beautiful tobacco stained grins the Hardgrass boys plum forgot about their work and found seats at the shaded picnic table. Mollie Kate cut extra large portions of cake, Mellshana poured tea and Mac Duff didn't say nothing else but made sure they had cookies aplenty. And to my dyin' day, I'll never know why they call that kid Mac Duff. Hit ain't on either side of the family ourn or that Yankees. I know I looked it up in them genealogical records... Nother of them great unsolved mysteries I reckon.

Back to the Hardgrass boys. They was so busy shovelin' in cake and cookies and gulpin' sweet tea Tom and his brothers was the last to know their exit was blocked by police cars.

Beth Anne said it wasn't the Lone Ranger or a Knight in shinin' armor that came to her rescue but Sheriff Tanner Hale was exactly what she needed. Seein' as how he was a Sainte Lillian's feller himself, Sheriff Hale let the Hardgrass boys finish their dessert before readin' them their rights and escortin' them to jail. Seems there was a stack of warrants knee high to a duck waitin' in his office.

Beth Anne and the kids got their piturs in the paper. Again! The second time. Beth Anne said Samantha Lynn's Mark done told her to be on the lookout for the Hardgrass boys and whut she should do. She said she was plum nervous fer awhile but figured livin' in Yankee land taught her a thang or two. My great nephew Mac Duff was quoted as sayin' he just knowed the sheriff deserved an extra merit badge for catchin' three bad guys.

As I reck'lect this is mostly all true. Does a feller good to get sech things offin his mind and on paper fer the history books. Guess about the only other thing I got to say is one of these days; I'll get around and tell Beth Anne I sent them fellers over. Be a shame to miss out on any reward money doncha' know.

Signed:

Jethro Patrick Parker, Beth Anne's only survin' uncle not countin' her pappy's sid, and I only know her aunts anyways.

Tale of Two Kitties

Spring in Michigan: After a winter hanging on long after it should have returned to the South Pole, it was spring. Almost overnight, which made it perfect, and even though days light was speeding toward sunset, I was walking home the long way, down a graveled country road. It felt so good to move without bumping into a desk, or facing another parent who couldn't understand the simple statement "Johnny has trouble sitting still." Where were they when the boy was home for goodness sake?" Thoughts, musings, memories all part and parcel of a fourth grade classroom. Loved the kids, loved teaching loved the peace and quiet time of reflection.

To my left a large just that day plowed field gave promise of summer sweet corn. On the first furrow, where great clods lay against unturned soil, black crows foraged for supper and fussed about fat worms -or lack thereof.

Time to think about something else like the red headed Muscleman boy pedaling towards me, one hand on the bike handlebars, another holding the helmet that belonged on his head. And it wasn't a week ago we'd had police at school assembly talking about bike riding safety and the use of helmets! What was Logan doing?

"Teachur lady!" he said.

I don't remember what I thought or said, but I do remember the sound of his voice; desperate, scared, pleading wrapped in those two words like he was throwing out a lifeline, reeling it in, tossing it out again.

. My questions disappeared when the handlebar hand joined the helmet holding hand and cupped something very small and softly golden.

I saw a red headed freckled faced boy holding something out to me. I saw the sun slowly sinking into a clear sky and felt cold wind with its promise of another frost filled night.

"Teachur Lady I found him three hours ago by the side of the road. My momma said she's allergic to cats and can't have him around. She said I could find him a home. I've been all up and down the road and there ain't nobody wants him. Mrs. Cowper said I shoulda left him in the ditch and Mr. Northline said I was on a fool's errand and everywhere I went people said no. I knows there's always cats in the dairy barn maybe he'd have a chance there, but mom told me I couldn't cross the highway Teachur lady you just gotta help."

I spoke truth. "Logan I don't need a dying kitten." Words said one thing, actions another. I held out a gloved hand and the little ball of soft yellow raised its small head and looked at me with two enormous amber eyes and blinked. Twice. Like he knew me, knew I would take him home. He tried to climb from Logan's hand into mine but was too weak to make the journey of two inches.

Suddenly, all I needed was a dying kitten. I took the small frail thing and cradling him in my hand tucked him inside my coat, over my beating heart. He gave the smallest meow I've ever heard and then from an inner reserve of strength, followed that with the soft contented purr of kitten music. It was not fear; it was a song that said he was now safe.

"Teachur Lady you gotta promise me you won't put him in the ditch to die."

Shocked, I said "Logan!" as in how could you think I'd think such a thing?" Satisfied he grinned, we hugged and helmet in place and both hands where they belonged, hero that he was Logan rode off into the sunset. Now, nothing else mattered except keeping this ball of fluff alive. At least he wouldn't die alone in a cold ditch, food for maggots and crows.

The girls looked for doll baby bottles. I warmed milk and white bread in a salad plate. He couldn't stand upright but he could crawl and crawl he did right into the bread and milk. Like Mr. and Mrs. Jack Spratt of nursery rhyme fame, he licked the platter clean. Then, remembering his manners, he rolled over and licked every drop and crumb from his pink tummy and paws. When we laughed at how his little round belly was so full it nearly reached the floor, he gave us a two eye blinker and a certified kitten grin. He was in on the joke.

Fourteen years later we would not laugh when his belly drug the floor, but we did not know that then. All that mattered that day, that hour was he lived and was full of milk, bread, and spirit.

My son, official name bestorer of all things bright and beautiful in our world, sprawled on the living room carpet with the object of our intentions. Girls and I tossed names. He said Fluffy and Puff Ball and Dan De Lion weren't fittin' for such a brave creature. "So name him then," girls and I said in unison. He said "Uggh, Ouch, and Wow." We laughed.

He said "Meathook."

We laughed longer and harder. "Surely you jest," said we.

"Exhibit A," said he, and pointed to his chest crisscrossed and marred by the claw work of a contented kitten making his bed on his chest. Meathook gave us a two eye blinker and went to sleep.

Kitchen lights came on during the night as wanna be Green Beret and hungry kitten bonded over warm milk.

During the week Meathook became Hookie, and the small bundle of purr bumped lead dogs and cats aside. Black Labrador Abraham Lincoln (aka tupid) who would have eaten cats for breakfast if he thought about it, took one look at Hookie and became his instant and devoted companion, slave and nap sight. Big black dog curled into ball, little yellow kitten centered in the warmth, napping together. If Abe woke first he lay watching Hookie, his large brown eyes glowing with devotion. Springer Spaniel Einstein Bear chased leaves if they came to close to his charge. German Shepherd Duffer offered his back for rides around the big mysterious yard. Old Tiger cat bathed Hookie with his sandpaper tongue then held him down to whisper family secrets. Josephine our orange tabby took one long look at him, another at us and without fanfare walked out of our lives. The kids said she was on a mission of vengeance, looking for the family that deserted Hookie. I never told them her mission ended at the driveway, or that stones in a flower garden covered her small grave.

Before his first great adventure began in the back yard, Hookie cowered between guardian dogs for at least five minutes. One tentative paw at a time he ventured into this mysterious world. Then like a real lion heart, he stalked bachelor buttons, swatted blades of grass, climbed waiting and willing dogs to reach first limbs of a maple tree and yowled louder than a cat three times his size when he couldn't get down.

His amber eyes flashed twice when we called his name, when we fed him, when he climbed our laps and sat on our shoulders. We knew cat speak enough to translate Flash one: "I love you," and two "I trust you."

When my son entered the Army, Hookie slept on his bed. Each night I would move him to mine and in the morning find him where he wanted to be.

Tiger was in his grave beside Josephine and Tasha became our newest feminine feline. A sassy bit of silky black fur, she wise enough to let Hookie boss her around. As I write I remember his call to her as they raced across linoleum floors in the dusty attic and our laughter as two unrecognizable cats raced to us for forgiveness and or help. Stripping wallpaper waited while they were dusted, brushed and restored to normal.

Hookie was there when my son came home from boot camp and through the years when he came home from wars, rumors of wars, and adventures in far away places. Always, soldier and Hookie remembered.

Hookie settled into a contented cat middle age, and put on weight. So much in fact we looked into cat weight watchers. The vet said Hookie was doing what old fat cats do, enjoying himself. Not to worry, the vet said. A week later, Hooky's skin was yellow. . Even the paws, inside his ears, his mouth.

Nothing worked.

We took him home and watched and waited.

The call came on a chilly afternoon in early spring.

Hookie was home waiting for me. Greeting me with his signature two eye blinker even as all he wanted was to quench his unbearable thirst. We could hear trapped liquid sloshing in his distended belly. I wrapped him in a new towel and held him close to my heart. He purred contentedly as we drove the last miles.

Very carefully we eased him onto thick grass in the animal clinic memorial garden. Happy to be outdoors he strained with his last energy to explore one last new place. Too weak to climb, he turned to me and I held him so he could touch greening leaves. He looked past them into the beautiful blue sky. We went indoors and immediately into a small side room. The kids spread the towel across the cold table and we all stood around him. Our hands covered him, his reassuring purring the only sound in the small cold room...

The Vet came in one door carrying a huge syringe. He looked at us, read our grief and walked out the other. "We'll never be ready," I said and once more we held Hookie and kissed him and whispered our love. Somehow in his great cat heart he found the strength to give each of us his signature message. This time when the doctor entered, I stood aside just enough for him to squeeze by. Hookie lay waiting, his tired heart beating like a drum tattoo with no rest between beats. He couldn't get enough air. He was so tired.

The needle went so quickly into Hookie's front paw his only reaction was to take his eyes from us and look intently at the doctor. Once again, the message from his amber eyes. Before peaceful death entered his bloodstream we called his name one last time. He opened his dying eyes and looked at me and blinked. Once. Twice, and then while his eyes were on mine, I saw the light leave.

He is buried on a sun filled slope above the creek.. Wrapped in the new towel, in his bed, in his coffin box, he lies where the grass grows, the sun is warm, and there is enough adventure to fill his heart.

It was a spring afternoon when we said goodbye. Fourteen years to the day when God gave me a nudge and told me to hold out my hand and give the small thing a place to live or die. Fourteen years from the day I first held him near my heart.

Two eye blinker Hookie.

Indiana Jones

Hookie was dead but his spirit lingered. We turned a corner and saw him in a chair; we heard a rumble and knew it was his song. Amber glows were everywhere. We lived in a house full of memories.

"Y'know," I said, there were a thousand days and as many ways that Hookie could have left us but it's just like him to do it when papers are full of free kitten ads." It didn't take them a second. "We can't" my girls said. "We must," I said

We answered every ad. We held black kittens, white kittens, black and white kittens, grey kittens, calico kittens, kittens of every stripe and hue, kittens in pet shops, in store windows and at the shelter. The very last day, the last time we looked we found one small soft cuddly yellow fellow who seemed to meet our needs. He gave my youngest daughter a once over and climbed her jeans. She melted just enough.

He looked like Hookie, He ate like Hookie, and he sometimes managed to sound just like Hookie. But he was not Hookie. He was nameless for two weeks.

One Sunday when we were tired of calling "Kitty kitty Nameless," my son did his duty. He said he could do it. We weren't all that sure. After all, he was out of practice, and other than nameless, we hadn't come up with anything in two weeks...

When we came home from church, the house was strangely quiet. Cats and dogs were in hiding. "Oh Lord!" I said as visions of disaster danced in my brain. We called nameless. "Kitty kitty kitty nameless." We opened tuna. We searched closets and cabinets and toilets and sinks for Nameless. There was no limp pile of lifeless cat fur, no bloody remains, nothing. At the upstairs linen closet I opened the door and called one last time. It was then we heard the faintest "Help me" meow ever recorded in history.

Nameless, the great snoopy adventurer had crawled into the closet, found a hole barely big enough, and went for it. Now, he wanted out. I wasn't ready to tear out a wall. My son said and I quote, "Get right back up here. Do you think you're Indiana Jones?"

A small cobweb smeared golden head peeked from the hole and a little tired kitten voice said "yessss" as he inched and wormed his way into safety. Naming him was the easy part.

Adjusting to a cat temperament so different than Hookies was another story. Learning to love him another. But we did. He made sure we did.

Having never been an outdoor boy, Indiana Jones was content with indoor adventures. His favorite was searching potted plants for buried treasure. He made sure the floors were swept clean. Drapes and sheers replaced trees. Blinds replaced drapes and sheers. He perfected the high jump and perched precariously on banisters, cabinet tops and window ledges. We considered cat Olympics

The dogs died. One after the other. Just like that. The dogs died. Tasha started acting like Hookie and, within a month, met the needle. This time it wasn't in me to find a replacement. When I took to my bed with chills and fever, Indiana Jones was there, his warm paws over my heart "He's Egyptian" someone said and told me how Egyptians considered cats possessed of healing powers.

Family came with their American Eskimo dogs. Hookie would have bossed them lovingly. Indiana Jones bossed them…They raced through the house cat chasing dogs all three enjoying themselves, all three shedding Only there was more cat fur. Lots more. Vet said he was allergic to the dogs and needed shots. Then his right ear became golf ball size. Indiana Jones didn't complain. He sat on my lap purring waiting for me to do something. Four hundred dollars later he was home with a drain tube in his ear and enough medicine to cure the black plague.

Allergy Shots didn't work. Long after dogs were banished, tufts of scaly encrusted cat hair decorated furniture, rugs, bedding. Different diet, different vet, different meds. Then the left ear became infected, swollen, and painful. The vet shook his head. Indiana Jones purred. Head under my chin, he purred. I held him in sunlight in the examining room and he purred while tears washed my face. The big syringe came.

Indiana Jones pulled one paw out of the towel and touched my hand and. I kissed his scaly head. "It's o.k., Jonsey its o.k". I lied. He looked at me and for the first time gave me a two eye blinker. "It's ok." I said as the light left his eyes. It wasn't. It will never be.

Patriotism

My sister Anna bein' a teacher and all always told me to focus more. She'd say, get one story or one project or one anything completely done before startin' another, but there's always so much to do. With my whittlin' and stories and sech, I jest take off doncha know?

Now about writin', to me, hit's like walkin' down a road you've never seen before and you gotta explore everything. Anyways, when I was telling about the roofers, I said a little bit about patriotism and it jest came to me, there's a lot more to say about that so now I'm gonna do er now.

Saint Lillian folks are so patriotic far as holidays go Memorial Day ranks right up there with Christmas and Easter. This feelin' started long before the Civil War. When that gawsh awful mess was over Sainte Lillian's veterans that wore blue or grey were buried side by side on Veteran's Hill. They was ours and it didn't matter none which side they was on in that war. Sainte Lillian honors its heroes. It's a big hill. There's always room.

The latest mound of wreath blanketed earth belongs to the Bollinger boy sent home from World War 11 with most of his brain gone. They patched him up, kept him alive at the VA Hospital up on that beautiful bluff there outside Saint Louis. He never woke up, never said anything never tasted another hamburger or saw another John Wayne Movie and that boy was some stuck on John Wayne. Rumor is posters and signed autographs and all his John Wayne souvenirs lined a whole VA wall.

Sainte Lillian never forgets its heroes. Folks from the VFW post and WW11 Mothers always visited our sojers at the hospital. We got us Korean vets and them from Vietnam and other fellers from every little bitty killin' war or police action all over the globe. Older them vets gets, more time they spend visitin'. Like they're rememberin, or maybe young again.

Plannin' for the big parade to kick off the Memorial Day ceremonies starts soon as the current parade is over. When that last float pulls into the VFW post, talk starts on what to do different and what to keep the same next year. For example, one year they plum forgot to get anyone to clean up after the horses. That never happened again. Memorial Day parades are work, and Sainte Lillian folks do their best.

Marching veterans are a big part of the parade. Till a year or so ago World War One Vets carried the colors. Now the few that's left come outa nursin' homes and ride as honorary Grand Marshals in front of the uniformed troops. Loosely identified that word uniform. Not a man or woman can wear the whole thing, but they manage a part, even if it's just a hat or boots or medals. "Uniforms shrink," they say.

The brotherhood-sisterhood: now doctors, lawyers, nurses, teachers, bankers, factory workers, store owners, farmers, preachers and drunks line up, settle in and work on cadence. Takes a block or two, but when they get to main street and cheering families their minds is back to another day when they came home from war. It's the flag, the music, the memories.

While floats, marchers and horses and all it takes to get a good parade line up at the VFW, the town gets ready. Lawn chairs take root on shaded streets. Families and neighbors band together, and kids don't have to be told twice to stay outa the streets. Wanting to be first to spot police cars and the big flags, they run up and down the sidewalks

Families share food and drink. Coffee and donuts make the rounds. Good old boys sold hot dogs one year and wanted to add beer the next but that didn't get any higher off the ground than a lead balloon. They was told right off to keep the Bud and or Schlitz t'home and be respectful of the event. They obliged. Settled on soda pop, hot dogs, wing dings and ice cream bars.

When the big bright flag, symbol of all that's good about America passes by, hands go over hearts and them that know how stand at attention and salute its passing.

High School bands do John Phillip Sousa proud. Candy rains from red white and blue floats as beauty queens in purty pastel dresses all dolled up and all wave like the princesses they are. After the last float passes, families join the procession to the cemetery and gather near Veteran's Memorial hill, the burying place of Saint Lillian's heroes since before the Civil war. Active military in full dress display the colors. Led by a church choir the crowd sings the national anthem. The VFW Chaplain offers a sincere and often tearful prayer of gratitude, remembrance and hope wars will end.

Families of active military place wreaths at the foot of the tall marble cross. With the acrid scent of gunpowder still on the breeze, buglers from four compass points render a haunting taps that echoes and penetrates. It's said that when the first notes sound, sleeping warriors know.

Stories about Sainte Lillian's heroes never wear out. A town favorite is about Private First Class Samuel Barrett Benable home from the war after VE day and very glad to become private citizen Samuel Barrett Benable. Yet glad as he was to be outa the war, he was so proud of his uniform and his country, he couldn't stop wearing dress khakis around town. Shopping with the wife Irene on Saturday, then double feature at the Bijou, and always to church on Sunday, Samuel wore that uniform. Spit shined boots, creases sharp enough to cut butter, tie straight, medals gleaming. Kept his regulation hair cut too. This particular Saturday Samuel and the wife were waiting to cross Fourth Street at the courthouse intersection. Samuel stood tears streamin' down his face lookin' up at the flag atop the courthouse. All of a sudden he walked smack dab into traffic and held out his hand. Cars speedin' by at 20mph just managed to stop. Tires screeched. Horns blared. Women screamed. Samuel stood there middle of the street, bawlin' his eyes out, and saluting Old Glory. Other veterans, some in uniform, some not decided to stand with him and honor the flag.

Samuel turned to the gathering crowd and made the first and last public speech of his life. He said every dad gummed time he saw that flag flyin' so free in the breeze he got all choked up and proud. He recklected way too many times when the thought of that flag and all it stood for was what kept him goin.' He said some folks 'd never know the pure pleasure of standin' in a street and seein' whole buildings, not just bits and pieces of walls and lots of rubble on the ground. Said it took him a long time to stop wonderin' if the next breeze carried a bullet with his name on it. Said he was there at the Battle of the Bulge, saw his friends disintegrate right before his eyes, went to liberate concentration camps and saw and smelt things he'd never be able to talk about and at the same time never be able to forget. Said it was a pure honor to march under that there Arch De Triumph over there in Paris, the Paris that's in France, and hear all the people shouting that "Vive le American." Took him awhile to make sense of all that parlavooin stuff but he got it down purty good when it came to eats and drinks. Not that there was much of either. Said he'd never in his life forget havin' his arm around a pretty little French gal and feelin' nothing but skin and bones. Probably would have said a lot more on that subject if the wife hadn't pulled away and stood there lookin' at him with the look every married man dreads more than tax day.

"Honeybun, sweetheart," he said.

She didn't budge, but veteran warrior Samuel out flanked her and took her in his arms. "I'll tell everybody here the best part of comin' home is knowin' we've done our part for Democracy and Christianity and Freedom. Right up there with that is bein' here at home with my wife, feelin' more than skin and bones when I hold her. I'm home. I've seen the world and I'm home. Home is where a feller belongs. Left a lot of fellers behind that'll never come home. Because they died, we can all walk the streets and worship our God and live our lives in freedom."

Samuel turned and looked at the gathering crowd where women wiped their eyes with lace bordered hankies as everyone stared at the flag. Samuel cleared his throat. "One more thing," he said, "God Bless America. Land that I love."

That's it. That's my story.
Jethro Patrick Parker signin' off